The Rabbi of Worms

The Rabbi of Worms

M. K. HAMMOND

RESOURCE *Publications* · Eugene, Oregon

THE RABBI OF WORMS

Resource Publications
An Imprint of Wipf and Stock Publishers
199 W. 8th Ave., Suite 3
Eugene, OR 97401

www.wipfandstock.com

ISBN 13: 978-1-62564-459-6

Manufactured in the U.S.A.

For EJS and JSH,
who made this work possible

Foreword

M. K. Hammond has written an extraordinary account of the eleventh-century epochal events that have so greatly impacted the history of Jewish-Christian relations. In light of current developments, those events seem especially relevant.

The setting is the Rheinland in the period before the First Crusade, which began in 1096 and culminated in the capture of Jerusalem in 1099. The author draws her inspiration from the life of the venerated sage Rabbi Solomon ben Isaac, also known as Rashi, who studied in Mainz and Worms before founding a yeshiva in Troyes. In creating a sense of historical authenticity, Hammond captures the positive and tolerant atmosphere that characterized the era just before the fateful events that followed the Crusades. She does this by depicting the lives of men and women in both the Jewish and Christian communities who exemplify the very best of those traditions and of human nature. For the moral voice for understanding the tragic turn of events at the end of the century, she turns to Rabbi Solomon ben Isaac and his teachings; he helps the protagonists in their quest to understand what was happening in the world around them and enables the reader to extract the very best and noble aspects of the two traditions.

The result of this endeavor is an historical novel that is informative, compelling, and inspiring. The descriptions of the Jewish Quarter in Worms, for example, where the story begins, is detailed and vivid enough to capture one's attention at the outset and to focus on the main characters: Josef, a Christian orphan whose route to learning and personal development is through a close Jewish friend who becomes his Hebrew tutor and mentor, Mosche, and his sister Miriam, whose life's quest is to be a fulfilled Jew through study and learning in addition to having a family and managing a household. Miriam's story resonates in many ways with women today in current traditional Jewish communities, and Rabbi Solomon's role in her development should be an object lesson for all rabbis today. Much of the story centers around the positive interactions of the two communities represented by the siblings and Josef. Those interactions include regular study sessions introduced via the teachings of the famed rabbi. One cannot escape the hopeful tone of this portion of the book, Part I: Torah study is important in both Judaism and Christianity, and serious students learn from their respective tradition to accept the other with respect and tolerance. The implication of that situation is that mutual understanding is the key to positive human interaction. The true test of that idea has a tragic outcome in the form of the beginning of the First Crusade, when centuries of mutual interaction and acceptance come to an end.

In Part II of this only partially invented story in which all the characters either are actual historical figures such as Rashi, King Henry, and Bishop John of Speyer or characters created to propel the narrative and allow the author to provide details of everyday life, the horrific details of slaughter of the Jews in town after town are recounted in great detail. The Jewish community is thus confronted with some of the most difficult decisions imaginable: to resist by force and create more killing, to commit suicide for the sanctification of God's Name, to publicly renounce their faith and be baptized, or simply to pretend to be Christian by learning a few prayers from the liturgy. As the survivors of these massacres move to new homes and new places in France, Hammond turns to the writings and rulings of Rashi on such matters to help the reader comprehend these awful choices. Josef's actions to assist Miriam and the survivors of her family achieve a new life in Troyes symbolize the hope that underlies this narrative and represent the Christian counterpoint to Rashi's tolerant views of other faiths, but especially Christianity. Despite the horror of the Crusades and ensuing descent into chaos that followed for all the children of Abraham, Hammond's positive account of what might have been, had the teachings of the Rabbi of Worms been observed and followed, provides a timely example for all who care about interfaith communication and peace in the Middle East.

Eric M. Meyers, Director
Center for Jewish Studies
Duke University
Durham, North Carolina

Pronunciation Guide

PLACES

Worms—pronounced "Vormce"

Mainz—rhymes with "pints" (Two pints make a quart.)

Speyer—pronounced "Shpire"

Rhein (River) —pronounced "Rine"

Troyes—pronounced "Twah"

Poitiers—pronounced "Pwah-tee-ay"

Köln—vowel sounds like "ea" in learn

PEOPLE

Mutti—rhymes with "sooty" (The fireplace is sooty.)

Mosche—pronounced "Moy-sha"

(Rabbi) Scholomo—pronounced "Shol-oh-moe"

Joakim—pronounced "Yo-ah-keem"

Eliel—pronounced "El-ee-el"

Frieder—rhymes with "leader"

(Bishop) Ruthard—pronounced "Roo-tard"

Ehud—pronounced "Eh-hood"

(Rabbi) Shmaya—pronounced "Shm-eye-ah"

Old City

Worms

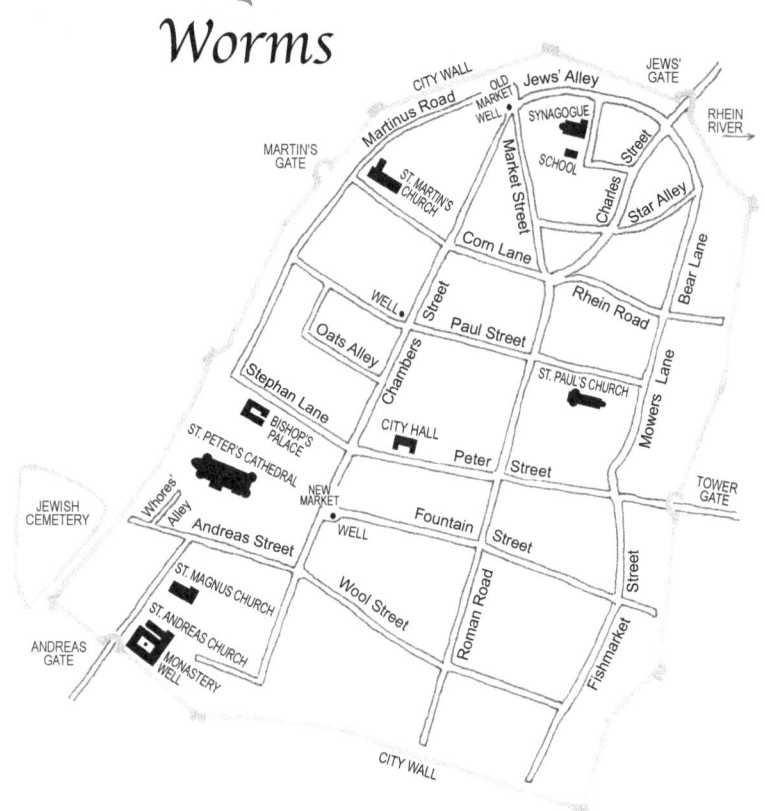

Medieval Europe

Baltic Sea

North
Sea

Rhein R.

LOW
COUNTRIES
• Köln
Trier • • Mainz
• Metz • Worms
• Speyer
Paris • CHAMPAGNE
• Troyes
FRANCIA
• Poitiers

• Clermont

HOLY

• Prague
Regensburg
Danube R.
• Vienna

ROMAN
Budapest •

EMPIRE

ITALIA
Adriatic Sea

• Rome

Mediterranean
Sea

PART ONE

4836–4846	Jewish Calendar
1076–1086	Christian Calendar

Chapter 1

They were lying in wait. Those horrible boys were waiting for him to pass through their territory, for another chance to make him cry. One time Josef had tried to find his way home by a different street, but he had become lost and wandered for nearly an hour, causing his mother much anxiety. Now he would simply lower his head and walk straight ahead, hoping they would not block his way.

He should have been accustomed to it by now, since he walked through their territory twice a week on market days and also on Mondays when he bought sewing supplies for his mother. But they always found new ways to torment him, and though he tried to ignore them, he could not. If he closed his ears to their taunts, they threw pebbles at him, and if he walked through the pebbles, they pulled his hair.

Today was Wednesday, and Josef was coming home from the market. He was carrying a small jug of milk and a basket of vegetables his mother had asked for. As he came down Market Street and passed the first house beyond Jews' Alley, he saw, out of the corner of his eye, the tall boy with big feet waiting by the doorpost. Josef noticed his feet because once the boy had stepped out and tripped him. But today the tall boy stayed where he was and gave out a shrill whistle. Josef looked straight ahead and kept walking.

Out of another doorway came the red-haired boy and the fat one. They walked beside him, one on each side, while the tall boy came up behind him and shadowed his steps. He got closer and closer until Josef could feel the boy's legs just behind his own at every step. All three started to chant, first quietly, but then growing steadily louder.

"Bastard, bastard, bastard . . ."

Two more boys joined the group, and the chanting became even louder. Josef did not dare try to run away because he might spill the milk, and anyway, they could run faster than he could. So he kept walking and tears began to fall off his cheeks, and the chant became, "Cry-baby, cry-baby . . ."

If only he could make it to the next corner where the old crooked man sat and begged, he felt sure they would turn their attention to that unfortunate man.

At last he reached the corner. One of the boys slapped his backside and sent him stumbling forward. He kept a tight hold on the basket and the milk jug, and only a small amount of milk splashed onto the road. Josef could feel the boys falling away from him but he dared not look back. Once before when he turned around and looked, the boys came running after him shaking their fists in the air.

He walked steadily forward for two blocks without turning his head to the right or left. After a few more minutes he saw the entrance to his house—only then did his taut body begin to relax. He passed the butcher shop on his left, then turned to lift the latch of the gate. He entered through an archway in the stone wall into a small unpaved courtyard, bordered on three sides by wooden buildings daubed with clay. Various shops occupied lower floors of the buildings, while Josef and his mother kept two small rooms on the upper level. He went into a hallway at the rear of the courtyard, climbed the steep, narrow stairway, and pushed open the door. There stood his mother with broom in hand.

"Josef, are you home so soon? I've not even had time to clean Frau Schmid's house."

"Yes, Mutti, I walked fast."

"Well, all right then. I suppose you're hungry?"

"Yes, Mutti."

"Bring the milk over here."

Josef set the basket on a small sideboard and carried the milk jug to a worn wooden table in the middle of the room. His mother filled a bowl with porridge and poured milk over it. Josef ate quickly and eagerly. His mother sat and watched and smiled a little when he looked up at her. Maybe this would be a good time to ask the question. It had been gnawing at him for a couple of weeks. But would she know the answer? He had never heard her use that word before. Maybe it was an unmentionable word, forbidden in the Bible. Would it be a sin if he said it? But in the end Josef's curiosity would not allow him to keep silent. All at once he blurted out, "Mutti, what's a bastard?"

He was not prepared for his mother's reaction. Her smile instantly vanished, and she took on that sad look, the look he had seen many times before but had never understood. In silence she stared at her son while the color faded from her face. Finally she spoke.

"Where did you hear that word?"

"Some boys on the street."

"Don't listen to them."

"No, Mutti, but what can I do?"

"Don't listen to them."

With that she picked up her broom and hurried toward the door. She did not stop to remind him of his chores as she usually did. She merely gave him a quick glance over her shoulder as she went out the door. Josef noticed that her eyes and cheeks were moist.

What was he to do? He had upset his mother, and now she would be in one of her gloomy moods for many days. He vowed he would try to be a good son and not do things that annoyed her. He would do all his chores without being told. And of course he would never again ask her that question.

Still, he had to find out what a bastard was, but who would tell him? Certainly not the boys on the street. They were the last ones he would ask. Could he ask old Wilhelm who lived across the courtyard? No, he might report back to Josef's mother. What about Anna and Lotti, the little girls he played with over in the next street? Anna was eight years old, two years older than he was, and she might know the answer. Maybe he would ask Anna. He would have to think about it. But now he had to do his chores and do them extra well.

By noon, Josef had carried kindling wood and hauled buckets of water to all the shops in the courtyard. The baker had given him a misshapen bun that was burnt at the edges. On most days, Josef would have stuffed it in his mouth and devoured it in a few seconds, but not today. He decided he would save it for his mother.

She was already fixing their midday meal when Josef returned home. A pot of potatoes was bubbling over the fire, with a few carrots and leeks adding color to the stew. It was the same meal they had yesterday and the day before and every day except Sunday. Sometimes the pot contained turnips and cabbage, but always they ate boiled potatoes. Frequently Josef complained. But today he would not complain.

They sat down, each with a bowl of potato stew, and ate in silence. After he had cleaned his bowl, Josef said with some hesitation, "Mutti, I brought you something."

His mother slowly raised her head and looked at him. Josef took from his sleeve the misshapen bun, now quite flat as well. He handed it to her across the table. She took the bun in her hand and stared at it for a few seconds until tears welled up in her eyes. Josef thought once again he had done something wrong.

"What did I do, Mutti?"

"Oh, Josef. It has raisins."

"Yes, Mutti. I thought you'd like them."

"But, Josef, it's your favorite. You take it back."

"Let's divide it. You eat half and I'll eat half."

They shared the bun, though Josef's mother pulled most of the raisins from her piece and pressed them into his. Before they went back to work, she put her arms around him and tenderly kissed the top of his head.

Some weeks later, as Josef was leaving the market square on a bright, clear morning, he felt the first warm breezes of summer surround him like a blanket. It was a wonderful feeling that made him want to skip all the way home. Of course he could not skip with his load of vegetables, so he began to whistle instead. He was turning his head from side to side, noticing colorful flowers blooming in upstairs window boxes, when he heard a sharp voice.

"Stop. Why are you whistling?"

He immediately stopped whistling but kept walking and looked straight ahead.

"I said stop! You better stop when I tell you to."

The tall boy jumped in front of him and blocked his way. Immediately five other boys came out from doorways and alleyways and surrounded him. One grabbed the basket out of his hand. The tall boy demanded, "Okay, bastard. Tell me why you were whistling. Are you a bird, or just a bird-brain?"

Josef stammered under his breath, "I . . . I'm not a bird. I'm a person."

"You hear that, boys? He thinks he's a person!"

"He's not a person, he's a bastard!"

The boys pushed Josef into an alley and up against a wall. They crowded close around him.

"Who's your father, bastard?"

"Tell us who your father is."

Josef remained silent.

"Hey, fellows, he can't tell us who his father is!"

"That's 'cause he's a bastard and he ain't got no father."

"I'll bet his mother's a whore."

Josef had never heard that word before, but he felt sure it was an ugly word. Tears filled his eyes and he cried out, "She is not!"

"Cry-baby. Look, he's crying 'cause his mother's a whore."

The boys began pushing him back and forth between them and calling out "Cry-baby" at each push. Josef heard the familiar chant echoing in his ears from all sides. Suddenly it stopped.

"Who's there?" came a quavering voice from the head of the alley. Josef knew the voice. It was Father Albert, the old priest who was nearly blind.

"Who's there?" came the voice again.

The tall boy whispered something to the others. All but one of them disappeared out the back side of the alley—they left the red-haired boy to guard Josef. He immediately grabbed Josef's wrist and told him not to move and not to say anything. He said the boys would come back and give him a "cudgeling" if he cried out. They stood silently with their backs against a wall for a few minutes, the red-haired boy keeping a tight grip on Josef's wrist. They heard no more from the old priest.

From the back side of the alley came the sound of footsteps. It seemed to Josef more like the sound of one person than like a whole gang of boys. Whoever it was walked up close to them and might have passed by without stopping, except that Josef gave out a short, involuntary sob.

"What's going on here?" asked the one who had just arrived.

"Get lost," said the red-haired boy.

"Let me hear from the other boy first."

Josef was too frightened to speak but he sobbed again.

"Okay. Let go of him, and if you won't tell me what's going on, then you just get out of here." With that the speaker clenched his fists and glared at the red-haired boy, who backed away slowly. From a safe distance, he threatened to return with his gang and beat them up. Then he spun around and ran.

The new boy turned to Josef. "What's your name?"

"I'm Josef."

"Well I'm Mosche. I'm nine years old, but my granny says I'm big for my age, and strong too. Where do you live?"

"Down Market Street, behind the butcher shop."

"Come on, I'll walk you home."

Josef found his basket. One of the boys had dropped it in the alley. He picked up the vegetables that had spilled out and carefully put them back in place. "Where do you live?" he asked as the two boys emerged from the alley.

Mosche pointed in the direction of the market square, but more toward the river. "Over there, in the Jewish quarter."

"Does that mean you're a Jew?"

"Yes, I'm a Jew."

"What's a Jew?"

Mosche laughed. "Well, my mother and father are Jews, and my sister. We read Torah and keep the laws and worship the Holy One."

"You can read?" asked Josef in astonishment.

"Yes. I started school when I was six years old. All the boys do. And some of the girls learn to read at home."

"I'm six years old, and I don't go to school."

"Do you want to?"

"I can't, because I have to haul water in the morning and help my mother in the afternoon." Josef hesitated. "Could . . . could you teach me to read?"

"Well, my father says it is the duty of every scholar to teach others. So I guess if you want to learn to read, I'll have to teach you. But you'll need to know Hebrew first."

"Okay."

"All right. I make deliveries for my father every morning except Sabbath. I guess we could meet early at the market and do lessons while we walk around."

Josef was becoming excited. "Yes! My mother mends clothes, and sometimes she asks me to return them to their owners. It would help her if I did *all* the returns. And some mornings I get sewing supplies and shop at the market. Could we meet every day?"

"Well, let's try it once or twice and see how it goes."

The following Monday morning Josef approached the market square apprehensively. Was this the morning they had agreed upon? Would Mosche be waiting for him out in the open, or would he conceal himself? What if they couldn't find each other? What if Mosche decided he didn't want to bother teaching a kid he met on the street?

When he passed the last buildings and emerged into the square, there was Mosche! He was waiting by the well in the middle of the square. Beside him was a small pull-cart loaded with hunks of cheese of all sizes, from slim wedges to huge wheels. Josef ran to meet him, holding tightly to the articles of clothing draped over his shoulder.

"I'm here!" he called out.

Mosche laughed. "I can see that. Let's get started. I usually go down Martinus Road toward the old prison, then over on Corn Lane and back up Chambers Street, with visits to some of the side streets. Sometimes I cut through an alley to Market Street, like I did the day I met you." After a short pause he added, "Who was that ugly red-haired kid?"

Josef winced. "Just someone who hates me."

"Well, don't worry about him. He won't bother you when you're with me."

The boys set out together to make deliveries. Mosche began his instruction immediately. "Okay, here's how it works. First you learn the Hebrew alphabet. Those are letters we use to make words. You learn how to pronounce the letters and what they look like. I brought my slate so I can draw them for you."

Mosche pulled from his cart a smooth, flat, rectangular board and made some marks on it with a piece of charcoal. "That's an *alef*. *Abba* starts with *alef*. *Abba* means 'dad'. You got it?"

"Yup."

"Okay. After you learn the letters, you put them together to make words, and then you put words together to make sentences. Then you start memorizing sentences, lots and lots of sentences, from Torah. Can you do that?"

"Yup. I think so."

"Good. We'll try it for a couple of weeks. Then if you want to keep going, you'll need to have a ceremony."

"What kind of ceremony?"

"An initiation ceremony. Every boy who starts school has a ceremony. Don't worry, it doesn't hurt."

As they traversed the streets, Mosche's instruction flowed quickly, and Josef soaked it up eagerly. Once they had made all their deliveries, the boys agreed on a day and time for their next meeting, and they parted. Josef set out for home in high spirits. Approaching the courtyard, he remembered he was supposed to stop at the sewing shop to get thread and patches for his mother. He ran back at full speed and returned home completely out of breath, but happier than he had ever been in his life.

The next afternoon, Josef went with his mother to St. Paul's Church where occasionally, on Sundays and holy days, they would sit at the back and listen to the Mass. Not today—there was no Mass this afternoon. Josef was helping his mother carry heavy linens back to the church. She had washed them, and now she would meet with other women to press and fold and put them away. It was a task she enjoyed, a brief respite from routine and a chance to chat with her few friends. Josef enjoyed it, too. He was expected to wait in a small garden beside the church.

A portion of the garden was bounded by the church itself, and the rest was surrounded by a high wall that shielded it from street noises and random intruders. For Josef it was the most peaceful, secluded place he knew. He would spend hours (or so it seemed) admiring the colorful flowerbeds and watching bees hurry from one blossom to the next.

But today Josef settled on his favorite bench and closed his eyes. He breathed deeply of sweet-smelling lilies and heard faint buzzing noises. The warm air made him drowsy. He could have fallen asleep had he not been jolted awake by the sound of the heavy iron latch opening and snapping shut.

Through the gate came old Father Albert. He was short and stooped, and his feet shuffled when he walked. His frizzy white hair pointed in every direction. As he drew closer, Josef could see his small eyes, set close together and bunched up in a perpetual squint. Father Albert hobbled straight to the bench and sat down beside Josef. Nevertheless, Josef was not certain the old priest had noticed his presence. The boy looked up and marveled at the network of wrinkles in the man's face, divided by deep creases. Slowly Father Albert turned his face toward the boy.

"Hello, little one."

"Hello, Father."

"Tell me your name."

"I'm Josef."

"And why are you here on this lovely afternoon?"

"My mother washes linens."

"Ah, yes." The old man turned his head and seemed to focus on the wall opposite, if he could see that far.

"Father, can I ask you a question?"

"Yes. What is it?"

"Can you read?"

Without turning his head back to the boy, the priest answered, "No, it was not deemed necessary for me to read. My work has always been with the sick and the lame and the poor. It's only those who teach or copy books or intone Scripture who require the skill of reading."

"Didn't you want to learn?"

"There was a time, when I was young, when I thought it would be wonderful to read the Scriptures and other works of literature as well. But it was not the will of God. My superiors determined I was to be a humble servant and not a scholar."

"Did you try to change their minds?"

"No, it was the will of God. I learned the prayers and doctrines and memorized certain formularies I would need in my work. The Father provides all that we need."

Josef mumbled quietly under his breath, "I haven't got a father."

The man turned and looked directly into Josef's face. "Nonsense, boy. You have a Father in heaven."

"I mean I haven't got a father at home."

"That may be so, but your heavenly Father loves you and cares for you just the same. And remember you call me 'father,' and the other priests."

Now Josef turned his head and looked intently at the wall. Should he ask Father Albert what a bastard was? He still was not sure what the word meant, although he suspected it had something to do with his mother. Would this simple old man recognize the word, and even if he did, would he explain it to a boy? No, it would be better not to ask a priest, in case it was a sin to say the word. Besides, if Josef asked about it, Father Albert might tell his mother.

When Josef looked up again at the old man, his eyes were closed. He seemed to be deep in thought or asleep. Josef remained silent until his mother came to get him and they went home.

Ever since he met Mosche, Josef was approached less often in the Market Street by those horrible boys. They stayed away from him entirely whenever Mosche was with him. Even when Josef ran errands alone, his schedule and his route were less predictable now, and he was frequently able to sneak through their territory unobserved.

One Saturday morning, however, they met him as he returned from the market. The tall boy stepped in front of him and walked backwards in Josef's path. "Well, if it isn't the bastard! What have you been up to, bastard?"

Josef kept walking.

"Hey, boys, look what I found!" Three others came out and walked alongside, chanting the usual refrains. "Bastard, bastard."

"Who's your father?"

"Tell us who sleeps with your mother!"

Josef stopped abruptly and looked straight into the tall boy's face. The others ceased their taunts and stared down at him. Josef said quietly, "My father is God."

The boys exchanged uncertain glances until the tall one burst out laughing. "His mother slept with God! Can you believe it?"

"Or maybe she slept with the bishop!"

"Naw, he's too good for her. I'll bet she sleeps with Jews. That's why this kid smells so bad."

Josef pushed his way forward and resolved to say no more. Some day he would understand the words they used and then he would be able to refute them. But now it was useless. He would just try to pretend they were not there.

As he walked down the block, the boys followed close behind. Josef could hear them talking about what they would do to anyone who gave them trouble in their territory. They would beat him until his eyes bulged out of his head. They would tear his arms out of their sockets. They told each other they were stronger and meaner than anyone else in the city. Josef was relieved when he crossed the next square and could no longer hear their boasting.

Late one morning the following week, Josef was resting in the courtyard by his house. He had already made deliveries and done a lesson with Mosche, and had just finished hauling water to the shops around the courtyard.

Now he was playing with the blacksmith's cat. He happened to look up and see Father Matthias, the young priest from St. Paul's Church, peering over the gate. Father Matthias lifted the latch and came through. He was a stocky, red-faced man with straight black hair.

"Hello, young man. You are Josef, aren't you?"

"Yes, Father."

The priest sat on a ledge of the stone wall and motioned for Josef to sit beside him. "I was passing through your neighborhood and thought I might have a word with you."

"With me, Father?" the boy asked incredulously.

"Yes. Old Father Albert spoke to me the other day and said you seemed to be interested in books and reading and that sort of thing."

"Yes, Father." Josef looked up at him eagerly.

"Perhaps some day you would like to be a priest and a learned man?"

"I want to learn as much as I can. If I didn't have to work all the time, I could go to school."

"There are no schools in Worms."

"The Jews have schools."

Father Matthias narrowed his eyes. "Who told you that? What do you know about Jews?"

"A boy I met. He said *all* the boys in his street start school when they're six."

Father Matthias assumed a serious tone. "Now, listen. You must not mingle with Jews. They are infidels and Christ-haters. We allow them to live near us because they are masters of commerce. It's all right to buy and sell with them but not to talk to them about other things. Do you understand?"

"I guess."

"And besides, it's not necessary for all boys to learn to read. In fact, it would be harmful. Most of what has been written is utter trash. The common people get all the learning they need from the creeds and what the priests teach them. Anything else is likely to undermine their faith."

Josef remained silent.

"Here is what we will do. In two years you may commence your study of Latin. I myself will instruct you. In the meantime, Father Albert will teach you creeds and doctrines so that you may be ready to read Holy Scripture with the right understanding." As he said this, Father Matthias leaned closer, and Josef could smell his breath. "If you make good progress in Latin, perhaps you may someday study with the monks at the cloister. We'll see if we can make a scholar of you."

The priest rose and opened the gate. As he was leaving the courtyard he said, "You may speak to your mother about this, but no one else. And, mind you, stay away from Jews."

Chapter 2

What was Josef to do now? His best friend Mosche was a Jew, and yet Father Matthias had told him to stay away from Jews. The two boys had been meeting early in the morning almost every day for several weeks. Josef helped Mosche unload heavy cheese wheels from his cart, and he had found other ways to be helpful as well. He wanted to do as much as he could to show how grateful he was for all that Mosche was doing for him.

Mosche had continued teaching Josef. Already they had worked through most of the Hebrew alphabet, up to the letter *tzadi*. Mosche had taught him many words, most recently words that began with *tzadi*, like *tzedaka*. It was the duty of every Jew, Mosche said, to practice *tzedaka*, to give alms to the poor and show kindness to the needy. It sounded exactly like what Jesus said. Hadn't his own mother told him that Jesus taught us to give alms to poor beggars? Father Matthias had said Jews were Christ-haters, but how could it be that Mosche would hate a man who taught *tzedaka*?

Suddenly Josef had an idea. He would ask Mosche if he hated Jesus. If Mosche said no, then they could still be friends. Maybe Father Matthias was wrong—maybe some Jews didn't hate Jesus after all.

At their next meeting Josef brought up the subject cautiously. "What would you think of a Christian who did *tzedaka*?"

"Perhaps he studied Torah," said Mosche, "and that would be a good thing."

"What if he was also a teacher?"

"You know that many of our rabbis are great teachers. We respect them above all others."

"Have you heard of someone called Jesus?"

"Yes, he was a Jew and a rabbi."

Josef could not believe his ears. "Jesus was a Jew? Then how could you hate him?"

Mosche looked at Josef with a puzzled expression. He seemed to be thinking how best to respond. "Who said I hate Jesus? He was just a man who lived a long time ago. His followers did some crazy things, but that doesn't mean I hate him."

Josef, who had been holding his breath, exhaled. "I'm glad," he said. "Now we can still be friends."

Mosche shrugged his shoulders. "Okay. Let's do our lesson."

When Josef returned home that morning, his mother was waiting for him at the gate. She looked agitated. "Josef, I must speak to you right away."

"What is it, Mutti?" Was she going to reprimand him for staying away too long in the mornings? Had she found out about his meetings with Mosche?

"You know times have been hard lately. Since the price of grain went up, everything else has been more expensive too." She sighed. "After we pay the rent and buy sewing supplies, we have barely enough left for food."

Josef was relieved to know the source of his mother's anxiety. "It's all right, Mutti. We'll gather more this year after the harvest. I'll stay longer in the fields, and fill more baskets and carry more loads."

"But it will be two months before harvest season is here. I've found a way to get a few more pennies each week. We'll rent out the back room to a boarder. There'll be less space for you and me, but it can't be helped. I've already moved my sleeping mat to your corner by the fireplace, and I found another stool to put at the table. He'll be taking most of his meals with us."

"Who?"

"The boarder. That's why I wanted to talk to you right away. He's already moved in. His name is Joakim."

Josef followed his mother across the courtyard and up the stairway. Once inside, he saw a middle-aged man with stringy hair and stubble on his chin sitting on a stool at the table. The man glanced up at them as they entered.

"Joakim, this is my son Josef."

Joakim grunted.

She addressed him again. "Our usual breakfast is porridge, but I put a bit of sausage over the fire for you this morning."

The man picked up his spoon. As soon as a bowl was placed in front of him, he began scooping large quantities into his mouth. His bowl was half empty before Josef and his mother began eating. Porridge and sausage disappeared together while Josef looked on wistfully. He wished he could have had just the smallest bit of sausage in his bowl.

Joakim wiped his mouth with his sleeve and eyed Josef's mother. He rose from the table, picked up his satchel, and went out, saying he would be back for dinner. Josef waited a few minutes and then said, "Mutti, I don't like him."

"Well, I don't like him either, but we need the money."

"I wish he wouldn't live here."

"We really need the money."

The following Sunday Josef had agreed to meet Mosche on Market Street, near the entrance to Jews' Alley. Customarily on Sunday afternoons, his mother went across town to visit her elderly aunt, and Josef was allowed to play with his friends during that time. He was glad to get away from his house now that Joakim lived there. The man spent his leisure hours snoring in the back room or loitering in the courtyard, and Josef found his company disagreeable.

Today was the day Mosche had chosen for the ceremony to initiate him as a new student. Josef did not know quite what to expect, although his friend had told him he would wear special clothes and eat special food. Josef arrived early at the place they were to meet. He stood at the corner observing Jews coming and going along the alley. He had never entered the street or paid much attention to the people who lived there, but now he could see they looked no different from the people he knew. Many of the women wore scarves and some of the men had beards, but these adornments were not uncommon in the city.

When Mosche walked up a few minutes later, he was holding a small child by the hand. "Sorry I'm late. This is my sister Miriam. I forgot how slow she walks."

Miriam looked up at Josef with wide, blue eyes. He was immediately struck by her intelligent, piercing gaze that seemed as if it might see into a person's soul.

"Is she going to have a ceremony, too?"

"No, girls don't do that," said her brother. "But we need a female person to help with your ceremony. The first thing we do is go to the synagogue."

The children walked less than a block down Jews' Alley before turning into a courtyard on the right side of the street. A three-story rectangular building stood before them. Josef noticed round arches over the doors and windows, similar to most of the churches he had seen. But the synagogue had no tall spires like a church—its appearance was simple and sturdy. The building and the courtyard were both made of stone, but quite different from each other. The rough-hewn stones of the courtyard, grey and of fairly uniform size, had been laid side-by-side on the bare ground, making an uneven surface. The synagogue stone was smoother and warmer-looking, consisting of pinkish-brown blocks of varying sizes, held together by white mortar. Large, powerful corner blocks and finely cut stones around the windows and doors made the building look interesting and beautiful.

The children entered through heavy wooden doors with panel decorations. Once inside, Josef saw more pink stone in the floor, along the lower part of the walls, and in columns rising from the center of the room. The upper walls and ceiling were whitewashed, and that, together with large windows of clear glass, gave the synagogue a bright, airy feeling, not like the dark, gloomy interiors of churches.

Mosche went first to a small cabinet at the back of the room. He took out a four-cornered, wool cloth with stripes across it and fringes on two sides. "This is a *tallit*," he said. "You wear it for this part of the ceremony."

Mosche wrapped it around Josef's head and draped the ends over his shoulders. He took Josef by the hand and led him to the other end of the room. Against the wall was a table with a silver lamp and a large, decorated box resting on it. "Here at the east wall, we keep the Torah scrolls in a wooden box called the *aron*. That lamp is kept burning whenever the scrolls are in the *aron* so we know they're there. Now we're supposed to read verses from the law, but since I'm not allowed to touch the scrolls, I'll say some verses I know by heart."

Assuming a solemn demeanor, he began to sway and chant.

"And the Lord spoke unto Moses, saying, Speak unto all the congregation of the children of Israel, and say unto them, Ye shall be holy; for I the Eternal your God am holy. Ye shall revere, every man, his mother and his father, and my Sabbaths shall ye keep: I am the Lord your God. Ye shall not turn unto the idols, and molten gods ye shall not make unto yourselves: I am the Lord your God. And when ye reap the harvest of your land, thou shalt not wholly reap the corners of thy field, neither shalt thou gather up the gleanings of thy harvest. And thou shalt not glean thy vineyard, and the single grapes that drop in thy vineyard shalt thou not gather up; for the poor and the stranger shalt thou leave them: I am the Lord your God. Ye shall not steal; neither shall ye deny another's property in your hands, nor lie to one another. And ye shall not swear by my name falsely, and thou shalt not thus profane the name of thy God: I am the Lord. Thou shalt not withhold anything from thy neighbor, nor rob him: there shall not abide with thee the wages of him that is hired, through the night until morning. Thou shalt not curse the deaf, nor put a stumbling-block before the blind; but thou shalt be afraid of thy God: I am the Lord."

Mosche stopped reciting. "Okay, that's enough. Do you have any questions?"

"What are 'gleanings'?"

"Just bits and pieces of crops farmers leave in the fields for poor people to pick up."

Josef remembered the times he and his mother had gone into the fields when their food supply ran low. He asked no more questions.

Mosche lifted the *tallit* off Josef's head, folded it carefully, and placed it back in the cabinet. "Next comes the fun part," he said. "We go to the teacher's house to taste the sweetness of the law."

The children followed Jews' Alley until they came to an old gate in the city wall. They went through the gate and walked a few hundred paces along the outside of the wall until they reached a small hut set against the stonework.

"This is your teacher's house," said Mosche proudly. "I don't really live here, but I keep my things here."

"Did you build it?"

"Not exactly. It was a shelter for shepherds, I think. But it was falling down, and I fixed it up."

The children entered the hut. A thick layer of fresh straw had been laid on the floor. Josef inhaled deeply the sweet aromas of the place. Was it the straw he smelled, or something else? Perhaps something freshly baked? In the corner he saw several rough, wooden boxes with various items stacked on top, a wash basin, some clothes, and plates of food.

Mosche pointed at the wash basin. "First you wash your hands and your face. Then put on a clean shirt and we'll start the second part of the ceremony."

Josef did as he was told.

"Okay," Mosche said. "Now I'm going to put honey on my slate, and you have to lick it off and say the verse that's written on the slate. Today we'll use ordinary language, but later you'll learn it in Hebrew." He dipped a stick into a small jar of honey and smeared it on a corner of the slate. "Now lick the honey and say these words after me: 'How much sweeter to my palate are thy sayings than honey to my mouth!'"

Josef licked the honey and repeated, "How much sweeter to my palate are thy sayings than honey to my mouth."

"Good. Miriam will help us with the next part. You're supposed to eat three cakes kneaded in honey by a virgin, and also some eggs and fruit."

"What's a virgin?"

"I'm not sure, but I think it means a young woman or girl. Anyway, my mother baked these cakes, and she's a good cook. Miriam will dip them in honey and feed them to you. Are you ready?"

"Yup."

Miriam picked up the cakes, dipped them in the jar of honey, and stuffed them, one after another, into Josef's mouth. Meanwhile, Mosche peeled three hard-cooked eggs and presented them to Josef, along with an apple and some blackberries.

"You eat while I say more verses."

"Can Miriam have some too?"

Mosche nodded and began reciting. "And he said unto me, Son of man, feed thy belly, and fill thy bowels with this roll that I am giving unto thee. And I ate it; and it was in my mouth like honey in sweetness. Open thou my eyes, that I may behold wondrous things out of thy law. Oh how do I love thy law! all the day it is my meditation. A lamp unto my feet is thy word, and a light unto my path. The opening of thy words giveth light, it giveth understanding unto the simple."

After Mosche finished his recitation, he joined the others in eating the berries that remained. When they were done, he said, "Now change back into your own shirt. For the last part of the ceremony, we go down to the river."

"I'm not allowed to get in the water," said Josef.

"Don't worry. We'll just go to the edge and look."

The children left the hut and walked down gentle slopes on a narrow pathway through fields and vineyards. They arrived at a promontory overlooking the wide river. A few small fishing boats were anchored against the steady current. Mosche explained to Josef that Torah is like water. "It feeds us, and refreshes us, and gives us life. Do you have any questions?"

Josef shook his head.

"Okay. Then I will say one more verse and the ceremony will be over. 'When Israel was yet young, then I loved him, and out of Egypt did I call my son.' That's the end. Now you're ready to be a scholar."

Josef beamed. The children stayed at the river bank, dangling their legs off the rock and watching fishermen cast their nets from stationary boats. Occasionally a large transport barge floated past, carried along by powerful currents. They said little to one another, but Josef could feel a strong bond growing between himself and Mosche. Here was a boy who loved what he loved and thought as he thought. He had never yet had such a friend. It made him feel he belonged, like he had a purpose and a goal other than just hauling water day after day. He hoped some day he could be a real scholar and know as many verses from Scripture as Mosche.

After a time, the children made their way back through the fields, entered the city gate, and passed into the Jewish quarter. Mosche and Miriam left the main road and went home, while Josef continued along Jews' Alley until he reached Market Street. He turned toward his house, feeling happy and confident. He would be a scholar! He would read many books and learn about everything under the sun! His world seemed much larger than it had before.

Walking along Market Street, he heard a familiar whistle. All at once, three boys jumped out and stood in his path. Josef stopped, looked up at them, and took a deep breath. When they started taunting him, he ignored them. He kept walking forward, not hearing a word they said, and barely noticed their pokes and jabs.

One morning it took longer than usual for Mosche and Josef to make their deliveries. They had already completed the daily lesson and were talking about other things. Suddenly Josef became serious and turned to his friend. "Do you know what a bastard is?"

"Yes. I think it's a person whose mother and father are not married."

"But what if a person has no father?"

"Everybody has a father. It's impossible to be born without one."

"What do you mean?"

"Well, a woman has to lie with a man before she can have a baby. Whoever it is she lies with, he's the father."

"So, if my mother is not married, that means I'm a bastard."

Mosche was silent for a minute. "I'm sorry. I didn't know."

The boys walked on without speaking, until Mosche said, "Listen. Our great rabbi Scholomo says that a man who teaches is like a father, and his students are called children. That makes *me* your father."

"You can't be my father. You're just a kid, like me."

"Not your *real* father, of course, but your teacher-father. Rabbi Scholomo says a teacher gives birth to a student and makes him a new man, almost like a new baby coming into the world. It's in Scripture, too. When the Lord commands a person to teach Torah diligently to his children, the rabbi says it means his students."

"Okay. What if I agree for you to be my teacher-father? What then?"

"Don't you see? You'll have two families, one with a mother and one with a father."

Josef wanted to think about this for awhile.

"Who is Rabbi Scholomo, anyway?"

"Rabbi Scholomo ben Itzhak. He lived in Worms and studied here for a long time. Everybody knows about him. He is such a wise man that people came here from all over the world to ask him questions, even Christians."

"Where does he live now?"

"He started his own school in Troyes. It's called a Jeschiba, where lots of scholars get together and talk about important things. But he comes back to visit his friends in Worms, and we still call him 'our rabbi.'"

"Have you met him?"

"Not yet. He lived here before I was born, and last time he came, I was sick. I'll meet him some day. Does the butcher shop near you have flies?"

"What?"

"Have you noticed any flies in the butcher shop near your house?"

"I don't know. Why?"

"Because Rabbi Scholomo lived in a house outside the Jewish quarter, near a butcher shop. People say the butcher shop never had flies. It could have been your house."

"What else do you know about him?"

"His parents lived in Worms before he was born. The old people in my neighborhood remember a story about his mother when she was expecting a baby. A runaway horse pulling a carriage behind it was galloping toward her, and she was afraid she would be killed, and the baby too. So she pushed against a wall behind her and it sank back and protected her. You can still see the sunken place in a wall near the synagogue."

"What happened then?"

"Her husband Itzhak was afraid she would be called a witch, and so he took the family to live in Troyes. That's where their son was born. He grew up and became our great rabbi. We still call him the 'rabbi of Worms.'"

"What makes him so great?"

"His knowledge and wisdom. He can speak five or six languages and knows all about science. And he writes notebooks that explain Scripture and other holy books. He makes words of Torah so clear that even my sister can understand."

Josef had much to think about as he walked home that day. Apparently he did have a father after all, but his father did not live with them. Who could it be? Why did the man not marry his mother? Mosche had offered to be his father (sort of) and give him another family. Josef would have loved to have a brother like Mosche, to go to school with him every day and to read books with him after school. The two of them together could meet the great rabbi from Troyes when he came to visit and maybe even hear him teach. There was so much to learn, and now that Josef could read simple texts, his desire was growing. He wanted to read and understand every book that was ever written. He wanted to learn from great teachers and have long discussions about books he read. But all this would have to wait. He had to work every day of the week except Sunday.

Only on Saturday afternoons was time set aside for him to meet with Father Albert and learn about Church doctrine. He had already memorized two things, the Our Father and the creed from Nicaea. The old priest had explained them as best he could. The Our Father contained seven petitions, he said, and they had talked about all seven of them. Seven must be an important number because Father Albert had told him he would learn seven beatitudes, and seven gifts of the Holy Spirit, and seven principal virtues. There was also a list of mortal sins he had to memorize. So many lists! Josef wished he could learn Latin right away and start reading, but Father Matthias had said he needed to learn

Church doctrine first. Well, at least Father Albert was a kind man, and funny too. Josef enjoyed spending time with him.

One Saturday afternoon in late fall, Josef met Father Albert in the garden by St. Paul's Church. When it was rainy or cold, they would do their lesson in a small room in the basement of the church. But today the sun was bright and the air was unusually warm, and so they met outdoors. At Father Albert's request, Josef recited the creed. For this lesson they would talk about Jesus Christ, the only-begotten Son of God.

"What does 'begotten' mean?" asked Josef.

"It means he grew in his mother's womb, like you did."

"Did Jesus have a father who was married to his mother?"

"Yes, his mother married a good man named Josef. You are privileged to share his name."

"Did he lie with her?"

"No, Josef did not beget the child. Rather, it was a miracle of the Holy Spirit. Jesus came down from heaven and entered the womb of the Virgin Mary."

"What's a virgin?"

"A virgin is a young woman who has never lain with a man."

"Then who was Jesus' father?"

"God is his Father."

"Like God is my father?"

"Not in precisely the same way. But we are all children of God, created in his image."

Josef was confused. Jesus' mother was married, and so the man was Jesus' father. But the man was not Jesus' father, because Jesus came down from heaven. God was his father, but not in the same way he was everyone else's father. And all of us were like the image of God. What could it mean? Josef shook his head and looked bewildered.

Father Albert chuckled. "Don't worry, my son. There are mysteries that even the great doctors of the Church cannot understand. But if you learn something very well and let it sit in your head for a long time, you may come to understand it better."

There was one question Josef wanted to ask that might have a simple answer. "Is it true that Jesus was a Jew?"

"Why, yes. He was the Messiah who had been promised to the Jews."

This raised more questions in Josef's mind. Why had Father Matthias told him Jews were Christ-haters? If they were, what made them hate one of their own people, their own Messiah? Why should Christians worship one Jew but be required to stay away from other Jews? Josef thought he'd better not ask any more questions. Father Albert might get annoyed with him, and besides, it was time to go home.

Late that evening, Josef was lying on his mat, thinking about his discussion with Father Albert, when he saw something that disturbed him. While his mother was cleaning and putting away dishes, Joakim, the man who slept in the back room, hovered around her. A couple of times he brushed against her, and once he curled his arm around her hips and put his hand on her belly. She pushed him away, but he got close again and mumbled something to her. Then he grinned and licked his lips before retiring to his room. Josef did not rest well that night.

Chapter 3

What could Josef do to protect his mother? He knew that Joakim had evil intentions toward her and that she would suffer if the man had his way. Speaking to his mother could have no good effect—she was determined to get extra income from renting the room. He would have to speak directly to Joakim, to tell him to leave her alone, and even to threaten him if necessary. Would he listen, or just laugh at threats from a seven-year-old? Josef had grown considerably taller and stronger in the past year, and he was more confident too. Yes, he would have to take a chance, in hopes that Joakim would listen and not get angry. The difficulty now was finding a time to confront the man while his mother was out of earshot.

The opportunity came a few days later, on one of the rare mornings when Josef was not making purchases or deliveries for his mother. She had gone out early to clean a neighbor's house. Josef was still lying on his mat, half asleep. As sunlight streamed through a small window, he reached into the hiding place he had found under a loose floorboard and pulled out a tiny scroll. Mosche had made the scroll from an unused scrap of parchment given to him by the rabbi—Mosche was always looking for something to write on. He had written out one of the psalms, and now Josef was trying to decipher the tiny letters.

After reading a few lines, he heard shuffling noises from the other room. Joakim must be waking up, he thought. Quickly he put the scroll back in its hiding place and rose from his mat. He pulled on his over-shirt and went to stir the porridge his mother had left in a pot over the fire. Joakim would want his breakfast as soon as he came out. Josef scooped out helpings of oatmeal porridge into bowls and set them on the table. He sat down to wait.

Joakim emerged from his room, looking groggy and disheveled. He came over to the table and began eating. Josef felt a knot in his stomach.

He knew if he tried to eat, the food would not go down easily, so he held his spoon and stared at the man sitting across the table from him. Suddenly Joakim stopped eating and eyed him suspiciously.

"Why aren't you eating, boy?"

"I'm not very hungry."

Joakim went back to his bowl. When he was nearly finished, Josef summoned every bit of courage he had and said quietly, "Don't touch my mother."

Joakim looked up at him. "What?" His mouth hung open, and the sight of porridge on Joakim's tongue made Josef nauseous. He looked away. "I said, don't touch my mother."

"Who are you to give me orders?"

"I'm her son, and you leave her alone."

"What if she wants me? Women like that always want a man."

Josef turned his head back to look at the man. "If you touch her, I'll do something to make you sorry."

Joakim snickered into his sleeve. He picked up his hat and bag of tools and walked out.

Josef now knew all the Hebrew letters. He had learned to read and pronounce many words during the months he had studied with Mosche. At first Mosche had copied texts on any scrap of wood or parchment he could find. Josef was soon able to read the daily prayers and recite many of them by heart, as well as certain short Scripture passages. By early springtime, it was clear he was ready to attempt longer texts. This would necessitate his having access to Torah scrolls and other writings.

The boys decided they would meet at daybreak, before making their morning deliveries, in the schoolhouse behind the synagogue. At that hour, none of the Jeschiba scholars would have arrived yet. The boys would be able to use the teaching scrolls in the classroom where Mosche studied. There they could read aloud to each other and recite passages they wished to commit to memory. Later in the morning when the boys walked the streets, they could use their time together for reviewing and discussing the day's readings.

This plan was working well. Josef made good progress reading through the first book of Moses. He loved hearing stories about ancient peoples and took special pleasure in the travel accounts of the patriarchs

Abraham and Jakob. Imagine mounting a camel and crossing mountains and wide-open plains and rivers! Mosche had told him to sway back and forth as he recited verses from memory, and he often pretended he was swaying on a camel's back while it loped along. The time they spent in the schoolhouse was enjoyable for another reason—Mosche frequently brought raisins, figs, and nuts for them to eat as they studied. He said students need encouragement and sustenance to keep up their enthusiasm for learning.

One morning they read about how the patriarch Josef was sold into slavery by his brothers. As they discussed the passage, Mosche told his friend not to worry, that Josef would survive and save his people from starvation. In fact, he would become a great man and a hero and chief assistant to the king of Egypt. "That must be why your mother named you Josef. She wanted you to be a hero like Josef, son of Jacob."

"No. My mother says she named me after Josef the carpenter, who was father of our Lord."

"What? How can you say that? The Lord has no father! He is the Creator of all!" Mosche covered his ears to shield them from further blasphemy.

Josef was alarmed. He shook his head vigorously and motioned for Mosche to uncover his ears. He would try to explain. "I didn't mean God had a father, only that Jesus did. We call Jesus 'Lord' because he was the only-begotten Son of God."

Mosche looked solemn. "You better not use the word 'Lord' that way anymore, at least not when you're with a Jew. There's only *one* Lord—it's the first thing our parents teach us. Any Jew can tell you that." He paused a moment and added, "Wouldn't you rather be named after a great, powerful leader than a carpenter?"

Another day, as they walked the streets, the boys discussed ritual sacrifice of animals. That morning they had read passages in the third book of Moses describing how Aaron and his sons were to slay a bull and present it as an offering to the Lord. Josef was fascinated to read how blood was thrown all around and flesh cut into little pieces. Even the head and fat and entrails of the animal were to be laid on the altar and burned. What a mess! His mother would have had a difficult time cleaning up. "Do Jews today kill animals and throw blood around?" he asked Mosche.

"I don't think so. We don't have a temple anymore so there's no altar to throw blood on."

"What happened to the temple?"

"The Romans burned it down. Then they made all the Jews leave Jerusalem."

"Why?"

"I guess they wanted Jews to follow the Roman religion instead of their own. It didn't work though."

"What did they do?"

"Wherever they went, Jews took the Torah with them. It was their protection against enemies who wanted them to forget about God. That's why we have to study Torah so much."

"What if people don't want to study?"

"Everybody's supposed to study. It's part of our religion. People who don't know Torah and don't teach it to their children can't be good Jews. Sometimes we make those people leave the Jewish quarter."

"Why can't they be good Jews?"

"Because you need to know the Law before you can obey it. In fact, everything we learn makes us better Jews. Our rabbi says all learning points back to Torah, and Torah points us in the right direction."

"What if there's no school in town?"

"One of the elders said a community with no school for children deserves to be destroyed. But I think every Jewish quarter has a school beside the synagogue. Some farmers live too far away to send all their sons to school, but they try to send at least one to live in town and become a scholar."

The boys went on with their deliveries. After unloading a huge slab of cheese on the back stoop at the residence of a town dignitary, they sat down to rest. Mosche said, "May I ask you a question?"

"Okay."

"Do Christians really kill and eat people in their churches?"

Josef frowned. "Where did you hear that?"

"Well, I heard someone say that Christians eat human flesh and drink blood sacrificed at the altar. So I figured somebody must be killing somebody else."

"It's not like that, really. The priest takes bread and wine and somehow changes it into the body and blood of Jesus. It still looks like bread and wine, so it's not as bad as it sounds."

"Do people eat it?"

"Some people do. We always sit at the back of the church and watch because my mother doesn't think she's worthy to go up to the front. But for the people who do go up, the priest takes a little piece of the bread and dips it in the wine and puts it in their mouth." Josef's eyes brightened and he looked excited. "I have an idea! I could take you to Mass at St. Paul's so you could see it for yourself."

"No! Never!" Mosche looked horrified.

"Why not? We can sit at the back near the door and go out quickly if anybody notices us."

"I can't go in a church. It would be a terrible thing for a Jew to go in a church."

"I don't mind going to the synagogue with you."

"That's different. There's nothing in the synagogue you would object to. But churches! You just have to believe me."

"Okay."

At Josef's next meeting with Father Albert, the old priest asked him to name the seven principal sacraments. After doing so, Josef asked, "Which of the sacraments have you had?"

"Let me see," the priest answered. "I was baptized as an infant, of course, and confirmed when I was a young man. Since then I have participated in the Eucharist many hundreds (or even thousands) of times. Hmm, what's next? Ah, yes, penance. Penance I have done, but I've not yet received unction. You've already learned that unction is reserved for the last days of life."

"You must have been ordained, though, because you're a priest."

"Yes, I received Holy Orders when I was twenty-five years old, more than forty years ago!" Father Albert paused and closed his eyes. "You may not know that I was married, even before my ordination. My wife was a dear woman who helped me in my parish work. Her nursing skills were well-known."

"What happened to her?"

"She died in an epidemic. Still a young woman she was, and very beautiful." Father Albert contracted his eyebrows and compressed his lips so that his face became a tight web of wrinkles.

Josef though he'd better change the subject. "How do bread and wine become the body and blood of Jesus?" he asked.

"That's a hard question. We know it happens because Jesus said so. He told his disciples at their last meal that they were eating his flesh and drinking his blood. But how does it happen? The scholars may figure it out, but I know I'm not smart enough to understand."

"Well, how come some people eat his body and blood at the Mass and some don't?" Josef asked.

"St. Paul says that anyone who eats the bread or drinks the cup in an unworthy manner profanes the body and blood of our Lord. So it's only those judged worthy who are allowed to partake."

"How can you tell whether a person is worthy or not?"

"You're full of hard questions today! God himself knows who is worthy, and he entrusts his special representatives with this knowledge. Sometimes people you would not expect are denied the sacrament. Our own King Henry, it appears, has recently been judged unworthy."

"If the king isn't worthy, how could anybody else be?"

Father Albert winked. "Perhaps the king will be worthy again by this time next year." Assuming a more serious tone, he said, "Between you and me, very few people are worthy, but the Church makes allowances."

"Will they make allowances for my mother?"

Father Albert laid his hand on Josef's head. "We must trust our church leaders to make these decisions. They're learned men and they know more than we do. Do you see?"

Josef did not see, but he thought he'd better stop asking questions. He crinkled his nose and nodded. What had he learned today from Father Albert? We are not wise enough. We don't know enough. Only a few learned men have knowledge, and we must trust them. But he wondered why it was that most Christians did not know enough. Why didn't they try to learn more? Why did they not have schools where they could learn to read Holy Scriptures? Why didn't they ask and discuss hard questions?

Josef did not go directly home. He wanted time to think. Mosche had told him that people should not study to gain riches and rewards or even to earn respect. Rather they should study for love, because the Lord commanded us to love him with all our hearts. Did Christians not love the Lord? They certainly didn't study the way Jews did. As he walked the streets, Josef wondered what it means to love the Lord. How can you love someone you can't see, or hear, or touch? How is love connected with learning?

Before long Josef found himself in the market square, just as the Saturday market was closing down. He watched vendors pack up their remaining goods and load their carts for the journey home. It was nearly time for dinner, and the air was growing cool. Reluctantly Josef set out for his house, which was no longer the peaceful place he had enjoyed as a younger child. Now it was inhabited by a disagreeable stranger who made life more difficult for him and his mother. At least he hadn't seen Joakim harass her in the last few weeks.

On his way down Market Street, Josef sensed he was being watched. He sighed, suspecting he would soon be confronted by those boys who were the other great annoyance in his life. He was right. One after another, the boys appeared on the edges of the street, shadowing him from a distance. What was their intention? It was harder now to make him cry, but still they had power to make him miserable. As he glanced from one to another, he saw something ominous. A couple of the boys were holding objects in their hands that flashed in the slanted light of the afternoon sun. Were they holding clubs, perhaps iron rods to hit him with? No, they had knives! This was more than annoyance—this was danger! Josef turned around and ran as fast as he could go. Four of the boys ran after him. He could feel them getting closer with each stride.

When he reached the corner, Josef turned abruptly into Jews' Alley. The boys seemed to hesitate for a moment, then came after him. He led them down the narrow street for about a block and tumbled into the courtyard of the synagogue. Here they caught up with him. Two of them grabbed his wrists and twisted his arms behind his back. The red-haired boy pulled out a knife and waved it in front of Josef's face. "You're going to come with us, bastard. We need blood for our clubhouse door, and you're going to give it to us."

Just then the doors of the schoolhouse behind the synagogue swung open, and a crowd of men, boys, and a few women streamed out into the courtyard. All nicely dressed, they were shaking hands vigorously with each other and repeating their friendly greetings all around. The red-haired boy quickly put away his knife. An old man approached him, clasped him warmly by the hand, and said, "Shalom, my son!" The other boys received similar greetings. They were soon surrounded by a boisterous mass of humanity. Josef was able to wrench free and slip away from the others. As the crowd grew louder and more animated, Josef saw the four boys backing out of the courtyard and into the street. He smiled when he remembered what Mosche had told him about Sabbath sermons and the loud discussions that followed. This was not all scholarly talk, Mosche had said, but mostly reports of news and the latest gossip. Well, anyway, it sounded like music to his ears.

Was Mosche here? Josef looked around but did not see him. He'd have to ask Mosche sometime if he could attend a Sabbath sermon with him. But he'd better go home now (by a different route than Market Street) before his mother started worrying.

Now eight years old, Josef had fallen into a routine that brought a sense of satisfaction to his life. Meeting with Mosche four or five mornings each week, he had made good progress in learning Hebrew and read-ing Scriptures. They had read through the five books of Moses and were currently working on Psalms and Prophets, committing many passages to memory. Once a week he was meeting with Father Albert to study Christian doctrine. While Josef did not always get satisfactory answers to his questions, he enjoyed the sessions with the kindly old priest. The situ-ation at home was not good but it was tolerable—the extra income from having a boarder live with them allowed greater variety in their diet, even occasional luxuries such as honey and butter (instead of lard) for their bread. The boys in Market Street still heckled him sometimes but no one had tried to confront him lately.

One thing had changed. Since Mosche's sister had turned six years old, she had decided she too was going to study Torah and Mosche was going to be her teacher. Miriam's determination led her to rise early and come with Mosche to their pre-dawn sessions at the school. To accom-modate the new student, Mosche went over material Josef had already studied. This was all right with Josef—he found he gained new insights when he reviewed texts he had read before. If the boys' delivery routes were not too long, Miriam came along and listened intently as Josef and Mosche discussed what they had read. Occasionally she added a com-ment. Josef had to admit she was amazingly perceptive for someone who was only six years old, and a girl!

One Sunday afternoon on a hot summer day, Josef was playing with Anna and Lotti, daughters of his mother's friend who lived near their house. Lotti was a bit younger than he was and Anna a couple of years older. They seemed to Josef rather silly, always wanting to play house. Anna was usually the mother, and he was cast in multiple roles: father, older brother of Lotti, infirm uncle, or soldier returning from battle.

Today he was the uncle, and the girls practiced their nursing skills. They made him a potion by crushing nettles and red currants together and brewing tea from the mixture. It tasted horrible. Once the cure was complete and their play ended, the children sat down to eat soft, warm buns, freshly baked by the girls' mother. After eating four of them, Josef thought he'd better go home to supper.

It was nearly dark but still sultry when Josef entered the courtyard of his house. As he climbed the stairs he heard some odd sounds, like bumping and scuffling. He ran up the last few steps and pushed the door open. What he saw made him grow pale.

Joakim was gripping his mother by the wrist and trying to pull her into the back room. Part of her dress had been torn off at the shoulder, and one breast was exposed. She was struggling and crying. The place smelled of wine. Several empty bottles were strewn around the room, and another bottle, tipped over on the table, was dripping the remainder of its contents on the floor.

It took Josef only a moment to apprehend the situation. He ran to a corner, picked up a broom, and started beating Joakim on the head and back. Without releasing his grip on Josef's mother, the man turned and kicked Josef vigorously so that he slammed against the wall. Josef came back, grabbed Joakim's free hand, and tried to pull him away. The mingled smell of alcohol and sweat was repugnant. After Josef dodged another kick, he pulled close to the man and bit his hand as hard as he could. Joakim howled in pain and finally let go of Josef's mother. He came after the boy, hit him repeatedly in the face, and threw him down. Then he stormed out of the room, cursing as he went.

Josef lay on the floor throbbing with pain. He put his hand on his cheek and felt blood. He wasn't sure if it was his own; perhaps Joakim had hit him with a bloody hand. In any event, the man was gone, and now he could rest. He would just lie on the floor for awhile and sleep.

When he opened his eyes, his mother was leaning over him, weeping and calling his name. "I'm sorry. I'm sorry," she sobbed over and over again. When he was awake enough to understand, she said through her tears, "I thought I could keep him off. Please, please forgive me."

"Yes, Mutti," said Josef. "Will he come back here to live with us?"

"No. Never. I promise we will never have another boarder like that man."

Josef remained at home for a few days, tended by his mother. One morning, quite early, they heard a tapping on the door. Josef's mother went to open it and there stood a young boy, several inches taller than her son.

"Is this where Josef lives?" asked the boy.

"Yes. Who are you?"

"I'm Mosche. Is Josef here?"

"Mosche!" shouted Josef from the corner where he lay. "Come in!"

Josef's mother nodded and stepped out of the way. Mosche came in, glanced around the room, went to the corner where his friend lay, and knelt beside him. He flinched at the sight of Josef's face, still swollen and bruised. "What happened?" he asked.

"I got in a fight with the man who used to rent the back room over there." He pointed to the door leading to the second room. "He's gone now."

"Well, I didn't know what happened to you. Miriam and I waited at the school a couple of mornings and then we went searching for you in the streets."

Josef's mother was standing over the boys, looking somewhat perplexed. Josef suddenly remembered she had no idea who Mosche was, or Miriam, and how they came to know each other. "Mutti, Mosche is my friend. We make deliveries together every morning and he's teaching me to read."

"To read?"

"Yes, Mutti! It's the most wonderful thing in the world, to look at marks on a page and see real words. And the words make sentences, and sometimes songs and prayers! And Mosche's sister is learning to read too. She's six years old and her name is Miriam."

Mosche pulled something from the front of his shirt and said, "I brought along a little scroll if you'd like to read it to your mother."

Josef took the scroll and gently unrolled it. He read a few words in Hebrew and translated them for his mother.

"Josef, you are a scholar! We must tell the priests."

Josef winced. "No, Mutti. Please don't tell the priests. It's different from what they teach, and they might not understand."

"Well, I don't know . . ."

"Please, Mutti. Mosche is my best friend, and reading is what I like to do best."

She smiled doubtfully, shook her head, and went off to fix breakfast. Mosche sat down close to his friend. He spoke into Josef's ear quietly but with great excitement. "I have some news! Remember I told you about Rabbi Scholomo? He's coming here in November! The granddaughter of his old teacher is getting married, and he's going to help with the wedding."

"Can we meet him?"

"I don't know. But we can see him in the wedding parade and maybe hear him in the schoolhouse. My teacher told us more stories about him, and we all went to see the place where the wall gave way to save his mother."

"Will you show me?"

"Yes, and I'll tell you the stories, too, as soon as you get better and come out again."

A few days later Josef was well enough to go out, and the boys resumed their lessons. One morning Mosche took Josef to see the indentation in the wall where Rabbi Scholomo's mother had been protected from a runaway horse and carriage. Afterwards, as they walked their accustomed route, the boys talked about the famous rabbi.

"When he was studying in Worms, he was a very poor man, "said Mosche. "My teacher said he had only a little food and no decent clothes."

"Didn't he have a mother or someone in his family to look after him?"

"He was already married, but his wife's family had no money either. Rabbi Scholomo wanted to understand Torah even more than he wanted to eat. He said students in search of knowledge are like doves going from one shelter to another looking for food. Except the students go from one Jeschiba to another to gain understanding."

"Did Rabbi Scholomo go to more than one school?"

"Yes, he studied in Mainz before he came here. After living here for ten years, he went to Troyes where his family was and started his own school. But his learning is so great that people say he must have traveled all over the world and talked with scholars in every country."

"If he could go all over the world, why did he want to study here?"

"He didn't come here at first. He went to Mainz because that's where the famous Rabbi Gershom had taught. Gershom was called 'light of the exile.' One thing that made him famous was his collection of books—he had all the Bible texts and the commentaries on the Law, and he wrote some new ones, too. His library was the best in the world, and his Jeschiba became the center of all Jewish learning."

"Did Rabbi Scholomo study with Gershom?"

"No, the learned rabbi died before he arrived. But Rabbi Scholomo's uncle was one of Gershom's students, and there were lots of his students who went to other cities to teach and start new schools. Two of them ended up at the Jeschiba here. That's why Rabbi Scholomo came to Worms."

"Do you know his teachers?" asked Josef.

"They've already died. But I knew one of them, the one whose granddaughter is getting married. His name was Rabbi Isaak haLevi."

"When Rabbi Scholomo is here again, will he study at the Jeschiba? Do you think he can learn anything from the new teachers?"

"It's more likely the other way around—the new teachers will learn something from him. Even when he was young as I am, Rabbi Scholomo asked really hard questions, and he told the teachers if he thought their answers were wrong. That made them mad! They asked if he thought he was smarter than they were. In the end he did become wiser than most of his teachers, except maybe Rabbi Jakov ben Yakar."

"Who's he?"

"He was Rabbi Scholomo's first teacher in Worms, the one he came to study with. Even after Scholomo had studied with many other great scholars, he still called Rabbi Jakov his 'master.'"

"He must have been a really good teacher," said Josef.

"He was. But he never wanted anyone to praise him for his work. He said only the Lord deserves to be praised. Rabbi Jakov loved the Lord so much, he swept the floor in front of the altar with his beard. That's what the old people say, the ones who remember him."

"I wish we could have met Rabbi Jakov."

"Me, too. But at least we'll get to see his greatest student. There will be other scholars coming to the wedding, too. In fact, lots of guests will be coming from all different places." He paused. "You know, they're all going to need places to stay."

On his way home, Josef thought how wonderful it was that such an important event would take place only a few blocks from his house. He had never seen a wedding before, and this one promised to be festive and grand. People would be coming from faraway places, wearing strange clothes and speaking languages he'd never heard. Suddenly Josef remembered what Mosche had said, that the guests would need places to stay. Did Mosche mean to imply that visiting Jews might stay with him and his mother? Were there not enough empty rooms in the Jewish quarter? Would his mother be willing to take in a Jewish boarder, maybe a poor one who could not afford a larger place? He would talk it over with Mosche. There was still plenty of time to raise the subject with his mother—the wedding was four months away. It would be hard to contain his excitement that long, but he would study more and try to be ready when the scholars came to town, in case he had a chance to talk with a man of great learning.

Chapter 4

Josef rose early one Saturday morning and left the house before dawn, without waking his mother. He didn't want her to know where he was going. She might not raise objections, but on the other hand she might, so it was better not to tell her.

It was still cool outside, but the damp, motionless air portended another hot August day. Josef walked quickly to the meeting place. His heart beat rapidly from the exertion, or perhaps from excitement. He was finally going to attend a Sabbath service at the synagogue! Mosche had told him what to expect and had explained some of the customs to him; nevertheless he felt he was entering an unknown world, full of mystery. Well, at least his friend would be sitting beside him.

Mosche was waiting for him outside the gate of the courtyard. In the dim light Josef could see only an outline of the building—the warm pink stones now looked dark grey. As the boys approached the synagogue, Mosche whispered, "We have to wipe our feet before we go in." He scraped his shoes on an iron rod near the door, removing the dirt. Josef did likewise. They went in.

"Men are supposed to cover their heads for prayer," said Mosche quietly as the heavy door closed behind them. He pulled out two small cloth caps from inside his shirt and handed one to Josef. "Put this on," he said.

The boys found seats in a rear corner and settled back to wait for the service to begin. After about half an hour, men and boys began to arrive. Most of the men wore long tunics hanging loosely around their bodies and wooden sandals on their feet, and all wore head coverings. Women and girls came in, too. They made their way to the rear corner opposite the two boys and disappeared behind a curtain. A few of the men carried small scrolls with them. After finding a place to sit on the bare, wooden benches, the men bowed their heads and began to recite. Mosche told

Josef to listen carefully—he might recognize some of the prayers he had learned by heart. Watching and hearing the men's quiet droning, Josef felt as if he were in a dream.

Suddenly he was startled by three loud knocks. The doors of the synagogue swung open and the Sabbath procession began. Leading the way were several older boys. Behind them came scroll-bearers holding great, large rolls of sheepskin. Following the scroll-bearers were several dignified-looking men with long beards. They must be rabbis, thought Josef. Little boys scampered along at the end of the procession, trying to keep up. A few of their fathers entered behind them and found seats.

When the procession reached the front of the room, the little boys ran back to sit with their fathers. The older boys at the head of the line peeled off to the right and left and stood beside the reading desk. One of the worshippers was called forward. He gently took the assigned scroll from the man who was holding it, cradled it in his arms, and kissed it. He carried it around to the older boys standing near the desk and allowed each of them to kiss it. Then these boys, too, joined their fathers in the congregation.

A cantor came forward and began to sing the opening prayers. The tune he sang was plain and repetitive, rising and falling by only a few tones. His loud, rough voice was not agreeable to the ear—in fact few seemed to be listening. Many in the congregation continued reciting prayers out loud. Others were speaking to friends seated near them.

When the cantor stopped singing, the man who had kissed the scroll took it to the reading desk and unrolled it. One of the bearded men, who Mosche said was the officiating reader, walked up and stood beside him at the desk. The first man read the selected passage, while the second leaned toward the scroll and followed along word by word, nodding to indicate his agreement. Even while the man read from the scroll, some of the men in the pews went on reciting their private prayers. Josef strained to hear what the reader was saying. In church, he thought, no one would dare talk out loud while the priest was reading Scripture! At least the men were speaking quietly—Josef was able to understand most of what was read. He didn't want to miss anything. The passage was from the second book of Moses. Josef had studied it with Mosche and so he knew most of the Hebrew words.

"And Moses said unto the Lord, Pardon, O Lord, I am not a man of words, neither yesterday, nor the day before, nor since thou hast spoken unto thy servant; for I am heavy of speech and heavy of tongue. And the Lord said unto him, Who has given a mouth to man? or who maketh him dumb, or deaf, or seeing, or blind? is it not I the Lord? Now therefore go, and I will be with thy mouth, and I will teach thee what thou shalt speak. And he said, Pardon, O Lord, I pray thee send some other person. And the anger of the Lord was kindled against Moses, and he said, Is there not Aaron, thy brother, the Levite? I know that he can speak well; and also, behold, he cometh forth to meet thee; and when he seeth thee, he will be glad in his heart. And thou shalt speak unto him, and put the words in his mouth: and I will be with thy mouth, and with his mouth, and I will teach you what ye shall do. And he shall speak for thee unto the people; and he shall be, yea he shall be to thee as a mouth, and thou shalt be to him as a god."

When the reading ended, many fathers in the congregation turned to their sons, touched their heads, and recited a blessing. Meanwhile, the reader rolled up the scroll and handed it to the bearded man beside him, who placed it on the altar beside the other scrolls. Now a younger man strode forward, said a brief blessing in Hebrew, and began to speak with an animated voice in ordinary, everyday language. Josef was glad for that—he would understand it better than Hebrew. Men in the congregation paid more attention now. The only distractions were occasional noises made by little boys.

"If we look for the literal or plain meaning in this passage, it is clear," said the speaker. "The Lord supplies exactly what we need in proportion to our need for it. Moses didn't speak well. The Lord said, 'I will be with your mouth and teach you what to say.' Moses asked him to pick someone else. The Lord said, 'I know that your brother Aaron can speak well. I will be with your mouth and his mouth, and he will speak to the people for you.' The plain meaning is simple enough: Moses needed a spokesman, and the Lord gave him one. But let us look more closely at the text. It says Moses was heavy of speech and heavy of tongue. What does this mean? It means words did not roll off his tongue, but sat heavily like lead pellets in his mouth. Speaking was difficult because his tongue was weighed down by words of fear, complaint, and refusal. However, the Lord would soon replace the words of lead with words of gold, still heavy but shining and beautiful.

"The Lord had given a mouth to Moses in the first place and promised to inspire his mouth, to fill it with good words and empty it into Aaron's ear. Aaron would be glad in his heart when he saw his brother

Moses again. Aaron had the willingness that Moses lacked. Each brother had something the other needed: Moses had words, Aaron had speech. Neither could do the Lord's work alone. This is how brothers should help each other and support each other. We are all of us brothers and should do likewise."

"But what if my brother tries to cheat me?" called out a man from his seat in the congregation.

"We should not squabble and fight among ourselves as some of you do far too often. Where does that lead us? It leads to death. Remember the first brothers, Cain and Abel. They squabbled and what was the result? As our great Rabbi Scholomo says, 'Cain quarreled with Abel and found a pretext to kill him.' It leads to death. We must work out our differences peaceably. You may appeal to an arbiter if necessary."

A man seated near the back spoke up, "My brother is always short of money, on account of his laziness. Should I give him charity when he asks?"

"That is for you to decide. Of course you must encourage your brother to work for himself and to support his family. But also remember that Aaron lifted Moses' hands high when he could not. 'When the hands of Moses became heavy, they took a stone, and put it under him, and he sat thereon; and Aaron and Chur supported his hands, one on one side, and the other on the other side; and his hands were steady until the going down of the sun.' And because of this, Israel defeated Amalek. Moses, in sympathy with his suffering people, would not sit in comfort, but on a stone, and Aaron would not rest while his brother needed help. Remember this when your brother needs help."

"Torah and Talmud are fine to study in the schoolroom," cried out yet another man, "but they are far removed from our daily lives."

"There you are wrong," said the preacher. "If you study the commentaries, especially the commentaries of our good Rabbi Scholomo, you will find that Scripture is truly for school *and* house. The Rabbi uses analogies and logic and stories (wonderful stories of real people) to teach us how to apply the text in our lives. We learn that the Bible is not only a book of law, but also a source of purpose and hope. It appeals to the heart as well as the head." When no more questions came, the preacher bowed his head and recited a poem in Hebrew. Josef thought he recognized it, perhaps one of the Psalms, about Israel's love for Zion and for the Torah that came forth from Zion.

After the preacher had finished, two of the bearded men opened the box on the altar and laid the scrolls inside. A man seated in the front row went forward with a taper and lit the oil lamp on the altar, to indicate that the Torah was in its place. More prayers were said.

When the bearded men sat down, a tall, slender man walked forward and faced the congregation. He was pale and not very steady on his feet. Trying to suppress a cough, he explained that his father had died and he did not have sufficient funds for the burial. Could anyone help him? A few hands went up. The cantor came down the aisle, approached each man who raised his hand, secured a pledge, and recited, "God bless Levi (or Samuel, or Elihu) who will contribute such-and-such to a charitable cause."

The cantor returned to his place at the front. He read aloud the names of donors who, over the past week, had redeemed the highest pledges, thereby purchasing the right to perform certain functions at the next Sabbath service. Everyone hoped to be selected, Mosche explained, for the honor of lighting the lamps or reading Torah. Some of those whose names were not called muttered their disappointment. The cantor raised his voice over the murmurs, reminding the congregation to return later with contributions pledged for the poor box.

Now an old bearded man stepped forward and stood in front of the altar. With both hands he was holding a large, silver cup. Josef knew the service was near its end. Mosche had told him that when the rabbi blessed the wine it was time for him to leave. Otherwise he would be caught in the crowd of people going toward the door and would have to pass under the rabbi's nose.

Yet Josef did not move. He was fascinated to watch the rabbi turn and lift the cup toward the altar, like a priest would do during the Mass. Josef wanted to hear the blessing, to know whether the words would be the same as the priest said, but just then he felt a sharp poke in his side. Mosche motioned for him to get out quickly. Josef tip-toed to the door, pushed it open a crack, and slipped through. He walked across the courtyard and found a spot beside the wall where he could watch people coming out. Soon the door opened. Just inside, Josef could see several of the bearded men standing, including the one holding the cup of wine. Every boy who came through the door took the hand of one of the bearded men and kissed it. The man, in turn, put his hand on the boy's head and blessed him. Then the boy was allowed to take a sip of wine from the cup.

Mosche went through the line with the others. Josef was eager to talk with his friend about the service; he was glad when Mosche broke away from the crowd and came over to him. They went out the gate and into the street.

"What did it taste like?" asked Josef.

"You mean the wine? It's good. Kind of sweet, but not as sweet as honey."

"Who was the preacher?"

"One of the scholars who studies in the Jeschiba. You were lucky he was the speaker—some of them are really boring."

"Why do people promise money instead of bringing it in their wallets?"

"On Sabbath day, we're not supposed to touch real money. So instead we make pledges. Later we bring our money to one of the rabbis, who passes it on to the people who need it."

The boys talked about other parts of the service as they walked slowly toward Market Street. At the corner, Mosche said he couldn't go any further.

"Okay. I'll see you on Monday. Will you go to Mass with me then?"

Mosche frowned. "I didn't promise I would go. I just said I'd think about it."

Josef made a wry face. "Okay. You tell me when."

Ten days later, on a Tuesday morning, Josef and Mosche sat at the back of St. Paul's Church. A few dozen faithful people, many of them old, had gathered near the front of the church for the early morning Mass. It was too dark inside to recognize faces across the wide expanse, and anyway, the boys were facing the backs of people's heads. Still, Mosche seemed uneasy. "What if somebody notices me?" he whispered to Josef.

"Don't worry. Nobody will."

"How much longer before it starts?"

"It's starting now. They just lit the candles and the priest is about to come through that side door."

Mosche sank down lower on the bench and put his hand over part of his face. A young priest came through a door near the front of the church. He was wearing a long, white garment tied at the waist. The priest walked quickly to the altar set against the front wall, and with his back to the congregation, began immediately to chant a nearly monotone series of syllables. Mosche looked at Josef with a curious expression, and Josef shrugged his shoulders. The priest droned on for a quarter of an hour, interrupted only by the occasional tinkling of a small bell. Mosche stopped listening after a while, focusing his attention instead on the decorations all around him. There were statues with gilded features, paintings of biblical scenes, and ornate wood carvings. The stonework here was more elaborate than in the synagogue, though drabber in color. After a time, Josef tapped him on the shoulder and pointed toward the front of the church. The priest was lifting, with both hands above his head, a small white loaf. He placed it on the altar. Next he picked up a grey cup, lifted that too above his head, and said some words the boys could not understand. Still facing the altar, the priest did something with the bread and took a drink from the cup. Finally, he turned around and faced the congregation for the first time. People started moving forward. With the loaf in his hand, the priest stepped out to meet them.

"We can go now," whispered Josef.

When the boys were outside, Mosche asked, "Is that all there is to it?"

"That's it. If we came on a Sunday or a feast day, there would be more priests and more stuff happening."

"That's even more boring than a bad sermon in the synagogue. What language was the priest speaking?"

"Latin."

"Can you understand it?"

"No. I'm supposed to start studying with Father Matthias next spring."

"Do all those people understand Latin?"

"No. Only the priests and a few others."

"What good is it if they can't understand it? How can they learn anything?"

"Maybe somebody explains it. The old priest Father Albert taught me some things about the Mass. I guess some of the other kids learn too."

"Who gets to eat the bread and wine?" asked Mosche.

"People who've been approved."

"What if somebody ate it who wasn't approved?"

"He would die, I guess."

"That sounds pretty bad. I think I'll stick to challah. It's safer."

Three months later, preparations were being made in the Jewish quarter for an important event. The granddaughter of the late Rabbi Isaak ha-Levi was to be married in the synagogue to a young scholar from Mainz. Not only would the groom's entire family be coming to Worms, but also friends and rabbis and scholars from other cities on the Rhein and elsewhere. Wormsers had not seen such bustling activity in many years.

Even the Christian community was affected. Large amounts of food and drink would be consumed, and much of it would come from shops outside the Jewish quarter. Also, the visitors would need places to stay. Many Christians living near Jews' Alley opened their doors to Jewish lodgers, although some wondered whether it was a proper thing to do. In spite of her misgivings, Josef's mother accepted the request of an elderly merchant from Troyes and his wife. They seemed harmless, and the extra income would be most welcome.

Eliel and Ruth were quiet, unobtrusive people. Neither spoke the local language; they communicated with Josef's mother by means of smiles and hand signals. Not that a great deal of communication was needed—the couple spent most of the day with their friends in the Jewish quarter. The only meal they took at the house was breakfast, and Mosche had given detailed instructions to Josef about what foods were allowable.

One morning Josef and his mother were sitting at the table with their two lodgers. They had nearly finished eating breakfast when Ruth turned to Josef's mother and asked a question in her native French, a language neither Josef nor his mother could understand. When they shook their heads, she repeated herself several times, and she took the edge of her skirt between her hands and rubbed vigorously. Still they did not comprehend. Eliel joined the exchange, but it was no use. Finally, in frustration, he pulled out his small Torah and opened it to the second book of Moses. He pointed at a passage of Hebrew text, perhaps hoping these Christians had a Bible of their own and would know what it said. Josef stared at the passage. "It says Moses came down from the mountain and blessed the people, and they washed their clothes. Mutti, I think maybe Ruth would like to wash her clothes."

"Oh." She turned to Ruth and said, "Wait a minute." She went to a cupboard and brought out two buckets and some soap. "Is this what you want?"

Ruth once again spoke some words in her native tongue, but this time she was nodding and smiling. At the bidding of his mother Josef went to fill the buckets with water from the well. Soon after he returned, Ruth began washing her garments.

Now Eliel began pointing to other passages in his Torah. To his astonishment, Josef was able to read all of them aloud in Hebrew. The man began speaking fast in Hebrew, but Josef waved his hands and shook his head. He could not understand modern vocabulary, especially when mixed with foreign idioms, and even the ancient words were unrecognizable if spoken too quickly. Once Eliel slowed down his speech and restricted himself to biblical Hebrew, Josef was able to get the sense of what he said. From then on, the four of them were able to carry on a sort of conversation. Ruth would speak in French, Eliel would translate into biblical Hebrew, and Josef would try to explain to his mother in German what was being said. Then the process would reverse itself. It was slow, but nevertheless it was real communication. The talk was punctuated with laughter when the translations seemed too outlandish.

A friendship developed. Ruth and Eliel began bringing gifts for their hosts each evening. First it was a loaf of challah, then a spinning toy for Josef, then some earrings for his mother. One morning, after their lodgers left for the day, Josef noticed his mother seemed agitated. He asked if something was wrong.

"Yes," she said. "We should not be accepting these gifts."

"Why not, Mutti?"

"They are Jews. We should not be too friendly with them."

"But they're lodging with us. They want to pay us for giving them a place to stay."

"Yes. We can accept rent payments, but no more. We don't want to owe them anything. It's not right to accept charity from Jews. You know I had doubts about all this in the first place. People say Jews lie and cheat and practice sorcery. If we profit from their devious ways, it might cause a terrible stain on our souls. I'm not sure we could ever be absolved."

"Oh, Mother, they just want to be friendly."

"You heard what I said. No more gifts. We're going to give back the things they gave us . . . except the bread, of course. I hope eating it hasn't polluted our insides."

A few days later Josef was turning into Jews' Alley for his pre-dawn study session with Mosche. Through the twilight he saw his friend running toward him. Out of breath and visibly excited, Mosche panted, "The Parshandata has arrived!"

"The what?"

"Parshandata. It means 'interpreter of the Law.'" Mosche leaned over and took several deep breaths. "You know, . . . Rabbi Scholomo from Troyes. He's here. He came in last night."

"Oh! When can we meet him?"

"It's not that easy. Everybody wants to talk to him. There's a long list of people who've requested judgment on hard questions, even some Christians, I think. Another thing—we can't use the schoolroom any more while he's here. It's reserved for him to use."

"That means we can't read any new texts. I guess we can talk about the ones we already read."

"Something better than that," said Mosche. "Rabbi Scholomo is going to teach classes every day, and he's going to give the Sabbath sermon tomorrow afternoon. That'll give us plenty to talk about."

"I'm supposed to have my lesson with Father Albert tomorrow. How can I get away?" Josef pressed his lips together. "I'll figure out something. Will you meet me here and let me go with you to the sermon?"

"Okay. I have to go back home now. There won't be any deliveries for awhile. We don't have enough cheeses, even for the wedding guests, so I'm going to help my father make some more. See you tomorrow."

The next afternoon, Josef went to St. Paul's Church for his weekly lesson with Father Albert. It crossed his mind that he might skip this meeting entirely and go straight to the Jewish quarter to wait for Mosche. But that might get him in trouble. Besides, he liked Father Albert and didn't want to disappoint him in any way. What could he say to cut short their lesson? He wouldn't lie to Father Albert, but he couldn't tell him the whole truth either.

Josef went to the garden and sat down to think. Soon Father Albert was at his side. Josef looked into his wrinkled face. "Father, I have to leave early today."

"Really?" The old man raised his eyebrows, creating more wrinkles.

"Yes, it's very important."

"Can you tell me where you're going?"

"Not exactly."

"Can you tell me approximately what you'll be doing? Maybe a little hint?"

Josef thought a moment. "Learning something."

Father Albert smiled. "Ah. Learning is good. But learning can occur in many different ways, some of them dangerous to body and soul. You're not going to climb a steeple, are you?"

"No, Father."

"Step on hot coals?"

"No."

"Handle snakes?"

Josef laughed. "No, Father, none of those things."

"All right then. You know the ten commandments and the seven deadly sins. If you promise to keep the first and refrain from the second, you may go with my blessing." He touched the boy's head.

"I promise. Thank you, Father." Josef jumped up and ran out of the garden.

Mosche was waiting for him when he arrived at Jews' Alley. "I'm glad you got here early. People are already going in. Let's find a seat before it gets too crowded."

The boys entered the school building and settled into a corner behind a large group of noisy men. It would be nearly an hour before the rabbi spoke, so Josef focused his attention on the conversations swirling around him. He heard words and vocal sounds that were completely foreign to him, in languages that were unrecognizable. He couldn't even imagine where these people came from. Maybe Mosche would tell him later. There was too much clamor to ask about it now. The noise had a hypnotizing effect that might have put the boys to sleep in other circumstances. Today, however, there was too much excitement in the air, and they were infected by it. After a time, the side door of the schoolhouse opened. Through the door came eight or nine men, some of whom Josef recognized from the synagogue service he had attended. Others were strangers. Which one was Rabbi Scholomo? Maybe it was the tall one with silver hair. There was another man whose beard hung nearly to his waist. Was it him?

The tall man with silver hair raised his hand as the others took seats behind him. The room suddenly became silent. The man announced that Rabbi Scholomo ben Itzhak would be giving the sermon, and that in order to be understood by as many as possible, he would speak in Hebrew. A murmur of approval went up from the crowd. The men near Josef and Mosche whispered to each other and nodded. The tall man recited a brief prayer and turned to face the men behind him. One of them rose. He was a slight man of thin build and less than medium height. His head was nearly bald and his beard neatly trimmed about six inches below his chin. Could this be Rabbi Scholomo? Josef looked questioningly at Mosche, who nodded eagerly. The rabbi came forward. He was assisted by the tall man in stepping onto a platform on which a stone chair had been placed. It was a beautiful piece of stonework, carved with geometric patterns on the back and arms.

The rabbi first addressed the crowd in the local dialect, saying he was grateful for the warm hospitality he had received. It was good to be back in Worms, he said, where the Lord had inspired him and provided the means for him to begin his interpretations of Scripture. He would speak today about those interpretations and about the commentaries he was compiling, not in order to glorify himself, but to show how the Law might be set before the people like a table of good food fully prepared for them to eat. With their indulgence, the rabbi said, he would sit while he delivered his sermon. He had walked a long way from Troyes and his feet were sore.

Once seated in the stone chair, the rabbi looked around at the eager faces before him, smiled, and closed his eyes for a moment. Then he began his oration. At this point it was more difficult for Josef to follow what he said because many of the Hebrew words he used were unfamiliar. Besides that, Josef missed words on account of coughing and other inevitable crowd noises. The rabbi's voice was strong and confident but not overly loud.

He began by saying that Torah is a portable homeland for the Jews who have been scattered around the world. It serves as sustenance when they are deprived, shelter when exposed, and armor when attacked. Therefore study of Torah should be of utmost concern to every Jew.

Josef understood this much fairly easily. As the discourse became more technical, he strained to hear and interpret the words he did not recognize. The general sense of the sermon was that Scripture could be interpreted in different ways. The two most important were *peshat* and *derush*. The rabbi himself preferred *peshat*, or plain meaning of the text. If a passage was simple and clear in its historical context, then there was no need to twist the words to find new meaning. On the other hand, if a passage was confusing, it might be necessary to introduce less literal interpretations. The rabbi spoke of *midrash* and *aggadah*, but Josef was not sure what these words meant. Sometimes it was useful, said the rabbi, to tell stories, introduce folklore, and give examples from everyday life.

These supplements would draw people into the text, making it comprehensible to those who were not scholars. Other ways to interpret Scripture were *remez* and *sod*, but these must be used with great care, he said, especially the latter. Again, Josef did not recognize or understand the Hebrew words. The rabbi went on to say that scholars should be wary of taking their interpretations too far, leading to foolishness. Students, he said, have an important role in scholarly pursuit—to ask questions. They should ask about anything and everything, all the questions that occur to them. They should not worry about looking foolish. They should not hesitate to challenge their teachers. Only by free discussion and investigation would their minds be sharpened. Not only would students' minds be sharpened but also the minds of their teachers, as their knowledge would be drawn out by persistent questions. Students themselves might have insights that would be helpful to their teachers, because, after all, even a master needs instruction.

After about forty minutes, the rabbi stopped speaking. Again he closed his eyes. The congregation remained quiet as the tall man with silver hair rose from his chair and stepped forward. He thanked the rabbi for his sermon and announced that their honored guest would now take questions from those in attendance.

Each man called out his question in the language he spoke most fluently. The rabbi answered in that same language when he could; otherwise he spoke Hebrew. Many of the questions and their answers Josef missed entirely, but a few he understood. One man asked when was the best time for a busy merchant to study Torah.

"You should study Torah not only at certain times but at all times. By this I mean keep the Law always before you in your mind's eye. While you work, while you eat, while you bathe, even while you relieve yourself. As a practical matter, it is good to appoint a regular time so that you may study a little today, a little tomorrow. And if you cannot study every day, remember that one day studying Torah is better than a thousand burnt offerings brought to the altar."

Another man asked who are the best teachers.

"To that question I have three answers, and I will tell you two of them. First, the Lord is your teacher. The Lord gives you his Torah, and through much labor you can make it your own. Second, the best and wisest teachers do not dictate to their students but rather guide them to come up with their own ideas. When you find this kind of teacher, your feet should wear out the steps to his door. The third answer is implicit in the first two."

Someone inquired which was more valuable to study, written law or oral law.

"You cannot say one is more valuable than the other, since both are part of the same divine teaching. Written law came first and therefore it is the beginning of wisdom. Oral law was compiled to help us interpret and understand written law. Commentaries have been written to give further clarification of both. All of these we study, interpret, and debate with one goal in mind, namely right conduct. Remember this: one who studies but does not practice righteousness is like a man who sows crops but does not reap, or like a woman who gives birth and buries her offspring."

The tall man came forward once again and said it was time to conclude the assembly. For the Jeschiba students, he said, there would be daily study sessions with Rabbi Scholomo. All Jews were welcome to attend his next Sabbath sermon. Would the rabbi now like to say a final word before the congregation was dismissed?

The rabbi looked out over the crowd of upturned faces, all eager to hear more. He said, "We are commanded to cleave to the Lord, but how can we cleave to a consuming flame, or a pillar of cloud, or a voice from above? We must cleave to what we can see and touch. Therefore if you cleave to Torah and to wise men who teach Torah, it will be the same as if you cleave to the Lord." Rabbi Scholomo recited a brief blessing, stepped down from the platform, and went out the side door with the other rabbis.

Once the boys were out on the street, Josef turned to his friend. "That was great!" he said.

"I'm glad you liked it. How much did you understand?"

"All the German, of course. And most of the Hebrew. Except certain words like *derush* and *sod*. Can you explain those things to me?"

"Not all of it. I'll try to find out more in the study sessions. We can talk about it next week. It's time to go home now."

Josef went up Jews' Alley toward Market Street. He was so excited by what he had just heard and invigorated by the cool night air that he fairly skipped along. A couple of bright stars caught his attention. Then, suddenly, he collided with something. Standing there at the end of the alley was someone who put his hand on Josef's shoulder and spoke in a familiar voice. "Hello, Josef," said Father Albert. "What did you learn?"

Chapter 5

Father Albert!" said Josef. "How did you know I was here?"

"I didn't know. But I suspected. When I make pastoral calls around the city, I see certain things."

"Like what things," asked Josef, looking warily at the priest.

"I've observed you walking and talking with a young Jew, a handsome lad with a quick and lively attitude about him."

"That's Mosche," said Josef under his breath.

"Yes, well, this Mosche fellow must be teaching you something. You seem quite absorbed in conversation whenever I see you together."

"Yes, Father. He's teaching me Hebrew."

"Hmmm. That seems a good thing. But you must be careful. Not everyone will recognize the value of what you are doing."

"Who do you mean, Father?"

After pondering for a moment, Father Albert said, "I think I've said enough about that. Come, let me walk you home, and you tell me what you learned today."

A few days later Josef met Mosche in the market square. He pulled his friend away from the crowded stalls and whispered, "Father Albert knows about our meetings."

"Is that a bad thing?"

"He says some people might not approve."

Mosche frowned. "Why not?"

"I think it's because they don't want me talking to a Jew."

"That's crazy! Are you going to stop being my friend?"

"No!"

"Good. Let me tell you what I learned this week." Mosche summarized for Josef the sessions he had attended on biblical interpretation.

He told, too, of the thoughtful decisions given by Rabbi Scholomo in response to questions by petitioners. "Somebody told me the rabbi was named after wise king Solomon who built the first temple in Jerusalem," he said. "I think our own Scholomo is the wisest man alive today. He seems to know everything."

"Really? Would he answer my questions?"

"If you can get near enough to ask, I think he would."

Josef wondered how that might be possible. How could he, a young boy who was not even a Jew, gain an audience with the great rabbi of Worms? Could he find out where the man was staying and sneak into his house? Could he stop him on the street? No, he would not be able to get through the crowds of admirers and petitioners. Yet he felt a strong urge to get near the rabbi, to see such wisdom up close, and to ask him questions that no one else could answer.

Josef lay in bed that night thinking about these questions. Suddenly it came to him: Ruth and Eliel lived in Troyes! They might know the rabbi personally! He would ask them if it might be possible to meet him.

The next morning Josef did ask Eliel, though he was not certain Eliel understood what he was asking. But the man nodded repeatedly and told Josef to wait for him at home after the midday meal. Josef waited out on the street, hoping his mother would not see Eliel return and the two of them leave together. They went to the schoolhouse and found it already packed with people. Rabbi Scholomo was sitting behind a table at the front, with a scribe seated on either side of him. Two men stood before the table, each making his case to the rabbi. When one or the other of them got excited and raised his voice, the rabbi waved his forefinger gently to calm the man. After he had heard both sides of the argument, the rabbi made a few notes, spoke briefly to the men involved, and stood to announce his judgment. As he spoke, the scribes beside him wrote quickly, dipping their quills repeatedly in ink pots and moving their hands gracefully over the pages. Without telling every detail of the case, the rabbi described the situation and outlined the general principles involved. He cited passages from Torah and Mishna. Finally he delivered a verdict directly to the two men standing before him. Neither seemed completely satisfied.

Other cases followed. There was constant movement in the audience as people came and left, but all present were quiet and attentive. Josef thought he would never have a chance to ask any questions of the rabbi or even get near enough to be heard. That was all right with him.

He didn't really want to stand in front of the table while all these people watched. His questions would seem silly. People would laugh at him. Someone might recognize that he was not a Jew. All at once he thought of Mosche. Was he here? Josef scanned the crowd but did not see a familiar face. No, it was better that he not be noticed. He would listen to one more case and then sneak out.

The next case was long and complicated. When it was over, one of the scribes rose and said the assembly would adjourn for two hours while the rabbi rested. Josef thought he would leave quickly before the doorway became jammed with people. At that moment, however, Eliel took his hand and started walking toward the front. They dodged back and forth through the crowd that was streaming in the opposite direction. People began talking excitedly, so that loud conversations echoed around the room. Josef's head was spinning. What was Eliel doing? Where was he leading him? They seemed to be going toward the table at the front, where a small knot of people had gathered. Rabbi Scholomo was standing in the middle, shaking hands and smiling as people greeted him. Was Eliel going to introduce him? They stood on the side, waiting as people made small talk with the rabbi. Seeing the great man up close (though he looked kindly enough) caused Josef's heart to beat faster. He became more and more nervous until it felt like his heart was in his throat. He could barely breathe. When all the other people had moved away, Eliel led the boy directly to the rabbi. The men spoke a few words in French which Josef did not understand, although he thought he heard his name mentioned. The rabbi turned to him and said (in German), "So! You are the little Christian who speaks Hebrew! My friend Eliel told me about you."

Josef could not force a sound from his throat, so he nodded.

"And how old are you, Josef?"

Still he could not utter a word. He held up nine fingers.

"It seems you are a silent scholar. That's not necessarily a bad thing. I know many a scholar whose tongue outruns his knowledge." The rabbi's smiling eyes had a calming effect on the boy.

Josef was finally able to speak. All in one breath, he said, "Do you know everything? My friend Mosche says you know everything."

With an amused look, the rabbi shook his head. "I'm afraid not. But the Lord often supplies answers to those who ask."

"Could you ask him a question for me?"

"What is it you'd like to know?"

"I need to know . . . (here Josef paused and took a breath) who my father is." There it was. He had said it. If anybody could answer the question, he felt sure it was Rabbi Scholomo. It was worth all the shame and embarrassment if only he could get an answer.

The rabbi shook his head again and looked directly at Josef. Now the man's face showed no sign of a smile, but his eyes were full of kindness. He placed his hand on Josef's head. "It seems you *can* speak after all! I am sorry your question is too hard for me. I have no answer. But from what Eliel has told me, you will be a fine scholar some day. You will find answers to difficult questions. I think you will make a name for yourself."

Josef did not know why, but he felt tears coming into his eyes. Was he going to be a cry-baby now? Would this be how the great rabbi would remember him? But he couldn't help it. He knew he was a bastard. He would never find out who his father was. Tears fell off his cheeks. Eliel put his arm around Josef and walked him to the main door. "Are you going to be all right?" he asked. Josef nodded. "Can you get back to the house by yourself?" Josef nodded again and went out.

Josef was glad he had not seen Mosche in the schoolhouse. He, Josef, had met the great rabbi face-to-face. He had had his chance to ask him anything in the world, and what was the result? He had started to cry. He had appeared utterly foolish. Josef hoped Mosche had not been in the audience, or if he was there, had left without seeing him. If Mosche didn't say anything about it, then Josef wouldn't mention it either. But the rabbi would always remember.

The next day was Friday, the day of the wedding. In spite of his shame and disappointment, Josef was excited. He had agreed to meet Mosche early in the morning to watch the wedding ceremony.

It began at dawn. A local rabbi and a group of men went to the house where the groom was staying. They called for the young man to come out. Some of the men in the crowd carried lighted torches and others had various kinds of drums and horns. The rabbi and the groom led a procession through the city streets, while those who followed waved their torches and played raucously on their instruments. Little boys ran behind the procession. Their sleepy siblings and elders watched and cheered from windows and doorsteps. The marchers arrived at the courtyard of the synagogue, left the rabbi and bridegroom there, and turned back toward the bride's house.

The bride and her attendants soon emerged from the house. A new procession formed, more sedate than the previous one. As the bride and her escorts approached the synagogue, the rabbi led the bridegroom forward to meet her at the entrance of the courtyard. He took the bride's hand and placed it in the groom's. Immediately their friends watching from the street began throwing small coins and grains of wheat at the young couple. Three times they chanted, "Be fruitful and multiply!" Then the pair walked hand-in-hand to the door of the synagogue and stood for a few minutes while the rabbi spoke to them.

Josef watched in fascination. He nudged his friend and whispered, "They don't look much older than you."

Mosche nodded. "The girl is probably fourteen or fifteen, and the boy a little older."

"Does everyone get married so young?"

"Most people do."

"Why were people throwing things at them?"

"It's supposed to make them have lots of children."

"Do they get to keep the money?"

"No, it goes to the poor. Watch what happens next."

Two men walked up to the groom and threw a hooded garment over his head and shoulders. One of them took the young man into the synagogue while the other led the bride out of the courtyard.

"Where's she going?" asked Josef.

"Back home to change her clothes. She'll look much different next time you see her."

"What about her husband?"

"They're not married yet. He has to wait in the synagogue until his bride comes back. It'll take her a couple of hours to get dressed (here Mosche grinned), so he's got lots of time to say his prayers."

"I need to deliver some things for my mother," said Josef. "I'll come back when I'm done."

At mid-morning Josef returned to the Jewish quarter. The main street had filled with people, rich and poor together, families with many children, old men and women, everyone speaking eagerly of the upcoming festivities. It seemed the entire Jewish population of Worms was assembled along Jews' Alley. But where was Mosche? Josef made his way to the gate of the synagogue but saw no sign of his friend. Well, that was all right. He would find a place along the street where he could see what was happening. They could talk about it later.

Josef found a spot and waited only a few minutes before he heard music in the distance. It was not blaring horns like he had heard at the groom's parade early in the morning, but gentle, sweet tunes more appropriate to a bride. As the musicians came into view, Josef could see pipes and flutes and fiddles of all sorts and sizes. Some of the musicians danced and some skipped in time with the music. Following them came a group Josef supposed to be the bride's family. They wore broad smiles on their faces and rich, brightly-colored clothes. Next came the bride's attendants, beautiful young women and girls dressed in flowing silk gowns. In the middle of the procession was the bride's litter—Josef had never seen anything so splendid.

Four men carried between them a little cabin balanced on two long poles. The cabin was open on all sides but had a shimmering pale blue canopy over the top, with silver fringes hanging from the edges. The platform, bride's chair, canopy, and even the poles on which these things rested were decorated with colored ribbons, flowers, and greenery. The bride sat motionless, looking a little frightened, amidst all the splendor. Over a plain white robe she wore a pale silk cape trimmed with fur. Garlands of white myrtle hung from her neck, and a loose white veil covered her hair.

Josef could not take his eyes off her. She was beautiful! He stared, unblinking, at the bride as she went by and barely noticed what came next in the procession. Perhaps it was some of the groom's friends. He thought he saw men carrying boxes and chests. Josef recovered himself enough to observe, at the very end of the procession, a small group of elderly men. They wore black and walked slowly, with great dignity. These must be the scholars, he thought. Yes, there was the tall man with silver hair and some of the others he had seen in the synagogue. And there was Rabbi Scholomo. Josef put his head down, hoping the rabbi would not notice him.

The procession wound its way through the streets, eventually arriving at the synagogue. Many of the onlookers drifted in that direction once the parade had passed them. Josef followed at a distance. He wanted to see as much as he could without being noticed. From a high place off the street, he could just make out near the synagogue door the young rabbi who had been with the couple that morning. The rabbi greeted the bride as she emerged from the cabin, took hold of her cape, and led her inside.

The rest of the ceremony and festivities Josef heard about later from Mosche. Inside the synagogue, the rabbi escorted the bride to a small platform in the middle of the room where the groom was waiting. The rabbi began by throwing ashes over the heads of the young couple, in remembrance of the destruction of the temple in Jerusalem. Four men took the groom's prayer shawl and made a canopy over the couple. Then the rabbi spoke the marital blessings. He asked two onlookers to be witnesses as the groom placed a ring on the bride's finger. After reading aloud the marriage contract and reciting seven benedictions, he offered the pair a glass of wine. Each took a sip. Then the bridegroom threw the wine glass against the wall, shattering it.

The groom's friends cheered loudly, picked him up, and carried him to the wedding house where he was staying. His new wife, left behind in the synagogue, was expected to follow in a more stately fashion. When she arrived at the house, her husband was waiting outside. He took her hand and placed it on the lintel above the front door. Then he handed her his hat, coat, and wallet, to show that he would fulfill his part of the marriage contract.

Inside the house, the wedding feast was already laid out. Mosche's description of the offerings—cold meat, fish, hard-cooked eggs, dried and candied fruits, potato pancakes, and crusty breads—made Josef's mouth water. If only he could have been there! There was singing and dancing, funny speeches, and a variety of games, and of course constant eating and drinking. The celebration lasted until nightfall. Next morning, special hymns were sung at the Sabbath service in honor of the newly married couple.

Now that the wedding was over, the visiting guests began to depart. Ruth and Eliel took their leave the following Monday morning, but not before paying Josef's mother a generous sum for their lodging. Rabbi Scholomo was going to stay another week, to hear more cases and to study with the Jeschiba students. Three days before his departure, having made judgments on all questions brought to him by Jews, the rabbi consented to hear cases brought by Christians and to give advice if he could.

Josef knew Rabbi Scholomo would be leaving soon. He wanted to hear the great man one more time and perhaps learn something new before the opportunity was gone forever. He and Mosche agreed to meet at the schoolhouse on Thursday afternoon. They entered quietly and found seats near the front. The rabbi was apparently concluding a case, speaking earnestly to three elderly women standing before him. When they left, he stood up and looked around the room. Seeing Josef, he gave a quick smile and nod of recognition. Josef felt his face getting warm. He glanced sideways to see if Mosche had noticed the rabbi's nod and was relieved to see his friend looking the other direction. He didn't want Mosche to know about his meeting with the rabbi.

When Rabbi Scholomo took his seat again, two men stepped forward. Once of them had a weary, shabby look about him. The other, a large barrel-chested man, introduced himself. "Mr. Scholomo, your Honor, I am a Christian, called by the name Frieder. I am employed as city clerk of Worms, which falls under the classification minor civil servant. May I present my case?"

"Yes, Mr. Frieder. Proceed."

"For fifteen years my wife longed for a child. When she finally conceived and a son was born, she was beside herself with happiness. But, sadly, the child died of a fever before his second birthday. There was nothing I could do to console my Claudia.

"When two years had passed, our maid servant, a young Jewess, gave birth to a daughter. Soon afterward, her husband died, and as she had no close relations in town, she and the child came to live with us. It was a great comfort to my wife to have a baby she could hold. Claudia helped raise the child and loved it as she would her own. The little girl Hanna is now nine years old and has lived with us almost her entire life.

"Just a month ago, her mother, our maid servant, took ill and died. Hanna's uncle, her father's brother, is here beside me. As her closest relative, he knows it is his responsibility to take the child into his house. Yet there are circumstances that would prevent it. This good man has a large family of his own, which he supports by cultivating a small farm about half a day's journey from Worms. The land is rocky and barely yields enough to feed his own children."

Hanna's uncle nodded slightly and hung his head lower.

Frieder continued, "But, your Honor, my wife and I have plenty in our house. We would be more than happy to keep her as our own daughter. In fact, I think my wife would be utterly despondent if Hanna were to move away. She lives for that child."

Now Hanna's uncle spoke for the first time. "I could not agree to such a plan without a rabbi's judgment."

Rabbi Scholomo had been listening attentively to all that was said. He seemed moved by the story, and, at the same time, deep in thought. First he turned to the uncle. "You were quite right to insist on a ruling in this case. Thank you for taking the time to travel so far to attend the hearing." The man nodded.

"Now, Mr. Frieder, let me ask you a few questions. What about the little girl herself? What does she say?"

"She is devastated by the loss of her mother, of course. It is my wife who has been able to comfort her the most. When I asked Hanna if she would like to live with her cousins out in the country, she ran straight into my wife's arms. It was hard to understand what she said through the sobs."

"But you are convinced she would like to stay where she is?"

"Yes, your Honor. All of her friends and her mother's friends live in Worms. It is the only place she knows."

"Pardon me for this blunt question, but would you and your wife want to make this girl into a Christian?"

"Yes, your Honor, we would want to, of course. But Hanna is already a Jew. She and her mother regularly sat with the women in the synagogue. Hanna already knows large portions of the Old Testament by heart. Even after her mother died, she has been going to Sabbath services every week with an elderly friend of her mother. We would make no attempt to change this practice."

"Does your wife agree in this? Would you both be willing to make a promise never to try to seduce the child into Christianity?"

"Speaking for myself, I would promise. I think my wife would do almost anything you asked, if only Hanna could stay with us."

The rabbi breathed deeply and closed his eyes. He asked one of the scribes sitting beside him to bring him a Torah scroll. After locating a passage, he said, "There is no question this girl Hanna is a Jew, and she must be raised as a Jew. Moreover, Judaism can be practiced only in the context of a Jewish family."

Frieder's shoulders slumped and he let out a sigh.

The rabbi raised his hand slightly and shook his head. He turned to the scribes and asked them to put down their pens. "This is a very difficult case, and I could be mistaken in my decision. Therefore, let the ruling not be publicized outside this community."

The scribes laid their quills on the table and leaned back in their chairs. The rabbi continued, "It is always easier to interpret the law strictly rather than to find a reason for leniency. Furthermore, close observation of traditional customs and practices often guards us against mistakes. For my own conduct, I find it best to adhere closely to every statute of the law.

"Yet we are also commanded to judge others in a spirit of righteousness and charity, and to weigh carefully the well-being of each individual involved. In a case such as this, the disposition to be charitable may lead to a lenient interpretation of the law. Such an interpretation can easily be misunderstood and abused. Thus we consider this ruling to be strictly local and not applicable in a larger sphere.

"For some time now, church and civil authorities in the Rhein Valley have been as generous to our people as we could expect. Half a century ago, Bishop Burchard of Worms encouraged Jewish commerce and allowed our people to practice their faith freely. The late archbishop of Mainz was another good man, mourned at his death by Christians and Jews alike. King Henry has given legal autonomy to Jews in some communities, and he is fair in his tax policies. The Christians in this region have demonstrated by their actions that they are reasonable people. Moreover, Christians are not pagans, but believers in their own way.

"Based on these considerations, it will be possible for the girl Hanna to continue to live with Mr. Frieder and his wife if the following three conditions are met: First, they must promise to make no attempts at conversion. Second, Hanna's Jewish education and Sabbath observance must continue without interruption. And third, her uncle must bring her into his family circle twice a year, for Holy Days and for Passover. This can take place at his farm or, more likely, here in Worms when the family comes to worship in the synagogue. Are there any questions?"

The two men standing before him shook their heads.

"Then it is up to you gentlemen to introduce Hanna to her uncle's family and to work out a method of communication between you. We close this case with a passage from the fifth book of Moses: 'As an eagle that stirreth up her nest, hovereth over her young, spreadeth abroad her wings, taketh them, beareth them on her pinions—The Lord alone did lead them.'"

Chapter 6

Josef pulled his cloak tightly around his shoulders. It was freezing outside. His hands were blue from the cold, and his feet felt the same, though he couldn't actually see their color through the thin leather shoes he wore. Listening to them crunch on the frozen snow, he wished the soles were thicker.

Adding to the sense of chill was his destination; he was on his way to study with Father Matthias. He had already attended lessons with the young priest almost every afternoon for three weeks, and that was enough to convince him he'd had enough. Latin was all right as a language; in fact it was easier than Hebrew. But Father Matthias was so different from Mosche as a teacher, or from Father Albert. He didn't seem to love the language or enjoy the interchange between teacher and student. Josef was supposed to study with him for three years!

Two other boys had begun their study of Latin at the same time. Michel, the rosy-cheeked son of a butcher, looked healthy and well-fed. The other boy, Stefan, was pale and sickly. His father was a member of the lesser nobility, though Stefan's clothes were as shabby as Josef's. Josef thought the other two boys rather dull-witted. During the first lessons, neither had been able to repeat the words Father Matthias pronounced. Only Josef had recited them in perfect order. Instead of seeming pleased, Father Matthias had frowned and made a sour comment. "One would think you had studied this before," he said, looking suspiciously at Josef.

"No, sir. But I like the sound of it in my ears."

"You needn't offer your opinion unless I ask for it," said the priest sharply.

Josef remained silent after that unless he was specifically asked to speak. Sometimes he couldn't decide what to say. Should he answer questions correctly or pretend he didn't know the answer, so he wouldn't seem too smart? Coming to no quick decision, he often became tongue-tied, and this caused Father Matthias to tap his wand on the desk. As difficult as the situation was for Josef, he felt it was worse for the other two boys, who, most of the time, did not know the answers.

On this day it seemed just as cold in the basement of St. Paul's Church as it was outdoors. A small fire burned in the grate behind Father Matthias' desk, but it hardly made a difference in such a large room. The boys kept their wraps on and shivered in their chairs. Father Matthias began his lesson with a prayer, as he usually did. It was in Latin, of course, and rather long. None of the boys had any idea what it meant. They stole sideways glances at each other as the priest droned on. He finished with a loud "Amen" and immediately opened a large, leather-bound book on his desk. "Since you seem incapable of learning verb tenses, I will have you copy letters. Perhaps your hands are smarter than your heads."

He wrote the letters INITIUM on a slate and propped it against the book, facing the boys. He gave each of them a slate. "Now copy this word. It's the first word of Mark's gospel. Write it as many times as you can, then wipe the slate clean and begin again. Once you've mastered this, we'll consider the second word."

The boys struggled to make their letters look like the ones displayed before them. It was easier for Josef than for the others since he had at least held a piece of chalk before. But all three were having difficulty balancing the slates on their laps and gripping the chalk in their frozen fingers. They wrote the word over and over until their hands ached. Finally, after thirty minutes, Father Matthias rose from his desk and sauntered over to observe their work. Their scratchy marks went in every direction. He shook his head and spat on the floor. "Pitiful," he said. "How could anyone expect me to make scholars of such clumsy half-wits?"

The boys practiced writing words every afternoon for many weeks. When they finally learned to form the letters in the word INITIUM, they were given another word, EVANGELII, to copy, followed by IESU and CHRISTI. Slowly and painfully, one word at a time, they worked their way through the first dozen verses of Mark's gospel. Occasionally Father Matthias would say something about the word they were copying, perhaps that it was a neuter noun in the genitive case or a participle of some verb. The boys had no idea what he was talking about, and he made no attempt to explain.

The butcher's son Michel did fairly well with his letters. He was strong and well-coordinated. Stefan had more difficulty controlling the chalk. When he fell behind the other two boys, Father Matthias made him stand and hold out his hands. Then he rapped him hard on the knuckles with his wand. Josef thought the punishment was unfair. Stefan was trying as hard as he could, and he obviously wanted to please the teacher. Michel, on the other hand, didn't seem to care. For him, drawing letters was a game, and he was playing along to humor this dull man. Sometimes he made rude remarks. Yet Father Matthias rarely punished Michel—Josef suspected this was somehow related to the packages Michel brought for the priest every week.

Spring came and the weather improved. All three boys wanted to be outside instead of stuck in the damp basement of an old church. One day Michel stood up and said, "I've had enough of this. I'm leaving." With that, he walked out. It was explained later to the other boys that Michel was required at home to help with the spring slaughter. However, he did not return at the end of spring, or summer.

Once Michel was gone, Father Matthias' mood grew worse. Stefan bore the brunt of his meanness, often suffering punishment for falling behind or giving a wrong answer. When Father Matthias left the room or turned his back for a few moments, Josef tried to help the other boy complete his work. Outside the classroom, after they were dismissed, he sometimes explained to him certain grammatical points. But Stefan seemed weak and dispirited and had trouble retaining information.

One day Josef discovered by accident why Stefan was so listless. Josef had brought with him half a loaf of heavy dark rye bread and was chewing on a piece while waiting outside the classroom for Father Matthias to appear. Stefan walked up and stood beside him. He said nothing and looked at the floor, though he occasionally allowed his eyes to glance sideways at Josef. Josef kept chewing and held out the loaf. "You want a piece?" he said with his mouth full.

"I can't," said Stefan.

"Why not?"

"I'm not allowed to beg."

"You're not begging. I'm offering."

"My father says we don't take charity. We come from a family of noblemen, and we should not demean ourselves."

"Okay. I can't force you to take it. Maybe it's not your favorite kind of bread."

Stefan was quiet for a minute or two before he coughed and said sheepishly, "Well, maybe a little piece."

Josef broke off a hunk the size of his fist and handed it to him. Stefan bit into it and swallowed hastily, hardly taking time to chew it properly. The hunk of bread disappeared quickly. Josef watched in amazement. He'd never seen anyone eat so fast! From then on Josef brought leftover food from home whenever he could and gave it to Stefan. He took care not to mention it to anyone.

Josef was spending less and less time with Mosche. His friend now attended school every day except Sabbath from mid-morning until late afternoon. Mosche was showing great promise as a scholar; therefore his father gave him fewer chores to do in order that he might spend more time at his studies. Mosche still made some early morning deliveries, and the boys managed to meet once or twice a week.

Miriam always came along. She had made good progress reading Torah at home in the evenings with her brother. By this time Miriam knew more Hebrew words than Josef and understood better the finer points of Jewish law. She was not content to hear Scripture translated into the common language, nor to recite certain selected biblical and talmudic passages that applied to household duties. Other women might be satisfied with those things. But Miriam loved to read and study the Hebrew text on her own.

One day, a holiday when school was not in session, the children met early to study and do errands. Afterwards they decided to walk to the river to watch boats go by. Their conversation naturally turned to school topics.

"What's it like, studying with Father Matthias?" asked Mosche.

"Boring. Except when he gets angry. Then it's really bad."

"What are you learning?"

"Mostly we memorize Latin words. He says later on, once we get the grammar through our thick heads, then we can learn some philosophy and science."

"Latin is the language of the Roman Empire. Why would anyone want to study the ideas of those murderers? Or learn their language, for that matter?"

"There's some good stuff written in Latin, like the Bible."

"The Bible was written in Hebrew, and that's the way it should be read!" cried Miriam, surprising the boys with her vehemence.

"It's okay, Miriam," said Josef. "Most Christians don't read anything at all. They don't know how."

"Don't you have schools?" she asked.

"No."

"What do the scholars do all day, and how do they earn a living?"

Josef laughed. "There are no scholars. It's not like the Jewish quarter."

"We have so many teachers we don't know what to do with them all," said Mosche. "All the young scholars need income while they study. But even the ones with teaching jobs are barely paid enough to live on."

"Who pays them?"

"In some towns the parents have to pay. Here we have a community fund that pays for all the boys, even the poor ones, to go to school until they're twelve. Rich people are expected to contribute most to the fund."

"With so many scholars around, you must have really good teachers."

"They're okay."

Here Miriam spoke up again. "That's not what you told me! You said your teacher doesn't know enough to be called 'Rabbi.' Some of your classmates call him 'Rabbozi.'"

"You're right. He's not very learned, or at least he doesn't show it. Instead of working and studying, he spends all his time complaining that the class is too big for him to manage without an assistant. He says elementary teachers are treated like slaves and given no respect."

"Is that true?" asked Josef.

"They're not as highly esteemed as the Jeschiba teachers, that's for sure. But they do get some money and they don't have to pay taxes. And they have time to study with the masters. That's what I want to do some day."

"Will you be able to?"

"I don't know. They say that for every thousand boys who begin studying the Bible, only a hundred will study Mishna, and of those just ten will study Talmud, and from them only one will be a rabbi. One thing I do know: if I'm allowed to study in the Jeschiba, I'll be happy to teach the younger boys."

"What about the girls?" his sister cried out.

"The girls too," said Mosche, patting her on the head.

"What are you studying now, Mosche?" asked Josef.

"Mostly Mishna. You and I haven't done that yet."

"What is it?"

"It's oral law collected by Rabbi Judah nine hundred years ago. They call it oral, and I guess it was at first, but it's all been written down since then." Mosche paused. When he spoke again, his voice conveyed excitement. "We've just begun reading through some tractates of the Babylonian Talmud. It's really hard, but to help us understand, we have notes made by the students when Rabbi Scholomo taught here."

"You're lucky," said Josef. "Even if your teacher isn't very good, at least you have good things to read. Father Matthias never lets us read anything except what we copy from his slate."

"Don't you have any books in your class?"

"Father Matthias has a few books, but he doesn't let us touch them. Mostly he teaches from memory."

"Our teachers are not allowed to teach from memory. They have to use a book or a scroll so they don't forget anything. Anyhow, it's nice to have books and scrolls nearby when we study."

"The church has a library, I think, but I've never seen it."

"We have a library at the school and any Jew in the city can use the books," Mosche said proudly. "One of the old rabbis says books should be our constant companions. But, since most of us can't afford them, we need a library."

"Oh, look!" said Miriam. "That boat is bigger than anything I've ever seen!"

"It's a barge," said her brother. "What you see is mostly cargo. It's loaded down with so much stuff that the deck is almost under water." The children watched in silence as several immense barges went by. Then Mosche asked, "If most Christians can't read, how do you make contracts for marriages and business deals?"

"We don't, unless a professional scribe writes them for us. Most of the time we just say an oath or go through some kind of ritual."

Miriam said she was hungry, and the boys agreed it was time to go home for lunch.

One day in class, Stefan was having more difficulty than usual completing the daily assignment. He repeatedly rubbed out what he had written on his slate and finally, in utter frustration, gave up. When called forward to show his work, he had only a few smudges on a dusty slate. Father Matthias' eyes became slits and he gritted his teeth. "You blockhead! Can't you do a simple conjugation? Put out your hands."

Stefan laid his slate on the teacher's desk. His hands shook visibly as he held them out in front of him. Father Matthias took his wand and rapped the boy's knuckles repeatedly until they bled. Stefan winced each time a blow fell, and tears were streaming down his face when he returned to his seat. Josef vowed to find more time outside of class to help Stefan learn his grammar. He couldn't bear watching his friend get beaten. It was all he could do to stay in his seat when it happened. He wanted to jump up and strangle Father Matthias. That would be a terrible sin, of course, but it might be worth it for one moment of satisfaction.

There were occasions when Josef tried to defend Stefan. Once, the priest was doing an oral drill with the boys. He called out questions and the boys were supposed to respond as quickly as they could. Stefan's nervousness caused him to stutter, and Father Matthias was beginning to get angry. Josef delayed his own answers, hoping to give Stefan an little extra time to think and calm himself. The next time a question was directed at Stefan, he gave a thoughtful answer, but not the one his teacher was expecting.

"That makes no sense," Father Matthias snapped. "Give me an answer that makes sense."

Stefan's countenance fell and he remained silent.

"I said give me an answer that makes sense!"

At this point, Josef could not restrain himself. "His answer must have made sense to him or he wouldn't have said it!" There was urgency in his voice, though he spoke quietly.

"What did you say?" asked the priest, his face becoming red as he turned to look at Josef.

Josef mumbled, "I said his answer makes sense to him."

"I'll have none of your cheek. Come up here right now."

Josef was required to hold out his hands for punishment. After ten quick blows he was allowed to return to his seat. His hands throbbed and red welts were beginning to appear, but he could bear physical pain better than watching Stefan endure another beating.

"Now, Stefan, you come forward," said the priest.

Josef looked at the other boy and saw that tears already filled his eyes. As Stefan began to rise, Josef jumped up and stood in front of him, with his back to Father Matthias. He gently pushed Stefan back into his seat and held him there. Behind him, he could hear and feel the man approaching.

"So that's the way it is. You think you can subvert discipline. Well, think again."

He lifted his wand and began striking Josef on the back and shoulders. Stefan cried out that he was the one who deserved punishment, not Josef. He begged for the man to please, please stop. After what seemed an eternity, Father Matthias returned to his desk and sat down. For ten minutes he sat staring straight ahead at nothing. The boys watched him, fearing another outburst. Finally the priest spoke, still without looking at the boys, saying they were dismissed for the day.

That evening at supper, Josef's mother noticed he seemed quieter than usual. "How are your studies coming?" she asked.

"Okay."

"You're so lucky, Josef, to have a teacher here in Worms. Some boys have to leave home to be educated. That would break my heart, if I couldn't see you anymore. Do you know how lucky you are?"

"Yes, Mutti." He reached for the bread to tear off another piece.

"Josef! What happened to your hands?"

"Oh, it's nothing. Father Matthias got angry today and I was punished."

"Josef, how could you? You mustn't misbehave! Please tell me you won't misbehave! You can't throw away your best chance to make something of yourself."

"No, Mutti. I'm not throwing anything away. Please don't worry."

In spite of her son's reassurances, she slept very little that night, anxious about his future and hers.

When Miriam was not helping her mother at home or doing errands with her brother, she lingered around the schoolyard. She wanted desperately to join the class of boys, to learn everything her brother was learning. From outside the schoolhouse, she could sometimes hear the lively discussions that went on in the classroom. It was tantalizing. Miriam was sure she knew Torah as well as most of the boys, but apparently it had crossed no one's mind (except her own) that she might participate in the class. Even Mosche did not like the idea when she broached it.

Nevertheless, she was able to persuade her brother to ask his teacher whether a girl could attend the class.

The opportunity came on a beautiful spring morning when the boys took breakfast out of doors during their break. Miriam was waiting in the schoolyard. When she saw Mosche come out, she ran to him and begged him to ask his teacher today.

"I don't know if today is the right day," he said.

"Come on. It's as good as any other day." She grabbed his arm and pulled in the direction of the schoolhouse. Just as they reached the door, the teacher stepped out. Miriam and Mosche dropped back. She poked him.

"Excuse me, sir," said Mosche. "My sister has a question. I mean, I have a question to ask for my sister."

"Yes? What is it?" he responded.

"Umm, might it be possible, I mean sometime in the future, for a girl to . . ." He hesitated and then burst out with the final words, "attend a class in the school?"

The teacher wrinkled his brow and frowned. Then he snickered and finally burst out laughing. The other boys all turned to see what was causing such mirth in their habitually dour-faced teacher. They drifted closer. Mosche was mortified at what happened next.

The teacher motioned for the other students to approach. "Come listen, boys. This silly girl thinks she can study with the boys! Apparently her brother has encouraged her in this crazy idea. How do you like that?"

The boys drew nearer still. A few of them whispered to each other and giggled, but no one ventured a scholarly opinion.

"Now pay attention, everyone," continued the teacher. "Let's put an end to this silliness once and for all. Women need to know only as much as will assist them in their household duties. They are taught particular prayers, customs, and portions of law that pertain to these duties. Hearing small selected passages of Scripture translated into the common language is good for them and quite adequate to their needs. In fact, that's all most women can take in." Then he turned to Miriam and addressed her directly. "Little girl, you spend your time learning tunes and hymns to sing on holy days. That'll give you something to do in your spare time. And save your pennies so that when you're married you can buy books for your husband to read."

Miriam ran out of the courtyard and did not stop running until she was completely out of sight. Mosche knew she would be sulking for many days. But he could not worry about that now. He would have to endure the teacher's disfavor and ribbing from the other boys. He wished his sister were less ambitious. Maybe he had done wrong in teaching her to read. Well, it was too late to change that now. The cat was out of the bag.

Josef learned about all this a few weeks later, when the children once again had some free time together. Miriam complained fiercely about the treatment she had received. "I can read as well as any of those boys in your class," she said to her brother. "Your teacher thinks all girls are stupid."

Josef addressed her. "Maybe it's better if you don't study with him. Teachers like that just make you miserable. I should know."

"Your teacher doesn't like girls either?" she asked.

"My teacher doesn't like anybody! Look what he does when he's angry." Josef held out his hands, discolored and scarred from recent beatings.

"That's terrible!" said Miriam.

"Oh, it's nothing, really. You should've seen my back after he hit me with his stick. It felt like I'd been trampled by an ox."

"I hate your teacher! He's a monster!"

"Don't say that, Miriam," scolded her brother. "We're taught to revere our teachers. Even when we disagree with them, we should speak of them respectfully."

"How can you respect someone who's so mean? The boys in your school aren't beaten like that, are they?"

"No," said Mosche. "Fortunately our scholars put restrictions on punishment. A strap may be used, but no marks can be left and no child injured."

Josef nodded. "That's good. Being afraid all the time doesn't make us learn any better."

"We just read one of Rabbi Scholomo's recommendations that says exactly the same thing. According to him, learning blossoms more fully from love of your teacher than fear of your teacher. He advises teaching with gentleness and sweet words. Verbal correction is better than a hundred blows, he says, and when physical punishment is used, it must never be severe or long-lasting."

"Right! I wish Father Matthias would read that."

"At least we have one teacher who believes it," said Miriam, looking again at Josef's scarred hands. "Mosche, tell me you will always be our teacher. Josef and I are lucky to have a teacher like you."

"Yes, Miriam. I'll teach you as long as I can, if you still want to learn."

"We do! Don't we, Josef?"

"Yes. For sure."

"The only thing is, I'm almost thirteen. You know I've already begun doing day-long fasts on holy days. The rabbis are considering whether I might be a candidate to enter the Jeschiba as a full-time student."

"That's okay. Then you'll know more stuff to teach us," said his sister.

"You don't understand. If I enter the Jeschiba, I won't have time to teach you."

"What? You have to be our teacher! There's nobody else!"

"I will as long as I can. Josef, I brought something for you to take home and study. My father gave it to me at the Purim festival."

"A book of Psalms!" Josef held it reverently. "Are you sure it's all right if I take it?"

"Yes, I can use the copy at school. But be careful with it, and don't let the mice eat it."

"I promise."

"I trust you."

"Thanks, Mosche. It's safe with me."

Chapter 7

Two weeks later Mosche began his studies in the Jeschiba. As he had predicted, his daytime hours were too fully occupied to allow regular meetings with Josef. He still read with Miriam in the evenings, although he had less time to spend with her as well. Knowing he would have a holiday at the end of the third month, Mosche arranged to meet Josef before sunup on that day. He wanted to take his friend to a place that had special significance for him.

They met at the entrance of Jews' Alley, along Market Street. Miriam came too. Waking early and seeing her brother preparing to go out, she had insisted he take her along. Following Mosche's lead, the children walked down Chambers Street toward Newmarket Square.

"Where are we going?" asked Josef.

"You'll see," said Mosche.

"The old market would have been much closer if you're going to buy something."

"I don't want to buy anything."

The children passed through Newmarket Square, where vendors had begun to set up their booths for the midweek market. Coming out of the marketplace, they could see on their right, in the dim light of early morning, the huge construction project that had been under way as long as they could remember. It was on the site of an ancient temple built by Roman settlers, later replaced by a Christian cathedral. Situated on the highest point of the city, the current structure was large and imposing. Its more modest predecessors had been torn down or destroyed by fire. More than fifty years ago, Bishop Burchard had begun construction on this cathedral, whose ultimate size they could only guess; it seemed to be undergoing perpetual rebuilding and extension.

Mosche led the others on a dusty path just south of the cathedral site. They looked in awe at the immense building looming over them, large parts of it sheathed in scaffolding. The children walked through the gate of the old city wall and at last reached their destination. Still within view of the cathedral, they stood looking over a field of gentle hills with a few trees scattered about. Covering the field lay a carpet of mist, partially obscuring the ground and giving the treetops the appearance of floating. It was a beautiful sight.

"What is it?" asked Josef.

"We call it '*Heiliger Sand*.' It's the holy soil where our forefathers are buried."

"Am I allowed to be here?"

"It's all right. Anybody can come in."

"Why is the burial ground so far away from where you live?"

"Some Jews live close by. But the synagogue and the school were built across town because most people don't want to be too near—contact with the dead makes them unclean. You see that basin over there? That's where we wash on our way out."

Mosche led the way through a wooden gate into the field, which was surrounded by a low stone wall. On a large stele beside the gate a Hebrew prayer had been inscribed. As the children walked toward a small plot of gravestones, Mosche stooped to pick up some pebbles. Miriam did the same.

"What are you doing?" inquired Josef.

"We always put rocks on our grandparents' graves. It's a sign of respect. Our rabbi told us the custom goes back to ancient days, when Jews lived in the desert. They piled rocks on graves to keep wild animals from digging up the dead bodies."

"That's awful," said Josef.

Mosche nodded. "We don't worry about that here." He and his sister approached two headstones and carefully placed their pebbles in a row along the top. By now the sun was up, the mist had evaporated, and the moist gravestones were gleaming brightly in the slanting rays of the sun.

"What are those pictures on the stones?" asked Josef.

"Over my grandparents' graves is a wheel. The same symbol was on their house, to show that my grandfather was a carter. That's how these graves are identified. See, there's a horseshoe for the farrier and bellows for the smith."

"Some of the headstones have writing on them."

"Yes. This one's for a man named Jakob who died a few years ago. Can you read it?"

"It's in Hebrew. Let me see if I can figure it out." Josef went closer to the stone and knelt in the grass before it. "It says 'This is the something-stone of Jakob,' and then there's a word I can't read. Then it says 'who died in the year'—I guess that's a date—'under the calendar. His soul rests in the bundle of life.' That's the best I can make it out."

"You got most of it," said Mosche. He pointed to words on the stone and said, "This means 'dead body' to show that it's a gravestone. After his name, it says he was a bachelor. The year he died was 4837 according to the Jewish calendar."

"Let's look at some others."

"Okay. Notice the funny names on some of them."

"Will you read them to me?"

"I'll let Miriam do that. She knows them all."

Miriam was delighted to be included in the conversation. Up to that moment she felt the boys had forgotten about her. She led them from one grave to another, reading the names written on the stones. "Hanna, Abram, Bella, Judith, Aaron, Bona, Speranza, Salo, Peruza, Bonafila."

"Those last ones are odd," said Josef. "Who would give their children names like that?"

"People who came from other places, like Toledo and Rome," Mosche answered. "I guess those names are normal for them."

"Why are they here?"

"Worms is a center of learning. Since a hundred years ago, our Jeschiba has attracted people from all over the world. We have a saying: 'Warmaisa is little Jerusalem on the Rhein.' Warmaisa is our nickname for Worms."

"I like being here in the cemetery. It's quiet," said Josef.

"It's a peaceful place and a holy place, and that's why I love it so much," said Mosche. "Now that I'm a full-time student, I won't be able to come here as often."

"Will you tell us what you do in the Jeschiba?" asked Josef.

The children found a comfortable place to sit under a large oak tree, and Mosche began recounting his recent experiences. "Once the rabbis decided I should enter the Jeschiba," he said, "they invited me and my parents to the schoolhouse. We talked a long time about what they expected of me (hours and hours of hard work) and of my family (encouragement and financial support). After that, all the rabbis put their hands on my head and gave me a blessing. They prayed that I might be worthy to study Torah and also that I should acquire wisdom and do virtuous deeds.

"Next morning at seven I went to the schoolhouse. Most of the Jeschiba scholars were there already and three of my classmates from school. The four of us sat together, not knowing what we were supposed to do. Before long, we heard the familiar sound of bells jingling on the fringes around the mantle of the Torah scrolls. One of the rabbis brought in the scrolls, read verses from Torah, and led us in prayers. Then we had some fun. The head rabbi told jokes and had us laughing for ten minutes. They say he does that every week. He's a short man called Rabbi Meir. He came over to us and introduced himself and told us who our tutor would be. We four new students were put in a group with four older boys. Each of us was assigned a study partner from the group to work with. Every day my partner and I are supposed to read an assigned passage, talk about what it means, memorize it, and then come together with the other three pairs and the tutor to discuss it.

"My study partner is a fellow named Amos. He's really smart. In fact, it makes me feel stupid because he knows so much. My father says that's the best kind of partner to have—he'll push me to learn more. I guess it's true. Anyway, I better get used to spending time with Amos, because we do everything together: read, study, pray, eat, rest. It's almost like having a wife! One thing he's already done, he's taught me to sing passages from Torah and Talmud, which makes them easier to memorize."

"What parts are you reading now?" asked Josef.

"We're working on Tractate *Berakhot* of the Mishnah, all about prayers and liturgy. It starts with a discussion of the *Shema*—you remember the prayer from the fifth book of Moses?"

"Hear, O Israel, the Lord our God is the One God."

"That's it. We're also working on a tractate called *Moed*, about Sabbath laws. There's another section about festivals that sounds really interesting. Our tutor said we could study it next if we want to."

"You get to choose what you study?"

"Not always. There are certain parts everybody has to do. But the teachers encourage us to give more attention to passages that interest us. Some of the writing is so clever and delightful I could spend all day on it. But really, everything we've read so far has been worthwhile."

"What about your tutor, is he any good?"

"Yes. Very good! He studied at Rabbi Scholomo's Jeschiba in Troyes. He knows lots about Torah and Talmud, and he also knows how to teach."

"What happens when you all meet together?"

"Well, sometimes our discussions get loud, with eight people trying to talk at once. It's kind of wild. The tutor lets us argue for a while. But then he guides the argument, so that we always come around to a reasonable conclusion. He uses the notes he brought back from his studies at Troyes and gives the clearest, wittiest explanation you could imagine. The whole thing is almost like a tournament, where we kick a ball around and he's our referee."

"Do students get mad if they lose an argument?"

"Nobody loses. Every suggestion is taken seriously and discussed completely. The tutor gives us reasons for everything. And he doesn't say you have to believe it. He quotes often one of Rabbi Scholomo's favorite passages of the Mishnah: 'A struggle that revolves around the book must end in love.' So we end all our discussions with a prayer for peace and friendship."

"Father Matthias would never let us argue about the Bible."

"We don't really argue about the Bible itself, but about interpretations of the Bible. The Talmud is called 'Battleground of Torah.' It contains ideas of many scholars, and they don't always agree. So we take sides and try to figure out what makes the most sense. The goal is to understand the meaning of sacred words in Torah."

"Do you do anything else besides study and argue?"

"Not much. We take regular breaks for prayer. And we stop to eat breakfast and lunch, of course, outside whenever the weather's nice. In the afternoon we have a rest period. Some of the boys go out and run around, but Amos and I are usually too tired for that."

Miriam had been silent through this entire discussion. Now she spoke. "Okay. I know what we'll do. Josef and I are going to be study partners. Mosche will be our tutor. After we argue enough, Mosche can settle the arguments. When he doesn't have time to meet with us, I'll ask him at night about anything we disagree on."

Josef looked doubtful. "Did you ever hear of a girl study partner?"

Mosche shook his head. "Highly unusual."

"Well who else are you going to find?" cried Miriam. "And who else am I going to find? We're both desperate."

The boys reluctantly agreed to give Miriam's plan a try. She and Josef were to meet three mornings a week, quite early, at the entrance of Jews' Alley. Whenever possible she would bring a scroll, or else she would copy out part of a text on a slate. The two children would find a secluded spot where they could argue in peace. Mosche would join them if possible, but he thought this would not happen very often.

One of the first passages Miriam and Josef studied together was found near the end of the first book of Moses. It described a time after the patriarch Israel and all his sons had followed Josef to Egypt, when Israel was old and sick and nearly blind. "And Israel perceived the sons of Josef, and said, Who are these? And Josef said unto his father, These are my sons, whom God hath given me in this place. And he said, Bring them, I pray thee, unto me, and I will bless them."

The new study partners found much to discuss in the passage. Josef thought it might apply to circumstances today, where young Jews cannot always be recognized, even by their own people. Sometimes they just blend in with everybody else, he said. Here in Worms, for example, he often could not tell who was a Jew and who was a Christian. Everyone spoke the same language and wore the same clothes. Maybe the world had grown old and blind so that it could no longer see the difference.

Miriam had another interpretation. She thought Grandfather Israel needed to be reminded who the little boys were because he had only first met them when he was an old man. The sons of Josef were born in a foreign land, like many other Jews. Throughout their history, she said, the Jewish people had wandered from one place to another, hardly ever finding a homeland where they were welcomed. Nevertheless, God always found them and (like the old man) blessed them.

The children argued for a time and tried to remember other passages from Torah and Talmud that would shed some light. They ended their session in considerable doubt as to the correct interpretation. Miriam said she would ask Mosche to tell her what he had learned from his teachers. In the meantime, she declared, they should memorize the passage and repeat it to each other. She recalled a bit of rabbinic advice Mosche had quoted to her: "One who repeats his lesson a hundred times is not like him who repeats it a hundred and one times." A complete knowledge of one passage, she said, will help a person understand other passages that come around.

As months went by, the two children continued to study together. Josef also attended Latin lessons with Father Matthias every afternoon but he much preferred the give-and-take of discussions with Miriam and, on rare occasions, with Mosche as well.

Miriam and Josef wrestled for several days with a passage from the third book of Moses: "And if a man maim his neighbor, as he hath done, so it shall be done to him; Breach for breach, eye for eye, tooth for tooth: in the manner as he has caused a bodily defect in a man, so it shall be rendered unto him." Miriam had difficulty reconciling this passage with her understanding of other commandments. God himself was kind and merciful, she said, even when he exacted justice. Oftentimes it seemed he demanded the same leniency from his people. This was spelled out quite clearly in an earlier passage from the Law: "Thou shalt not avenge nor bear any grudge against the children of thy people; but thou shalt love thy neighbor as thyself: I am the Lord." How, then, could such cruel punishment be required against an offender who may have acted from momentary anger, never intending to put out a man's eye or break his leg? Some members of the community seemed to delight in taking an eye for an eye or a tooth for a tooth. It made them feel righteous, Miriam thought. But for her it was different. Seeing anyone in extreme pain just nauseated her.

Josef could not shed much light on the question, except to say that Christians were as likely as Jews to resort to cruel punishment. Fortunately, Mosche was able to meet with them one Sunday afternoon. He had recently studied these texts and was eager to share what he had learned. His tutor had stated over and over, Mosche said, that education should enhance both intellect and character. The Bible was a source of ethics as well as information. To be truly wise, the tutor had said, a person must learn to read the Bible in light of everything he knows about this world and about human nature. Instead of interpreting every word literally, scholars should find ways to capture the spirit of the words in order to apply them appropriately. Sometimes harsher action is required than the text calls for and sometimes less harsh. Rabbi Scholomo was able to make this distinction. According to Mosche's tutor, the rabbi taught his students that "an eye for an eye" did not require maiming the offender, only that he make restitution for the injury he had caused. This could be done by paying money to compensate for loss, as one would do if a slave were injured and unable to work for a certain time.

How did the rabbi come to this conclusion? In the *Gemara* there appear to be good arguments on both sides of the question. One writer asserts that adjoining Scripture passages should be read and considered for comparison. In this case, verses found before and after the "eye for an eye" passage indicated that a man who kills a person shall be put to death, but a man who kills a beast shall pay compensation. Therefore a man who merely causes injury may also pay compensation, since he has killed no one.

A later writer says it would be unjust to take an eye for an eye in all cases because one person's eye may be large and another's small. Perhaps the offender should be permitted to pay compensation in this case? Then it must be so in all cases, since the text states "ye shall have one manner of judicial law." Other scholars refute this argument. What happens if a small man kills a giant, they ask, or vice versa? On the basis of previous discussion, how could the murderer be put to death? Yet Torah requires that he be put to death. Thus it follows that an offender who takes away sight should have his sight taken away.

But another writer asks what should be done if a blind man puts out another man's eye? How can the law be strictly applied? If retaliation cannot be exacted, is the offender to be set free? And another asks what happens if a dying man murders a healthy man? Is the dying man truly punished by taking his life?

Rabbi Scholomo considered all these arguments. His final proof, Mosche told the others, was found in the text "in the manner as he has caused a bodily defect in a man, so it shall be rendered unto him." The word "rendered" implies giving something into the hand of another, such as monetary compensation. Therefore, the law need not be enforced literally.

Miriam was delighted with these arguments and with the final conclusion. Josef was impressed that Mosche was learning (from his tutor) interpretations given by Rabbi Scholomo. It followed that he and Miriam would be, indirectly, students of this great teacher. Josef wished Mosche had more time to spend with them.

Josef had been studying Latin with Father Matthias for more than two years. Stefan still struggled to master the grammar and memorize texts, but he did learn to read and could do it fairly well. Nevertheless, it was clear that Josef was by far the superior student. The relationship between teacher and pupils was by no means warm, but they had settled into a routine that allowed the boys to work at their own pace with minimal interference. Father Matthias rarely resorted to beatings now, perhaps because he discovered they were ineffective.

One afternoon Father Matthias asked Josef to stay a few minutes after the lessons were concluded. The priest looked rather smug and self-satisfied, and Josef could not imagine what the man would say to him.

"Josef, you are my star pupil," he began. "I've been asked by city officials to advise you of an excellent opportunity. The mayor's office is looking for a secretary to keep records and write documents. They were thinking of hiring a Jew for the position, but fortunately I stifled that idea. I told them I could recommend an honest Christian who would be less likely to take advantage of them. They seemed grateful. You'll be paid a small salary, of course. But even more important, this will allow you to make connections with the right people, and we could all stand to benefit. What do you think?"

"Which people do you mean?"

"People with power and money, of course."

"When would I work?"

"Right away. The need is immediate."

"No, I mean what hours of the day?"

"What difference does that make? In the mornings, I think."

"I work for my mother in the mornings."

"Don't be silly. Your mother can find other children to run errands. She'll be proud of you, working at a real job. Besides, people in your position can't afford to pass up a steady income, no matter how small."

Josef thought about this point. It was true that he and his mother lived on the edge of poverty. While they had never actually gone hungry, there had been weeks and months when all they could afford was barley bread and a bit of lard. Few lodgers had rented the extra room lately, and those who did stayed only a short time. His mother was still loathe to let the room to Jews, who would likely have stayed longer and paid better. Yes, it was true they could use some additional income. But that was not foremost in Josef's mind. What he was primarily thinking about was his morning study sessions with Miriam. He had grown to love the time they spent together reading, discussing, arguing, bickering, sometimes laughing, and occasionally discovering a great truth. It was the best part of his week, the time he looked forward to most. He had come to admire Miriam almost as much as her brother for her intelligence, wit, compassion, and even for her stubbornness and petulance. Both children were busier with chores than they had ever been, but they had clung to those three precious mornings each week. Would he be forced to give them up if he worked in the mayor's office?

Josef was so deeply immersed in his thoughts that he didn't hear Father Matthias tapping vigorously on the desk with his wand. "All right, young man. Stop your daydreaming and listen. I told the town clerk you would be there first thing tomorrow morning. Do you know where city hall is?"

"Yes, it's over that way a couple of blocks, toward Newmarket."

"That's right. You're to ask for a man named Frieder. He'll show you around and explain what they expect you to do. And mind you, do it well, whatever it is. Your performance will reflect on me. I recommended you for this position—don't make me look like a fool. We both could profit by this if you show them you're a careful and diligent worker. Is that clear?"

Josef nodded and muttered, "Yes, it's clear." He left the church feeling dejected. He would have to find Miriam that afternoon, to tell her the bad news. They were supposed to meet tomorrow morning and he didn't want her to wait for him in vain. He decided he'd better go immediately to the Jewish quarter to look for her, before his mother could set him to work on some lengthy task. He knew where the family lived and would go to her door if necessary. But he also knew a couple of other places where she liked to spend her free time, a meadow just outside the city wall and a small grove of trees behind the schoolhouse. He would look there first.

Josef hurried through the streets, taking a back way to avoid passing by his own house. He approached the rear of the schoolhouse and was about to enter the grove when he noticed Jeschiba students outside taking what he surmised was their afternoon break. There was Mosche sitting under a tree! Beside him sat an older-looking boy, leaning back against the tree trunk. The two of them were talking and laughing about something that must have been exceedingly funny. Josef stood transfixed—what he would have given to be part of that scene! Suddenly he noticed Mosche was looking at him and even nodding his head. Josef did not wish to speak to Mosche just now, or to meet his study partner. He quickly turned up the street toward the city gate. If he was lucky, he would find Miriam in the pasture outside the wall.

There she was! Josef hurried over to her. At first she didn't look up from the scroll she was reading. When she did, a look of surprise came over her face. "What are you doing here?" she asked.

"Looking for you."

"Why? What's happened?"

"It's terrible. I have to work tomorrow morning and probably every morning from now on. They want me to keep records at city hall. We can't meet any more in the mornings."

A look of dismay came over Miriam's face. She turned her head away and didn't say anything for a long time. Finally she said, "You're the only study partner I have, and now you're quitting."

"I can't help it! It's not my choice. Besides, my mother and I need the money."

"Study is more important than money."

"I know that. Maybe we can find another time."

"Like when?"

"Sunday afternoons are supposed to be my free time. Sometimes my mother expects me to visit her friends, but I'll tell her I can't do that any more."

Early the next morning Josef presented himself in the office of Frieder, City Clerk of Worms. Frieder was a large, burly man with a gruff voice but kindly eyes. After leading Josef on a brief tour of city hall, he set the boy to work at a small table in one corner of his office. Josef was expected to copy long, detailed documents, most of them having to do with property ownership. For the first weeks and months of his employment, Josef did little else. It was boring work, yet Josef came to enjoy the bustle of city government and the company of his boss.

Some days it was necessary for Frieder to inspect properties outside the city wall. On these excursions Josef usually accompanied him, carrying his surveying tools and writing implements. Going out through the southwest gate of the city one day, they passed by the Jewish cemetery. Frieder motioned as they went by. "Do you know what this plot of land is?" he asked.

"It's a cemetery."

"Yes. In fact it's a burial place for Jews. They've had a community here for three hundred years. Some of the graves are quite old. My department is responsible for administration of this land, but for the most part we leave it alone. The Jews do some minimal upkeep and we try to stay out of the way."

"Have you ever been in there?" asked Josef.

"Many times. It's a peaceful place with a certain atmosphere I can't describe. You could say it inspires reverence I guess. Would you like to go in?"

Josef nodded. He was glad to be back in this beautiful place. But he dared not tell Frieder about his previous visit or his Jewish friends. He didn't know if Frieder was one of those people who hated Jews and avoided them for fear he might be contaminated. Even if Frieder felt differently, it was better not to bring up the subject. Word might get back to Father Matthias, and then there would be trouble.

Josef's doubts about Frieder's attitude toward Jews vanished after he'd been working for the man about a year. The work was more varied now, as the boy had gained his boss's trust. He was asked to take dictations of letters and keep records of tax payments, among other things. Today Frieder was dictating a letter to the city clerk of Mainz. He had received word from this man that the Jews of his city were looking for a new place of residence. They had been living in fear since a fire burned down most of Mainz's Jewish quarter. The Jews claimed it was accidental, but the burghers of the city accused them of attempting to damage adjacent property owned by Christians. The city clerk of Mainz said he suspected the Jews were guilty, but even if they weren't, he would be glad to be rid of them. Would it by possible for the Jewish community in Worms to take in these other Jews, at least temporarily?

Frieder's response was as follows: "To my most esteemed colleague, City Clerk of the Municipality of Mainz, from the occupant of the same office in Worms, greetings!

"Pursuant to your request concerning relocation of Jews, let it be known that we the citizens and city officials of Worms have no objection, in principle, to the presence of additional Jews in our community. We find their commercial activities conducive to our economic prosperity. However, it is an incontrovertible fact that the living conditions of Jews in this city have suffered of late due to overcrowding. Houses along the Jews' Alley and surrounding streets and lanes are completely filled with residents. Furthermore, the active Jeschiba in Worms attracts hundreds of scholars from the Rheinland and beyond, sometimes swelling the local Jewish community to twice its normal size. We are therefore unable to incorporate in our city the entire Jewish population of Mainz. Jews with family connections in Worms could perhaps be accommodated, assuming the number were no more than ten or fifteen.

"If I might be so bold as to propose another solution: it has been reported to me by certain friends in ecclesiastical circles that the bishop of Speyer might be receptive to an influx of Jews. His Reverence Bishop Rudiger is said to be a broad-minded man with good understanding of economic matters. He would know the benefits attendant upon a Jewish presence in the business community. With all due respect, I suggest you apply to the bishop of Speyer.

"Submitted in faithful service by Frieder of Worms."

Frieder looked solemn as he folded and sealed the letter Josef had transcribed. After placing it in the outgoing basket, he returned to his desk and sat motionless, gazing at the wall. Josef thought this might be a good time to ask something he'd been wondering about. "Why would the Jews of Mainz burn down their own neighborhood?"

Frieder flinched slightly, startled out of his thoughts by the boy's question. "I don't know. The accusation is probably false."

"Why would someone make up a story like that?"

Frieder pursed his lips. "It's hard to explain. Jews are permitted to live in our cities and even to practice their faith, yet at the same time, we are warned to keep away from them. People who don't know Jews spread outrageous stories about them. Sometimes they get violent."

"Who does?"

"Well, for example, my father told me about something that happened when he was a boy. The king tried very hard to convert Jews and make them Christians. When this failed, he became angry. Rumors and accusations flew about. It was said that Jews had willfully misinterpreted their own Scriptures in order to deny Christ. The labels 'Christ-killer' and 'deicide' were frequently heard. A few went so far as to say every Jew was an agent of the devil. When people get ideas like that in their heads, it's hard to restrain them from violence. Jews were expelled from their home villages. Some of them suffered bodily harm and a few were killed."

"Did that happen here in Worms?"

"No, not in Worms. But in villages to the south. A similar situation occurred in the Moorish lands not too long ago."

"Will the Jews in Mainz be safe?"

"I hope so. Things have been fairly calm lately—I pray they will stay that way."

A few weeks later, Josef met Miriam for a study session. They had observed that the grove of trees behind the school was rarely occupied on Sunday afternoons, and this is where they met. Josef was noticeably excited. "Miriam, did you hear what happened in Speyer?"

"No. Was it something bad?"

"Not at all. The bishop, whose name is Rudiger, told the Jews of Mainz they could come to live in Speyer. I know you heard about the fire in Mainz and how the Jews are afraid to stay there. Well, now they have a place to go!"

"Are you sure it'll be safe?"

"Yes. The bishop has written a contract. I heard about it from my boss at city hall. They'll have their own district outside town with a wall around it. They're allowed to hire guards and defend their property."

"How are they going to earn a living?"

"The bishop promised they could do business anywhere in his domain. It's an amazing contract! He said the chief rabbi would be judge of the Jews. And he even gave them land for a cemetery that they could keep forever!"

"It sounds good. I just hope it works. You know my uncle lives in Mainz."

Just then Josef heard something behind a small clump of bushes. It sounded like giggling. He walked over to investigate and was surprised to find someone he knew. First he saw Lotti, the daughter of his mother's friend who lived near their house. Behind her and slightly more hidden was her older sister Anna.

"What are you doing here?" asked Josef, showing annoyance in is voice.

Anna came forward with her hands on her hips. "We followed you here. We wanted to know what you do every Sunday afternoon. In case you forgot, you used to visit us on Sundays until you got too snobbish."

"It's not that. There are just other things I need to be doing."

"Like what?"

"You wouldn't understand."

"Well, you better tell us or we'll ask your mother what you're doing."

Josef sighed. He introduced the girls to Miriam and told them that they read and studied books together. Anna and Lotti wanted to look at the book they were reading and hear what some of the words meant. They noticed that Miriam wore a woven shawl and wanted to know where it came from. They talked to her about their new clothes and the handwork they were learning to do. Through all of this, Josef was thinking how little time he and Miriam had to study together. Today was lost, and perhaps other Sundays as well. What could he do to keep the girls happy and still find time to meet with Miriam? Could they locate a secret meeting place? Would the girls try to follow him again? Would they talk to his mother if they couldn't find him? Josef needed time to think and sort out the situation. He offered to walk with Anna and Lotti back to their house. When they arrived, he couldn't help but notice the sweet aroma of cinnamon cake the girls had baked earlier in the day. Josef was easily persuaded to stop with them and take an afternoon snack.

Chapter 8

From then on, Anna and Lotti often showed up behind the school on Sunday afternoons. Occasionally they would listen in silence while Josef and Miriam discussed a biblical text. Usually, however, they interjected comments, or worse, tried to change the subject entirely. They loved to talk about clothing and food and people they knew. Josef was frustrated that the limited time he was able to spend with Miriam was now largely wasted. But what could he do? If he asked the girls to leave, they might complain to his mother. The consequence could be a complete end to his study sessions with Miriam. It would be better to make the best use of the time they had and hope the two girls would eventually lose interest and stay away.

One day Anna came by herself. She said Lotti was at home helping their mother prepare for visitors. Some cousins who lived on a farm in the country were coming that afternoon. Anna was not looking forward to it. Her eighteen-year-old cousin was a boorish fellow with straw-colored hair sticking out in every direction. He seemed to think she should find him attractive. He was the last person in the world she wanted to spend time with, but her mother insisted she be there. Anna told the others she was allowed to leave home only to pick up a cut of lamb at one of the shops in the Jewish quarter. She thought it was all right to stop briefly and say hello.

Josef and Miriam were both relieved when Anna left. Now, at last, they might have a long afternoon to devote to their studies. The young scholars decided they would go somewhere else, to a place where no one could possibly disturb them. After some thought, Miriam suggested Mosche's hut outside the city wall. It was an old shepherds' lodge Mosche had fixed up years earlier but rarely had time to visit since he had entered the Jeschiba. Josef thought this was a good idea. He remembered having gone to the hut for his initiation ceremony almost eight years ago. It was a happy memory, leading to many other happy memories of time spent with Mosche learning to read and studying texts. Miriam had been there, too, at the initiation ceremony. She was a tiny little girl at the time, and now she was twelve years old! Josef tried to think what she looked like back then, but all he could remember were her piercing blue eyes. She still had those, of course, but now she was grown into a slender, tall girl with ivory skin and smooth dark hair. Not like Anna and Lotti, ruddy-faced girls with thick reddish hair and sturdy limbs. Miriam looked more delicate somehow, like a finely carved statue.

The two set out immediately for the hut. Upon arrival, they found the place in disrepair. Some of the wooden slats were hanging loose, and part of the straw roof had fallen in. They fixed the roof as best they could and cleaned out the old straw and other debris that had collected on the floor. Josef tried to jam the slats back in place while Miriam stacked some old wooden boxes to make a small table near the window. It was nothing fancy, nor was it especially comfortable when they sat on the floor, but at least they could be alone for a few hours.

Miriam suggested they read a text from the first book of Moses that she and Mosche had been working on at home. It was the story of Noah and the flood. Mosche had been able to answer most of her questions, citing what he had learned in the Jeschiba, but still there were certain points she could not understand. She opened the scroll she had brought along and read some verses.

"And the earth was corrupt before God; and the earth was filled with violence. And God looked upon the earth, and behold, it was corrupt, for all flesh had corrupted his way upon the earth. And God said unto Noah, The end of all flesh is come before me; for the earth is filled with violence through them, and I will destroy them with the earth. Make thee an ark of gopherwood, rooms shalt thou make in the ark, and shalt cover it within and without with pitch. But I will establish my covenant with thee; and thou shalt come into the ark, thou, and thy sons, and thy wife, and thy sons' wives with thee. And Noah was six hundred years old when the flood of waters was upon the earth. And Noah went in, and his sons, and his wife, and sons' wives with him, into the ark, because of the waters of the flood."

The first part Mosche had explained well, though Miriam still found the conclusion troublesome. All flesh would be destroyed because of the corruption and violence that prevailed in Noah's time. "All flesh" included guilty people, innocent people, and even animals. This seemed harsh to Miriam (as it surely must have done to those who were swept away by flood waters). She had asked her brother why such drastic action was needed. Mosche compared those days to a plague, when pestilence had spread so far and wide that everyone was infected. Their corruption was manifested in deceit, idolatry, and sexual perversion, as well as violence against their neighbors, including murder and robbery. Thus God's word no longer held sway. Society as a whole had become degenerate. Just as townspeople dispose of bodies, burn clothing, and scrub houses in time of plague, God cleanses the earth of moral pestilence. It is inevitable in such circumstances that even innocent people suffer.

Mosche's explanation of the next part was rather technical. Scholars had observed what seemed like Noah's reluctance to believe God. He and his family enter the ark "because of the waters of the flood." Why do they wait until the waters actually began to rise? Is Noah skeptical? Is he disobedient? The scholars believe that God's mercy also reveals itself in the passage. First Noah goes in with his sons. His wife and sons' wives enter after that. It must be that they are kept apart during the entire forty days of the flood so that Noah has a second chance to show his faithfulness. This time Noah succeeds. Why is this separation of men from women pleasing to God? Mosche said in times of terrible distress, when the whole world is in turmoil and trouble, one cannot live a normal life as if nothing were the matter. All people must share to some extent in the sufferings of others.

Miriam found she could grasp the thread of these scholarly arguments, but she nevertheless objected to the violence in the story. Mosche's explanation was fine for scholars who looked at the situation from far away, across continents and centuries. But what if they had been there? What if their own families were drowning? Would they talk about "cleansing" if they saw their children cry out and sink in the swirling waters?

Josef could not offer much comfort or explanation. He guessed that maybe God saved the little children and took them straight to heaven. At least drowning was a quick death and they didn't suffer very long. The parents would suffer more, but maybe they deserved it. Only God knew that, of course. Josef hoped all people got what they deserved.

Miriam also wondered about Noah's "second chance" at obedience. What's so terrible about keeping men and women apart? She thought this would be a good thing. "The boys I know are snobs," she said. "I'd rather be with girls and women anyway."

Josef grumbled, "Thanks a lot."

"Oh, I don't mean you. You're not like the others. You don't mind talking to a girl like she's a real person."

"Well anyway, I think men and women prefer to be together when they're married."

"What for?"

"Umm. It's hard to explain. When they love each other they do certain things."

"Like what?"

"Like kiss and hug and smooch."

"Girls kiss and hug each other."

"Not the same way. Maybe you should talk to Mosche."

"I guess so. I need to find out all about marriage. I'm going to get betrothed."

"What?" Josef could hardly believe his ears. "You're only twelve years old!"

"Yes, the betrothal won't happen until I'm thirteen, and my parents said the wedding could wait a couple of years after that. But they've already picked out the man."

"Who is it?"

"The leaseholder of a sheep farm outside the city. They say he's rich."

"Have you met him?"

"Not really, but I've seen him at synagogue. He's stocky and bald and looks a lot older than me."

"What happens if you don't like him?"

"It's too bad, I guess. In this community parents always find husbands and wives for their children. We're not even supposed to give our opinion."

"I can't imagine *you* not giving an opinion."

"It wouldn't do any good. Luckily my parents are pretty sensible."

"Once you're married, I guess we can't study together?"

"Probably not. But it's still a few years off."

"I'm getting a new Latin teacher sometime soon," said Josef, deliberately changing the subject.

"Good! I don't like the one you have now. At least I don't like what you told me about him."

"He's not so bad. He doesn't beat us any more."

"Who's your new teacher?"

"I don't know yet. Father Matthias told me and Stefan he's taught us all he can. He says we should join the older boys at the Saint Andreas cloister over near the cathedral."

"That's close to the cemetery."

"I know. I'll be required to live at the cloister and then I can visit the cemetery whenever I want. Maybe we could meet there sometimes."

"It's possible. Let's get back to studying."

The two friends became so absorbed in the text they were reading that they failed to notice the daylight fading. All at once they were surprised by voices some distance away. They stopped to listen. The voices sounded like men and they were getting nearer. Josef and Miriam involuntarily drew closer together until their shoulders were touching. Was it shepherds coming to reclaim their hut? Were robbers prowling outside the city wall? Josef's fears were alleviated when he recognized one of the voices as Mosche's. The other voice he didn't know. In a minute Mosche's head appeared in the doorway. He quickly turned back and called, "Papa, she's here."

A tall, broad-shouldered man soon walked up to the doorway. With arms folded across his chest, he spoke reproachfully. "Miriam, you should have been home hours ago! Your mother and I have been worried about you! We looked everywhere. Luckily Mosche thought to come here. What do you think you're doing?"

"Oh, Papa. We're just studying. I'm sorry I didn't think about what time it was."

"Well, you need to be thinking about that." He paused to look at Josef. "Who is this young man?"

"It's Josef, my study partner. I told you, Papa, there was someone besides Mosche who reads Scripture with me."

"Yes, but you didn't tell me it was a handsome young man." He turned to Josef. "I am honored to make your acquaintance, Josef, although I wish the circumstances had been different. Do I know your parents?"

Josef stuttered. "N...no, sir. I...I'm not a Jew."

"Not a Jew? Studying Torah with my daughter? Out late with her, away from the protection of her family? This is not an auspicious beginning to our acquaintance." He reached over and took Miriam by the hand. "Come, daughter. We must get home quickly before your mother faints from worry." He led his daughter out and they disappeared in the twilight. Mosche stayed a moment longer. He looked at Josef, shrugged his shoulders, and patted Josef's arm before following his father and sister.

Left alone, Josef wondered if he was in trouble. Would someone report this incident to his mother? Maybe she was already out looking for him. Would Miriam be allowed to study with him ever again? Would her parents be suspicious of his intentions? Yes, it was true they had stayed out too late this once, but they had been studying! How could anyone be suspicious of two people studying the Bible together? Josef looked around and noticed that Miriam had left her scroll. He tucked it under his arm and set out for home.

As it turned out, Josef worried needlessly, for he and Miriam were allowed to continue studying as before. Mosche had been able to smooth things over with their parents. He explained to them who Josef was, how they had met, and how long they had studied together. Miriam was permitted to meet him on Sunday afternoons, but only in the grove behind the schoolhouse. She was always careful to end their sessions well before dark and go directly home.

Anna and Lotti came frequently. Much to Josef's dismay, they seemed to regard these meetings as social events. Sometimes they brought freshly baked bread with fruit jam, or cheese-filled pastries, or cinnamon rolls to share with their friends. Josef had to admit these were delicious. He never ate such delicacies at home. When the girls had food, they often spread a cloth on the ground for a "proper picnic," as they called it. Other times they brought items from home to show Miriam: trinkets they had bought at the fair, snippets of beautiful fabric they had picked up at the tailor shop, or jewelry they had made from stones and shells. While Miriam expressed some interest in these items and seemed to enjoy the girls' company, Josef thought he sensed her growing impatience. With their time together so limited, Josef himself was extremely frustrated by this distraction from their studies. On some occasions they never opened a book or read a verse, and he felt the afternoon was wasted.

One day Josef met Miriam in the grove when the other girls had not yet appeared. He was eager to begin reading, but she seemed preoccupied with something else and perhaps slightly amused.

"Let's try to get some studying done before the others show up," said Josef.

"Oh, don't worry. They're not coming today."

"How do you know?"

"They came to see me during the week. I don't know how they found me, but they did."

"What did they want?"

"You'll think it's silly. When they came up to me, the girls were giggling so much they could barely talk. Anna finally managed to say that both of them were in love with you. Since I was your friend she asked me to find out which one you liked better. They think you're the handsomest boy in town."

Josef couldn't help smiling a little.

"Well, which one?" asked Miriam.

Josef shook his head. "Neither one," he said. "In fact I like you best because I can talk to you. You're interested in the same things I am."

Now it was Miriam's turn to smile and shake her head. "I can't tell the girls *that*."

"Well, tell them I like them both the same amount. Can we study now?"

A few months later, Josef was sent to live at the Saint Andreas monastery, built beside the old Roman wall on the southwestern side of the city. His mother was not happy that her son no longer lived under the same roof with her, but at least she was able to visit him twice a week in the square outside the cloister. Josef and his fellow student Stefan shared a tiny cell, furnished with two narrow cots and a small table. On the table was a washbasin the boys filled each morning with freezing water from a well in the center of the monastery courtyard. They quickly fell into the routine of the monastery. They woke early to join the community in morning prayers. After a meager breakfast and an hour of study, Josef was allowed to pursue his work at city hall. The small salary he received now went directly to the monastery coffers to pay his expenses. Later in the day the boys joined the monks in the refectory for their midday meal. All were expected to remain silent during the meal while a chapter of Scripture was read aloud. An intense afternoon study session was followed by daily chores and another community meal. The boys prayed with the monks during the office of Compline just before going to bed, but they were not expected to rise for Matins during the night.

Most of the boys attending the monastery school came from out of town. A number of them were younger sons of landowners or noblemen, whose elder brothers would inherit the family estate. Josef concluded from their jokes and remarks that they all expected to become priests, and he was a little surprised to learn that Stefan shared this expectation. Was everyone assuming he himself would follow the same course? He wasn't exactly sure he wanted to be a priest. There would be certain advantages, such as roof over his head, plenty of food, a chance to read books and talk to scholars. Yet the works they read and the topics they discussed here at the monastery seemed tedious and dry compared to what he was used to. Reading Hebrew Scripture and rabbinic commentaries was fun, full of interesting stories, real-life examples, jokes, puns, and sage advice. The monks here always wanted to talk about dogma and doctrine. After two months, he was already tired of it.

The worst thing about living in the monastery was confession. Since they had moved in, Josef and Stefan had been allowed to eat the bread at Mass. The monks made it clear, however, that they boys were to confess their sins before going to Mass. Now before divine service on Sundays and holy days Josef had to stand in a dark corner of the church and speak to a priest. He was expected to ask forgiveness and list all the sins he had committed in the past week. He knew their names, of course, things like envy, lust, and sloth. But when would he have had time or opportunity to commit them? Josef did not assume he was free of sin (Scripture warned against that!), but he had no idea what his own sins were. So he made up something. He pretended he had said angry words to his mother, or was envious of another boy's leather shoes, or took extra sugar at mealtime. Each time he went in it became harder to invent a new sin. It occurred to him that if he were a priest, he would have to sit and listen to stories made up by boys like him.

For the first time in his life, Josef felt lonely. When he was little, he had never strayed far from his mother, who even now (at a distance) showed great solicitude and affection for him. As an older boy he had one good friend, Mosche, and really that was enough. He just needed one person to share his thoughts and concerns with, to laugh with, to stand with him against the world. For the last couple of years, since Mosche had entered the Jeschiba, Miriam had been his friend. As much as Josef missed having her as a study partner, he missed her more as a companion. Since he had come to live at the monastery, they rarely saw each other. A few times, when he left the cloister to go to his job or to meet his mother, he thought he saw Miriam on the street some distance away. On one occasion he got close enough to recognize her for certain. As they approached each other, neither knew what to say. They stood staring at one another. Finally Josef said he'd like to talk to her. Miriam nodded and said maybe they could meet sometime in the cemetery. From then on, Josef went to the cemetery whenever he had free time. He spent hours sitting among the gravestones, thinking and dreaming. For many weeks, Miriam did not show up.

As time passed Josef was the target of increasing harassment from the other boys at the monastery. They seemed to resent him for two reasons: he was not of their social class, and he was a better student than they were. The latter point was particularly irksome to them because he was a couple of years younger than most of them. Stefan did his best to defend Josef. But his efforts in that direction were weak and dispirited, like the boy himself. Stefan had become more sickly since he took up residence in the cold, drafty monastery. He stayed in his cell most of the time when he was not required to be in class or at meals. He coughed a great deal and sometimes spit up blood.

Tensions seemed at this time to be increasing across the town and the whole region. The fall harvest had yielded less than usual, and now food supplies were beginning to run low. The early summer harvest was still months away. In fact, it would probably be delayed because the fields were now too soggy to begin spring planting. This had been the wettest winter anyone could remember, and even now the rain continued to fall. Josef heard disturbing stories from his boss Frieder at city hall, stories of grocers refusing to extend credit to long-time customers and people accusing their neighbors of stealing food. More disturbing to him were grotesque tales that seemed to Josef as if they must be totally false or hugely exaggerated. A young mother, for example, had confessed on her deathbed to participating in witchcraft. Frieder had dictated for the city records details of the case as related to him by the local magistrate. It seemed the woman had suffered many years from tuberculosis. She had one child, a daughter, who was also sickly. Desperate to keep the child alive, she wrapped the little girl in a blanket and secretly carried her to a doctor in the Jewish quarter. The woman acted against her husband's wishes and her priest's advice, and she was terribly ashamed of her transgression. Yet for many months she kept silent as her daughter's condition steadily improved. But the woman's health continued its slow decline. She saw this as punishment for her deceitfulness. Finally, as she lay dying, she confessed to the priest that her daughter had swallowed magic potions prepared by a Jew. She wanted desperately to know that God forgave her and would not punish the child for its mother's sin. She was able to give the name of the Jewish doctor.

The official reaction from church and city government was minimal. An inspector from city hall visited the doctor to ascertain that his methods were in keeping with standard practice, and they were. That was not the end of it, however. Word of the woman's confession leaked out, and certain elements of the town population decided to take action. At first, they came in the middle of the night and drew skulls and hex signs on the outside walls of the doctor's house. After rumors of his witchcraft circulated more widely and grew more fantastic with each telling, unsavory-looking men were seen lurking in his street. When they began to follow and frighten his children, the doctor forbade the children from leaving the house. One day the entire family disappeared. It was assumed they moved out into the country or to another town, and things seemed to calm down after that. Frieder hoped the whole affair would soon be forgotten.

One cold Sunday afternoon in late spring, Josef left the cloister and walked to the Jewish cemetery. The sky was dark and a heavy mist hung in the air. Josef's mood matched the weather. He wanted a couple of hours away from the monastery to reflect on unhappy events in his life and in the town. He had a favorite place in the cemetery near the far wall that was almost like a small cave. The ground was slightly depressed and thick shrubs grew on the sides and over the top. In his little grotto he would be shielded somewhat from the weather. As he approached the spot, Josef sensed something was different. Perhaps the grass nearby was flattened, or some twigs had been broken off at the entrance; at any rate, he was not surprised when he looked between the bushes and saw another person. His mood improved immeasurably when he saw that it was Miriam.

"Miriam! How did you find this place?"

"I watched you come here a couple times."

"Why didn't you stop and talk to me?"

"It seemed like you wanted to be by yourself. I guess I didn't really have anything to talk to you about, either."

"But you're here now." Josef frowned. "Is everything okay?"

Miriam paused as she tried to find the right words to say what she wanted to say. Finally she spoke. "Josef, things are getting worse for us."

"In what way?"

"Strange men have been coming into our neighborhood. They paint marks on houses and leave excrement on doorsteps, and someone left three dead dogs by the door of the synagogue. We don't know what it means."

"I heard there was vandalism when that doctor was accused of sorcery," said Josef, "but I thought it stopped when he moved away."

"No. It's gotten worse. What frightens me most is that some of them stay around and harass people who are on the streets at night. Mosche was out late one night and two men jumped in front of him and shoved him and called him a 'dirty Jew.'"

"What did Mosche do?"

"Nothing. He was too stunned. The men ran away."

"Then it's okay. As long as no one gets hurt."

"But don't you see? Next time Mosche will be ready to answer. He's not afraid of anything or anybody. He'll do something that makes them really mad. Josef, I'm afraid."

"You don't need to worry. Those men are just a bunch of thugs. The citizens of Worms are reasonable people. They don't approve of hoodlums and vandals."

Miriam shook her head violently. "No! You don't understand! There's no one and nothing that will protect Jews." She bit her lip and tears welled up in her eyes.

Josef couldn't answer this assertion. He stared at Miriam for a full minute as more tears came and she started shaking. Not knowing what else to do, he put his arms around her and held her tightly. When she stopped shaking and turned her face up towards his, he pressed his lips to hers. He didn't want to let her go. At first she was still, but after a few moments she struggled to get loose. Once she succeeded, she stepped back and away from him. Her face was still wet.

"Josef, you can't do that. It's wrong. I'm betrothed to another man."

He hung his head as she turned to go. He watched her disappear in the rain that was now falling steadily. He noticed beside the path some small purple flowers that had been trampled or beaten down by the rain.

Over the next few weeks, Josef thought a great deal about Miriam. He missed her more than ever and longed to see her again. He also thought about what she had said. He was still convinced that the citizens of Worms were sensible and compassionate people. They would not allow violence to get out of hand. Take Frieder, for example. Here was a city official who clearly had no interest in persecuting Jews. He was in a position to influence other people's behavior. If trouble broke out, he could stop it. On the other hand, there were certain silly notions floating about that would not go away. How could people believe that Jews were witches who cast spells with an evil eye or savages who ate Christian children? The church did not teach these crazy ideas—at least Josef had never heard anything like this from a monk or priest. Yet they did say that Jews had once known the truth but were now in error, and that Jews had killed their own Messiah. But that was a long time ago! Jews living today had nothing to do with it. If only the people of Worms could talk to Jews who live here and get to know them better, they would not believe these silly stories. Here was another problem. Church leaders tried to keep Christians and Jews apart. They kept reminding people not to eat with Jews or socialize with them. Josef knew he would have been in trouble if the monks found out he had friends who were Jews. Were they afraid Christians would turn into Jews if they got too close? He himself had studied with Jews, eaten with them, lived under the same roof with Jewish lodgers, received gifts from them, and even kissed a Jewish girl, and he was still a Christian! Josef wondered what the civil authorities said about socializing with Jews. Did they support what the Church preached? He would look for an opportunity to ask his boss Frieder about these things.

Chapter 9

Frieder assured Josef that he personally saw no reason to avoid associating with Jews. Furthermore, he knew of no civil ordinance that forbade contact between Christian and Jew. However, numerous Church directives spelled out what was permissible and what was not. In general, the Church followed policies laid down by the first Pope Gregory. Nearly five hundred years ago he had assailed Jewish theological error and stubbornness but nevertheless protected the legal rights of Jews. Since then, Christians had been permitted civil and economic dealings with Jews, but little else. In the intervening years, more specific rules had been set down by popes and bishops, although these rules were inconsistently enforced across domains and dioceses. Their own King Henry, Frieder told Josef, tended to be lenient toward Jews, but this was one of many areas in which the king and the Church were in conflict. In fact, King Henry and the most recent Pope Gregory had argued constantly about who had authority over whom.

"Listen," said Frieder to Josef one morning shortly after he arrived for work. "I have business to transact in the Jewish quarter. How would you like to come along?"

Josef was startled by this proposition. He stared at the floor, hoping that his boss would not detect his sudden confusion. Of course he had no objection to spending time there, but what if he ran into someone he knew? Suppose Mosche greeted him like an old friend, or one of the rabbis recognized him? Could he remain anonymous? Could he pretend he was in unfamiliar territory? Josef hesitated to refuse the offer because that too might arouse suspicion. He continued staring at the floor.

"Well, you don't have to go," said Frieder. "It's just that you seem so interested in everything related to the Jews. I thought you might like to meet some of them up close."

"Yes, I would. Only . . ." Again he hesitated to speak.

"Only what?"

"Only that's near my old neighborhood and I might run into someone I know."

"Like your mother, for instance? Don't worry. I'll explain that we're on official business."

As they made their way through town, Frieder told Josef he was going to inspect a house prior to issuing a deed of purchase. The new owner was one of the local rabbis, and Frieder wanted to ask him about another matter as well. He had heard that the great teacher from Troyes, a rabbi named Salomo, was in residence for a couple of weeks. Frieder had had some dealings with this famous rabbi before and wondered if a meeting with him could be arranged. This disclosure left Josef once again stunned and speechless. Frieder was certainly talking about Rabbi Scholomo, who had patiently tried to answer Josef's stupid, childish questions and then watched him break down in tears. The very thought of that episode made his face warm with embarrassment. He hoped Rabbi Scholomo would not be available to meet with Frieder today.

When they arrived in the Jewish quarter, Frieder led the way to the property in question, a few doors down from the synagogue. After surveying the exterior, he knocked on the door and held a brief discussion with the new resident about the purchase of the house and its condition. He was invited inside to complete his inspection. Once their signatures were affixed on the deed, the two men proceeded to talk about other things.

"Have you suffered any more vandalism in your neighborhood?" asked Frieder.

"Not in the last week," answered the rabbi. "It's more sporadic than it was earlier."

"That's good, I suppose."

"Not necessarily. People don't know what to expect. We're all on edge."

"It would help if you could identify the culprits. Then we would give them a good scolding." The rabbi was silent so Frieder continued. "I wanted to ask you about something else, too. Where could I find the visiting rabbi? I'd like to follow up on some business I had with him a few years ago."

"He's over at the school now, talking with some of the students. It sounded like quite a lively discussion, from what I heard. You can look in if you like."

At the schoolhouse Frieder opened the door quietly, stuck his head in, and motioned for Josef to follow him. They sat down on a bench about halfway to the front. Near the far corner, the rabbi was engaged in a spirited debate with five or six youths. Whether from curiosity about the topic of discussion or simply from politeness, Frieder made no attempt to interrupt. At any rate, he and Josef sat and listened for many minutes.

"Our forefathers came here many years ago with the Romans," said one young man. "Why are we still not welcome?"

"Oh, we are more than welcome," said another, "as long as our money helps the local economy. But if our money loses its usefulness, then so do we."

A third young man spoke up. "My father says the world's economy is changing. There are new towns growing up everywhere, and they need money to operate. He says we Jews are in an ideal position to be lenders and merchants because we're educated and honest and we speak an international language. He thinks Jews' position in society will get better and better."

"It's true we have some advantages," said the second youth ardently. "But the gentiles use our differences as a reason to look down on us. They need us, yet they hate us."

"Hate is perhaps too strong a word," interjected the rabbi. "We have good relations with many of our neighbors. Our economic dealings with them are based on mutual confidence. Adjustments are often made to accommodate our beliefs, such as changing market day from Sabbath to mid-week."

"Yes, Rabbi, but all of that is to *their* advantage. Once they find a way to get on without us, they will."

The rabbi smiled and shook his head. "We have lived in harmony with gentiles for many years. Our connections with them are more than merely economic. In Champagne, where I live, for example, the noblemen and clerics often hire Jews as scribes and entrust them with all their correspondence. Some Christian scholars study Hebrew with Jewish teachers, and several have lately consulted with me about scriptural interpretations. You may find this hard to believe, but some of the young priests in Troyes asked if we could teach them our synagogue songs, which they now sing with great gusto."

"But you know they write different laws for us and for them. They make it impossible for Jews to hold positions of power and authority."

"Perhaps. Even that is changing somewhat. In Champagne, Jews are major land-owners. By virtue of this, they are granted a position in the court of Count Thibault. Some have been appointed ambassadors, tax collectors, and civil administrators. Even better for us is the autonomy we have been granted in fiscal and judicial affairs. Our own people control court judgments, payment of fines, immigration, and all religious concerns in the Jewish sector."

"Well I think that's just part of their plan to keep us off by ourselves. They don't want to get too close to us 'dirty Jews.'"

"My young friend, have you forgotten that we see ourselves as a people apart? We live by faith, and our faith inspires a way of life. As a community in exile, we hold to the Law through study, remembrance, and sacrifice. If we should sometimes meet with difficulties, we turn them to our advantage. The psalmist says, 'It is well for me that I have been afflicted, in order that I might learn thy statutes.'"

Another youth asked, "Should we then isolate ourselves completely from gentiles? Should we find another place to live, to be a people *far* apart?"

"No, my son. The first book of Moses tells us God created the earth 'in the beginning,' before any nations were established. Therefore all land belongs to the One who created it, and he gives it to whomever he pleases. For now he has put us here. We must have dealings with the people among whom we live. The prophet Jeremiah said to the exiles in Babylon, 'Seek the welfare of the city whither I have banished you, and pray in its behalf to the Lord; for in its welfare shall ye fare well.' Thus it is better for us to cultivate peace with our neighbors insofar as we are able. The story of Johannan ben Zakkai is instructive. Do you remember learning about him?"

"Yes, Rabbi. He was the scholar who founded the very first Jeschiba many centuries ago."

"Correct. But do you know the circumstances? No? Well let me tell you. He was in Jerusalem during the Roman siege, when pestilence and starvation threatened the entire population. Inside the walls, the city was controlled by Jewish zealots who vowed never to surrender or negotiate. Death was staring them in the face. Yet Johannan eluded death to carry on his scholarly work."

"How did he do it, Rabbi?"

"It's a memorable story. Disciples of Johannan ben Zakkai pretended he had died of the plague. They put him in a coffin, sealed it, and carried it out of the city, past the unsuspecting Roman guards, and straight to the tent of the Roman general! This general, Vespasian, was known to be a shrewd, ambitious man. When the disciples opened the coffin, Johannan emerged and immediately prophesied that the general would one day become emperor of Rome. In return for this good news, Vespasian offered to grant one request. Johannan asked that he be allowed to establish a school in Jabneh, a town northwest of Jerusalem, and that scholars from Jerusalem be allowed to join him. The request was granted."

"What happened after that?"

"Scholars came, and the academy became known as 'Vineyard of Jabneh' because the first meeting was held in a vineyard. For more than six decades the school flourished. Scholarship blossomed. Judaism was preserved. All this because Johannan ben Zakkai was able to negotiate with Romans, who were the cruelest of oppressors."

"Are you saying, Rabbi, that we should accept oppression?"

"No. But when it happens, we can find a way to survive and even thrive. Who knows but that gentile laws might not work to our advantage? We are allowed free travel and trade that are forbidden to Christians. We are granted property rights, and we have educational opportunities that most Christians do not enjoy. We belong to a community that spans three continents, unified by religion, language, and law. It is a privilege to be a Jew."

The students were silent. Until now Josef had been listening in utter fascination. The topic was interesting enough, but what captivated Josef's attention was the openness of the discussion. These students were boldly questioning and voicing disagreement with a respected teacher. This would never happen at the monastery school! Now he thought of something else. What if Mosche were one of the students? If they acknowledged one another it would be awkward. How could Josef explain their relationship to Frieder? He strained to see the students, some of whom were sitting with their backs to him. None of them really looked like Mosche; in fact these young men seemed older. Josef was relieved. It was only the rabbi who might recognize him, and that was by no means certain. Their meeting had occurred six or seven years earlier, when Josef was a little boy. He looked quite different now, with darker hair and fuzz on his chin.

At that moment the rabbi looked up and saw the two of them sitting patiently in the middle of the schoolhouse. He said a few words to the assembled students, who then rose and began collecting their things. When the last one had left the room, the rabbi walked over.

"Hello, my friends. May I do something for you?"

Josef noticed that the rabbi gazed at him for a few moments and raised his eyebrows slightly. He then smiled with pursed lips but gave no other sign that he might have recognized Josef.

"Yes, your Honor," said Frieder. "I am Frieder, city clerk. A number of years ago you made a ruling which allowed me and my wife to keep our little girl, our adopted daughter. Do you remember?"

"Yes, I do. And how is the little girl getting along?"

"Hanna is thriving. But she is no longer a girl. She's a young woman, and a very attractive young woman at that." The rabbi smiled and nodded. Frieder continued, "She and my wife have grown very close. Nevertheless, we know the time is coming when Hanna must leave us. She's nearly sixteen years old, an age when many young women are already married. Up until now, she's had no suitors from the Jewish community. Her uncle is not well enough known to local families nor is he here often enough to arrange a suitable match. Also, I believe he has no money to offer as dowry. As you know, it would be impossible for me to negotiate a betrothal, but I'm willing to supply funds for a dowry if this can be done in secret."

"You are very generous, Mr. Frieder. Perhaps we could accept an anonymous donation to the community fund for that purpose. I will consult with local rabbis to see how this might be accomplished. Rest assured, your name will not be mentioned. And if Hanna is as attractive as you say, there should be no difficulty finding an eligible young man."

Frieder smiled.

"Was that all you wished to speak to me about?" asked the rabbi.

"There's one more thing. I want to thank you for your kindness. Because of your ruling, Hanna has had a loving home and my wife has known what it is to be a mother. We are very grateful. Is there anything at all we can do to thank you?"

The rabbi's answer was immediate. "Help a Jew in trouble."

The two men made arrangements for the dowry money to be delivered, and the visitors departed. Josef went straight back to the monastery, since it was already time for the community's midday meal. He entered the refectory quietly and took his seat, hoping the priests would not notice or ask any questions.

As the months passed, Josef's cellmate, Stefan, became weaker and weaker. Some days he did not leave his bed. It fell to Josef to act as caretaker, bringing Stefan food when he missed meals and reading lessons with him when he was not strong enough to study with the other young men. Josef did not mind the increasing isolation; in fact he rather preferred it. But it was becoming harder for him to watch his friend in this condition. Stefan kept a basin beside his bed into which he spat blood and mucus. His coughing fits went on for hours, it seemed. Josef wondered that no doctor came to see Stefan, to give him medicine for his illness. His family never came to see him either.

In the hours they spent together, the two friends sometimes carried on long conversations. This usually happened when Stefan was in one of his "bubbly moods," as Josef described it to himself. Stefan would suddenly emerge from his lethargy, full of energy, looking cheerful, almost ebullient, with rosy cheeks and glowing face. Then he would talk fast and with great enthusiasm. On one such day, he said, "Josef, do you remember those days when we first started learning Latin with Father Matthias?"

"Yes. Not the best memories in the world."

"Oh, but for me they are! It was so wonderful when you met me after class to help me learn the grammar. You were such a good teacher! Didn't I ever tell you how much I enjoyed that?"

"No."

"Well, I did. I felt in those moments that you loved me. You focused your attention completely on me and really wanted me to understand everything you understood. Sometimes it seemed like you climbed into my head and saw things exactly as I saw them."

"I never thought anything about loving you."

"Believe me, I felt more love from you than I ever felt at home. For them I was just another mouth to feed. When you were teaching me, I could see it was important to you that I succeed. Not just to please Father Matthias, but because my mind would be opened up."

"I still don't see what that has to do with love."

"No? Well, it seems to me that you really did love me. Not all teachers love their students. Maybe that's what makes a good teacher."

They talked for another hour about their experiences with Father Matthias. They were able to laugh about things that seemed horrible at the time. Even the memory of his beating them took on a comic complexion. As usually happened after these energetic episodes, Stefan suddenly stopped talking and lay back on his bed, utterly exhausted.

On other occasions the two talked about education in a more abstract sense: What good was it? Who should be educated? What should they be taught? Was all learning equally valuable?

"I think it's all good," said Josef. "People should be able to study whatever they want."

"Even if it's heresy?"

"As long as someone explains why it's heresy. The students can discuss the subject from different angles until they understand it and see why it's wrong."

"That would be dangerous," said Stefan. "What if the students don't understand it completely? What if they start to believe something that would endanger their eternal souls?"

"But that's exactly why we need *more* education, not less. So people can think better."

"Most people will never be able to think. People like peasants and laborers and women, for example. They don't have the capability."

"I know a girl who can read."

"What? You're joking, aren't you?"

"No. She reads Hebrew better than I do."

"You can read Hebrew?"

"Listen, Stefan. You have to promise never to tell anybody, okay?"

"Okay."

"I have a friend who's a Jew. He taught me to read Hebrew. It's his sister I'm talking about."

"That doesn't count. Jews are already damned so it doesn't matter what they read or study. Other people have to be careful. It's the Church who should decide what's right to believe and to read." Stefan began coughing. When he recovered, his voice was raspy and barely audible. "What I'm really afraid of is that I'm not smart enough to understand the doctrines. If my beliefs are wrong, I'll go to hell."

"No, that's not right. Remember what you said about teachers who love their students? God is our teacher. He teaches us new things every day, so he must love us. He can't expect us to understand everything all at once."

Stefan shook his head. "I may not have time to learn what I need to know."

Josef tried to reassure his friend. He told him what he had learned about the search for wisdom and righteousness. He repeated Mosche's claim that one who directs his eyes, his heart, and his ears to Scripture is already on the right path. When the text says the deaf shall hear and the blind see, this means that even a man who cannot read will be rewarded if he searches diligently. The seeking itself is the beginning of wisdom. After that, each person draws water from the well the Lord has given to him. Josef tried to explain these ideas in a way that Stefan would understand. He wanted to convince him that scholarly shortcomings would not keep him out of heaven. Stefan seemed somewhat comforted by these arguments, and he soon dropped off into a peaceful sleep.

Over the next few weeks, however, Stefan became more agitated. He suffered night sweats as he tossed restlessly in his bed. When awake, he was more listless than ever, while his eyes and his mind wandered in every direction. Josef reported all this to the priests, who sometimes looked in and said a blessing. Early one morning Josef noticed that Stefan's eyes were glazed over and his breathing was uneven. He ran out to tell someone. Soon three priests entered the cell. They brought with them a cross, a dish of water, a cruet of oil, and a small box. One of the men sprinkled water all around and recited prayers in Latin. *"Pax huic domui et omnibus habitantibus in ea . . ."* The others responded with an antiphon. *"Benedic, Domine, domum istam et omnes habitantes in ea . . ."*

Josef had never heard these words before but he understood them to be a blessing over the house and those dwelling in it. The priests continued chanting as one of them sprinkled water over Stefan. Other prayers followed, including psalms. When these were concluded, the man with the cruet stepped forward. He dipped his finger in the oil and made a sign of the cross on Stefan's eyebrows, while saying, *"Ungo te in nomine Patris, et Filii, et Spiritus sancti . . ."*

"By this anointing may the Lord in his tender mercy forgive you any sins you have committed through the sense of sight."

He dipped his finger again and touched, in succession, Stefan's ears, nostrils, lips, and hands, each time reciting an appropriate form of the anointing prayer. Thus any impurity of body or soul connected with the five senses was wiped away. Now the priests knelt beside Stefan's bed and motioned for Josef to do the same. They all said together the "Our Father" and the Creed. One of the priests said words from the Mass that Josef recognized. He opened the box, took out a morsel of bread and held it before Stefan's mouth. Josef did not expect Stefan to respond, but miraculously his lips parted slightly. The priest gently inserted the morsel onto his tongue and recited more prayers. Stefan coughed a little. A final blessing was pronounced, followed by a thanksgiving. The priests solemnly rose, nodded to Josef, and left the cell.

When it was time for Josef to go to his work at city hall, one of the priests came back to sit with Stefan. Upon his return from work, Josef found this man conferring with another just outside the cell.

"Where will the boy be buried?"

"In the pauper's grave. His family has no money."

"You'd think they could scrape up a little for a proper burial."

"No. This boy was the youngest son. The older ones have taken what little there was."

Suddenly they noticed Josef looking at them with questioning eyes. "The boy died," said one. "The sextons are just now preparing to carry him away."

Josef moved closer and looked in through the half-open door. Stefan was completely wrapped in a coarse, woolen cloth. The sextons laid him on a board, lifted it between them, and carried it out of the cell. As they disappeared down the hallway, Josef asked, "Is that all?"

"We have no money to pay for funerals."

"But can't we honor him in some way?"

"A Mass will be said for his soul."

"What about his body?"

"You remember what Scripture says? 'Consider the lilies of the field. King Solomon in all his glory was not dressed even as one of these.'"

Josef was lonelier than ever. While he and Stefan had not been close friends, they had spent a good deal of time together in recent months. They had discussed many topics of mutual interest and had confided in one another to some degree. At the very least, Josef had lost an ally against the ill-will of the other students. None of them had shown any inclination to be his friend. Meanwhile, the monks and priests kept mostly to themselves, interacting with their pupils only in ecclesiastical and academic matters. While caring for Stefan, Josef had rarely left the monastery except for three hours each morning when he went to work.

Now suddenly he had more time on his hands. Since Stefan's death, the cell, and in fact the entire monastery, had a melancholy association for him. He wanted to escape. He began visiting the Jewish cemetery again, spending what time he could walking among the gravestones or sitting in his hideaway.

One warm, clear day in late summer he was delighted to see Miriam coming through the gates of the cemetery. He ran to greet her. She seemed surprised to see him. "You haven't come here for a long time," she said.

"I've been too busy to come."

"Studying Latin?"

"Yes, but also taking care of Stefan." Miriam waited for an explanation. "He's the other boy who studied Latin with Father Matthias. I think I told you about him, the boy who was always sick."

"Is he okay?"

"He died."

The young people were silent for a few moments, each contemplating how quickly a life can be snuffed out.

"Well anyway, you're here now, and I'm glad you are."

"You're glad?"

"Yes, Josef. I've missed you. There's no one to study with me now."

"Mosche stills helps you, doesn't he? You can read by yourself and work with him in the evenings."

"No. Mosche is a real scholar now. He lives with a family whose boys he tutors."

"But you still read, don't you?"

"No. My mother is teaching me to spin and weave and cook and all the things I'll need to do when I'm a wife. She says the time for play is over."

Josef frowned. "Has your marriage date been set yet?"

"No. I keep putting it off. I'm lucky, I guess, that Ehud is a very patient man—he seems in no hurry to complete the marriage."

"I would be, if you were betrothed to me."

Miriam blushed. "Josef, don't say things like that."

"Okay. But it's true. Have things improved any in the Jewish quarter? I mean, have the troublemakers left you alone?"

"It's better than it was. Our commerce with Christians is thriving after the good harvest this summer. Relations get better when people have money to spend."

The two friends decided they would try again to meet on Sunday afternoons to read and study together. In the cemetery or the nearby fields, they would have quiet and privacy. Josef felt new hope that maybe his life would not be dreary all the time.

Chapter 10

Just a week later, Miriam and Josef were walking together through the cemetery. Miriam led the way, pointing out her favorite tombstones and occasionally stopping to read an inscription. Josef followed, watching her intently. He felt happier than he had in many months.

"You see the two raised hands on this stone?" asked Miriam. "Can you guess what that means?"

"I guess it's the symbol of someone's occupation. Probably a man who worked with his hands, like a sculptor or a woodcarver."

"Wrong. It's a member of the Kohen family. They were temple priests in Jerusalem, and today many of them are rabbis and teachers. The raised hands give a blessing."

Josef thought how remarkable it was that even in death a rabbi could bless passers-by. It was especially nice that he and Miriam stood together and received a blessing on this beautiful autumn afternoon. He wished it would never end.

Miriam walked on to another grave. "This one I never understood," she said. "It says, 'He died as he lived, under shadows. In life and in death, darkness.' It sounds awfully gloomy."

"Maybe he worked underground in a silver mine. It's a dark place but not so gloomy."

"It is if he died there. But I think it's another kind of darkness. Maybe he was unhappy all the time. Or uneducated. Either one of those would seem like darkness." Then glancing at the sky she added, "Let's do some reading before we get caught in the dark."

The two companions found a grassy hillock and sat down. Before they opened the psalm book Miriam had brought with her, Josef said, "Did you hear that King Henry is coming to Worms?"

"Really? Why should he come here?"

"Well, he's been here at least three times before. My boss told me King Henry was crowned in Worms twenty years ago, when he was only fifteen." Josef grinned. "That's my age. Do I look old enough to be king?"

"You're being silly. Tell my why he's coming now."

"I'm not exactly sure, but he really likes this town. The citizens protected him once when he got in trouble with the Church."

"What kind of trouble?"

"He was always arguing with the pope about who should pick new bishops. The pope sent an army to try to force King Henry to give in, but it didn't work. The people of Worms fought off the army. That was about ten years ago—the king was so grateful he said no one here had to pay taxes."

"No one, really? I knew some Jews didn't pay taxes. But I thought the law applied only to Jewish merchants who did long-distance commerce. You know the king likes foreign foods and other stuff imported from the east."

"No, I didn't know that," replied Josef. "What else have you heard about him?"

"He stood up for us when the pope gave orders to push Jews out of public jobs. We like King Henry. He's good to us, and so are the bishops he appoints."

"Do you want to see him? I heard he's going to attend a Christmas Mass in the Cathedral. We could probably sneak in at the back."

"Yes! Just tell me where to meet you."

"Okay. The only problem for me might be getting out of the monastery. Some of the monks hate King Henry. But I'll find a way to get past them."

Josef and Miriam read only one psalm together before it was time for her to go home. Josef did not return immediately to the monastery. He went for a long walk alone through farm fields near the cemetery. He wanted to prolong the pleasure and excitement he felt at seeing his friend again. Over the next few weeks Josef found that he was constantly thinking about Miriam. It made him happy to think of her, yet at the same time not happy. How could he explain it? He just wanted to see her again, that's all. Was she feeling the same about him? Did she *ever* think about him?

Josef went to the cemetery as often as he could, and sometimes found her there. She seemed to him rather distant, as if keeping him at arm's length. He didn't dare touch her, or even get close, for fear she would be offended and stop coming. Between reading sessions they talked more about the history of their city and how the Jewish and Christian parts had grown up side by side. Josef had learned a great deal from his boss Frieder about the early Roman settlement, referred to in documents as *Civitas Vangionum*. Later on, the emperor Charles the Great was married in Worms, and it became one of the most important cities in his empire. More recently the powerful Bishop Burchard founded monasteries, built churches, and laid the cornerstone for the new cathedral (still under construction). The monastery where Josef lived and studied had been constructed under the bishop's direction, just beside the old Roman wall. Josef himself had seen some of the Roman inscriptions still visible after many centuries. In the last decade, King Henry had again made Worms an important center of government. He summoned the German bishops to Worms to stand with him against Pope Gregory. Now he was returning, perhaps to reassert his authority now that the pope he opposed had died.

Miriam was able to tell Josef something about Jewish history in the town. Jews had been in Worms for at least three hundred years, she said. In this century two scholars from Mainz, the great rabbis Jakov ben Yakar and Isaak haLevi, had settled here and taught in the Jeschiba where Mosche now studied. It was a thriving school, one of the best in the world. The current synagogue was nearly as old as the cathedral, its cornerstone having been laid some fifty years ago, and anyone could see that the style and handiwork of the two buildings were quite similar. Miriam could not explain why the corners of the synagogue were not square, but she supposed there was a good reason for it. The community was proud that a gate in the city wall had recently been designated "Jews' Gate." It was the portal through which goods were transported to and from the river by Jewish merchants. But most of all, Jews in Worms were proud of their code of laws, enforced by twelve leaders chosen from among their own people. Josef thought this was admirable.

As the weather grew colder, the two friends continued to meet, although their sessions were shorter. Finally the Advent season came, and the town folk began making preparations for the king's visit. It was thrilling to watch: decorations were put up, fairgrounds cleared, living quarters prepared. Not only the king would be coming. He would bring a royal entourage of knights, foot soldiers, cooks, blacksmiths, counselors, and attendants of various kinds. The palace on the north side of the cathedral would house the royal family, but other visitors would spill out into the town, requiring goods, services, and lodging. Everyone would be affected in some way.

Josef thought he'd better explore the cathedral thoroughly to be sure he and Miriam could find a place to observe the king. Frieder had told him the royal party would be seated in the west choir, at the opposite end of the building from the main altar. They would be separated from the rest of the congregation by a screen. (It had a small opening through which the king and his consort could view the celebration of the Mass.) If the king wished to enter the cathedral in a public procession, he would come in through the main north portal. However, there was also a private entrance from the palace into the west choir, in case he did not wish to be seen. On previous visits, King Henry had made a grand ceremonial entrance into the cathedral, much to the delight of his subjects. But the political situation was more delicate and dangerous now, Frieder had said. The king might feel it was risky to present himself openly in a large crowd. That would make things more difficult. How could he be sure he and Miriam would see the king? They would normally enter through the south portal with the rest of the townspeople. Even if they stood in the western end of the cathedral, they could not see him through the screen. In his explorations Josef found a possible solution to his difficulty. The western end of the cathedral was still under construction. The towers on each side of the west choir were only half built, and a temporary roof covered that part of the building. Yes, he thought, this might provide a way in. But he still had to find a place where they could stand and watch without being seen. He would have to spend more time looking around.

Excitement in the city mounted as Christmas Eve drew closer. Bakers prepared fancy pastries; butchers slaughtered and dressed their best livestock; merchants brought in extra wares; women washed and hung out linens and festival clothing; even the children were unusually helpful and on their best behavior. A general invitation had gone out to all inhabitants of the region, noblemen as well as peasants and town folk, to attend the Christmas Eve Mass and the Yule feast which followed.

At last the long-anticipated day arrived: Christmas Eve! Josef was happy and excited for a number of reasons. The Superior of the monastery had declared a free holiday for the students. Perhaps he was an admirer of King Henry, or else he simply realized the futility of trying to keep the young men secluded on a day like this. At any rate, Josef was allowed to leave the monastery for the entire day without having to sneak past anyone. He looked forward to seeing the king's entourage; it would be a splendid spectacle even if the king himself stayed out of sight. A beautiful, festive Mass would end the day, and it would be followed by a sumptuous meal to welcome Christmas morning. But best of all, Josef would spend several hours this evening with Miriam. He had arranged to meet her at Newmarket Square just before sunset.

Josef left the monastery early and found the streets already teeming with people. Peasants on foot and farmers in donkey-carts were streaming in from the countryside, wearing their best holiday clothing. The donkeys wore tinkling bells around their necks, and some of the men brought lanterns which clanked as they swayed back and forth. Parents and older children carried the little ones who had grown weary of walking. Josef recognized a few tradesmen and students he had seen in the Jewish quarter, although for the most part they blended in with the townspeople. Occasionally a procession of noblemen on horseback and their families in horse-drawn wagons passed by, attracting admiring glances from the crowd.

About mid-morning Josef was chewing the last bit of a penny-loaf he had bought from a vendor, when he was startled by a sharp sound. It was the blare of a trumpet. He looked around and decided it must have come from the nearby market square. Immediately he took off running to see what was going on. A crowd was gathering around the trumpeter, who wore a vest with the royal emblem on it. Beside him stood another servant dressed in a long tunic with royal insignia. This man held a scroll before his face and read out in a ringing voice: "Hear the decree of Emperor Henry, the fourth of that name, concerning a Truce of God." He paused while the milling crowd grew quiet. "In these days of tribulation, oppression, and danger which afflict the holy Church and ourselves, we are striving to promote, with God's help, the cause of peace. To this end we have declared, with full agreement from clergy and people, that beginning in Advent of this year until the end of Epiphany, and from the season of Lent through the octave of Pentecost, as well as on feast days and apostles' days, this decree of peace shall be observed. Our purpose is that people who travel and those who stay at home may enjoy security from assault, robbery, and murder. Therefore, on these dates proclaimed, no man shall presume to carry weapons such as sword, whip, or lance, or to injure another with any kind of weapon, nor shall anyone wear armor, unless he travel to a place where the peace is not observed. In such case, he may harm no one except he be first attacked and must defend himself. When he returns he shall once again put down his weapons."

The speaker then listed the designated punishments for violating the decree, depending on who committed the offense and its severity. Nobles and freemen would be expelled from the kingdom and their estates confiscated. Slaves and peasants would be flogged or beheaded or have their right hand cut off. He continued reading: "If anyone strive to oppose this pious decree, he shall be denied salvation of the Church, participation in the Eucharist, and visits by Christian neighbors, unless he come to his senses. Punishments are to be inflicted not only by noblemen and officials, but also by the people in common when they see violators of the holy peace. They must take care to show no favoritism or secrecy but to enforce justice openly in public. Furthermore, traveling merchants, farmers at work, women, and clergymen shall enjoy continual peace, every day of the year. Amen."

Josef watched while the trumpeter and speaker climbed down from their makeshift platform. They packed everything into a pull-cart and walked away, Josef presumed, to read the proclamation in another part of town. What would be the effect of this "Truce of God"? King Henry might feel himself safer from his enemies if they were not permitted to carry weapons in his domain. Jewish scholars and merchants might travel more freely without fear of assault (although robbers were still a hazard). Life in town would probably not be affected much at all. Nevertheless, Josef was pleased by the spirit of the decree.

Since he had no specific plan for the day, Josef decided to remain in the market square. Watching the throng of people come and go would make the time pass more quickly until sunset, when he was supposed to meet Miriam. Minstrels and jugglers roamed about providing amusement, and vendors from out of town sold unusual items. There was plenty of activity here to hold his interest. As evening approached, the air grew colder. Flickering candles began to appear in windows of shops and homes. A few stars came out and sparkled in the clear sky. Josef hoped Miriam would arrive soon, before darkness made it harder to find her in the midst of so many people. A moment later she was at his side, having approached him quietly and unseen.

"Miriam, when did you get here?"

"Just now."

"Where were you?"

"Across the square behind the cloth vendor. I was watching the crowds, just like you. Before that some of us were waiting at the east gate by the tower. We were hoping to see the king make his entrance, but he didn't come."

"I haven't seen him either. Some of his servants were here this morning. They read a royal decree about putting down weapons and keeping peace."

"Yes. They read the same thing in the old market by Jews' Alley. After we heard it, Mosche said he wanted to see this great king who was protector of the Jews. That's when Mosche and I and a bunch of our friends went to the city gate."

"Well, I'm still hoping we can see the king in the cathedral. I have a plan."

The two friends watched as giant torches were lit around the market square. Soon these torches would lead a procession into the cathedral courtyard. In anticipation, more and more people crowded into the square. And what a mix of people it was! Peasants and townspeople wearing their most colorful clothes, kitchen maids in frilled aprons, wealthy merchants and landowners wearing pastel silks and multicolored brocade. Suddenly a bell clanged. The sound came from above, and their heads turned instinctively to look up at the dark silhouettes of the two east towers of the cathedral looming overhead. In the cold night air, the ringing was magnified and multiplied by echoes off nearby buildings. This was the signal for the procession to begin. Strong men unfastened the torches from their stands and carried them to the south end of the square. People began drifting in that direction and formed a ragged line, as wide as ten people. Slowly the mass of people followed the torches through the streets to the courtyard within the cloister on the south side of the cathedral. Most of the people passed through the courtyard and straightaway into the cathedral.

Miriam and Josef lagged at the very end of the procession. When they came into the courtyard, the sharpness of the cold night air was softened by the warm aroma of roasting and baking that wafted out of the chapter house. They could hear the clatter of dishes and see through the windows the festive decorations inside the hall. Josef began to imagine the fully laden tables that would await them after the Mass. The two friends lingered in a dark corner of the courtyard until everyone else had gone into the cathedral and the torches had been extinguished. Then

Josef took Miriam's hand and led her through the darkness until they reached the southwest corner of the building. As they approached a large wooden door, Josef whispered, "We're going in here. It's a tower that's still under construction." Slowly he pulled the door open and they slipped in. The memory of wonderful aromas in the courtyard was suddenly erased, as the acute smell of animal waste and rotting trash filled their nostrils. The ground was covered with straw. In one corner lay a pile of manure and in another a rotting trash heap. Miriam held her nose. "What's all this?" she asked.

"It's called Donkeys' Tower because donkeys are used to haul stuff up inside. They walk up this ramp and carry stones and tools for building the upper levels. Once we get above this level, the smell won't be so bad."

"Let's go quick."

Josef told Miriam to watch where she stepped as they made their way up the sloping, straw-covered spiral passageway. It was hard to see with only a little dim moonlight coming through narrow slits in the circular walls. Most of the manure had been removed from the path, but they still saw (and smelled) a fresh pile here and there. When they reached a certain level, Josef stopped.

"We're going out here on a little walkway. When we get through this door, we'll be over the west choir. You can look down through the railing and see where the king is supposed to sit. Once he comes in, we have to be completely quiet and still. Okay?"

Miriam giggled. "What if I have to sneeze?"

Josef shook his head and tried to look exasperated.

The walkway was about forty feet above floor level. Standing behind the balustrade, Josef and Miriam could see the west choir just beneath them, or they could look over the screen into the nave of the cathedral. For a few moments they feasted their eyes. Hundreds of tallow candles mounted on poles gave a warm glow to the red stone pillars and walls. Garlands and wreaths of fresh pine and cedar boughs adorned the walls. Red and gold bunting was hanging from the capitals of the pillars. The entire cathedral was full of people. Near the front, a few rows of chairs had been set up, but most people were standing. Josef had never seen the place so full. The two friends sat down to wait. The balustrade in front of them now blocked their view of the nave, but they could see through the slits into the west choir below. A few feet overhead was the flat wooden ceiling which temporarily covered this unfinished section of the cathedral. As they waited, Josef inhaled deeply the fragrance of burning incense mingled with the smell of evergreen boughs and tallow candles.

Now, Josef thought, the priests must be coming in. He could hear shuffling feet and chanting. As the procession made its way down the aisle to the altar at the far end of the building, he could imagine the throng of people bowing and crossing themselves. He was glad to be out of sight, not obliged to act out rituals that Miriam might find embarrassing or offensive. But where was King Henry? The Mass was going to start and he was nowhere in sight. Perhaps he had been delayed on the road or had decided not to come. The cathedral was now hushed, the priests and people silent, and even the building itself seemed to be waiting. After what seemed like an eternity of anticipation, they could hear the main north portal swing open on its hinges. When the creaking stopped, Josef heard gasps and murmurs from the crowd, as well as clattering of armed men. The king's procession was coming across the nave toward the west choir and would enter through the opening in the screen. Josef and Miriam froze in their places. Soon they saw below them knights in glittering mail shirts taking their positions around the walls, followed by two or three maids in splendid dress. All stood, waiting for the king and queen to enter. Naturally the royal couple came at the end of the procession.

Josef and Miriam were in a perfect position to observe the king. He was dressed in unexpectedly simple garments: a robe with embroidered decorations around the sleeves and lower hem, fastened with a gold clasp at the neck. His head was bare. The queen wore a more elaborate gown and a head-covering, similar to her maids-in-waiting but adorned with precious stones. The royal couple came into the west choir through a door in the screen, faced the altar, and crossed themselves. The king spoke softly to his consort, telling her he had attended the Christmas Mass here as a boy, and again several times as a young man. His voice echoed off the stone walls. Josef distinctly heard him say that the famous Bishop Burchard was entombed in this part of the cathedral, and he told her other particulars about the place as well. Finally the royal couple knelt briefly and took their seats. Only then did the maids seat themselves. One of the knights gave a signal to the ministers that the Mass could begin.

The two onlookers could not hear the priests very well and could not see them at all. Occasionally they heard the tinkling of a bell. But in truth they were more interested in watching the royal party just below them. The king seemed quite attentive to the Mass. From the raised floor of the west choir he could observe through openings in the screen what was happening at the altar. He crossed himself at the appropriate times and knelt when a priest came to offer the Eucharist. Josef thought he looked like a regular person, not so grand as he had imagined. When the service ended, the king and queen quickly left through the private door leading out of the west choir. Their attendants followed. Josef and Miriam exhaled slowly from relief that they had not been discovered. They found their way down the dark, sloping passageway and back to the empty courtyard of the cloisters. The people had not yet come out of the cathedral. Josef led the way to the chapter house. "Let's go in. We'll get first choice at the feast."

Miriam was hesitant but finally followed her friend inside. The tables were laden with rich foods: stuffed hens, roast boar, carp, trout, and eel baked with savory vegetables, piles of fruit and cheese, and flasks of wine in all colors from deep purple to ruby red to golden-white. Josef's mouth watered.

"I can't stay here," said Miriam.

"Why not?" asked Josef.

"I can't eat this food."

"But everybody's welcome."

"You don't understand," said Miriam. "Most of this would make me sick to my stomach. We don't eat this kind of food." Miriam walked out of the chapter house through the courtyard, and into the street. Josef followed her. "You go back and get something to eat," she said.

"I don't need to eat."

"But there are lots of things you like."

"I'm not hungry any more."

"I need to go home now or they'll start to worry."

Before Miriam could slip away, Josef reached for her hands. They were cold, and she shivered slightly. "When can we get together again?" he asked. Miriam pulled free and gave him a disapproving look. "Next Sunday," she said and ran off.

Josef returned to the monastery with his head and his heart full of the day's activities.

Chapter 11

Life in the monastery brought new misery for Josef. He was compelled, ever since Stefan died, to spend more time in class and at meals with the other young men. They continued to resent his academic prowess, and now they found additional reasons to dislike him. It was obvious that he came from a lower social class. Rumors now began to circulate about his questionable parentage and the company he kept. It was painful enough to hear whispered remarks as he passed, but even worse to find notes stuck in his papers or stuffed under his cot. They were always unsigned, written in crude Latin, and often illustrated with vulgar pictures. Some of them implied he was leprous from having shared a cell with the dead boy. Others accused him of being a dirty Jew in disguise. What cut deepest were allusions to his mother "the whore" and references to himself as "fatherless cur." This was an old wound reopened. How had they found out where he came from? Most of the students had lived in outlying villages or estates before taking up residence in the monastery. Was their innuendo pure speculation? Or had they talked to people who knew him as a child? Did they know about his Jewish friends? What was the source of their malice?

Adding to his distress, it seemed to Josef that the monks and priests also showed antipathy toward him. No recognition was given for his academic accomplishments. He was assigned the most menial tasks, such as scrubbing floors and cleaning out latrines. Meanwhile the other students were progressing through the ranks of minor orders and given jobs appropriate to their stations. The harder Josef worked at his studies and his janitorial duties, the more he was ignored. No one suggested that he serve as an acolyte or lector or even as a tutor for weak students. Not that he cared much about it, but he wondered why this was happening. Was it a consequence of his lack of wealth and connections? Or maybe his illegitimate birth? He tried to figure out why they allowed him to stay at all.

Probably it was because he provided income for the monastery through his job at city hall. Yes, that must be it. Even some of the high-born students didn't contribute to their upkeep, so he was helping to pay for them. He thought briefly about quitting, but where could he go? Certainly not home to his mother. She would be mortified if he squandered his opportunity to "better himself." No, he would stay a while longer and try to endure the unpleasantness.

The time Josef spent away from the monastery became ever more important and precious to him. His work at city hall was usually boring but not disagreeable. Frieder was a good boss. Sometimes they went out together to inspect houses or survey land, and during those times they carried on interesting conversations. One day Frieder talked about the city's efforts to protect people who were subject to persecution. He said city officials had to walk a fine line between doing what was right and stirring up resentment and ultimately more trouble for those they wanted to protect. Josef felt this applied to his situation at the monastery. If he kept quiet and out of the way, at least things wouldn't get any worse.

Josef continued to meet with Miriam most Sunday afternoons. They read Scripture together, but often their discussions would turn to personal matters. Miriam's parents were putting pressure on her to marry soon.

"What's their hurry?" asked Josef.

"I'll be fifteen at my next birthday. Most girls are married by then."

"You're not like most girls."

Miriam shrugged. "I wish I was a boy. Then I could do what I really want."

"Such as?"

"Study in the Jeschiba to be a scholar, like Mosche. Spend all my time reading and discussing Torah. Learn finer points of the Law. But women aren't allowed to do that."

"You told me women recite prayers at home. They must have learned something."

"Not much. Most fathers teach their daughters just enough to ask a blessing at mealtimes. Lots of girls do it from memory. The rest learn to read and pronounce Hebrew, but they don't know what the words mean."

"But there are some women who do more than that. You said the head rabbi's wife reads Torah and says the same prayers as the men."

"She's a special case. She helps her husband find tutors for the students and plan out their studies. Besides, she's got servants to help with the housework."

"What does that have to do with it?" asked Josef.

"She couldn't do the appointed *mitzvoh* with blessings if she was busy all the time spinning and cooking and doing women's work."

"At the beginning of the fifth book it says Moses gave the words of Torah to *all* Israel. That means women too."

"I'm glad you know that, Josef. Most men ignore it."

"Couldn't you at least study Torah with the rabbi's wife?"

"Maybe. But I want to do more than that. I want to study Mishnah and Gemara and all the commentaries of the rabbis. But women are forbidden."

"How come?"

"They think we'll get too smart. Ha! Maybe we'll outwit our husbands."

"You'll do that anyway."

"Yeah. Ehud is not the brightest man in the world."

Josef shook his head. "Why can't you break the whole thing off?"

"You don't understand how these things work. Parents make the decision, based on what's best for the girl and her whole family. They consider the man's occupation and his property and his prospects. It's complicated. Anyway, my parents already signed the *ketubbah*."

"What's that?"

"The marriage contract. My father and brother and all the witnesses read it in a ceremony and agreed to the terms. Then they turned it over to my husband."

"Don't call him that."

"We're as good as married. Ehud promised to abide by the *ketubbah*. He's already wearing his ring."

Josef glanced at Miriam's hands. "Well you're not wearing one."

"No, I'll get mine when we live together."

"That might not be for a long time."

Miriam sighed. "Josef, it's going to happen. We'd have to get a divorce to stop it now. My parents would have to pay a huge fine if they broke the contract."

"Look. You remember reading in Torah about Moses' mother and sister? They didn't obey the Law. They were supposed to drown the baby

Moses, but they put him in a basket instead. His sister's name was Miriam, like you. She wasn't afraid to go against the rules."

"That was different. She was breaking Egyptian law, but not God's law. And she didn't go against her parents."

Josef and Miriam had many such discussions. They confided to one another about difficulties and disappointments in their lives. As winter ended and the days grew longer, they were able to stay later on Sunday afternoons, reading and talking.

One day Miriam said, "Josef, I'm afraid."

"Of what?"

"Of being married."

"You think your husband will beat you?"

"No, he's nice enough."

"What then?"

"I really don't know. Maybe just the change in how I spend my time. There'll be so many things I can't do . . . things I enjoy."

"Is that all?"

She hesitated. "No. What I'm most afraid of, I think, is that I won't love Ehud. My mother says you can learn to love a man, but I don't think I can. He'd have to earn my respect first. The only men I really respect are scholars."

"Are your parents still pushing you to get married soon?"

"Yes. They want me to do it before Passover. The rabbis here don't allow weddings between Passover and Pentecost. If I can hold off until Passover, then I'll have seven more weeks at least."

Josef nodded.

On a bright, sunny afternoon in April, following two days of rain, Josef was sitting on a low section of the wall overlooking the Jewish cemetery. High grass clumped around the gravestones glistened with moisture and stirred softly in the warm breeze. Daffodils and wild irises in great abundance appeared as a colorful carpet over the open spaces. Josef was thinking how little time he had spent with Miriam in the last few weeks. They had met only twice, and briefly. At those meetings they had read a little and hardly talked at all. He yearned to see her.

Suddenly there she was, standing beside him. He looked up at her, stunned to see the object of his daydreams, more beautiful than he had ever seen her. Their eyes met and she took his hand. Neither said anything as they walked across the cemetery. Where was she taking him? They passed through the gate and out into a nearby field. Still holding hands, they came to a thicket of trees at the far edge of the field. His fingertips were tingling and he wondered whether Miriam could feel it too. They entered the thicket by a pathway that led to a small clearing. Still without speaking, Miriam sat down on a blanket of long, soft, pale-colored grass and looked up. Josef stood over her, every sinew and tendon in his body taut and trembling. She motioned for him to sit beside her. What was happening? Was it a dream? Josef took both her hands in his and kissed her softly on the lips. Then he kissed her harder. The two embraced and held each other for a few moments that seemed to Josef like an eternity of ecstatic joy. He had never felt anything like this before. He wanted the feeling to last forever and knew that in some way it would.

Without thinking he found himself gently removing Miriam's blouse. He put his head on her bare breast. She held his head in her hands and stroked his hair. His heart was throbbing. He kissed her again and she returned his kiss. After that, neither tried to restrain the emotion they had held back for so long.

Sometime later, Josef was holding Miriam in his arms. He touched her lips with his finger. "Miriam, I love you." She lowered her eyes and did not answer. "Miriam, tell me that you love me. I know you love me."

She gave a slight shake of her head. "It's impossible," she said with downcast voice.

He pleaded with her. "I want to marry you. I'll talk to your parents and tell them how much I love you."

Quietly she dressed herself. Looking back at Josef, still lying in the grass, she repeated, "It's impossible." Then she went away, walking toward the cemetery.

Josef lay still, wondering if he had been dreaming. He had never known such ecstasy, yet now he was distraught. What could he do? He could not now go back to the monastery. He would be utterly preoccupied and distracted. Should he follow Miriam and try to talk to her? No, that would be useless. She was bound by her parents' decisions. Maybe he could talk to Mosche? Yes, he would do that. He would make his case and convince Mosche to talk to their parents. But where could he find Mosche? Miriam had told him that her brother did not live at home any more. He might be anywhere in the Jewish quarter. Josef decided he would do whatever he had to to find his friend. This was the most important thing in his life.

He hastily pulled on his clothes and began running. Before he reached the city wall he turned north and ran through farm fields. He wanted to keep clear of the monastery and cathedral precinct, where he might be recognized. When he reached Martin's Gate on the north side of town he was completely out of breath. Nevertheless he pushed on, walking and holding his side. Passing through the gate into the old market square, he made his way to Jews' Alley. For the next few hours he wandered through the streets, looking in the face of every man he passed, searching for the one he knew. Several times he went to the synagogue, hoping to find a gathering of men, but no one came. Even after nightfall Josef stumbled around the streets, until he was completely spent. Finally he slumped against the wall in a corner of the synagogue courtyard and fell asleep.

At daybreak he was awakened by a small boy nudging his shoulder. The child held out a coin for him to take. Josef was confused and shook his head. "What's that for?"

"It's alms for the poor, sir."

Josef looked around, trying to remember where he was. "I'm not here to beg. I'm looking for someone."

"Who, sir?"

"A scholar named Mosche. He's a tall man with kindly eyes."

"Yes sir, I know him. He's praying in the synagogue."

"Would you tell him someone wants to speak to him?"

"Yes sir."

The boy ran off and entered the synagogue. Josef stood up and straightened his clothes. After a few minutes, he saw his old friend walking toward him. Mosche looked him up and down and laughed. "What happened to you? I thought you were a beggar who had too much wine."

Josef looked serious. "You could say that. Not that I drank too much wine. But I am here to beg your help."

"You know I'll help you if I can. What do you need?"

"Can we find a place to talk? Off by ourselves?"

Mosche led the way to the grove of trees behind the schoolhouse. "No one comes here early in the morning. We won't be interrupted."

Josef spoke tentatively. "Mosche, I don't know exactly how to say this, but it's about your sister."

"What's she done now?"

"Nothing. It's just that . . . I love her."

"Well so do I, even if she does have a gigantic stubborn streak."

"No, I love her more than anything else in the world. I could never love anyone else. Do you understand?"

Mosche shook his head.

"I want to marry her. I know she's betrothed to someone else. But I'm sure she likes me more than him. I'll do anything. Please, please talk to your parents. Try to convince them I'd be a good husband."

Mosche scratched his head. "This is truly astonishing. You're a Christian. You have no property or income to support a wife, much less a family. And you want my parents to break a legal contract so you can marry my sister?"

"I know it sounds crazy. But please . . ."

"Our rabbis wouldn't approve. Your priests wouldn't approve."

"It doesn't matter. I can't live without her."

Mosche sighed. "Look. I think the chances are almost zero, and I'm not sure I like the idea myself. But I will talk to my father. Just don't get your hopes up."

"Thank you." Josef gave an involuntary sob. He bit his lip as tears welled up in his eyes. His friend patted him on the shoulder. "Calm down, Josef. Let's get you cleaned up a little bit." They went to a trough behind the synagogue. Mosche drew water and Josef splashed his face.

"Wait here a minute," said Mosche. He came back with a leather pouch containing two loaves of bread and a large piece of cheese. "Let's eat breakfast." Only then did Josef realize how famished he was. Eagerly he bit into one of the loaves and broke off bits of cheese to eat with it.

Josef went directly from the synagogue to his work at city hall. Frieder noticed immediately that his young assistant was disheveled and preoccupied.

"Are you all right?" he asked.

"I didn't sleep very well," Josef answered.

"Can I help with anything?"

Josef shook his head. He pretended to take an interest in the papers on his writing table. He began copying documents but found he made more mistakes than usual. It was hard to keep his hand steady. Frieder must have noticed his continuing agitation. After an hour or so, he suggested that Josef take the rest of the morning off work.

Josef was grateful for Frieder's sympathy and generosity. He immediately set out for the cemetery. From there he walked to the little clearing, the place where he had at long last expressed his love for Miriam (and she for him, he thought). It seemed like a dream deep in his memory. Was it only yesterday? He could hardly believe it had happened at all. Yet his heart was beating just as hard now as it had then. He sat down in the grass and tried to think, but his mind was muddled. He lost track of time. Suddenly he remembered that he would be expected at the monastery for mid-morning prayers and lessons. He jumped up and began running toward the gate of the city wall. As he got closer, he slowed down. There was no reason to hurry, he thought. After all, he had missed the evening meal and vespers yesterday, not to mention breakfast this morning. He knew he was already in trouble. What would it matter if he was late for another session? He would slip in as quietly as he could, but he knew some kind of punishment awaited him.

After the noontime meal was over, one of the monks came to his seat and tapped him on the shoulder. He motioned for Josef to follow him. Silently they walked through the gloomy cloisters until they came to the Superior's room. He was seated behind a large desk, examining a parchment. Josef stood before the desk, shifting nervously from one foot to the other. Finally the master looked up at him and said, "Josef, where have you been?"

"I'd rather not say."

"You'd rather not *say*? You missed two meals and two devotional offices. I believe you were out all night. This is not acceptable behavior." Josef hung his head and remained silent. "All right, Josef. I suspect you spent the night in a tavern, or perhaps in a brothel. It's what young men do. But we are different. We must overcome those urges. Do you understand?"

Josef nodded.

"I am assigning penance and putting you on notice. You will recite the 'Our Father' and 'Hail Mary' fifty times in the presence of Brother Karl. If I hear of any more foolishness, you will be expelled."

For the next few days, Josef tried to concentrate on his work. It was futile. Whether attending class, studying alone in his cell, or working with Frieder on city business, his thoughts inevitably turned to Miriam. Even while kneeling at prayers or occupied with housekeeping duties, he pictured her in his mind, although in the latter case at any rate, his hands were busy and productive. His preoccupation was so great that he no longer noticed the contempt of the other students, which only grew worse as he withdrew further from them.

After four days had passed (although it seemed like a year to Josef), he was lying on his cot following the noonday meal, daydreaming. There was a soft tap at the door. Josef pulled himself up to a sitting position and called, "Come in." The door opened a crack and a hand appeared, holding a small scrap of parchment. "A messenger brought this for you earlier today," said the bearer. Josef ran to the door, took the letter, and nodded to the monk who had delivered it. He closed the door and held the parchment in his trembling hand. Slowly he unfolded it. The writing was in Hebrew. It said: "Sorry Josef. I talked with my father. He said it was out of the question. Miriam and Ehud are to be married this morning."

For a moment Josef stood stunned, as if hit by a blow to the chest. He could barely breathe. His thoughts raced. With no clear plan, he ran out of his cell, through the cloister, and into the street. Then he started running wildly, paying no attention to what he passed, knocking over a street cart that was in his way, until he reached the Jewish quarter. There he found the usual festivities associated with a wedding. People lined the streets, loudly talking and laughing. Raucous music could be heard somewhere in the distance. Josef mingled with the crowd, trying to blend in and hide his agitation. The music came closer. The nuptial parade was approaching. Josef scrambled to find a spot along the roadway where he could watch without being seen. The parade was passing. He saw the attendants and the family go by. Then Miriam herself, carried on a canopied platform by four young men. She looked beautiful. Yet Josef thought her smile showed a hint of sadness. She glanced toward where he was standing. Did she see him? Immediately she turned away and looked in the other direction. The rest of the wedding party passed by. Josef followed after the procession, hoping to see her again. Maybe he could catch her eye or even talk to her for a moment, to find out how she was feeling. Was she miserable? Did she still love him? A hundred times he had turned it over in his mind, and he was certain that for one day at least she had loved him. He stayed as close to the parade as he could, jostled along by the boisterous crowd. As he approached the synagogue, he caught just a glimpse of Miriam's back as she disappeared through the door.

Afterwards Josef couldn't remember how the next hour passed, except that he was miserable. When the doors opened again, he saw a group of men and the groom, beaming with pleasure, hoisted on their shoulders. A homely, heavy-set, middle-aged man. Why him? It was not right. Josef thought no one could love Miriam as much as he did. Then everyone else came out. Josef could not see Miriam in the crowd. He followed at a distance as they pushed through the streets. By the time he reached the groom's house, the bridal party was already inside. Josef stared at the house. Suddenly he realized the truth. This was Miriam's home. She would live here forever as someone else's wife. She would care for that man and raise his children. A wave of despair passed through him. He, Josef, might never see her again. And she wouldn't ever think about him.

For the rest of the day Josef wandered aimlessly around the city. Later on, he could not remember anything of where he had gone or what he had done. As evening approached it occurred to him that he would no longer be welcome at the monastery, since he had left again without permission. He didn't care. There was no reason for him to go back there. But where could he go? Last time when he stayed out overnight, the Superior assumed he went to a brothel. That sounded like a good idea. He knew where the prostitutes were, in the alley just below the cathedral precinct. He would go there a little later, after it got dark. In the meantime he would try to scrounge up some food. On the cobblestones of Newmarket Square, he found some stale bread and pieces of raw potato, but this hardly satisfied his hunger. He was terribly thirsty as well. Someone had left a half-rotted, leaky bucket by the well, and he was able to draw enough water to drink his fill. After that he felt a little better. He sat down beside the well and dozed.

When he woke with a start, a full moon was high in the sky. He recalled something Mosche had told him years ago, that weddings are best held at the time of the full moon. Would this bode well for Miriam's marriage? Right now, he thought, she must be lying with her husband. He gritted his teeth. He couldn't bear to think about it. Josef pulled himself up. He would take comfort where he could find it. Tonight he would visit a prostitute for the first time in his life.

He made a wide circle north of the cathedral and came into the whores' alley from the west side. There were five or six ladies standing about in tight clothes and gaudy jewelry. Josef hugged the wall, hoping to remain inconspicuous, as he stared at the women and tried to decide which one to approach. Then it occurred to him—he had no money.

Women did this job for income, not for pleasure. What could he do now? He covered his face with his hands and let his back slide down the wall. There he sat with his head hanging between his knees. After a few moments, a light hand touched his shoulder.

"Hey, boy, what's your name?"

Josef looked up and saw standing over him an older woman, not unattractive, but with greasy skin and painted eyelids.

"Come on, what's your name? I'm Hilda," she said.

"Josef," he whispered.

"Well, Josef, I'm not going to bite you. Are you looking for a trick?" He shook his head. "It's okay," she said. "The young ones never admit it. Why don't you come with me?" She took his hand and pulled him to a standing position. He followed her into a dirty little room. The floor was nearly covered by a large wooden bed frame and straw mattress. "Let's sit," she said. He sat. "Is this your first time?" she asked.

"I'm sorry. I shouldn't be here," he said. "I have no money."

"No money, he tells me. So why are you here?" Josef hung his head and said nothing. "Do you want to talk about it? I can see something's bothering you."

"The girl I love . . . she, she got married today."

"Oh. One of those cases. Look, you're cute and I've got nothing else to do tonight. I could give you some comfort. But you have to promise not to tell your friends. I don't need a bunch of young stallions knocking at my door with no money."

Josef nodded.

"Take your pants off."

He did as she asked. She began fondling him and rubbing her body against his. She exposed her breasts. They were large and loose, hanging almost to her navel. Josef noticed wrinkles on the women's neck. He was becoming aroused, but this was not what he wanted. It was nothing like his experience with Miriam. He didn't want this memory to blot out the other one. "Stop," he said.

"What's the matter, honey? Got cold feet?"

"Not exactly. It's just not what I want to do."

"This old girl's not for you? Look, I'd offer to get you a younger girl, but you've got no money."

"No. It's okay."

"I may be past my prime, but some of the young guys think I'm pretty good."

"No, really. It's not you. You're nice. I like you just fine."

She smiled with her eyes and patted his hand. "All right, honey. Do you want to talk about your girlfriend?"

Josef told the woman all his experiences of the past week. He opened his heart to her. Before the end, he was sobbing and shaking. She put her arms around him and held him until he became calm. "Put your pants on, Josef. I'll find you something to eat." She returned with a platter of cold meat and buttered bread and a large mug of beer. "Eat this. You'll feel better." She watched while he quickly consumed it all. "Now you better get home to your mama. She'll be worried."

"I can't go home."

The woman sighed. "This is turning out to be a costly trick. You stay here and sleep. I'll bunk with one of the other girls tonight."

She left him alone and he lay down on the straw bed. He slept soundly and woke at dawn. Before going he wanted very much to leave something for the woman who had been so kind to him, but he had nothing of value with him. All he had was the scrap of parchment Mosche had sent him. He carefully laid it at the head of the mattress. The woman would not be able to read it, of course, but Josef hoped she would accept it as a thank-you token. He stepped out the door and immediately looked up to see the cathedral towers looming overhead. At this moment he was glad he had not defiled himself. That would only have made him more miserable. Now he had to figure out where to go and what to do next. For him the best place to think was the cemetery. He would go to his little covered grotto and try to come up with some ideas.

Three hours later Josef still had no plan. He didn't know where he would live or get his meals. He didn't know if his employment at city hall would continue, now that he had left the monastery under shameful circumstances. The only idea he had was to go see Father Albert. Josef had always liked his old tutor and found him sympathetic. Maybe he would know of an empty room where Josef could board in exchange for labor.

He set out for St. Paul's Church, choosing his route carefully to keep some distance from the monastery. When he arrived at St. Paul's, Father Albert was nowhere to be found. Josef went into a dark corner of the church and waited. After an hour or so, Father Albert approached the altar with another priest to conduct the noon Mass. When it ended, he went out the side door. Josef lingered until the last worshippers had left and then hurried to look for his old friend. He found the priest removing his vestments in the sacristy. He knocked lightly on the open door. "Hello?" he said tentatively.

Father Albert looked up and squinted. "Josef? Is that you?" After hanging his alb on a wall hook, he approached for a closer look. Then he gave Josef a bear hug. "How are you, my boy? What's going on at the monastery? Tell me everything!"

"Well . . . that's why I'm here." Josef hesitated. "Can we talk?"

They went to sit on a bench in the walled garden beside the church. Josef told Father Albert about his troubles at the monastery, how the other students taunted him and the monks held him in low regard. He said he'd stayed out a couple of nights and got in trouble with the Superior. He stopped short of mentioning Miriam or his visit to the prostitute. Nevertheless, Father Albert surmised that certain things were left unsaid.

"Is there no possibility, then, that you could return to St. Andreas Monastery?" he asked.

"No, there's no way."

"What about your mother?"

"She'll say I threw away my best chance at success. I could never go back and live with her."

"Let me think. You're pretty well educated already. Is this something you want to carry on with?"

"I guess so."

Father Albert sat quietly for a few minutes. He scratched his head. "I have an old friend who's abbot of a monastery in Poitiers."

"Where's that?"

"West of here, in the region of Poitou, south of Brittany. My friend could teach you a great deal."

"That's part of Francia. I don't speak the language."

"With your knowledge of Latin, you can learn it quickly."

"How would I get there? It must be ten days' journey from here."

"It's a great distance. But if you want to go, we'll find a way. Traders and scholars sometimes travel back and forth. I've put aside a few pennies that might buy a certain degree of protection on the road. You'll need travel provisions, too."

"I don't want to take your money."

"Nonsense. I saved it for just such a reason as this. Now let's decide where you can stay in the meantime."

It was determined that Josef would sleep in the crypt underneath the church. To earn his meals, he would do odd jobs around the place. Father Albert encouraged Josef to contact his boss at city hall and keep working there if possible. It turned out Frieder was happy to have his young assistant back at work, even for a limited time. Josef's continued employment there had two beneficial results. Now that he was no longer living at the monastery, he would receive his wages directly. And Frieder had knowledge of travelers who entered and left the city. He would notify Josef of any groups he heard about who were going across the mountains to the west.

Chapter 12

Four weeks later, Josef was informed by Frieder that a group of merchants would be departing Worms in the middle of May and carrying their wares to the summer trade fairs in Champagne. They would not, however, be going as far as Poitiers. Josef could travel with them only about half-way to his destination, and then he would be on his own. Did he want to set out with such uncertain prospects? Frieder pointed out two advantages of going with this group. First, they would be crossing the mountains at the most favorable time of year, when rivers would be free of ice and nighttime temperatures quite bearable. Second, these merchants were mostly Jews, who enjoyed the protection of King Henry in his domain and the counts of Francia in theirs. While they might encounter bandits along the way, their travel documents would be respected by everyone except the most brazen and desperate.

Josef did not hesitate in making up his mind. He would take this chance to escape the town of his birth and leave behind all the turmoil in his heart and soul. Now he had just over two weeks to make preparations. First, he would have to inform his mother. That would be the hardest part. She would be losing her closest living relative and sole means of support in old age. Who knows whether he would ever return? His preference at the moment was to get as far away as possible and never think about this place again. Next, he would need to assemble supplies for travel: sturdy shoes, extra clothes and blankets, dried meat and other non-perishable food, and as much money as he could scrape together. He already had the coins Father Albert had given him, as well as his salary for the last few weeks. Perhaps he could earn a bit more running errands in the marketplace.

The day of departure was fast approaching. Josef could hardly sleep at night, so stirred up was he. Frieder had introduced him to a couple of the merchants in the trading party, and they told him some of their plans. The initial part of the journey would be by river. They would load their wares on a barge and travel the Rhein northward toward Mainz, then follow a smaller river westward until it was no longer navigable. At that point they would purchase donkey carts and trek through the mountain passes. Finally they would cross the great plain of Champagne to reach the important trading center of Troyes, where they would participate in the St. John's Day fair. Josef recognized the name of the city. It was Rabbi Scholomo's hometown and the site of his Jeschiba. Mosche had spoken admiringly of the many learned scholars of Troyes and the outstanding work they did. This added to Josef's excitement. Perhaps he could spend a few days in the city and quietly slip into a study session or two.

His preparations for the journey were almost complete. He had spoken with his mother, and the encounter had been surprisingly calm. Father Albert offered to come along, which helped smooth the waters. He explained that Josef had advanced in his studies to a point where new teachers would be beneficial. The abbot of Poitiers was an exceptionally learned man who had gathered other bright young men around him. Learning to speak French, Father Albert told her, would also give Josef an advantage if he were to pursue a vocation in the church. His mother nodded and remained silent as she tried to understand what the old priest told her. She had never been one to question the pronouncements of a clergyman. Josef himself said barely a word.

Now it was time for him to make his final farewell. He hoped this meeting would be as free from strife as the last one. He found his mother sweeping the steps leading up to her rooms.

"Mutti, I'm leaving tomorrow."

"Tomorrow! Why so soon?"

"I have to go when the merchants are ready. All the arrangements have been made."

"Can't you wait and go with some other merchants?"

"There may not be another group leaving this summer."

"Josef, I can't bear it. You're all I have." She clutched his shirt and tried to pull him close. He resisted.

"Please, Mutti, don't make this harder than it needs to be."

She clung to his sleeve and started crying. He waited a few moments, then pried her hand loose and held it in his own. "Listen, Mutti. I'll send letters to Father Albert at each stage of the journey and another when I arrive in Poitiers. He'll find someone who can read them to you so you'll know I'm safe. Now, really, I have to go and get ready for the trip."

Her weeping gradually ceased. She turned her teary eyes up to his face and said, "Can you wait just one minute?" He nodded and she ran up the stairs. She soon returned with a small packet. "It's some of your favorite honey cakes. Maybe you'll remember me when you eat these."

"Mutti, I'm not going to forget you." He took the packet and kissed her tenderly on the cheek. Then he turned and walked away, afraid to look back. Later, when he opened the packet, he found that his mother had slipped in three coins from her hard-earned wages.

The first part of the journey was uneventful, yet for Josef it was thrilling. Floating silently down river, he saw the world opening before him. On the banks he observed castles, villages, vineyards, and people of every description. Though he tried to make himself useful on the barge, running errands for the captain and helping the crew load and unload cargo, he spent most of his time watching the countryside go by. The grand city of Mainz seemed to go on forever. Its shoreline was noisy and bustling, and buildings were taller than in Worms. The sights made Josef eager to see and visit other large cities.

Once his party disembarked, the going became harder. They were eleven men in all, including seven Jewish merchants (one of whom had brought his twelve-year-old son), two Christian merchants, and Josef. The six wagons they purchased were barely large enough to carry their goods, piled high and secured with tarps and ropes. Donkeys pulled while the men walked alongside. For a time they followed the dwindling river upstream as it led them higher and higher into the mountains. During this stage of the journey, they relied on their own provisions, eating and sleeping outdoors, sheltered at night from the elements by makeshift tents. Josef rather enjoyed the adventure of a long hike in the open air, except that his feet became terribly sore. In part, this was caused by his shoes wearing thin. He learned from the others to wrap bands of cloth around his feet for extra warmth and padding. He decided, when they reached the next town, he would buy larger shoes to accommodate more padding.

Gradually the mountainous terrain leveled out. The road became wider and smoother. Now the travelers moved faster and measured their progress by the towns they passed through. The merchants had friends at every stopping point, fellow Jews who would feed them, lock away their wagons for the night, re-supply them for the next leg of the journey, and, on occasion, offer them a roof to sleep under. Most importantly, however, the local people advised the traveling merchants on the safest route to follow, in some cases providing an escort through dangerous country.

Josef had no idea what dangers they might face, aside from rough roads and rickety bridges. One day he learned firsthand. The party had stopped at midday to rest and refresh themselves. They were in a wooded area, not far from a small stream that formed a series of pools. Some of the men unharnessed their beasts and led them to the stream. When the animals had drunk their fill and the men had replenished their water skins, they went back to the road. Only Josef and the merchant's son stayed behind to soak their feet and splash around a bit. Suddenly they were grabbed from behind by large, rough hands. One hand covered Josef's mouth, while a strong arm over his shoulder held him like a vise. He struggled briefly but was quickly dealt a sharp blow to the head. After that he cooperated. A large band of ruffians, perhaps fifteen or more, came out of the woods and made its way to the road with the two captives. Many carried knives and sharp farm implements. They approached the wagons and shouted at the men in a language Josef did not understand. Clearly they were demanding something.

One of the merchants stepped forward. With no discernible fear, he spoke to the intruders in their own language. After some discussion, the spokesman for each side retreated to confer with his companions. The man Josef took to be the head bandit sent three of his men into the woods, while a couple of merchants approached one of the wagons. They dug under piles of cloth and leather goods and pulled out a sheet of parchment. Speaking to the head bandit once again, the merchant spokesman held up the parchment and read from it, or rather translated it into the other's language. The bandit nodded to the men who were holding Josef and the boy. They loosened their grip and gave each one a shove towards the wagons. Still, everyone waited. The travel party made no move to resume their journey. The band of ruffians stood watch with weapons raised. Josef was confused by the situation, but he did not dare ask questions. Finally, after twenty minutes or so, the three who had been sent into the woods returned, accompanied by a heavily armed man on horseback. He and his horse were dressed in a grand manner, with fringes and badges on their garments (though their costume was less colorful than the knights Josef had seen in Worms). The rider dismounted. One of the bandits held his horse while he came forward to inspect the travel document. He looked at it suspiciously and eyed the merchants one by one. He walked by the wagons, lifting some of the tarps and probing the goods underneath. Finally he remounted, said a few words to the others, and rode away. The entire band quickly disappeared into the woods.

Once the episode was over, Josef asked many questions. He learned that the band of men (and the knight as well) were indeed robbers. They preyed upon travelers who crossed into "their land." However, they feared retribution from the local lord if they attacked Jews. Why were Jews so favored? Through the years Jewish merchants had made arrangements with landowners and noblemen to guarantee their security. In the open country, this meant paying regular fees to the local lords. Closer to the cities and commercial centers, the counts and dukes took it upon themselves to protect traveling merchants. They knew, after all, that they would gain ample revenues from the trade fairs.

The company had been on the road about fifteen days when they arrived in Troyes. Thanks to the hospitality of Jews along the route, Josef had spent very little of his money. He had bought a new pair of shoes at a good price and paid for ale and wine and some food, but otherwise his stack of coins was intact. He would stay in Troyes for a few days as cheaply as he could. The next part of the journey, he knew, would require more of his own resources. He felt well endowed to proceed. First, however, he wanted to see what this city had to offer.

Through the influence of one of the merchants with whom he traveled, Josef was able to rent an inexpensive room near the main market square. From there he explored the city. Troyes was a large settlement on the River Seine that functioned as capital and trading center for the region of Champagne. Its streets were narrow, with overhanging gables blocking out much of the sunlight. The prevailing shadows, the crowds of people pushing through the streets, and the bleating and baying of wandering livestock all contributed to a feeling of confusion and disorder that Josef was not accustomed to. This city did not present a bright, well-scrubbed face like the town where he had grown up. Yet Josef found it all stimulating. Even the putrid smell of tanneries reminded him that this was a city of commerce, a hub of merchants and Torah scholars from faraway lands, bringing not only wine, salt, grain, textiles, and leather goods to exchange, but new ideas as well. The fair would go on for fifteen days, and Josef determined he would stay until it was over.

On the northeast side of the city, near the banks of the river, the counts of Troyes had established their residence. The current occupant of the castle was Count Thibaud (or Theobald, as German-speaking visitors referred to him). Local Jews, living here under the count's protection, had built their synagogue in the shadow of his castle. Many Jews dwelt nearby. However, the Jewish quarter in Troyes was not so clearly defined as in Worms. Some Christian families and even a church or two were located in the district, while Jewish families had houses in every part of town.

Josef went to the synagogue, hoping to find out when Torah study sessions would take place. He could not understand the French language, of course, but found he could communicate in Hebrew. The Hebrew dialect here was different from what he knew, as it incorporated many words borrowed from French; nevertheless, he could usually get the gist of what was said. He approached a boy with a slate who appeared to be three or four years younger than himself.

"Are you a student at the Jeschiba?" he asked.

"Yes. Except we call it Yeshiva. Where do you come from?"

"Worms on the Rhein River. I came with merchants. Will there be any public lectures and discussions while the fair is going on?"

"Yes, eventually. After the vendors put out their goods. All classes are canceled until the rabbis get their booths set up."

"The rabbis have things to sell?"

"Of course. They have to make a living like everyone else."

"Where I come from, rabbis are paid for teaching."

"Not here. At least not enough to live on. Even the head of our Yeshiva keeps vineyards."

"What's his name?"

"Rabbi Salomon. He has other names, too. We call him Hamoreh, our teacher. The town folk call him Rabbenu Shalmo."

Josef smiled. "You say he keeps vineyards?"

"Yep. Some of the best wine in Champagne comes from his vats. Christians pay top dollar to get it for their idol worship. It's much superior to the polluted grape juice they make."

Josef ignored these remarks. "When do you think Rabbi Salomon will start teaching again?"

"In three or four days, I would guess."

For the next three days, Josef wandered the city and its outskirts. He had no particular object in mind but to hear and see and taste as much as he could. Some of the languages he heard were strange to his ear, including (he assumed) Italian and English. Discussions focused for the most part on commercial matters such as price and quality, but Josef thought he overheard people talking about scientific theories and art collections as well. The goods on display at the fair were fascinating: bottled wine, spices from Asia, fine parchment, wrought metal pieces, jewelry with sparkling stones, and delicate silk fabrics. Josef bought a small remnant of royal blue silk as a gift for his mother. He would send it back to Worms with the returning merchants. Another outstanding feature of the fair was the food. Josef tasted delectable meats and pastries, as well as tropical fruits he'd never heard of before.

Once the fair was well underway, the local rabbis entrusted all commercial dealings to their wives and children. Nevertheless, they did not resume their usual teaching at the school or tutoring of younger children. Instead they offered lectures and discussion sessions for Jewish merchants. This was the only opportunity some of the visitors had to interact with scholars of Torah and Talmud. Josef found his way into many of these sessions, especially the ones led by Rabbi Scholomo. Mosche would be envious if he knew! It was hard for Josef to hear and understand everything, since he sat at the very back of the room, trying to be inconspicuous. Also, many of the questions from the audience were posed in French, and so he had to guess from the answer (in Hebrew) what was being asked. Still, Josef was thrilled to be observing once again the intellectual give-and-take of sharp, inquisitive minds.

After a week, Josef was beginning to feel quite at home in the synagogue and schoolhouse. He arrived and left with visiting businessmen and exchanged greetings with a few of them as they came in. One day, before the start of a lecture on Proverbs to be given by Rabbi Scholomo, Josef heard someone call his name. At first he ignored it, thinking there must be another Josef in the assembly. Then he felt a tap on the shoulder, and looking around, saw the rabbi standing behind him.

"Hello, Josef. I've been observing you all week."

"Rabbi Scholomo!"

"Yes, it is I. Surely you recognized me from our earlier meetings?"

"Well, yes, but . . ." Josef was completely tongued-tied.

The rabbi smiled and said, "Stay after the lecture and we'll have a chat."

Josef sat as if paralyzed. Sweat poured from his head and chest. He had not expected to be recognized, much less singled out. The merchants sitting around him were all looking at him, and a couple patted him on the back. He could not concentrate on the lecture or the discussion that followed. After it was over, he stayed in his seat. Gradually the hall emptied. The rabbi motioned for him to come forward to the lectern. Collecting his papers, Rabbi Scholomo said, "Come. Let's have a talk." Josef followed him into a small room containing a table, two chairs, and shelves of books, more books than Josef had ever seen collected in one place. They sat down.

"Now, tell me, how are things in Worms? I haven't been there in months."

Josef took his eyes off the books and looked into the rabbi's kind face. He took a deep breath. "Not too bad, sir. They were expecting another good harvest this year."

"Splendid. What about you? Do you still find time to read Hebrew with your friends?"

"No, sir. I was a full-time student at St. Andreas Monastery. Now I'm on my way to study at the Abbey in Poitiers."

"Ah. That's what brings you here. What do you intend to do with all this education, if I may ask?"

"I don't really know. Many people expect me to be a priest. That may be the only path open to me, since I have no skills."

"Nonsense. You are young and bright. You can be a scholar, a theologian if you like, and still practice a trade. We have a saying: 'Without worldly pursuits, there can be no Torah.' I myself am a vintner."

"Yes, sir. They say you make excellent wine." Josef shrugged his shoulders. "Sometimes I think I should give up studying entirely and just be a farmer. It would be a simpler life."

"Yes, it would. But we have another saying: 'Love Torah, and for its sake be a fool and a simpleton, leave your business, and pursue your studies.'"

Josef laughed. "You have too many sayings, Rabbi."

"Perhaps. But wisdom cannot be encapsulated in one idea. We need paradoxes to explain ourselves and our condition. You, for example, are developing your intellectual powers. You might become a priest and exert tremendous good influence on your Church. On the other hand, you might be a businessman or city official and exert even more influence. The key is to remember what is truly important."

"And what is that, sir?"

"To love the Lord with all your heart, all your soul, and all your might."

"The *Shema*. I've heard it before. But how am I supposed to do it?"

"For now, learn as much as you can. Find a master at whose feet to sit." Josef sighed. Thus far his teachers had been uninspiring. The rabbi continued, "You're going to a good place. It is said that the abbot of Poitiers is a wise and compassionate man. He will help you. You will find that, in the right setting, the life of the mind has certain attractions."

"And if I get bored?"

"You won't, if you ask questions constantly. This attitude also protects you against false teachings, which can become deeply entrenched. Remember to think—always. If you blindly accept what your teachers say, you may find yourself obliged to justify and defend lies. Worse yet, you might teach them to other people."

Josef nodded. "But I still can't decide what I want to do."

"It's all right. Keep listening for guidance. The name Josef, your name, is revered in the old covenant and the new. Both men of that name had visions from heaven. And, you remember, they paid careful attention to what was disclosed."

Josef leaned forward, somewhat startled. "Rabbi, how is it that you know about people in our gospels?"

The rabbi raised his eyebrows. "We Jews are a curious people. We read and we study, sometimes to better understand our adversaries. Now let me tell you one more of our sayings: 'Iron sharpens iron.' Whatever difficulties you encounter can make you stronger."

"Thank you, sir. You've been very kind. I should not take any more of your time."

"One more thing. My wife and I always invite visiting scholars for a meal in our house at the conclusion of the fair. Will you join us?"

Quickly Josef shook his head. "No. No, really. I'll be leaving Troyes immediately when the fair ends. I am honored by your invitation, but I really can't."

The rabbi nodded. "As you wish. But you must accept a small gift." He lifted a thin scroll from a basket beside the table. "Our young scribes-in-training practice their script on fragments of parchment. Here is a section of my commentary on the fifth book of Moses."

Josef couldn't believe his good luck. He thought again of his friend Mosche. "Thank you, Rabbi. I will read it carefully."

Two days later, Josef was on the road to Poitiers. He fell in with a small caravan of merchants going in his direction. After a few days, they took a different road, and Josef was on his own. All went well at first. He walked steadily onward, stopping only to buy bread in villages along the way and rest at night under shelter of trees and shrubs. He was rounding a curve in the road when he saw before him a group of men laughing and talking among themselves. One of them saw him coming and made a crude remark, eliciting hoots from the others. Josef was confused. Should he turn around and run? Should he keep walking calmly past them? In the end he simply stopped and stared at them. One sauntered over and said something in French. Josef shook his head and pointed at his mouth. The man shouted a few words to his friends. They came closer, and Josef noticed that some of them carried clubs and poles. He turned and started running back the way he had come. The men followed in pursuit. Josef twisted his ankle and went sprawling in the road. In a minute they were on him, grabbing and poking at him, tearing off his coat and shirt, and delivering blows to his head. When they were done, they kicked him over the side of the road into a ditch.

After a couple of hours, Josef awoke, sore all over. He touched a welt on his head and winced in pain. He felt clotted blood on his forehead. When he tried to get up, his ankle gave way. With his arms and his good leg he pulled himself out of the ditch and back to the road. Then he thought of his pack, containing his extra clothes and blanket and utensils. It was nowhere to be seen. His shoes and shirt were gone, too, and the pouch in which he kept his money. What was left? He was still wearing his breeches. That was all they had left him. Wait a minute. Josef felt his left thigh. The parchment was still there! The scroll Rabbi Scholomo had given him. Josef had wrapped it around this thigh inside his pants so it wouldn't get crushed in his pack. In spite of his losses and his injuries, he felt grateful. But what was he to do now? He had no idea how far it was to the next village, and, anyway, he couldn't walk. Maybe he could crawl or drag himself a short distance, but to what purpose? To search for water. His dry throat was telling him he must find water. He looked up the road and saw a slight rise. Maybe the band of robbers had been waiting at a bridge to cut off anyone who would go across. It was worth a try. With pain and difficulty, Josef pulled and pushed himself along the road until he did indeed come to a bridge. With renewed thankfulness he tumbled down the banks and lay on the edge of a gently flowing stream. He plunged his throbbing head in cool water. It felt wonderful! He drank and drank and was much refreshed. He quickly decided he would stay here and await his fate. Either someone would come along and help him or he would die waiting.

For two days no one came. Josef's stomach rumbled, then ached from hunger. He tried eating some grass and weeds growing along the banks of the stream, but that was no good. He kept watching the road, even as he felt weaker and less hopeful. Finally he saw in the distance a man leading a horse-drawn wagon. He pulled himself up the bank and waited. Slowly the man came closer, and Josef observed that both man and beast seemed quite old. The horse's head hung low and the animal moved forward only with much coaxing. As they pulled even with Josef, the man stopped and stared. He said a few words to his horse.

"Hallo," said Josef. "I don't speak French. Can you help me?"

The man asked him something. Josef shook his head. "Sorry, I don't understand." He held up his leg and pointed to his ankle. "My ankle is hurt. And I'm awfully hungry." He made motions as if eating. The man nodded and took a small loaf of bread from his satchel. He gave it to Josef. "Thank you, thank you. Merci." He ate ravenously.

The man continued staring at Josef and spoke again to his horse. The horse whinnied. When Josef had consumed the last bit of bread, the man pointed at him and then at the wagon. Josef immediately nodded and clambered aboard. The wagon bumped along for hours, making him conscious of every bruise and sore spot. At last they pulled up to an old farmhouse, much in need of repair. A white-haired woman stood waiting in the doorway. She said a few words to her husband. He extracted two small coins from his stocking and handed them over to her. Then he nodded at Josef and explained how he had found him.

For nearly a month, Josef lived with the old couple. They fed him well with fresh vegetables, milk and cheese, eggs from their henhouse, and bread baked on the hearth. Josef quickly learned enough French to communicate. As his injuries healed, he helped with farm chores, weeding and harvesting, tending the cow and chickens, and making repairs to the house. He felt useful and appreciated. One day the woman approached him while he was working in the vegetable garden.

"Josef, you are like a son to us," she said. Josef looked up and smiled. "We had a son once," she continued. "His name was Jean-Pierre. He was a good boy who would've looked after us in our old age. But it was not to be."

Josef brushed the dirt off his hands. "What happened?"

She spoke in a hushed voice. "Typhoid fever. He was just twenty." Josef shook his head in sympathy. The woman's voice became more animated. "But now the good Lord has sent you to us. You can be the son we lost. Don't you see?"

Josef closed his eyes, trying to decide what to say. He loved these people. Their way of life was physically demanding, but also wholesome and satisfying. He felt sure they would turn the farm over to him if he stayed. Yet he could not stay. He knew his vocation lay elsewhere. He had a little education and he wanted more. How could he explain this to country folk who never left their own farm except to sell produce in the next village? What could he possibly say to make them understand?

"Thank you, Maman. You are most kind." He looked into her haggard face. "In the city where I come from, there are priests and monks who are educated. Some of them taught me to read Latin and a little Greek."

"Yes, that is well and good. But too much learning will make your head explode."

Josef smiled. "My head is hard like a rock." He took her rough hand in his. "Maman, it pains me to say this, but I will have to leave you before too long. When your old man found me, I was on my way to Poitiers to study at the abbey. I need to learn more so that some day I may become a priest or a teacher. Do you understand, Maman?"

The woman's shoulders slumped. "Then you are not the one we have been waiting for. We must wait a little longer. Surely the Lord will provide help for us." She turned and slowly plodded back to the house.

Josef stayed another two weeks. When he left, the old farmer insisted on going with him as far as the main road and, once there, gave directions to the nearest village. His wife prepared a large sack of food for him to take along. The rest of the journey to Poitiers was difficult but uneventful. When his food ran out, Josef hunted or scavenged. He remembered when he was a little boy, how his mother took him along to glean in the fields around Worms. He knew what crops to look for and which parts were edible. Except in extreme hunger, he took only from fields that had already been harvested. When he finally approached the walls of Poitiers, he was tired and hungry and sun-burned. In the dusk of twilight, the city looked grey and gloomy. Nevertheless, Josef felt a surge of hope and resolved to make a new beginning.

PART TWO

| 4852–4865 | Jewish Calendar |
| 1092–1105 | Christian Calendar |

Chapter 13

Miriam was worried about her brother. He seemed anxious all the time. It was certainly lamentable that his wife had lost two babies to miscarriage. But did Mosche's anxiety make things any easier for the unfortunate woman? Johanna was again suffering the discomforts of pregnancy, her third in four years. Could Mosche not see how hurtful his behavior was to her well-being (and his too)? He was constantly running back and forth between the synagogue and his house, always ready to panic if anything seemed amiss. Miriam would speak to her brother and try to make him calm down.

On a hot day in summer, Mosche appeared at her door. He seemed excited. "Miriam, I've got some surprising news for you."

She motioned for him to come inside. "I'm glad you're here. I've been wanting to talk to you. Can your news wait a minute?"

He frowned and fidgeted on his feet. "I suppose so."

"Look, Mosche. Ever since I've known you, my whole life long, you've been one of the calmest, most level-headed people I know. But recently you've done nothing but worry. It doesn't help matters."

"That's easy for you to say. You've got a fine, strapping son and two beautiful daughters" (he glanced at her midsection) "and another baby on the way. If only my wife bore children so easily as you."

Miriam closed her eyes and exhaled slowly. "Mosche, I know it's been hard for you. But if you torment yourself, and Johanna too, with worry, then neither of you will survive to raise your children. Please, if you can't be calm, can you at least hide your anxiety from Johanna? Don't go home so often during the day. Let her rest."

Mosche pursed his lips. "All right, Miriam. I'll try. It won't be easy."

Miriam kissed her brother on the cheek. "Now, what's your news?" she asked.

"I heard Josef is back in town."

Miriam's face became flushed but she said nothing.

"His mother is very ill, perhaps at the point of death. Someone apparently sent word to him. He's staying with her in the rooms on Market Street, where he used to live."

"Will you try to see him?"

"I wouldn't mind. But you know he's been away for six years. Who knows what he thinks or feels about anything. Maybe he'd rather stay away from us."

Miriam nodded in agreement. She sat down and began rummaging through her sewing basket. Mosche took this as a signal that it was time for him to go. He had intended to stop by his house to see how his wife was doing, but after Miriam's reproof, he decided to go straight back to the synagogue.

Miriam wanted to be alone so she could think. What would it be like to see Josef again after so many years? He was, after all, her first love. And before that he'd been a good friend to her and her brother. Ever since she could remember, she'd looked up to Josef as a thoughtful, intelligent person who might have become a first-rate scholar. He was a little naïve sometimes and less assertive than most of the scholars she knew. But this was part of his charm and one of the reasons she had fallen in love with him. Now he was back. Would her peaceful existence be disturbed? She had been quite happy, hadn't she, over the past six years? And even if she couldn't honestly say she felt a passionate attraction for her husband, was she not very fond of him? And appreciative of his kindness? Ehud had always treated her gently and considerately. To the children he was a devoted father, showing no partiality and not even a hint of suspicion. Admittedly, he was not an especially observant person, but how could he fail to see it when others remarked (in his presence) how different their son looked from the girls? It was hard not to notice. Aaron had curly reddish hair and green eyes, while the girls were dark-eyed with smooth black hair. Yet Ehud doted on them all, Aaron just as much as the girls. Such a happy family and, she had to admit, a good marriage.

What if she met Josef on the street? How would he react? What would he think about her children? Would he suspect anything? She and Josef were much older now and more in control of themselves. Or were they? Would all the emotions they had felt six years ago come flooding back? Now Miriam was agitated. She did not fail to see the irony in the situation. When Mosche stepped across her threshold, she had done her best to make him calmer. At the same time, he had brought news that made her anxious. She hoped she could regain her composure before Ehud returned.

Just then she heard noises in the next room. The children were waking from their naps. Usually she would try to finish some chores or rest a few minutes until she was sure they were wide awake. But not today. It would be a relief for her to have them running around. With all their needs to be met, there would be no time to fret about Josef's return. Once they were cleaned and fed, she would play games with them until their father came home.

A few weeks later, Mosche knocked on his sister's door. He was smiling and holding a piece of parchment in his hand. Miriam welcomed him with a kiss. "Sister, I've seen Josef. He actually came to find me at the synagogue. Look what he gave me."

Miriam took the parchment and scanned its contents. "Is it a commentary on Torah? The script is not familiar to me."

"Yes. From Rabbi Scholomo himself! Josef met him during his travels. The rabbi gave him this and he saved it especially for me."

"That was thoughtful. Have you read it?"

"Yes, it concerns the *Shema* and the sentences that come just after. Let me read you what it says. First there's the quotation 'Hear, O Israel . . .' about loving the Lord with all your heart and so forth. Then comes 'And these words which I command thee this day shall be in thy heart: And thou shalt teach them diligently unto thy children . . .' You recognize the text, I'm sure."

"Yes, those are familiar words," said Miriam.

"I have worried about this passage because I have no children of my own to teach. But listen to what Rabbi Scholomo says about it: 'These are the disciples. Everywhere do we find that disciples are called "children," as Moses said to the people, "Ye are children to the Lord your God . . ." and even as the disciples are called children, so the teacher is called "father," as Elisha said to Elijah, "My father, my father, the chariot of Israel!"' Rabbi Scholomo is saying that a teacher's students are his children!"

"Interesting idea."

"For me, it's a great relief," said Mosche. "It reassures me that God is providing children for me. Even if my wife never bears a child who lives past infancy, I already have many sons in the Jeschiba, and I will have many, many more."

Miriam raised her eyebrows. "I wish you had a few such daughters."

Mosche rolled his eyes. "Miriam, you never change." He patted her shoulder. "I think I didn't properly thank you for the sisterly advice you gave me last month. I've tried very hard to be less anxious and it *has* made things better between me and Johanna. Now that I've seen what Rabbi Scholomo says about teachers and students, I think I'll worry even less. By the way, Josef sent his greetings."

"He did?"

"Yes, and he wanted to know how things were going with you."

"What did you tell him?"

"That you're happily married with three children. He's had an interesting time since he left Worms."

"Doing what?"

"He went to the abbey in Poitiers, but didn't really know what sort of place it was. At first he thought there would be no other options except preparing for priesthood or life in a monastery. He found out otherwise."

Miriam looked inquiringly at her brother.

"It turned out the abbot was a jolly old fellow with many interesting ideas. After interviewing Josef, he decided to put him to work, first as a Latin tutor to the sons of a local nobleman. Josef said he enjoyed teaching and observing life on the estate, though the family treated him little better than they did their farm hands. Meanwhile at the abbey he studied philosophy, theology, and Greek, taught by monks or the abbot himself."

"I'm sure he enjoyed that."

"He did. But once the abbot found out Josef knew Hebrew, everything changed. Suddenly he was elevated to the position of scribe, translator, and teacher of Hebrew at the abbey. His former teachers became his students. That was all it took to convince Josef that his chosen profession would be teaching. Whether to do that as a priest or a layman, he could not decide, and so he put off the decision. The abbot supported him completely."

"Did he continue to study Greek and the other subjects?"

"Yes. Eventually he studied Latin grammar, rhetoric, and logic as well. Occasionally the monks discussed other topics, such as music, astronomy, and mathematics. As I said to Josef, these things are completely foreign to me."

"Maybe he'll teach you what he's learned?"

Mosche laughed. "That would take years. You know my time is completely taken up with Torah and Talmud. It's enough to keep any man occupied for a lifetime."

"Did Josef say how his mother is doing?"

"She is quite ill, in a great deal of pain. She was able to recognize Josef when he first appeared—he was thankful for that. Now I think she is barely conscious." Mosche got up to leave.

"Thanks for stopping by, brother. Don't make your 'children' work too hard."

Over the next few weeks, Miriam tried to stay busy. She didn't want to think too much about Josef. Yet she couldn't help it. Her thoughts kept drifting back to the time they had spent together, reading, discussing Torah, talking about personal matters. She also thought about her children and her husband, and about the sanctity of marriage. A passage from the fifth book of Moses came into her mind, as it had many times in the last six years: "If a damsel that is a virgin be betrothed unto a man, and a man find her in the city, and lie with her: Then shall ye lead them both out unto the gate of that city, and ye shall stone them with stones that they die; the damsel because she cried not for aid in the city; and the man, because he hath done violence to his neighbor's wife, and thou shalt put away the evil from the midst of thee." Miriam knew this passage applied to her. While she and Josef had actually been outside the city wall when it happened, she did not cry for help, nor did she want to. She was guilty. But did she regret her actions, her tacit expression of love for Josef? What was to regret? Perhaps if there had been some terrible outcome, she would have been sorry. Women in the community who gave birth to a harelip or a cripple often attributed it to their own sinfulness. Mosche's wife, for example, had searched her past for the sins that caused two stillborn children. Scripture told them that Bathsheba's child died after it was conceived in adultery with King David. Miriam was indeed grateful no horrible punishment had resulted from her sin. On one level she repented her actions because she knew they were wrong. The community would have condemned her if they knew. Yet still she could feel no regret.

Now, however, things were different. She was wife to a good man and mother to his children. Nothing must be allowed to jeopardize their marriage. Miriam resolved to keep her thoughts and actions in check. If she met Josef, she would treat him as a friend and nothing more. In the meantime, she would focus her attention on her family.

Miriam's life went on as usual. She was happily occupied with her children, and Ehud remained as gentle and placid as ever. Josef's return to Worms might have slipped her mind entirely, had not Mosche from time to time mentioned seeing him. One brisk fall morning she was coming out of Jews' Alley on her way to the old market. She carried a large basket and wore a shawl around her head and neck as protection from the cold wind. Walking along Market Street, she heard footsteps coming up behind her. Someone tapped her lightly on the shoulder.

"Excuse me, ma'am. I think you dropped this."

Miriam turned to see a man holding out a small leather purse that she recognized to be her own. She raised her eyes to thank him, but no words came out. It was Josef standing before her. He also stood silent for a few awkward moments. Finally he said, "Miriam, I'm sorry. I didn't know it was you."

She smiled. "And if you had known? Would you have left the purse on the ground?"

"No, of course not. I would have found another way to return it. I've been trying to stay away so as not to intrude on your life."

"Well, now that we've met, it's all right to speak to one another. Which way are you going?"

"To the market."

"So am I."

They turned and began walking slowly along Market Street. Miriam spoke first. "Mosche said your mother was very ill."

"She was. She died two weeks ago."

"I'm sorry to hear that. What will you do now?"

"For the time being, I'm going to stay in her rooms. I want to see if I can get employment around here as a tutor or teacher."

They walked on without speaking for some minutes. Josef cleared his throat. "Mosche told me you were happily married?"

"Yes, very happy."

"And you have three children?"

"That's right. They're with their grandmother." Miriam was glad she had left the children with her mother. It might be awkward if Josef saw them and started asking questions.

He suddenly stopped walking and said, "Look, Miriam, I'll go back home if you want. I can come to the market later."

"It's all right, Josef," she replied. "I don't mind talking with you."

They walked on. After a few minutes of silence, he said, "May I ask about Mosche? He seems changed somehow, more subdued than he used to be."

Miriam nodded. "Did he tell you his wife lost two children to miscarriage?"

"No, he said nothing about that. He did tell me she's expecting a child. How long have they been married?"

"Four years."

"Mosche seems very emotional about his marriage. He told me what a great blessing it was to him. He must love his wife dearly."

"He does. And we all agree she's a sweetheart. But not having children is a great disappointment to him. He always assumed he could plan out his life and everything would fall into place."

As they approached the market square, Josef offered to meet her later and carry her basket home for her. Miriam expressed thanks but declined the offer. That evening she reflected on her meeting with Josef. It was a great relief to her that she no longer felt attracted to him. There was a cordiality between them, and admittedly a little awkwardness, but that was all. Now she knew for sure that her marriage to Ehud was right and good. From the beginning, her husband had taken to heart his responsibilities in this "holy covenant" (as the rabbis called it). He had honored and protected her as a woman, yet treated her as a partner in day-to-day affairs. Furthermore, he had allowed her a certain degree of freedom. Never had he objected to her reading or attending sermons and discussions at the schoolhouse. He didn't mind if she left the children with their grandmother, and he even offered to watch them himself on occasion. What pleased her most was that Ehud now took a greater interest in scholarly endeavors. He had always been a pious man, but lately he spent more time at the school, considering points of Law with the other men. She had certainly underestimated his intellectual capabilities. Miriam remembered a passage from Talmud: "A good and virtuous wife expands a man's character." In her case, it was mostly the reverse: his goodness and virtue had made her better. Whether she had any effect on him she could not say. But she hoped she'd inspired him just a little.

On a snowy evening in midwinter, Miriam delivered her fourth child, a son. Ehud celebrated the next day by taking a holiday from his work. He rose early in the morning, washed his hands and face in preparation for prayers, and recited psalms of thanksgiving. This day he would go twice to the synagogue. In the morning he would make a special visit to offer additional prayers of thanks. Later he would take his older son to the evening service, as he often did on week days. Young Aaron was already showing promising signs that he would be a scholar, and his father did all he could to encourage him in that direction.

Miriam lay in bed, weary but overjoyed to have another son. Her little girls doted over the baby, patting his head and whispering in his ears, while Aaron stood watching solemnly from the corner of the room. An hour or so after her husband left for the synagogue, Miriam heard the local *shammash* announcing their happy news from the street corner. Now that the community was informed of the birth, she could expect gifts to begin appearing on her doorstep. It was indeed a joyful day, yet she felt a touch of sadness. Her brother would hear the *shammash* today and again on the eighth day when the circumcision was announced. Mosche would certainly be reminded of the two children he had lost, as he was every time a birth occurred in the community. Yet there was new hope. Johanna was now six months into her pregnancy, longer than she had ever carried a child before. Miriam resolved to say a prayer every day, a plea that the child would come to full term.

Because it was such a cold winter, Miriam decided to prolong her time at home from the usual five weeks following childbirth. She would bathe in the *miqveh* on the customary day, of course (it would be freezing cold!), but after that she would not resume her normal activities. In her role as translator and interpreter for women attending synagogue, she would certainly be missed. Her husband's wool shop, too, would lose an extra helper while she was away. She never spent more than two or three hours there on a given day, but her presence allowed Ehud more time to deal with customers and merchants outside the shop. Fortunately, he had found a reliable foreman for his sheep farm in the hills west of the city. Ever since their marriage, Miriam reflected, Ehud had become a homebody, spending far more time in town than at the farm. She, too, found more pleasure in domestic life. In her youth, Miriam never thought she would want to stay home all day with children, but she was truly looking forward to it. Even with her outside activities curtailed, there would be plenty to keep her busy. After all, she now had four children, a husband, and a household to look after.

Ehud soon fell into a pattern of going to the synagogue twice every day. Now that Aaron was six, he attended school with the other boys. His father walked with him early each morning to the schoolhouse and stayed on with the other men to pray, study, and discuss Torah. Aaron was so eager to learn and practice the faith that Ehud thought it best to take him to services every evening. Miriam was delighted to see father and son encouraging each other to be devout Jews. Meanwhile, she did her part. On Fridays, she cleaned the kitchen thoroughly, kneaded dough, prepared savory meats, and carefully planned the Sabbath meals. When the men arrived home after the evening service, a white tablecloth had already been laid. Miriam herself lit the Sabbath lamp and recited the appointed prayers. With great glee, Aaron welcomed to the meal the two angels who, according to legend, followed a man and his son home from the synagogue. These family meals were some of the happiest times Miriam could remember in her life.

Chapter 14

About ten weeks later, when the first purple crocuses had just poked through the snow, Mosche knocked vigorously at Miriam's door. On seeing him, she could tell immediately that he was exuberant.

"Miriam, I have a son!" His voice was loud but hoarse. He looked bedraggled.

"Can you come in for a minute?" she asked.

"No, I want to get back to Johanna as quickly as I can. She had a hard time of it all day yesterday and most of the night."

"Is she all right?"

"Getting better. Her mother's with her. And the midwife is still there, too. I'll come back tomorrow and tell you more. I need to go by the synagogue now and report the news." He jumped off the front stoop and began running.

"Don't forget your thanksgiving prayers!" Miriam called after him. She stood watching as her brother disappeared around a corner. It was good to see him happy and excited, the way she remembered him from childhood.

But Mosche did not come the next day, or the next after that. When he did return, he seemed subdued. Miriam invited him inside.

"We've missed seeing you these two days, brother. There's nothing wrong, I hope?"

"The boy is not robust. I've spent many hours praying in the synagogue."

Miriam sighed. "My prayers will be added to yours," she said. They sat quietly for a few moments. Then she said, "Mosche, you haven't even told us your son's name."

"His name is Nataniel."

A quiet smile came over Miriam's face. "Gift from God," she said. "How is Johanna doing?"

"She's recovering very well. She said to thank you for the cakes and swaddling cloth. And also to make sure you know when the *berit milah* is scheduled."

"Yes, thank you. We'll be there. Ehud found out from the rabbi when it would be."

"I've invited Josef to come."

Miriam looked startled. "It's a little unusual, isn't it, to invite a Christian?"

"Yes. But he's been a good friend. He came by to ask about Nataniel, and we talked a long time."

Four days later, Miriam and Mosche's extended family and many friends gathered in the synagogue for the solemn covenant ceremony of *berit milah*. Early that morning the *shammash* had announced to the community that a child would be circumcised on this day. After broadcasting the news from street corners, he knocked on doors of those most closely connected to the family. Many were already awake, anticipating the festive occasion.

When Miriam first saw little Nataniel, she was stunned. Even with prior knowledge that he was "not robust," as Mosche put it, she was unprepared for what her eyes told her. The baby was small and pale, with raised cheekbones protruding from its tiny face. Bald spots on Nataniel's head were interspersed with patches of stringy black hair. What she could see of his arms and legs twitched in jerky motions. It was like looking at a withered old man wrapped in swaddling bands. She couldn't help comparing his appearance with that of her newborn babies, who had been pink, chubby, and fuzzy-headed.

The ceremony began when Mosche lifted his son from the arms of the godmother and carried him across the room. He handed him to the *mohel*, an experienced surgeon who would perform the operation. First, however, the *mohel* set little Nataniel in a tall chair with massive armrests and said, "This is the chair of Elijah the prophet, of blessed memory." Miriam recalled that Elijah was regarded by ancient rabbis as the angel of the covenant, whose spirit was present at all circumcisions. Next the *mohel* lifted the baby onto a cushion held in the godfather's lap. This was a good thing, thought Miriam, that someone other than nervous parents should hold the baby while surgery was performed. After reciting certain blessings, the *mohel* undressed the child and proceeded to cut off the foreskin. He worked deliberately with a steady hand. Immediately he put his lips on the wound to draw off the blood. A linen cloth was wrapped carefully around Nataniel's middle, and he was dressed. Once again the child was handed to his father, who took him tenderly in his arms and said another blessing. Miriam detected a slight unsteadiness in Mosche's voice as he spoke the traditional prayer: "O Lord, who hath favored us with the commandments and hath commanded us to bring our sons into the covenant made with Abraham, we ask thy blessing on this child." More prayers were said, and the child was given the name Nataniel ben Mosche. To conclude the ceremony, a hymn was sung by all those in the synagogue.

Now came the celebration! The crowd made its way to the school-house, where the large assembly room doubled as a dance hall. Tables were already spread with delectable foods, and more platters kept appearing. Wine was brought up from the cellar beneath the hall. A small band played festive music, inspiring some of the energetic young men to show off their dance steps. Before the party became too lively, the officiating rabbi raised his hands for silence. He motioned for Mosche and his family to come forward, while he invited the little children in the hall to move closer so they could see the baby. Miriam's three older ones scampered forward, as did a dozen others. Everyone watched as Mosche carried a small crib to the center of the room and set it down. Johanna walked by his side, carrying a large Torah scroll. The rabbi took the scroll, blessed the boy again, and prayed that he might study and uphold the Law. He turned to Johanna, handed the scroll back to her, and enjoined her to use all her skill in making a cloth Torah binder for her son. It went through Miriam's mind that she should offer to help Johanna with this task, as she had made two before for her sons. These wraps were customarily made from the bloodstained linen cloths used to bind the circumcision wound. Most were relatively simple, but Miriam had embellished hers with embroidery, giving the name, date of birth, and words of blessing for her sons. Perhaps Johanna would want to do the same.

Mosche led his family to a corner of the room, ending the formal ceremony. The party soon became noisy and spirited. Miriam looked around at the crowd. She saw her older children playing tag with their father. The baby was asleep in a cloth pouch on her stomach. She strolled over to one of the tables and picked up a couple of blintses. They were her favorites, filled with currant jam. While eating, she saw Josef standing in a far corner with two other men. It looked as if they were engrossed in serious conversation. She walked toward them to see if she could tell who the men were. Now she could see they were the Levi brothers. These were two men she disliked intensely, arrogant, brash, and belligerent. What business could they have with Josef? She moved a little closer, hoping to hear some of their conversation. Over the noisy festivities in the hall, she was able to distinguish sharp, spiteful words directed at her friend. It was worse than she feared. The brothers were quoting from the *Sefer Toledot Jeschu*, a bitter satire on the life of Jesus. She had once seen a copy that was passed stealthily from hand to hand around the community. Some people found it amusing, but to Miriam it was sickening. Its object was clearly to stir up contempt and hatred toward Christians and their faith. The book defended the execution of Jesus, mocked his miracles as sleight of hand, and dismissed the so-called resurrection as an elaborate deception. Jesus himself was painted in caricature. His mother was said to have been raped. Those who followed him were called "apostates," and the Christian sacraments equated with idolatry. What must Josef think? He had probably never heard such venom from Jews before. Would this make him think less highly of them, perhaps leading him to believe some of the less charitable opinions held by Christians? Miriam continued to watch from a distance, fearing that her intervention might provoke a scene. The brothers seemed to be challenging Josef to respond, yet he remained surprisingly calm. Occasionally he nodded and said a few words. The conversation came to an end, upon which Josef abruptly left the hall.

Miriam was embarrassed. She gritted her teeth. Her anger seethed at those two idiots who used this joyful occasion as an opportunity to sow discord. When could she tell Josef how sorry she was? Certainly she could not visit him at his house. Later she would ask Mosche to seek him out and speak for both of them. Josef must not be allowed to think all Jews shared these hateful sentiments.

The next day Miriam visited her brother and his family. After looking in on the baby and sharing motherly advice with Johanna, she took Mosche aside and told him what she had witnessed. He promised to speak with Josef about it. Later that week, he came to report on his visit.

"I've been to see Josef," he said.

"Was he upset?"

"Yes, very upset. But not for the reason you think. He dismissed the Levi brothers' assertions as 'silly prattle.' He said it was no worse than the crazy stuff Christians say about Jews. In fact, Josef enjoyed the *berit milah*. He was impressed by the ceremony. And of course he liked the food—said it was a 'breakfast to remember.'"

"I'm relieved to hear that. But then what was he upset about?"

"He met someone yesterday, someone he'd never seen before."

"Is that unusual?"

"Let me give you the story the way Josef told it to me. Then you can decide what you think. About mid-morning he was in the courtyard by his house, getting ready to carry water buckets to some of the other residents. You know he's doing whatever jobs he can find to make a few pennies."

Miriam nodded.

"Well, suddenly there was a clomping of hooves and a clatter of gear as an armed knight rode into the courtyard. Without dismounting, he surveyed the area, made some remark under his breath about 'nothing changed,' and then asked Josef if a woman named Agnes still lived there. You remember, that was Josef's mother's name. He told the man no, she didn't. The knight asked if he knew where she was, and he said yes. At that point, the man dismounted and tied his horse to a post."

"Who was the man?" Miriam asked.

"I'll get to that. Josef observed him carefully. He was a handsome man, even dashing, with smooth manners. He asked for a cup of wine, but Josef had only water to offer him. The man said he was passing through Worms on his way to a tournament and thought he'd try to find an old acquaintance, someone he'd spent a good deal of time with. That was Agnes, of course. He boasted that she had been a beautiful young woman, one of many he'd known. But Agnes was special. He had felt genuine affection for her. Somehow she got the impression he would marry her and take her to live on his family's estate. Women are so silly, he said. Of course he couldn't do that. Josef asked him why not. The man looked scornfully at Josef. 'Because she was a low-class wench,' he said with an impatient voice. 'Besides, I already had a wife. But of course Agnes didn't know that.' Then he made a sarcastic comment about women not understanding men's affairs."

Miriam grimaced. "What a cad."

Mosche nodded in agreement. "Can you guess where this is going?"

"I'm afraid so," she answered.

"Well, the knight chattered on while Josef listened. The man's wife had died recently and he was looking for comfort. He said his 'little

Agnes' had always been good in bed, in fact, much better than his wife. He might even want to take her home now to be his mistress, if she was still as good-looking as he remembered. 'Tell me where I can find the old girl,' he asked. Josef told him she was dead. The man gave an involuntary jerk of the head. He asked all about the circumstances of her death and concluded with the question, 'Who are you, that you know so much about this dead woman?' 'Her son,' he answered. This gave the knight pause, and he looked more closely at Josef. 'Her son?' he asked. 'I never knew she had a child.' He seemed to be considering in his mind certain possibilities. Finally he said with contempt, 'Don't get any ideas. Even if we are related, which I doubt, you won't get your hands on any of my fortune. Your mother probably slept with scores of men. You could never prove you were my whelp.'"

Miriam groaned and put her hands over her face. "What happened then?"

"Josef stood with clenched jaw and stared at the man. He told me it was all he could do not to strangle him. He was sure this man was his father and yet he wanted nothing at all to do with him."

"Did the swine get away without being strangled?"

"Yes, he left quickly. Josef never found out the man's name, but he didn't care. He said he's better off not knowing."

"Maybe so," said Miriam.

It was weeks before she heard any more about Josef. When Mosche saw him again, he learned that Josef was still having difficulty finding gainful employment. Father Albert had asked him to teach the catechism class for young children at St. Paul's Church, which he was happy to do, but there was no salary. He inquired about working again at city hall and was told that he might be hired occasionally for special projects. Apparently Frieder now had two full-time assistants, one to help with paperwork and another for field work. There were two places in Worms where Josef's skills in reading and writing would be truly valued, St. Andreas Monastery and the Jeschiba. Yet it was certain that neither institution would hire him. The only paying jobs he could find were menial labor, of the sort his mother had done all her life. He would have to be satisfied with that for now.

Miriam spent as much time as she could with Mosche's family. She took her children frequently to visit their new cousin. When she could find a babysitter, she went without them. Although Miriam was three years younger than Johanna, she nevertheless had considerably more experience with infants. Her sister-in-law was insecure about her own abilities and seemed grateful for any advice and assistance she could offer. But Miriam had another reason for spending time there. She loved to watch Mosche with his little son. Her brother doted on the boy, carried him around everywhere, and spoke to him in the sweetest voice possible. It was a side of her brother she had never seen. Probably his tenderness was magnified because he waited so long for a child of his own. But there was another reason, too, for his gentle watchfulness. Little Nataniel was not thriving. He was quite small for his age and often had trouble breathing. It sounded as if his lungs were full of water. Miriam was sick at heart each time the baby suffered a coughing spell. His parents could do nothing more for him, the doctors said, than pat him on the back in hopes of getting the fluid to settle. Miriam guessed from comments she overheard that one or the other of Nataniel's parents stayed up with him all night.

Life in the Jewish quarter went on as usual. Even as regional leaders, lay and clergy, issued decrees granting certain rights to Jews, the Church in Rome continued to hold overarching influence. The first Pope Gregory had declared that, while Jews should not be treated with violence, yet they enjoyed no rights except those specifically granted by law. In the 500 years since his decree, little had changed. A few enlightened leaders of Church and State had advocated kindness to all. In rescuing Jews from injustice, the good King Louis (the first of that name) said that Christian teaching exhorts mortals to take inspiration from Divine mercy in their relationships with everyone, regardless of beliefs. His words gave new hope to persecuted people of all faiths. But more common were statements like those of Bishop Agobard of Lyons, who said Jews were under a curse and clothed with it as with a garment. "They are cursed in the town and cursed in the countryside; cursed when they come in and cursed when they go out; cursed are their children and their livestock; cursed are their houses, their barns, what they drink and what they eat, and even the crumbs that fall from the table. And none of them shall escape from this horrible, this ghastly, curse of the Law, except by Him who became a

Curse for us." The bishop believed the curse had entered into the bodies of Jews "like oil into their bones."

Still, life went on. In good times, Jews enjoyed amicable relations with their Christian neighbors. In tense times, they kept to themselves. Always they were required to follow certain rules, such as to refrain from working on Sundays and to stay off the streets during Holy Week. The chosen head of the Jewish community, ironically called the "Jewish bishop," was charged to enforce these rules. He and his council of elders also saw to it that their own laws were observed. For a minor (but serious) infraction against Torah, a man might be given a beating before his congregation, followed immediately by corporate prayers for atonement and forgiveness. For a major infraction, a person could be expelled from the synagogue, cut off completely from family and friends, and treated as dead. In general, Jewish settlements along the Rhein were well-ordered communities.

One problem faced by Jews in Worms and all across the region was overcrowding. Their population increased, yet their streets, houses, and meeting places did not expand. The cramped Jewish quarter was not permitted to annex additional land in the city. Construction of new synagogues was forbidden by Church law. Thus more and more people squeezed into the same spaces. Apartments that previously held one family now held two or three. Worshippers at Sabbath services spilled out into the courtyard or adjoining buildings. Somehow the people endured these conditions. Strict adherence to their laws prevented chaos from breaking out.

Miriam and her family were lucky. Ehud's father had been a prosperous merchant, traveling eastward for long distances to trade in wool and linen cloth. As his wealth grew, he invested in property. Thus the family held title to three houses in Worms, connected to each other and to the city wall behind. For now, at least, Ehud and his wife and children occupied the entire upper floor, consisting of three large rooms, in one of the houses. Miriam knew this could change at any time. It might become necessary for more family members to move in with them, but until then, they would enjoy the relative spaciousness of their home.

Nevertheless, when weather permitted, Miriam found it more and more desirable to take her children outdoors. Aaron and the girls were bright and energetic and curious about everything. They loved walking in the streets and, even more, running in the fields outside the city wall. On days when Aaron was not in school, they often set out early with a picnic lunch and hiked down to the river. On one such day in early spring, Aaron ran ahead while Miriam carried the baby in a pouch on her back and held each of her girls by the hand. They passed through Jews' Gate into the fields, following a footpath toward the river. After a delightful morning examining flower buds and insect larvae, they settled on the banks of the river to eat lunch and watch the boats go by. Within a few minutes, clouds rolled in and heavy drops began to fall. Miriam quickly put the baby back in his pouch and gathered up the other children for the walk home. The rain became steady, and her littlest girl started to cry. Miriam picked her up and hurried clumsily up the path. Aaron was trying his best to pull the other girl along, but they walked slower and slower, and finally Miriam had to stop and wait. She saw a man in the distance walking toward them. Should she appeal to him for help? He drew closer. With a mixture of relief and dismay, she recognized that it was Josef. Miriam quickly explained to him what had happened. Immediately, he lifted one girl in each arm and led the group as fast as they could go uphill to the city gate. They stood under its shelter and watched as the rain came down harder and harder. Miriam turned to her friend.

"Thank you, Josef. You came along at exactly the right time."

"I'm glad to help."

"How did you happen to be crossing the field just then?"

"I recently started working for a farmer, keeping his accounts. Once or twice a week I go out to the farm and look things over."

"So you found a job at last? Mosche said you'd had some trouble with that."

"Yes, but it's not enough to live on. I have another job, too. The old priest, Father Albert, hired me as part-time sexton at his church. Between the two, I earn enough so I can eat."

"Good thing. I know you like to eat."

The rain continued to fall. Miriam glanced at her children. They had invented a game, touching as many stones in the wall under the gate as they could reach. Little Eva, only three, was having a hard time keeping up with her older siblings. She was standing a little apart, her lower lip protruding and her eyes glistening. The pitiful scene brought a smile to Josef's face. Quickly he scooped Eva into his arms and lifted her high above the other children. She reached out and put her hands on the wall, telling her brother and sister she had touched highest.

"You like being up high?" asked Josef.

Eva nodded and giggled. Josef set her on his shoulders and went back to stand beside Miriam.

"Look, Mama, how big I am!" said Eva.

"I can see that." After a minute or two, during which the older children resumed their game, Miriam turned again to Josef. "You lived a long time in an abbey. Did you consider full-time work with the Church?"

"You mean priesthood?" Josef hesitated. "No," he said finally. "The abbot in Poitiers taught me a great deal about the Church. And about myself. I've come to love and appreciate the faith, but that's not my calling."

"I think you should be a teacher, like Mosche," said Miriam. Josef smiled and nodded. Then she asked, "Have you seen him lately?"

"Yes, he's quite a family man now. He said everyone should marry and have a family. It certainly suits him well."

"It does. I love to watch him with his son. But I worry, too."

Josef said he knew what she meant. The rain finally let up, and Miriam led her children home, thoroughly tired out and wet from the day's adventures.

Chapter 15

Late one afternoon, as Miriam descended the stairs of her house with her children in tow, she heard a soft voice calling from one of the rooms on the ground floor. It was her mother-in-law's room. Miriam quickly turned and knocked on the door, opening it slightly. The voice bade her come in. The three older children scampered ahead of her and ran to a figure seated in the corner.

"Grandmama, we're going to visit Papa at his shop," said the older girl.

"That's lovely, sweetheart. Give him a kiss for me, won't you?"

"Yes, Grandmama. We're taking him his supper, too. Your kiss can be his dessert."

The old woman laughed and blew a kiss to the child. With a more serious expression, she turned to her daughter-in-law. "Miriam, I'm worried. I sent Sofi out this morning to pick up a few things at the market. She hasn't come back. It's not like her to be away for more than an hour or two."

"That is worrisome. Most of the vendors at the market know her. I'm sure they would bring her home if she were injured or confused. Shall I stop by the market to inquire?"

"Yes, please. And mention it to Ehud when you see him. I can barely get along without that girl. I don't know what I'll do if she's gone."

"Don't fret, Mama. We'll look after you if need be." Miriam shepherded her four children toward the door. As they walked to the market, she considered the situation. Sofi had been with the family for nearly twenty years. Ehud's father had found her on one of his trading expeditions to the east. He had seen her on the street, a beggar child no more than eight years old. Apparently an orphan, she looked malnourished and had bruises on her arms and legs. The wealthy merchant took pity on the child, brought her home, and made her a part of his family. As time passed, they expected her to learn the local language, but she never said a word. At first they thought she might be deaf or simple-minded. Neither of these proved to be the case. Regardless, she was a willing child, and helpful. Ehud's mother taught her as she would her own daughter, first to do simple household chores and to select produce at the market. Later Sofi learned to cook and sew, and eventually to do fine needlework. Yet still she did not speak. After Ehud's father died, his mother depended entirely on Sofi to do her shopping, prepare her meals, and help her move about the room. Mama still had strength enough to stand on her own, but her lack of balance made walking difficult.

What if Sofi never returned? Would Miriam be saddled with more responsibility? Her children now ranged in age from two to eight. Aaron was in school most of the day, but in the evenings he still needed help with his lessons. The next oldest child, Susanna, almost seven, was quite responsible—she could keep her younger siblings amused and happy for an hour or two. Even so, Eva and Daniel required much of Miriam's time and attention. If only Susanna were a few years older, she would make an excellent companion and helper for her grandmother. But why was Miriam fretting about a situation that might not arise? In all likelihood, Sofi would be found. She would return to the old woman and all would be well. Yet Miriam had an uneasy feeling. Something serious must have happened. Sofi seemed quite happy in her home and had never wandered away before.

Miriam carried the youngest child in one arm and led the others, linked by their hands, into the market square. She spoke with vendors she knew, inquiring if Sofi had stopped by that morning. Several had seen her and noticed nothing amiss. Finally one woman told her she'd seen a friendly young priest talking to Sofi, and she thought they left together. It had attracted her attention because the young man was carrying a large pastry and a pail of fresh strawberries. Miriam groaned.

"Sofi loves strawberries. Did you see which way they went?"

"I think towards St. Martin's Square."

Miriam couldn't haul her children all through town looking for Sofi. Anyhow, too much time had passed, and there wasn't much hope of finding her right away. She would tell her husband what she had learned. He could follow up later, after he closed the shop or perhaps early tomorrow morning. At least Sofi was not wandering around the city by herself. Miriam hoped the young priest was honest and decent. Sofi might be strong enough to fight off a bodily attack, but she had no defense against smooth words.

That evening Ehud inquired at St. Martin's Church. It was the church nearest the Jewish quarter, built on the site of a Roman prison. According to rumors, a dungeon still existed under the church, a horrid place where ecclesiastical enemies were kept in chains. Ehud had never seen any evidence for this. Still the church had a certain menacing aspect for Jews, as it had a reputation for enthusiastic proselytism. Ehud spoke with a senior cleric of St. Martin's, who gave him no definite answers. The priest suggested that he wait a few days and see if the situation resolved itself. Ehud suspected the man knew more than he was telling him.

Miriam was not happy to hear what her husband reported, but what could they do? Civil laws protected Jews and their servants from kidnapping, but strictly speaking, Sofi was neither a Jew nor a servant. As an unofficially adopted member of the family, she occupied some indefinite grey area. Besides, they had no proof the young priest had kidnapped her—she may have gone willingly. They would simply have to wait and hope Sofi was safe. In the meantime, Miriam would spend as many hours as she could with her mother-in-law. When her presence was required elsewhere, she would leave one of the older children with their grandmother. In an emergency they could find Miriam or call on one of the neighbors. It was fortunate that Ehud's mother lived in the same house they did, just two floors down.

On the fourth day, Sofi returned. She was completely out of breath from running, and her eyes were red. She seemed apprehensive. It was evident Sofi had been unhappy in her captivity, if that's what it was. A short time later, someone knocked on the door. Miriam was angry when she opened it and saw a young priest standing there.

"What do you want?" she asked.

"Excuse me. I followed a young woman to this house."

"What business do you have with her?"

"She is a member of my flock. I baptized her myself."

Miriam glared at him. "It's against the law for you to seize any of our people and secretly baptize them."

"But she came willingly. She raised no objection to the baptism. She's had her three days to deliberate, as the law requires, and still has not objected. So I conclude she has forsaken your corrupted law for the one true Faith."

Miriam was furious. "This woman cannot speak! She's never said a word in her life. Surely you could see something was wrong with her."

"There are many deaf and dumb people who are faithful Christians. As I said, she willingly submitted to baptism. Now it is for the ecclesiastical authorities to decide what is best for her."

"Isn't that perfectly obvious? Sofi came straight back here, once you released her. This is her home, where she feels secure. If you try to take her away, we will fight you in every way we can."

The priest folded his hands together and bowed slightly. "We shall see. We shall see."

Miriam shut the door in his face. She was seething. Now she must gain control of herself. There was much to be done. First she must try to comfort Sofi and reassure her that none of this was her fault. The poor woman's normal routine must be restored as soon as possible. Then she must consult with Ehud about what to do next. Where could they turn for help and advice? Mosche might have some good ideas. He kept up with civil affairs and knew the parts of King Henry's edicts that applied to Jews. Maybe they could ask Josef for help. Yes. As a young man, he had worked in city hall. More recently, Miriam had heard him mention friends in local government. Perhaps Josef could steer them in the right direction. For now they would keep Sofi at home behind locked doors. Miriam herself would do the shopping and other errands for her mother-in-law. She must alert the neighbors to watch out for strangers lurking in the neighborhood. They should all be vigilant until this senseless dispute was settled.

By the following week the story had been widely circulated. Mosche communicated what he knew to Josef, who spoke to his former employer Frieder at city hall. Shortly thereafter, Frieder came with Josef to Miriam's house. Immediately two women and a man from the neighborhood confronted them and asked what they were doing. Josef said a few words in Hebrew. One of the women recognized him and told her companions it was all right. The visitors found Miriam at home and arranged a time for Frieder to come back and get more information from the family.

When Frieder returned, he had already made inquiries at St. Martin's Church. The young priest in question acknowledged having baptized Sofi and holding her at the church for three days afterwards. He told Frieder he was concerned for her soul. Somehow he had found out that Sofi had been taken (perhaps kidnapped) from her homeland, brought to Worms as a child, and raised in a Jewish household, but that she was actually of Magyar extraction. Therefore, he assumed she must be a "natural-born Christian." To deny such a person the salvation of the Lord would be a terrible crime. The young priest was aware that King Henry's charter to the Jews of Worms forbade the baptism of their sons and daughters against their will. Yet this was a special case. Surely the king's magistrate would recognize that. If, however, the ruling went against him, the priest would gladly pay the fine of twelve gold pounds into the king's treasury. This was but a small price to pay for a human soul. The woman was now a baptized Christian, and nothing could change that fact.

After relating these particulars to the assembled family members, Frieder asked if they knew any other details that might pertain to the case. He was seated in the ground floor residence of Ehud's mother, conducting an informal interview with her, her son, and her daughter-in-law. They had asked Sofi to go upstairs and stay with Miriam's children, who were now in bed. Ehud confirmed what the priest said about Sofi's origins. Ehud's father had seen her on the streets of Budapest. When he brought her home she was thin, bruised, and melancholy. She rarely smiled and never spoke (even to this day). Ehud had been a teenager at the time, somewhat carefree. Having this girl in their household opened his eyes to the misery experienced by people in other parts of the world.

He went on to say that it took Sofi many months to adjust to her new life. In the first year, the family observed that the girl picked up extra food from the table when she thought no one was looking. She would hide it away against future hunger. Gradually she came to realize there was always plenty of food, and the hoarding stopped. Ehud's parents showed her a love she'd never known before. At first she only stared at them with her deep-sunk grey eyes, but later she learned to smile. This was her primary means of communication. Now she seemed reasonably happy most of the time, but fragile. Any changes in routine seemed to upset her. Miriam confirmed this and said that Sofi had broken down and wept several times since her recent ordeal. Surely removing her from the family would cause her great distress.

Frieder pondered the case for a few minutes. Then he spoke slowly and deliberately. "Everything you have said is likely to arouse sympathy in whoever judges this case. However, I don't think it will affect his ruling. King Henry's charter states that Jewish children are not to be seized and baptized against their parents' will. But the legal claim here is far from clear-cut. First of all, the person in question is an adult, not a child. Second, she is not a natural-born daughter of this family. And third, she apparently went willingly to be baptized and has not repudiated the baptism."

"But she can't speak!" said Miriam with frustration in her voice.

Frieder took a few deep breaths. Looking directly at Miriam, he said, "I know that. As I said, the magistrate is likely to be sympathetic, but he may have no choice in the matter. If the Church authorities insist on removing her from this household, they will probably have their way." Everyone looked somber. After a minute or two, Frieder spoke again. "There is a possible way out, but the chances are slim."

"Tell us," said Ehud. "We're willing to try whatever you advise."

"If you can make the court consider the young woman to be your servant, even while you treat her as an adopted member of the family, she might be able to stay. Jews are permitted to have Christian servants if they make no attempt to convert them to Judaism and if they allow them to practice the Christian faith."

Until now, Ehud's mother had said nothing. She spoke quietly, as if not wishing to be overheard. "It's true," she said, looking at her son. "Your father didn't want anyone to know, because the idea was so abhorrent to him. But it's true. Sofi was sold to him as a slave, sold by her own father. She was not an orphan at all. She was simply a mistreated little girl, forced to beg on street corners and do even worse things to get money for her parents. Your father told no one but me. We kept the secret all these years because we didn't want Sofi to find out what sort of people she came from." The speaker lowered her eyes and said no more.

Frieder's mind worked quickly. "This might be the fact that saves her. The laws about slavery are spelled out clearly in the charter. A Jew's property, including slaves, may not be taken away from him, or must be restored double. Furthermore, if a pagan slave is taken for baptism, the perpetrator must pay three silver pounds into the king's treasury. The slave is then returned to his Jewish owners, but henceforth is considered to be a Christian."

"We were under the impression that Jews could not own Christian slaves," said Ehud.

"That has been the Church's policy all along. But King Henry's charter supersedes those laws in this district. The only legal problem which might arise would be positive proof the girl was baptized in her home country. In that case, your father would have purchased a Christian slave, which is still not permitted in the charter. However, it's exceedingly unlikely that proof of such a baptism could be found."

"So what do we do now?" asked Miriam.

"Well, you understand I have no authority to judge a case like this—it must be put before the king's magistrate." Turning to Ehud, Frieder continued, "You will be the plaintiff, bringing suit against the man who took your slave for baptism. You'll be required to make a public oath of honesty and to bring two witnesses, one Jew and one Christian."

Ehud seemed discouraged at this news. He would be bringing charges against a priest of the Church, and he needed a Christian witness. "Is it possible?" he asked.

"Yes, it's possible. I'm willing to stand in as your Christian witness. My word as a public official might have some influence. In presenting the case, you must acknowledge publicly that the woman is your slave. And if you win, you must recognize that she is considered to be a Christian, entitled to practice the faith. It will be up to you to make sure she does not work on Sundays, and that she observes fasts during Lent, and so forth. Can you do this?"

Ehud looked at his wife, then his mother. They all nodded their assent.

When the king's magistrate was next in Worms, he considered the case. The first witness, Ehud, described what had happened. A local rabbi then vouched for the honesty and good character of the family. Frieder began his testimony by reading aloud those sections of the charter pertaining to slaves in Jewish households and followed up by explaining how the law applied in this case. Finally, the young priest told his side of the story. Almost immediately, the magistrate gave his ruling. He told the priest that henceforth he must find out more about the circumstances of those he would baptize. And he ordered the young cleric to pay three silver pounds into the king's treasury.

In the end, though, everyone was satisfied with the outcome. Sofi, now officially a slave, continued to live in the house and care for Ehud's mother. On holy days, the young priest or his delegate came to escort her to St. Martin's Church. Sofi learned to enjoy the services and took pleasure in these regular outings. When strawberries were in season, the priest always remembered to bring her some.

The next time Miriam saw her brother, she questioned him about King Henry's charter to the Jews of Worms. She was fascinated that a written document could be so effective in protecting the rights of a people, especially Jews. When had it been issued? Was there any precedent? What were some of the other articles in the charter, besides those concerning slaves and baptism? Mosche had read the document and discussed it with other scholars. He told his sister it had been issued about four years earlier. Naturally it had taken many months for its contents to be widely disseminated. One of their own learned men had undertaken to translate it from Latin into Hebrew, so that Jews everywhere in the kingdom could read it. As to precedents, there weren't many that he knew of. Bishop Rudiger of Speyer had offered a charter to the Jews several years before this one. The provisions of that document had mostly to do with rights of self-defense and employment. The charter helped lure Jews to Speyer from Mainz, a city where they had suffered persecution. King Henry must have noticed the economic benefits that immediately accrued in Speyer, because shortly thereafter he issued a more sweeping charter to the same community. It was on that document that the charter to the Jews of Worms was modeled. Mosche described some of its provisions.

"Jews are allowed to own land and houses inside or outside the city wall," he said. "Our merchants may travel toll-free throughout the empire. We can sell goods in the city and exchange silver, as long as we don't set up shop near the mint house or wherever the mint masters might conduct business. We have the right to sell certain products to Christians, including wine, dyes, and medicine. Those are the main points I can remember concerning property and trade."

"It seems fairly comprehensive," said Miriam.

"Yes. Another related point I forgot to mention is that Jews' houses and horses are not to be commandeered by armies or officials passing through Worms. What I find most heartening, however, are the parts that protect our community from violence. Jews may not be tortured with a burning iron, hot or cold water, or the flogging whip. We cannot be imprisoned without just cause. If someone plots to have a Jew killed, both the plotter and the killer are heavily fined or otherwise punished."

"Brother, this is truly remarkable. Could it be that we're finally safe?"

"Some of our best thinkers feel that way, and I tend to agree. But others have doubts. They observe that each one of the 'magnanimous' policies in the charter serves the economic interests of King Henry. Where self-interest is the primary motivator, laws might be changed in an instant, or simply ignored."

"How do these policies benefit the king?"

"Jews make money and pay taxes. They spur trade and prosperity. Therefore, it follows that removal of a Jew by death or imprisonment diminishes the economic engine. In fact, fines for torture, murder, or detainment of a Jew are paid, not to the victim, but to the king himself. Apparently he's the one who has been wronged and suffers most, even if a Jew loses his life. One of my colleagues in the Jeschiba refers to us Jews as 'slaves to the treasury of the king.' Still, I'd rather have protection for the wrong reasons than no protection at all."

"Are there any parts of the charter that are prompted by reason and fairness instead of economic interest?"

"I think so. The articles dealing with justice among ourselves seem quite reasonable. A dispute between Jews is to be judged by a Jew. To some extent we've always done this, but now it's officially authorized. We choose our own judges, who are then formally appointed by the king. In cases between Jews (and even when Christians are involved), a Jew may appeal to the king if he feels a verdict is unjust. Most remarkable is that when members of both faiths are involved, no person can be convicted except by testimony of Jewish and Christian witnesses together."

"Will our testimony be given equal weight?"

"If we swear according to the laws of Torah, our word is supposed to be accepted."

"At least they recognize that Jews are devout and honest and deserving of justice," said Miriam. "Who knows? Some day we might be treated like regular citizens."

"We might. But so much depends on events beyond our control."

"What do you mean?"

"You remember a few years back when plague broke out, certain people said Jews had poisoned the town wells. Then when crops failed, they accused us of casting a spell. Why would we do such a thing? Does it help us when people get sick or go hungry? I guess if the moon fell from the sky, someone would blame us. We're different, and therefore we're suspect."

"Most people don't believe that stuff."

"You're right. But such accusations linger in their minds and arouse suspicion. Then when something else goes wrong, they react irrationally, with a ferocity that's out of proportion to the situation."

"There are many Christians of good will who would try to prevent wrong-headed acts. Think of Josef, and some of the tradesmen we know, and the city clerk who helped us with Sofi's case."

"Yes, it's true. And there are Jews of good will, including most of our friends. However, there are people in both camps who stir up trouble. We can't do much to hold back hateful Christians. What we *can* do is encourage our fellow Jews to be more circumspect, so as not to give our enemies any pretext for acting badly."

"Anything in particular you're worried about?"

"Maybe. I heard that some Jewish vendors at the market were successful enough to accumulate a good bit of capital. Using that to support themselves, they lowered their selling prices. This had the effect of driving out competitors who couldn't afford to sell cheaply."

"And that's so unusual?"

"Well, it might have been all right, except that a few of the more unscrupulous vendors, once they had the market to themselves, raised prices again, even higher than before. They think they're being clever, but they're trading short-term gain for long-term harm. In the end, it's not good business if you stir up resentment among sellers and buyers."

"Short-sighted, I would say," added Miriam.

"Jews, more than anyone else, must be completely fair and honest. First and foremost, because it's an obligation of our Law. Beyond that, we have to follow the rules written by Christians. Some of our people take too much for granted. They want more privileges and profits than are officially sanctioned. I've heard of Jews bribing their servants to work on Sundays. This sort of thing causes rumors that we are converting them to Judaism. The rumors get worse when people like those odious Levi brothers mock the Christian faith. Have these Jews forgotten who has the power and weapons and armies on their side? Things can change in an instant so that our lives become intolerable."

"Brother, please don't get upset. Our lives are not intolerable. There's a fair amount of friendly contact between the two communities. We've seen Jews and Christians exchange gifts, and celebrate together with wine and dancing, and play with one another at games of chance. And we have a charter issued by the king himself that protects us from the whims of our enemies. Our own small victory is a good example. Ehud and I still rejoice at keeping Sofi in the family. There's much to be thankful for."

"I know," replied Mosche. "I keep reminding myself."

"Now, tell me how your little son is doing?"

Mosche smiled. "He's doing well. We just celebrated his second birthday."

"Let's agree to be optimistic for our children's sake," said Miriam as she rose to leave.

Chapter 16

"What does it mean?" Miriam asked her brother one evening a few weeks later. She sat beside Johanna in the front room of Mosche's house. Johanna was rocking Nataniel in her arms, singing softly to him, while Miriam worked with needle and thread, mending her family's clothes. Her children had gone to bed early, giving Miriam an opportunity to visit her brother.

"I don't exactly know," said Mosche. "The word 'crusade' is new to me. I can tell you what some of my colleagues at the synagogue have overheard, but they don't understand it either."

Miriam leaned forward. "Go on."

"Apparently Pope Urban declared that all Christians should unite to take Jerusalem back from the Muslims. Recently it's become more and more difficult to make a pilgrimage to visit the places they consider holy."

"What stands in their way?"

"Well, you know the Egyptians ruled Jerusalem for a hundred years. They put limits on who could visit and when. That was an annoyance to Christian pilgrims. But then about twenty-five years ago the Seljuks conquered the city, and things got worse. The new rulers tore up some of the venerated sites and mistreated those who tried to defend them. There was violence on both sides. You know how people's religious convictions can drive them to extreme behavior."

Miriam nodded. "How on earth does the pope think he can push out the Muslims?"

"That's what we're all wondering. It would be a huge undertaking to get a big enough army assembled and transported the distance, to say nothing of food and shelter and supplies along the way. I think it's impossible."

"Is all this likely to affect us in any way?"

"It shouldn't," said Mosche. "Jews are not required to provide lodging for traveling soldiers or to donate supplies of any kind. Who knows but that our merchants might profit from a little extra business."

"I think we should try to find out more. Why don't you invite Josef to come over and tell us what he knows?"

Mosche agreed and said he would do it soon. He gently lifted his son, who had fallen asleep, from his mother's arms and carried him to his bed, leaving the women to talk of other things.

Josef came over the following week. He had discussed the situation with Father Albert, who knew some details, and his former boss Frieder, who knew a great deal more. Father Albert was vaguely optimistic that the many squabbling Christian factions could be unified by a crusade. Frieder thought the whole enterprise would come to no good. Mosche and Miriam asked many questions.

"What do Christians squabble about? Don't they all believe in the same things?" asked Miriam.

Josef raised his eyebrows. "Yes and no. It's very complicated. Do you really want to hear what divides Christians from one another?"

"Can you explain it briefly?"

"I'll try. The biggest split right now is between East and West. That's the one that worries Father Albert the most. It got really serious about forty years ago, when bishops in the Greek Church and the Roman Church couldn't agree on the words of the Creed, which is our statement of beliefs. There were some differences of interpretation."

Mosche smiled. "When Jews have different interpretations, they argue. Once the argument is over and nobody's mind is changed, they sit down to eat."

Josef laughed and said, "I remember. Miriam and I used to argue over Scripture, but we were still friends. Anyway, there's more to it than that. The pope would like to be head of the entire Church, but the bishops of Jerusalem and Constantinople don't like the idea. Father Albert thinks if they unite in fighting a common enemy, they might overlook their differences."

"Do you think they could fight side by side?" asked Miriam.

"Yes, I think so. The eastern empire has been under siege for a long time, and some of the emperors have turned to Rome for help. Until now, none of the popes has responded enthusiastically."

"What's different about this pope?"

"Pope Urban is very idealistic. He called together hundreds of bishops and knights last fall to the town of Clermont in Francia. They say he was passionate in asking them to free the land of Jesus from the infidels. Many pledged right then and there to defend the honor of the cross. To show their devotion, they pinned crosses to their clothes. The pope also appealed to princes and counts and barons in his territories to stop quarreling. I suppose if they all march off to Jerusalem, they won't be fighting against each other. But more importantly for the pope, they'll increase the power and influence of the Roman Church in the east."

Mosche looked thoughtful. "I wonder what our own King Henry thinks about all this."

"Frieder asked the same question. You know the king has had continual disagreements with popes since he was a young man. At one time, King Henry tried to depose Pope Gregory. That pope turned around and excommunicated the king and some of his bishops and then chose a new king to take his place. It was a mess—nobody knew who was king or pope."

"What about the present pope?"

"The king doesn't get along with him either. Pope Urban made an alliance with King Henry's son against his father."

"Then I doubt the king will support the pope's policies, whatever they may be," said Mosche.

"That's probably true. Frieder thinks that's why the pope went to Francia to raise his army. He couldn't get much support here. A French bishop named Adhemar has been put in charge of the army."

Mosche pursed his lips. "Can we be sure King Henry will hold on to power when the pope has a big army at his disposal?"

"No one knows," replied Josef, "and it's one reason Frieder is skeptical about the whole operation. He suspects the pope's motives are more complicated than they seem on the surface."

Mosche's expression became more solemn. "If King Henry is deposed, who will protect us Jews?" The three friends were silent for a moment. With more animated voice, Mosche said, "Well, enough of that." He turned to his friend. "Josef, we haven't told you yet that Rabbi Scholomo is coming back to Worms. He'll be here in a couple of weeks, as soon as the mountain roads are clear enough to pass. You'll want to see him, I think?"

"Yes, for sure. Let me know when he's teaching."

Miriam was excited to be able to attend study sessions with the visiting rabbi. She and her husband had agreed on a schedule: Miriam would attend morning sessions while Ehud watched the children. They would go together in the afternoons, leaving the older children to watch over the younger ones while they were napping. Ehud would take Aaron to services in the evening. Miriam was grateful that Ehud was willing to close his shop for the entire week Rabbi Scholomo was in town. Many of the merchants asked their wives to run their business while they attended to scholarly pursuits. Her husband never did that. He knew how important it was to Miriam to learn as much as she could. Ehud was proud of his educated wife, and she loved him the more for it.

On the first day, the discussion focused on Talmud. One of the young men in attendance had heard an accusation that Jews favored the Talmud over the Bible. Was there any truth to this? Why would Christians have this perception? Rabbi Scholomo responded that some Christians were looking for any excuse to malign Jews, and this sounded like just such a case. Nevertheless, since the question had been raised, he would address the relative importance of Torah and Talmud.

"To shed light on this subject, we must go back to ancient times," said the rabbi. "When God created the universe, he had Torah in mind; therefore the whole of creation is connected with the teachings of Torah. Part of the divine plan was that Israel would bring all peoples of the world under sovereignty of the One God. For this to be accomplished, it was needful that Torah be widely read and understood. Here is where Talmud comes in. The 'oral law,' as we call it, was allowed to be written only because Torah was being forgotten. The Lord would not allow such a calamity to happen."

"Did he appoint a prophet like Moses to remind us?" asked a boy sitting near the front.

"Not one, but many. Torah was given to Moses in an instant on Mt. Sinai. But Talmud came slowly over a period of ten centuries. First in the land of Israel and later in Babylonia, scholars formulated interpretations of Torah that infused new spirit into the ancient writings. These newer works were collected and recorded for all to read, becoming known as Mishna and Gemara, or all together as Talmud."

"Did they all agree with each other?" asked the same inquisitive boy.

The rabbi chuckled. "Not at all. Some rabbis interpreted the law narrowly; others gave broad and flexible explanations. But all were guided by the principle that no interpretation should contradict the plain meaning of the text. And all made decisions based on understanding from their hearts, not simply from their heads."

"So which is more important, Torah or Talmud?" asked the first questioner.

Rabbi Scholomo shook his head. "That is the wrong question to ask, my son. Torah is sacred, and Talmud is also sacred because it opens our eyes to the meaning of Torah. For us Jews, faith inspires a search for knowledge, and Torah is the knowledge which is the foundation of our faith. In our search, we are bound to consider all reasonable interpretations of Torah. As it says in one of Solomon's proverbs, the understanding of a man's heart must be drawn out from within him as water is drawn out from a deep well."

"So understanding Torah is the ultimate goal?" asked another man.

"It is true that the goal of scholars is to understand Torah," said the rabbi. "To say it is the ultimate goal, however, is misleading. We strive to understand Torah so that we might live in accord with God's will. Talmud helps us to do this, telling us how to apply Torah to our everyday lives. So you see there is a practical reason for studying Talmud: to make us better Jews. It is a great blessing that we have these writings."

"How did they come to us here, and when?"

"Traders and traveling scholars brought manuscripts from the academies of Babylonia. About a hundred years ago, the great Rabbi Gershom of Mainz collected and verified the texts. That is why we call him 'Light of the Exile.' Rabbi Gershom enlightened the eyes of Jews in the diaspora. Many scholars in this region still consider themselves to be disciples of his disciples."

Looking around the room, Miriam felt privileged to be one of only two or three women in attendance. Indeed, this was the first time she'd participated in a study session with Rabbi Scholomo. She had heard him deliver sermons during his earlier visits, but never before had she witnessed his interaction with other scholars and town folk. It was extraordinary. He answered every question directly and sincerely. His sympathy, intelligence, and clarity of expression made him an outstanding teacher for pupils at any level. Everyone in the room, from ten-year-old children to learned rabbis, seemed spellbound by the speaker. Miriam thought of her own children. The two older ones would certainly gain something by attending these sessions. They might not understand every word, especially the Bible passages quoted in Hebrew, but these could be explained to them later. Aaron and Susanna were younger than anyone present at today's session, but Miriam knew they would sit still and pay attention. She resolved to bring them along the next morning and send them again with their father in the afternoon. She would stay home with the younger children during naptime so that her son and daughter could hear the voice of this great man.

Next morning at the study session, a question was raised about the image of the suffering servant in Isaiah's writings. The questioner had been told by Christian friends that this was a representation of Jesus, the Messiah, who suffered and died. He thought his friends might be trying to convert him, and he didn't know exactly how to respond.

"First of all, my good man," said Rabbi Scholomo, "do not dispute with Christians, or with sectarians, or with Jews who depart from the faith. People who are set in their beliefs (or in disbelief) will not be won over by arguments. As to the suffering servant, he might be identified with Isaiah himself, or with another of Israel's prophets. My own feeling is that the servant stands for the nation of Israel, in ancient times and modern. Later this week, I shall give a sermon on precisely this topic. I hope you will attend."

Another man, who was a wine merchant, asked the rabbi what to do about aggressive missionary activity. One of the local priests had been rather assertive when he came to the shop to buy wine. "You say we shouldn't argue with Christians, Rabbi. How should I answer this priest, who insists on telling me his interpretation of our Scripture?"

"It's a delicate question. As you know, sacred writings, especially prophecy, can be interpreted in many ways. We try always to keep in mind the plain meaning, the most immediate intentions of the writer. And yet there are sometimes deeper, metaphorical meanings as well, a fact that Jewish scholars readily acknowledge. At times, we might even consult with Christians for assistance in explaining a difficult passage. It is said that Hai Gaon, the great scholar of Babylonia, once referred a Jewish student to a Christian priest who had good understanding of the Psalms and was able to shed light on a particular question. In Talmud we find the statement, 'One who imparts a word of wisdom, though he be a non-Jew, still deserves to be called wise.' Christians are not idolaters, after all. When they speak highly of Jesus, they're thinking of the Creator of heaven and earth. Nevertheless, I refute the claim that Hebrew Scripture carries any reference to this man Jesus, who lived hundreds of years after the Scriptures were written. When Christians force their unwarranted ideas onto unwilling ears, I can only conclude their action proceeds from arrogance."

"Yes, Rabbi, I agree. And I'd like to tell that priest what I think."

"Be cautious," responded the rabbi. "We do not wish to bring hostility upon ourselves. You must judge whether this man can bear criticism and whether he can discuss rationally a subject so near to his heart. Our Scriptures teach peace and harmony among families. I take this to mean all the families of mankind."

"But, Rabbi, if someone picks a fight with us, can't we fight back?"

Rabbi Scholomo closed his eyes and paused for a few moments. He spoke slowly, choosing his words carefully. "Remember when the Lord commanded Moses to build an altar, he said it must be built of unhewn stones. Do you know why? Because the altar of our faith is made to prolong life, not to shorten it. Therefore the stones of the altar must not be touched by a sword, an instrument that shortens life. Doing so would profane the sacred altar."

The wine merchant shook his head. He said nothing, yet he did not seem satisfied with this answer.

The rabbi continued. "In the third book of Moses, the Lord says, 'If ye walk in my statutes, and keep my commandments, and do them: Then I will give peace in the land, and ye shall lie down, with none to make you afraid; and I will remove evil beasts out of the land, and the sword shall not pass through your land.' Do you not see that without peace, there is nothing, because peace is equal to all the other blessings added together?"

Miriam looked around the room. Many in the audience were nodding in agreement. Josef, too, sitting in a far corner, seemed happy with the answer. Miriam turned to her two children sitting beside her. They had been so quiet during the discussion that she all but forgot they were there. She sensed they had been paying attention.

A penetrating voice came from the rear of the hall. All eyes turned to see a thin, taut young man whom Miriam did not recognize. "Rabbi, what is happening in your homeland? It is said that the pope is assembling a huge army in Francia."

"Yes, I've heard the same. This, we hope, will not affect us. The pope himself seems somewhat sympathetic to Jews. You remember, he condemned King Philip, who tried to expel the Jews of Paris. We in the district of Champagne live under protection of the counts, a so-called 'royal peace.' Our rights seem secure. And yet others in the region are not so fortunate. For example, Jews in Chartres have been prevented by the bishop from participating in local government and forbidden to act as witnesses in civil court. The people protested, but to no avail."

The young man, standing against the back wall, spoke again. "That's only the beginning, I think. I've just come from Mainz, where I'm a student. Our chief rabbi Kalonymus is clearly worried by recent developments. He sent a message to King Henry, asking him to reassert his protection of Jews in the Rheinland. The king is far away in Italia, perhaps too far to help us."

A murmur went up from the crowd. Someone called out, "Tell us what you know." A few others shouted their agreement with this proposal. Rabbi Scholomo conferred with another rabbi, and the two invited the young man to come to the podium. He seemed nervous. Rabbi Scholomo patted his arm and spoke kindly to him. "Peace to you, my son. Please introduce yourself to us and relate any news you think it would be useful for us to know."

The young man looked around the room full of inquiring faces. He turned to the rabbi, who nodded reassuringly. "My name is Franck," he began. "I have studied for the past three years at the Jeschiba in Mainz. As you know, scholars and students come from many places to visit that city. We are in frequent contact with the Jews of Köln, in particular, and they in turn have close ties with communities to the north and west. In the last year, there has been a stream of immigrants to Köln, both Jew and Gentile, from the low countries. Apparently the coastal region has been suffering from pestilence and famine, prompting many to leave. As long as the numbers remained small, this posed no serious problem for the community in Köln. But over the winter, more and more people came, and a larger portion of them were tramps or escaped convicts or troublemakers. Things got ugly."

The young man paused and looked again at Rabbi Scholomo. Miriam heard people in the audience ask each other, "What could he mean?" and "Does this have anything to do with us?" A few people spoke up and urged him to continue. Miriam wondered if what he had to say would be appropriate for her children to hear. She thought about taking them home but decided against it. It would be good for them to learn what goes on in the world, no matter how unpleasant. At any rate, they would eventually find out about the ugly side of life. After another nod from the rabbi, Franck resumed his narrative.

"There is a hateful spirit in some of the new immigrants, especially when they gather in groups. The usual accusations against Jews always come to the surface: Jews keep company with the devil. Jews trample on bread stolen from the churches. Jews killed Jesus and, like Cain who killed his younger brother, should be compelled to wander the earth. Naturally such people blame Jews for all the evil in the world. This includes the famine in their own country."

"How are the people of Köln reacting to the mean-spiritedness?" asked a woman sitting near Miriam.

"I haven't been there, you understand. All this comes to me second or third hand. But the reports agree. Jews are getting nervous. They fear it might take only a little spark to incite violence. There is a new factor recently introduced that is especially worrisome. It might influence the general population who normally are willing to coexist with Jews."

Again Miriam wondered if she should take her children away from this discussion. Now, however, she was curious about what the man would say next. Perhaps she would leave after a few more minutes.

"As you may know, Pope Urban has issued a call for Christians to free the land of Israel from Muslim rule. One of the holiest places for Christians was a church built on the site where their prophet Jesus was supposedly buried. They call it Holy Sepulcher. More than eighty years ago, the church was destroyed. In the same year, plague and famine brought desolation to much of the world. By some wild turn of the imagination, people are connecting these events and blaming Jews for everything."

"How's it possible?" someone called out.

"It makes no sense, of course," said the speaker. "But I've heard several theories. Some say an unknown Jew sent a letter to a powerful prince in Babylon, urging him to destroy the church. Others say a group of Jews conspired with the Moors of Spain to tear it down. What they all agree on is that 'Jewish treachery' was behind both destruction of the church and the plague."

Miriam decided at this point to take her children home. She couldn't tell by looking at them how much they understood of the young man's testimony. She soon found out. When it came time to return for the afternoon session, Susanna seemed anxious.

"Mama, do I have to go back to the schoolhouse with Papa? I'd rather stay here with you."

"Why is that, Sweetheart? I thought you liked listening to the rabbi."

"I don't want to hear any more scary talk."

Aaron was standing nearby. "I'm not afraid. I'll go with Father and we'll learn how to protect you and Mama from danger."

Miriam smiled at the courage of her son. It reminded her of her brother, completely fearless at that age—and still today. Aaron attended all subsequent study sessions that week, but Miriam could not coax her daughter to return. On the last day of Rabbi Scholomo's residence in Worms, he was to deliver a sermon in the afternoon. Miriam assumed her husband would take Aaron, according to the usual schedule. When it was time, Ehud approached her.

"I will stay home with the little ones, Wife, while you take Aaron and Susanna to hear the final sermon."

"But it's your turn to go, dear. And Susanna is happier to stay home."

"It's important for her and you to hear what the rabbi will say. I've spoken with Susanna and assured her that only the good rabbi will speak, and he does not bring bad news."

Miriam once again marveled at her husband's thoughtfulness. She gave him a grateful smile and a kiss as she left the house with her children.

Chapter 17

Rabbi Scholomo began his sermon with a passage from Isaiah: "Behold my servant, whom I will uphold; my elect, in whom my soul delighteth: I have put my spirit upon him, that he may bring forth justice to the nations. He shall not become fatigued and not be faint, till he have established justice on the earth; and till the coastlands shall wait for his law." The rabbi paused and looked around the room. "Who is this faithful servant of whom the Lord speaks? Might the prophet Isaiah be referring to himself when he writes these words? Or perhaps to another prophet, such as Jeremiah or Ezekiel? Let's read a little further before we decide. 'I the Lord have called thee in righteousness, and will lay hold on thy hand, and will keep thee, and appoint thee for a covenant of the people, for a light of the nations; To open blind eyes, to bring out from the dungeon the prisoner, and out of the prisonhouse those that dwell in darkness.' When the Lord speaks here of a call to righteousness, a covenant for the people, and a light to the nations, he is surely thinking of Abraham, our father, whom he chose for this purpose. When he speaks of bringing a prisoner out of the dungeon, he is reminding us of Josef, sold into captivity by his brothers, who upon his release from prison, opened their eyes and became an agent for their deliverance from death by famine."

Miriam glanced at her children. Both leaned forward, listening intently. The rabbi continued, "Yes, the servant is not one man, but many. All the sons and daughters of Israel who are faithful to the Law, seek justice and righteousness, and attempt to dispel darkness are servants of the Lord. The prophet Isaiah, one of the foremost of these servants, warns us that with service may come suffering. The one he describes is treated shamefully, beaten, spat upon, and rejected. Is this what we can expect?

"Perhaps. You have heard the reports of our young friend from Mainz. It seems we are living in perilous times. We must prepare ourselves for whatever comes. As people who are called to bring forth justice, we must cling to our Law. Yet we must also remain obedient to civil laws, because as one of the ancient rabbis said, 'The law of the land is law.' It is imperative that we avoid confrontation with Christian neighbors: do not break a promise, do not utter insults or slander, do nothing that might bring accusations of sorcery, and do not cheat. Defrauding a Christian is perhaps worse than defrauding a Jew, because our duty is to sanctify the Divine Name to all the world. Take refuge in the Law, obey its precepts, but do not stop there. Apply yourselves to the cultivation of peace. Harmony will be our defense. Concord will keep us safe.

"The Lord promises to uphold his faithful servants so that they do not become weary or faint. He tells Moses, 'Behold, there is a place by me, and thou shalt stand upon the rock.' This I take to mean that God has a place ready for us, where we can hide and be protected from injury. The Lord compares himself to an eagle looking after her young. 'As an eagle stirreth up her nest, hovereth over her young, spreadeth abroad her wings, taketh them, beareth them aloft on her wings: so did the Lord alone lead him.' Like a mother bird, God sheltered the Israelites in Egypt and bore them away, and he is able to do the same for us. Hold these assurances close to your hearts. Dear friends, resist violence and cherish peace. Study Torah so that you might draw upon it as a fearless man draws out his sword. And yet, if trials and suffering come in spite of this, let us resolve to receive them with a peaceful spirit and love in our hearts. Let us not rebel against God, nor complain that Torah does not protect us from suffering. For there is no such thing in this world as reward for keeping the commandments. If you suffer, follow the example of our forefathers, and our entire nation, named the Suffering Servant. We must serve God and fulfill his commands, not from fear, but from love."

Miriam turned to look at her children. Aaron was sitting on the edge of his seat, watching the rabbi. Susanna leaned back and looked around the room, but she showed no sign of anxiety. This sermon had been well worth hearing. Miriam was glad her children were present. She wished her husband could have heard it too. It might be a long time before Rabbi Scholomo returned to Worms.

In the days that followed, the Jewish community in the city drew together each week to hear the latest reports and consider what action might be necessary. They met Wednesday afternoons in the schoolhouse, as many as could break away from their work or studies. Miriam watched approvingly as her brother led discussions and became the effective leader of the assemblies. She was especially proud to hear him called "Rabbi Mosche," a title he had earned in the Jeschiba. Doubtless, his students used the title every day, but Miriam had never heard him addressed this way.

Reports trickling in from Francia and the northern Rheinland were disturbing. They seemed more serious than the usual accounts of robbery and hostage-taking attributable to the general lawlessness of the day. Church leaders were evidently trying to channel the endemic violence to a common purpose. They encouraged preachers to inform their people of the crusade and arouse them to action. While the crusade had no stated anti-Jewish purpose, yet there was a danger. Complaints against Jews resurfaced, and some clergymen were not averse to repeating malicious rumors. Civil authorities had thus far been able to maintain order, but would this continue? Indeed, stories circulated about an attack twenty years earlier in Spain, directed at Muslims, but resulting in the massacre of Jews. Local authorities had been powerless to stop the rampage. And now, French Jews sent warning letters to their brothers in the Rheinland, and asked for their prayers. A monk, known as Peter the Hermit, had gathered a band of supporters and led them across Francia. He claimed to have a letter from Jewish leaders, saying Jews should supply provisions for his eastward march. In return he would speak well of them. His subtle threat had its desired effect, as Jews along the way were coerced to give food and money in an effort to forestall violence. In some cities, Jews offered payment to churchmen and secular leaders in exchange for promised protection.

Bishop Adhemar himself was preaching the crusade. In his capacity as appointed head of the enterprise, he was attempting to organize a proper army. More unsettling by far were the popular preachers, like Peter the Hermit, who followed in the bishop's wake. They attracted adherents who were not soldiers, but unemployed laborers, or vagrants, or worse. The sermons given by these wandering clerics were sometimes incendiary, sometimes bizarre. The old accusation of "blood libel" came up, the claim that Jews sacrificed Christian children and used their blood in the Passover ritual. As people who kept to themselves, Jews were called secretive and deceptive. One preacher maintained that Jews sold to Christians only dregs from the wine cask and meat considered inedible for themselves. Another denounced Christians who preferred hearing Jewish scholars to their own preachers. One of the strangest sermons touched on the miraculous behavior of a goose. A woman had raised the creature from its earliest days, and consequently it followed her everywhere she went. The woman said her goose understood that she was joining the crusade and had decided to go with her, praise be to God! Whether in regard to this fowl or another, a leader named Count Emmerich said he was putting his faith in a certain goose to guide him to the Holy Land. The count believed the goose and its companion, a goat, were infused with the Holy Spirit. Emmerich himself received a revelation from heaven, telling him he would lead his troops to victory and receive a crown for his noble actions.

Miriam could not take these last items seriously. How could anyone believe such fantastic tales about barnyard animals? She and Mosche laughed about them when they met in private. There were other reports, however, they did not laugh about. According to some sources, roving crusaders had taunted and threatened Jews in Francia, telling them they must either convert or die. A French count named Godfrey swore he would not begin his journey to Jerusalem until he had avenged the blood of Christ in his homeland. This he would do by shedding the blood of Israel until not a remnant was left bearing the name of Jew. Statements of this sort were troubling. The Jewish communities in the path of the crusaders must prepare themselves for whatever might come.

The first action taken by the assembly at the schoolhouse was to write a letter to King Henry, asking him to renew his commitment to protect Jews. While the king himself was far away and could not, in any case, defend all his Jewish subjects scattered about the empire, nevertheless he could influence barons, noblemen, and bishops to take up their cause. If enough Jews appealed to the king, as the rabbi in Mainz had already done, he would be convinced there was cause for concern.

The next step decided upon by the assembly in Worms was to approach local leaders. A delegation would be sent to the bishop and to the heads of city government and business establishments. It was hoped these leaders would be willing to defend their Jewish neighbors on humanitarian grounds. But if not, the community would pool its resources and pay for protection.

"Suppose they take our money and still don't protect us?" asked one skeptical member of the assembly.

"We hope the situation never advances that far," said Mosche. "Still, we should prepare for every eventuality. If the community as a whole cannot be guarded, then we must resort to individual options. Some of you have Christian friends who might be willing to take you into their houses. Sympathetic priests might be persuaded to offer shelter in their churches. Perhaps the cathedral and the bishop's palace could be opened to larger groups who wish to remain together."

"You're depending too much on the gentiles," said the skeptic. "Why can't we stay in our houses and defend ourselves?"

"You are free to do that. If there's violence, each family will have to make a choice. Some of you may wish to leave the city."

"And go where?" asked a young woman with a baby in her arms.

"To the countryside. To the villages. One might survive for a time with the help of strangers, then return when the trouble has passed."

"There you go again, depending on gentiles. What makes you think they care anything about us?" asked the skeptical man.

"You'd better hope they do," answered Mosche. "If we're attacked, we'll need every friend we can get. This is no time for bravado. A sensible humility will serve us better."

Mosche was showing his cool head. Miriam felt sure he was as worried as anyone. All the horrible possibilities must have been going through his mind. Yet in public, under the pressure of leadership, he demonstrated a calm rationality. He wore his mantle well.

When Mosche saw Josef, he asked how Christians were reacting to the pope's proclamation. Josef said people he knew didn't seem concerned, one way or the other. The bishop of Worms had on several occasions preached about the crusade, trying to drum up local support. He had emphasized Pope Urban's promise of absolution to anyone who took part. All their sins would be instantly pardoned when they set out on this grand adventure to free the Holy Land from infidels. Some of the parish priests spoke on the same theme, giving elaborate details of glories to be heaped upon the crusaders. Naturally in their sermons, they painted Muslims (and Jews as well) as sworn enemies of God. Josef asked one of the priests how it could be that these worshippers of God who were forbidden to swear could be God's sworn enemies. The priest smirked and said, "Exaggeration, even fabrication, can sometimes serve the truth." This statement confirmed Josef's predisposition—he wanted nothing at all to do with this crusading venture. Frieder had predicted the whole thing would come to no good. In fact, Josef told Mosche, Frieder was taking extra precautions in regard to his adopted daughter, a Jew, now married with children of her own. He had insisted that the daughter and her entire family learn to recite the Our Father. Then if anyone came looking for Jews, they could fall on their knees and say the prayer. Intruders would assume they were Christians and leave them alone.

Josef asked Mosche why, if Jews feared the crusaders, they did not appeal directly to the pope for protection. Pope Urban had shown no hostility toward Jews. In reply, Mosche said it would be awkward for Jews to appeal to the Church in Rome for anything. They might ask for help from an individual clergyman whom they knew and trusted. But the Church hierarchy had always been suspicious and antagonistic toward Jews, and not open to reexamining its position. On the other hand, some of the bishops King Henry appointed were friendly to Jews. The king himself had responded quickly to recent petitions for protection. He had ordered the authorities in his kingdom to put Jews in secure places should violence break out. Mosche was grateful to King Henry for his willingness to take action, often in contradiction to the highest Church authorities. All in all, he said, Jews in the Rheinland preferred to take their chances with secular leaders and local citizens, rather than trust their safety to the Church.

News from Francia was getting worse. While the official army of crusaders was not scheduled to depart until August, groups of peasants had assembled in response to the traveling preachers. Inflammatory words brought out huge mobs that quickly became uncontrollable. Their frenzy was fed by such statements as: "Before we set out on the long road against God's enemies to the east, let us not ignore his worst foes, the Jews, who are before our eyes," and "First accomplish vengeance for the Crucified One on his enemies who stand before you, and then you shall fight the Ishmaelite," and "Whoever kills a Jew has all his sins forgiven him." The Jews of Rouen were the first to be slaughtered. They were driven into the churchyard and given the choice: be baptized or die. Those who refused baptism were immediately killed. The same murderous action was reported from Metz and other cities. In some places, the mob demanded a bribe; if one was not forthcoming, they looted and burned the Jewish quarter. Then they enforced the vile choice between death and baptism.

Messengers who escaped these cities brought word that these "wandering enemies" were pushing relentlessly eastward. Peter of Amiens (the one also known as 'the Hermit') had already reached Trier. He was traveling barefoot, wearing coarse clothes, riding a donkey and carrying a huge cross. His dramatic appearance created a sensation, attracting ever larger crowds. Disorderly groups led by priests named Volkmar and Gottschalk caused more havoc, and mobs following Counts Godfrey and Emmerich were on the march as well. Jews throughout Francia were fasting and praying, and they requested more prayers from their brothers in the Rheinland.

Meetings in the schoolhouse in Worms became increasingly somber. Participants began every session with prayers for those who had been attacked and those who would be. Choices were becoming more clear for Jews in the path of the crusading mobs.

"Let's consider the options before us," said Mosche one day to the assembled group. "It's reported that the crusaders spare the lives of Jews who are willing to undergo baptism."

Immediately a clamor arose. "Never! Never!" came a shout from the back of the room. "I will not allow my family to join in pagan rituals."

"We must not forsake the covenant of our ancestors," said another man.

"What is this ritual you speak of?" asked a young woman.

Mosche waited until the room was quiet. "Baptism is a washing ceremony. It is supposed to cleanse a person from sin. I believe it is the initiation rite for becoming a Christian."

The woman spoke again. "Every month I bathe in the *miqveh*. Could I not regard this 'baptism' as another ritual cleansing, and then forget about it?"

For a moment, no one said a word. Then whispering began, and louder expressions of opinion. The man in the back spoke up. "No! If you agree to their initiation, then you have played the harlot with them. That is apostasy."

Mosche again waited for complete silence. He took a deep breath. "Each of you will have to look to his own conscience," he said. "It's a difficult decision. Some say it's possible for a person to wash his body but not his heart. For me, that would be impossible. Submitting to baptism would betray my faith in the Holy One of Israel. But you must decide for yourselves."

"We will not do it!" someone called out, and most people murmured their agreement.

"You know the other options," continued Mosche. "Leave the city, and wait for the crusaders to pass through, seek refuge from Christian neighbors; ask for sanctuary in a church or palace; or stay in your home and defend yourself. Families will undoubtedly choose different paths, and that is a good thing. Should violence overtake us, God forbid, we would hope that a faithful remnant might survive. By dividing the community, we increase the likelihood that it will endure." Mosche now had the attention of everyone in the room. "Talk over these things at home. Decide what is best for your family. And remember what Rabbi Scholomo told us: 'Work at making peace. Avoid discord among yourselves, and if at all possible, with those outside our community. That is our best defense.'"

Later Mosche and Miriam and their spouses discussed the situation. Ehud was the most optimistic of the four. "The Christian merchants and tradesmen in this town are good people," he said. "We've worked hand-in-hand with them for many years, to everyone's advantage. I think they would defend us against outside threats."

"If they could," said Mosche. "But we don't really know what's coming. It's better to plan for the case when everything goes wrong."

"Well, if Miriam agrees, I think we'll just hold out as best we can in our own house. With four children and an elderly mother, it would be difficult to uproot ourselves."

Miriam nodded to her husband. "What about you, Mosche?"

"Johanna and I have decided to leave Worms and look for shelter in the countryside. Depending on what happens in the city, we may keep going."

"What do you mean?"

"We might travel east, to find a new home, a place to raise Nataniel in peace."

"But Mosche, you can't leave the Jeschiba! How could you survive if there were no scholars where you live?"

"If no scholars are to be found, I'll teach the children, beginning with my own son. We'll start a new Jeschiba."

Miriam couldn't help but admire her brother's courage. Yet she was alarmed at the thought of losing him. "Mosche, our family has never been separated before. It would be too hard to bear."

"Perhaps it won't happen," he replied softly. "But what is true for the community is true for families as well. Splitting apart may be the best way to preserve a remnant."

Chapter 18

Early in May, Miriam was awakened by soft tapping on her door. She lay motionless for a few moments, waiting to see if it was a dream. No, she heard it again, this time a little louder. After a quick glance assured her that Ehud was still sound asleep, she rose quietly from her bed. Who could it be at this hour? Through the window the sky still looked black. She made her way to the door and felt for the latch. Before opening it, she whispered, "Who's there?"

"It's me, Mosche," came a muffled response.

"What's the matter?" asked Miriam after she opened the door and saw how distressed her brother looked.

"You and Ehud need to come as quickly as you can to the schoolhouse. Get Sofi to come upstairs and stay with the children."

"But what is it, Mosche? Tell me."

"There's no time. I have to go wake up others for the meeting."

"Please! You can't leave without telling me something."

"A messenger from Speyer. Bad news. But don't speak of it. The last thing we want to do is start a panic."

Miriam woke her husband and went downstairs to find Sofi. In less than half an hour, she and Ehud arrived at the synagogue. A few others were making their way across the courtyard toward the school in back. No one spoke. Upon entering the schoolhouse, Miriam immediately recognized Franck, the student from Mainz, standing at the front of the room. Beside him was an older man whom she'd never seen before. Everyone who entered stood silently, perhaps too sleepy to converse. Only Franck and the stranger spoke quietly to one another. As the minutes passed, tension in the room increased. A few more people arrived, looking frightened and disoriented. Finally Mosche came in, followed by half a dozen others. He quickly made his way to the front of the room. "Please, everyone find a seat," he said. "Our visitors have an urgent message for us.

You remember Franck from Mainz, who visited Worms earlier this year when the great rabbi was here. His companion is Ruben of Speyer."

Franck stood and addressed the crowd. "We will not detain you long. You'll want to return to your homes quickly after you hear what we say." He took a deep breath. "Since I left Worms, I have been acting as a courier for communities along the Rhein, because I believe our people must be kept informed of the grave dangers they face. Five days ago I entered Speyer just as Count Emmerich was approaching from the south. His mob of followers, not worth calling an army, was rowdy and undisciplined. Anyone who saw them could have predicted trouble. My friend Ruben will tell you what happened, as he is more familiar with names and places in that city."

Ruben rose slowly and faced the crowd. His bearing was solemn and dignified. "Good people of Worms, I am a cloth merchant, formerly a resident of Mainz, but for the last twelve years happily established in Speyer. Four days ago, on Sabbath eve, our head rabbi received word of a plot. Certain citizens of the town were conspiring with the newly arrived crusaders to attack Jews in the synagogue. Consequently, the rabbi called us early for Sabbath prayers, recited them quickly, and dismissed us just as the sun was coming up. When the evil men learned they had been tricked, they seized the first Jew they saw and killed him. In all, eleven of our people died that day." A gasp went up from the crowd. "Yes, it is horrible. But it could have been worse. We're fortunate to have friends among the leaders of the church and city government. The good bishop John, when he heard of the violence, immediately sent a regiment of soldiers to quell the mob. He brought many Jews into his castle. Though some of us offered him money to pay for lodging and protection, he refused to accept it. Then he rounded up the local ringleaders of the plot and cut off their hands."

People in the room began murmuring among themselves. Someone called out, "Would the bishop of Worms shield us from the mob?"

Ruben shook his head. "I cannot tell you that. You know the situation here better than I do. All I can say is that the two bishops I've known in Speyer have been good and pious men, who valued the achievements and abilities of our people. Bishop Rudiger first invited Jews to the city and granted them certain rights and privileges. His successor Bishop John has shown himself eager to preserve friendly relations between our peoples. The Jewish quarter has always been regarded as a separate township, answerable directly to the bishop. Some Christians in the city find this special treatment irksome, but most go along willingly. As I said, we Jews of Speyer are fortunate."

Ruben sat, and Franck rose again to speak. "The most distressing news we have to report is that Count Emmerich is heading north. The mob might arrive here in two or three days. You must prepare a defense. I myself am returning to Mainz to stand and fight in the city of my fathers."

The two visitors left, and the crowd began again to whisper and murmur among themselves. Mosche raised his hands for silence. "The time is short. It is imperative that each family have a plan of action in case we are attacked. Today you must lay in supplies, bury or hide sacred objects, and devise a way to carry money or other valuables hidden on your persons. You may have to pay for protection. In answer to the question that was raised, Bishop Adalbert of Worms is not an ally of King Henry, nor of the Jews. It's unlikely he'll enforce the king's edict to protect us unless he sees some benefit to himself. One final word of caution: the crusaders may attack on the Sabbath, as they attempted to do in Speyer. If you must defend yourself, do not be bound by Sabbath restrictions. Rabbi Scholomo has written that man was meant to *live* through precepts of the Law, not die through them. Now, go to your loved ones."

Nothing happened that day or the next. But on the following day a few of Count Emmerich's party came into Worms and met with some of the townspeople. It was no coincidence, Miriam felt sure, that trouble started soon after. Someone dug up a fresh corpse and dragged it through town, saying it was a Christian killed by Jews. Furthermore, it was alleged that these Jews had boiled the body and thrown the cooking water into the town wells to poison the citizens. The crusaders and local people who were allied with them quickly armed themselves and sought revenge.

Miriam's family, together with Sofi and Ehud's mother, locked themselves into their apartment on the third floor. The day before, Miriam and Sofi had carried home a week's supply of bread, vegetables, and salted meat. Meanwhile, Ehud had taken their silver plates and goblets for safe keeping to vaults under the synagogue and procured a few sharp tools that might serve as weapons. Their location adjacent to the city wall was more secure than most, owing to its proximity to the guard tower at the Jew's Gate.

Not everyone was as well prepared. Some Jews still walked the streets, seemingly unaware of the danger they faced. The marauding bands quickly found them and showed no mercy. Miriam could hear their cries and imagine what was happening. She kept her children away from the windows for fear they might witness murder and then dream about it afterwards. It was reported later that crusaders broke into several houses and killed those inside. This rampage went on for two days. After that, an eerie silence prevailed on the streets of the Jewish quarter.

The children were behaving very well under the circumstances. Aaron recited Torah to his younger siblings and helped them memorize short passages. Miriam read to them from a small book of poems, love songs, and laments for Zion that Ehud's father had acquired on one of his trading expeditions to the East. Much of the poetry recounted deeds of heroism by Jews struggling to survive. Miriam devised games for them to play and crafts to work on, but after six days she was running out of ideas. The hours dragged on and the children were becoming visibly restless. Besides, the food supply was nearly exhausted. It would soon be necessary to go out. That evening, Ehud proposed a visit to Mosche for information and advice. On the way, he said, he would try to find food, bread if nothing else, to satisfy them for a few more days. Miriam was afraid of his going out at night and convinced him to wait until morning.

He left at dawn, and his family waited and worried until the sun was high in the sky. When he finally returned, he carried an armload of bread and a small sack of potatoes. The children climbed all over their father, covering him with kisses.

"Well, my children, if this is the reward for bringing such meager foodstuffs, what will you do when I bring you sugar candy?"

"Oh, Papa, can you get some?" asked little Daniel, the youngest child.

"We'll see, my son. One day, when the troubles have passed, we'll have a feast of sweet things. Now I must talk to Mama, so you children take a loaf of fresh bread and share it with Aunt Sofi and Grandmama."

Ehud and Miriam went to the back room and spoke quietly together. "I've seen Mosche. He's been busy these last few days."

"Is he all right? I've been so worried he wouldn't have the patience to stay hidden."

"Yes, he's fine. You're right though. He came out of hiding as soon as the streets were calm."

"What was he doing?" asked Miriam.

"Organizing, as usual. Several people had already been admitted to the bishop's palace. Mosche led a delegation of community leaders requesting that more space be made available. After what happened, people are afraid to stay in their houses. Hundreds of them are looking for refuge."

"How did the bishop respond?"

"He said he'd make room for them, but he couldn't promise to protect them. Chances would be better, he said, if we all accepted baptism immediately. Then the delegation went to some of the leading merchants. One or two offered their own houses as sanctuary. Others said they would avenge the blood of any resident of Worms, Jew or Christian, shed by the crusaders."

"That's a small sign of hope, I suppose."

"Mosche doesn't see it that way. He says vengeance won't do us any good once we're dead. Really, it looks like there aren't any good options. Those who go to the bishop's palace will be crowded into an empty hall with no beds or sanitation facilities. It'll be noisy and dirty. Storing enough food for all those people is another problem."

"What are we going to do?"

"Staying home is risky, but it might be best for us. While things are quiet, we can bring more food into the house. We'll all go to the market this afternoon. The children need to get out into the fresh air."

"Do you think it's safe?"

"As safe as it's going to be for some time. The other thing I learned from Mosche is that the larger part of Count Emmerich's horde is about a day's journey from Worms."

"Is there any hope of keeping them out of the city?" Miriam's voice became more anxious.

Ehud shrugged his shoulders. "There's always hope. Mosche's delegation handed over a large sum of money to the merchants and asked them to negotiate with Count Emmerich. And besides, after what happened in Speyer, the count might be leery of tangling with another bishop. It would be easier to take the money and go on his way."

"But the current bishop of Worms has never been a friend to us. If King Henry were here with his army, I'd feel safer."

"Yes, wife, but his empire is too big to govern, much less protect."

Soon the family ventured out into the streets, running errands and visiting friends. Many houses were already empty, the residents having fled to the countryside or to the bishop's palace. Ehud and Sofi spent the afternoon carrying food supplies to the house, while Miriam led the children around the Jewish quarter, looking for interesting playthings to take home. They stayed outdoors as long as they could, until the light began to fade. Then they all locked themselves into the house again, to wait out the storm.

Four days passed. During those days, Miriam heard people go by on the street beneath the windows of the house. Some were running; others moved slowly as they led small children or pulled clattering handcarts. Occasionally a shout rang out. Once she thought she heard heavy footsteps running close by, perhaps a crowd of people. On the fifth day, around noon, there came a loud, rapid knock at the door. Miriam and her husband looked at each other. He quickly motioned for her to take the children to the back room, where his mother and Sofi stayed most of the time. Ehud picked up a metal shaft and a knife and stood silently in front of the door. The knocking resumed, only this time it sounded like banging with a fist. He and Miriam had discussed what they would do if raiders came into their house. First he would plead with them and offer them money. If that failed, he would fight them off as long as he could, while Miriam and the children made their escape. They would squeeze through the back dormer window onto the top of the city wall adjacent to the house. There they would hide or make their way into another residence nearby. Under no circumstances would they consider suicide, which some of their neighbors had contemplated as a last resort. Suddenly the banging stopped. It sounded as if someone slumped against the door and groaned heavily. Ehud listened. Yes, he heard someone say Miriam's name over and over. He turned the latch and opened the door a tiny crack. There was Josef, collapsed on the floor of the landing, looking wild and distraught.

"What are you doing here?" asked Ehud.

Josef, turning his head up, looked a little surprised. "You're here, then?" he said with a husky voice.

"Yes. Get yourself inside. Quickly now." Ehud latched the door and went to get his wife. "Now tell us why you're here?"

Josef stared at Miriam for a moment. "I was afraid you were . . . taken away or something. It's horrible. You need to find a hiding place."

"It's okay, Josef," said Miriam. "We decided to stay here until it's over."

"You can't. They'll come and get you."

"How do you know?"

Josef hung his head and held out his arms. "Can't you see the blood on my hands? I had a chance to save someone's life and I refused. I'm as bad as the killers."

"What are you talking about?" asked Ehud.

"Yesterday," said Josef. "A young woman came to me in the street and took hold of my shirt. She wouldn't let go. I asked her what she wanted. She said she'd seen me in the Jewish quarter and knew I was friendly with Jews. She wanted me to give shelter to her family." Josef closed his eyes. "I told her I had no room to keep them. But she didn't give up. She said they didn't need much space—it was just herself and her husband and three little boys. They would bring food with them." Josef looked briefly at Miriam and then at the wall behind her. "I could have taken them into my rooms. But I told her to go to the bishop's palace for protection. I said I couldn't fight a mob. She said the bishop wouldn't protect them. She fell to her knees, still clinging to my shirt. 'If you won't take us all,' she said, 'just take the boys. The oldest one will look after the others.' She showed me a purse full of gold coins. I told her I didn't want her money. I finally got loose from her and walked away as fast as I could."

"Maybe she found another safe place," suggested Miriam.

"No," said Josef, his voice shaking. "She went home. This morning I found the bodies. The invaders dragged them out and killed them on the street." He looked hard at Miriam and her husband. "They'll find you and do the same."

Miriam put her hand over her mouth.

"Will you come with me?" asked Josef. "The back room at my place is small, but I think it would be safer than staying here."

Miriam and her husband exchanged a few words while Josef stared at the floor. Finally she said, "It'll take us a few minutes to get ready. You know there are eight of us, including Sofi and Ehud's mother."

Josef nodded. "While you get things together, I'll run over to Mosche's house, to see what he's doing."

Ehud took Josef's hand. "Thank you, my friend. We'll be ready when you return."

Miriam quickly explained to the children that they would be going to another place. She filled a few sacks with food and other essentials. Meanwhile, Ehud spoke with his mother and Sofi. He encountered unexpected difficulty.

"No, my son. I will not leave this house."

"But, Mother. It's too dangerous. The thugs will break down the door. Who knows what they might do to you."

"What would they want with an old woman?" she answered. "You know I would only slow you down. Take Sofi and the children. They still have some life ahead of them."

Sofi shook her head violently. She moved closer to Ehud's mother and linked arms with her.

"Not you too, Sofi," said Ehud with a groan. "Maybe you'll listen to Miriam." He went to get his wife. She also had no success in convincing the two women to leave the house. She turned to Sofi.

"Now listen, Sofi. You are a Christian. If the rioters come here, you must show them you're not a Jew. Fall on your knees and cross yourself, or whatever it takes. They shouldn't harm you. When you get out, go to your church, and someone will look after you."

Sofi shook her head again and held tighter to the old woman. Against this solid wall of resolve, Miriam and her husband could see that further argument was useless.

When Josef returned, he was out of breath. "We must go quickly. Some of them are coming this way."

"What about Mosche?" asked Miriam anxiously.

"His house was empty. They must have escaped."

Miriam and Ehud strapped supplies on their backs. Josef picked up one of the children, Ehud another, and Miriam took the two oldest by the hand. After a hasty farewell, they made their way quietly down two flights of steps and into the street. It was impossible to take the most direct route to Josef's house. The lower section of Jew's Alley was overrun with angry-looking men carrying torches in broad daylight and sharp weapons. The family slipped through a narrow passageway into the grove behind the synagogue. They waited while Josef looked for a safe path to his rooms off Market Street.

"It's no good," he said upon his return. "The rioters are gathering on the main street near my house. We have to find another place for you to stay until they're gone." Miriam pulled her children closer to her. "The choices are few," said Josef. "My suggestion is to make our way to the cathedral. There are some good hiding places in that huge building. Besides, it's a holy place. The crusaders might be more restrained on sacred ground."

"What about the bishop's palace?" asked Ehud.

"No. Part of the mob was milling around there earlier today."

The small group found its way through back streets and alleyways to the cathedral. They were about to enter through the south portal when Miriam suddenly stopped and looked around the empty courtyard. "What about the Donkey's Tower?" she asked Josef. "Can we get in?"

"Let's try it," he replied.

The old wooden door stuck tight, but the two men were able to push it open. Inside, the remains of garbage and manure piles on the ground floor gave off a sickly-sweet aroma. The spiral walkway was still intact. Quickly the company climbed the sloping path until they reached the first landing. There they rested. Josef said he'd go out and scout around the cathedral. Also, he would try to find out what was happening in the Jewish quarter. He promised to return to them that night, after the sun went down.

Miriam and Ehud took turns reading aloud to the children from a small book of Psalms that Ehud had stuck in his shirt as they were leaving home. After a quick supper, the children begged to be allowed to explore their new surroundings. To their delight, the spiral walkway led them high into the tower. Miriam found an open space about half-way up where they might sleep. This far above ground level they would be less likely to be heard, if someone were searching the cathedral for Jews. She cautioned the children to be as quiet as they could, then she left them and descended with her husband to the base of the tower. The two spoke quietly to one another while they awaited Josef's return. Outside the tower, they heard frightening noises, shouting, jeering, and heavy footsteps. Ehud put his arm around Miriam and told her how fortunate he felt to have her as a wife, like Isaak in the Bible whose marriage was made in heaven. But he was luckier than Isaak, he said, because he didn't have to travel so far to find his wife. They talked about the holy covenant of marriage and the joys and trials of parenthood. For a long time they sat just quietly together.

When Josef finally showed up, rather late at night, he was not alone. With him was a boy who looked to be about fourteen years old. He had blood on his shirt and was trembling visibly. Josef explained he'd found the boy outside St. Paul's Church. There had been violence in the neighborhood, and he was sure the boy had witnessed some terrible things. So far, the boy had not spoken about it. Could he stay here with them until, perhaps, some relatives might be found? Miriam agreed immediately and took the boy by the hand. She learned his name was Marcus. After coaxing him to eat some bread and cheese, she walked him slowly up to the level where her children were sleeping. She sat with him until he, too, was asleep.

Miriam returned to the lower level and heard the men talking together. When she appeared they both became silent, looking at her with solemn expressions.

"What is it?" she asked.

"The worst you can imagine," said Josef.

"People killed?"

"Many people killed. There was mass slaughter at the bishop's palace. The courtyard is full of bodies. Houses have been looted and the inhabitants murdered. Only a few people who consented to baptism were passed over."

"And those who found good hiding places," added Miriam quietly.

"Yes. You'll have to stay here. I'll try to come back in a few days with food and water." After a quick farewell, Josef disappeared into the gloom.

Chapter 19

Several days passed, and Josef did not return. With another hungry mouth to feed, the family's food supply would quickly run out. But more worrisome was the water. Even with careful rationing, their reserves would soon be used up. Against her motherly instincts, Miriam allowed no washing whatsoever; every drop was to be drunk. With limited water intake, the children were complaining of dry throats. But what could they do? It was much too dangerous to go out just yet. They could still hear marauders roaming the streets, yelling ugly things. Where was Josef? He must know the situation. Perhaps he had been injured or even killed. Perhaps he would never return. Miriam's heart sank. Would she and her family die right here, too weak and dehydrated to even attempt an escape? No, she should have known her husband would not allow that. On the fourth day, Ehud proposed to go out.

"It's all right, my dear. Things will have calmed down a bit. I'll go out in the middle of the night with water jugs."

"Where will you go?" asked Miriam anxiously.

"I think there's a well in the courtyard at the Andreas Cloister. If I can't get in there, I'll go to Newmarket Square. Both are close by, so I can be back within an hour."

"And if you're not back by then?"

"You're not to worry. If anyone seems to be following me, I will not give away your hiding place. I might have to delay my return. In that case, I'll try to hide the water jugs outside the tower. There's a recess in the wall, just to the left of the door, I noticed on our way in. If I'm not back in a couple of hours, look there."

Ehud fixed a crude latch on the inside of the door and instructed his wife to lock it when he went out. That night he succeeded in filling the water jugs. He was back within an hour, as he had predicted. Nevertheless, Miriam waited tensely on the lower level the entire time he was away.

Sleep was out of the question. By the time he returned she was trembling with fear. He put his arms around her and held her while she sobbed, finally overcome by her worries. It was good that the children were asleep. She wanted to show herself strong to them. Tomorrow the whole family would celebrate by taking a long drink and washing their faces.

Next morning the children were as happy as Miriam had ever seen them. They all drank until she thought they would burst, and then they drank some more. Each face was scrubbed until it shone. After this little extravagance, Miriam would start conserving again, but today they would enjoy the abundance of water. Still there loomed the question of what they would eat. Apparently, the public wells were accessible, but would Ehud be able to find food? Would anyone sell to a Jew? Had the townspeople turned against them during this tumultuous time? Or were they too intimidated to have any dealings with Jews?

Ehud went out several more times at night. He brought back water each time but no food. Now all they had left was a bit of bread and a few raw turnips. Miriam and Ehud discussed what they should do next. Should they try to escape to the countryside? No, that would be too slow and dangerous, since the younger children needed to be carried. Should they wait longer and hope Josef came with food? Maybe they could hold out for a few days, but then they would be too weak to attempt anything else. The violent noises they had heard outside the cathedral had nearly ceased now; Ehud thought it might be safe to go out in the town when the sun was up. He decided to try the next day to find a vendor who would sell food to him. Whatever he acquired he would conceal in the recess beside the tower door. He would not, in any event, leave or enter the tower during daylight hours, for fear of being seen. That night Ehud kissed his wife goodbye, and she implored him to be cautious.

Over the next two days, Miriam saw nothing of her husband. At night, however, she checked the recess in the wall and found evidence of his success. First came eight loaves of heavy, dark rye bread, hidden in a clump of cut branches. The next delivery included a piece of hard salami, a large bag of carrots, and a folded paper containing sugar candies! How did he do it? Miriam thought her husband must have worked a miracle. The children would be so pleased to have sweets! But she herself could not celebrate. In fact she wasn't sure she could eat. Her stomach was empty, gnawed by hunger, yet she had no appetite. All she could think about was Ehud. Now they had enough food and he must come back to them. Surely he would come tonight, and then everything would be better. She and the children would pray all day today, and tomorrow if necessary, for his safe return.

He did not come that night, nor the next. In spite of her fatigue, Miriam was unable to sleep soundly. She woke at any small noise, and immediately her mind started racing over the horrible possibilities of what might have happened to her husband. On his fourth night away, Miriam arose and went down the spiral walkway to the ground floor. She couldn't lie still any longer and didn't want to wake the children. Besides, she might hear Ehud if he came by with another delivery of food. Even though they used one corner of this lower room as their latrine, the smell was not so terribly bad. A good supply of straw had been left behind, and she had shown the children how to cover their excrement. Miriam settled herself on a pile of straw in the opposite corner.

She was dozing lightly when a noise awakened her. Instantly she was fully awake. Where did the noise come from? She hoped with all her might that Ehud would walk through the door. But no, the sounds came from above. Someone was coming down the sloping walkway. Perhaps one of the children had noticed she was gone and come to look for her. She listened hard but did not recognize the footsteps as one of her children's. It must be Marcus, coming to relieve himself. When he entered the room, she stood and told him she would leave if he needed to use the latrine. He said no, he just wanted to come sit with her. For many minutes they sat quietly in the dark, with only a little moonlight shining through a slit in the stone wall. Marcus began to sob, and Miriam put her arm around him.

"Do you want to talk about it?" she asked in a gentle voice.

He nodded but could not speak through the sobs. After a time he said, "My family . . . they're all dead."

"Are you sure?"

"Yes, I was there. I saw it."

"You don't need to tell me about it if you don't want to."

"We lived across the street from St. Paul's Church. My father worked at the church as a groundskeeper. There was an old priest there named Albert who was always kind to us. His eyes were weak, and my mother thought maybe he couldn't see that we were Jews. But I think he knew. Anyway, he used to give little presents to me and my sisters. Nothing much, but sometimes a bit of fruit or a homemade toy." Marcus paused, struggling to move his mind from those happy childhood memories to what would happen later. "When the troubles started, we waited at home as long as we could. But the rioters heard there were Jews living nearby, and they were going from house to house looking for us. We made a run for the church, and the old priest took us down into the crypt. He told us to be as quiet as we could. He said we could stay until the danger was passed. But someone had seen us go into the church."

Again Marcus struggled to recount what happened next. "I was so scared. We could hear a noisy crowd arguing with the priest. They came closer and closer. We could see some of our neighbors at the head of the crowd, people we'd known for years and years. But they looked different, full of meanness and hate. Albert stood there, between us and them. He told them we hadn't done anything wrong. Murdering innocent people, he said, would not help the crusade. They should be ashamed of going after their own neighbors, especially defenseless women and children. He talked to them about what their Jesus would expect them to do. Meanwhile the men stood with knives and clubs in their hands, looking angrily at us, even as the old priest kept talking. Finally a few of them at the front turned around and motioned to the others. They left, grumbling to each other on the way out."

"The priest saved your life."

Marcus sighed heavily. "What good did that do?"

"At least we know some of the townspeople listened to reason."

"You haven't heard the end of it. The priest stayed with us that day and the next. He brought us food and asked if there was anything else we needed. He talked seriously with my parents, asking their forgiveness for the behavior of his fellow Christians. He had hoped the crusade would direct people's anger and energy toward a noble cause, but instead it made them crazy.

"Then another mob came, much bigger than before. We could hear the uproar from where we were hiding. They were taunting a youth named Yitzak, telling him he needed to repent of his unbelief and be baptized. Someone in the crowd remembered that other Jews were hiding in the crypt. They came to get us. The old priest tried to stand in their way, but this time they knocked him over. We were dragged into the church and told we should witness a baptism and submit to it ourselves if we knew what was good for us. Poor Yitzak, who couldn't have been over twenty, had a cord tied around his neck. His face and arms were bloody. They had dragged him through the streets from the bishop's palace to the church. He was barely alive. One man put his boot on Yitzak's chest and told him this was his last chance to accept baptism. The young man stared up at him and moved his head weakly from side to side. The crusader pulled his sword and shouted, 'Their ancestors crucified God! Why should we let them live? Let our swords begin their work here, before we make our pilgrimage!' I turned my head away. I couldn't watch. Then they pushed us to the center of the mob. The man with the sword asked if we would be baptized. My father said no and a melee broke out. We tried to stay close to each other, and somehow the old priest got in among us. My father fell on top of me after we got separated from the others. I lay as still as I could, until suddenly someone shouted that the priest had been killed and everyone should get out of the church quickly. They all left, except me and the dead bodies. I pushed my father's body aside and saw that my mother and sisters were dead too. I was dazed, but eventually I went out on the street and sat there until your friend found me and brought me here."

Miriam and the boy sat quietly for a time. She stroked his hand. "Marcus, you'll be part of our family from now on. Whatever happens, we'll stay together and protect each other."

Marcus nodded. After a few moments he said, "I'll be a big brother to your children, now that their father is gone."

This was a stab in Miriam's heart. She was not yet willing to give up hope that Ehud would return. She resolved to stay where they were until their food supply ran out.

A week later Ehud still had not returned. They had eaten most of what he brought, but not the sugar candies. Aaron convinced his brother and sisters to save them until their father came back. He said having sweets would help them celebrate when the whole family was together again.

Marcus had gone out several times in the past week to fill the water jugs. He reported that the streets at night were quiet and practically empty. The crusaders must have continued their drive to the north, leaving the town of Worms bloodied and dazed. It would probably be safe now for the family to make a run for it. Yet Miriam did not want to leave until she found out what happened to Ehud. Now that their food supply had nearly run out, they would need to make a decision soon. Either she would have to go looking for food or the family would try to make an escape. She and Marcus would talk about it that evening after the children were asleep.

Around sundown, while the family was eating the last remnants of stale bread, Miriam thought she heard a tapping on the door below. Her heart leapt with the thought that Ehud might be alive after all. She scrambled down the sloping walkway and stood just in front of the door, waiting and listening. Yes, someone was knocking. She whispered through a crack in the door, and an unintelligible answer came back. Slowly she slid the latch back and pulled the door open. It was Josef. Miriam's face fell, and her eyes filled with tears. Josef came in quietly and closed the door behind him. He waited a few minutes before speaking.

"Miriam, I'm sorry I didn't come back sooner."

She shook her head but said nothing.

"The night I left you, there was a huge riot. The crusaders were raiding houses, killing people, stealing whatever they could get their hands on. It was barbarous." Josef hung his head and put his hands on his forehead. Miriam noticed now that his arms were wrapped up to the shoulders in stained, wet, bandages. A loose, sleeveless shirt hung on his back. All she could see of the skin on his neck and hands looked red and raw.

"What happened?" she asked.

"I was burned."

"How?"

"When I saw what was happening, I went to the Jewish quarter. Jews' Alley was a scene from hell—bodies in the street, people screaming, plunder and pillage everywhere. Even the synagogue was sacked. I went inside. Curtains were torn down, furniture smashed, and windows broken." Josef paused, trying to recollect what else he had seen. "The Torah scrolls were on fire. I'm not exactly sure, but I think I tried to carry them outside. All I remember is waking up in the courtyard. My old boss Frieder was standing over me, putting a wet rag on my face."

Miriam spoke softly. "I remember Frieder. He helped us when Sofi was kidnapped."

Josef nodded. "He brought me to his house. His daughter took care of me. My arms were burned and I had a fever. They say I was convulsing and hallucinating. That's why I didn't come, Miriam. I'm sorry I didn't help you. As soon as I remembered where you were, I came. Here, I've got food and water for you."

Miriam shivered. "You're too late, Josef," she whispered.

"What do you mean? What's happened?"

After a long silence, Miriam said, "Ehud went out to get food for us. He didn't come back."

Josef put his head in his hands. "Miriam, I'm sorry." He tried to look into her face, but it was too dark to see anything. "What about the children?"

"They're okay. A little hungry and discouraged. They miss their father."

"You need to get them away from this place."

"Yes, but how can I do that?"

"There's a way. Frieder's daughter is a Jew." Josef explained to Miriam how Frieder and his wife had raised Hanna from childhood and adopted her. During the riots, she and her family had taken refuge in Frieder's house, and the crusaders didn't find out about it. "Anyway, Hanna's family is leaving Worms, along with a few other survivors. They'll be heading west, to Francia. The violence there has been less severe. It's reported there are large communities of Jews still intact."

"Are we to be refugees, then?"

"It's the best way to assure your safety. Besides, there's nothing left here for you. The synagogue and the Jeschiba are destroyed. Where would your children be educated?"

"Yes, you're right. But it's hard to leave when I don't know what's happened to Ehud, and Mosche, too. All my relatives and friends live in Worms." They sat quietly for a few minutes. Miriam sighed. "So what do we do next?"

"Hanna and the others are making preparations now. They hope to leave in the next day or two. Shall I tell them you'll join them?"

Miriam hesitated for a moment. "Yes. I'll talk to the children about it in the morning."

"There's one more thing you should know about, Miriam. It's not much, but a tiny scrap of good news is better than nothing. While I was lying in bed from the burns, Hanna told me about something that happened during the riots. After the assault on Jews at the bishop's palace, the mob marched to the Jewish cemetery. Frieder had anticipated this might happen, and he was waiting for them at the gates when they arrived. The rioters were shouting ugly words about 'digging up Jew bones' and 'pissing on holy sand.' Frieder stood his ground. Hanna said her father claimed authority over town property. Anyone who set foot on this land, he said, would be charged with trespassing. He demanded to speak with their leader. When a scruffy Frenchman came forward, Frieder told him that the pope himself had a special interest in preserving cemeteries, and if anyone wanted to destroy it, they should seek permission from him. That was enough to send them away."

"So at least dead Jews are allowed to rest in peace," said Miriam.

What Josef didn't tell her, but she would soon find out, was that hundreds of other dead Jews had recently been buried beside their forefathers in the cemetery. The survivors had put off their departure to Francia to accomplish that task.

The next morning, Miriam told her children they would be leaving. Aaron tried hard to be brave, but the younger ones all cried and whimpered. They wanted to know what would happen if their father came looking for them and they were not there. Miriam told them not to worry, that if he were alive, he would find them. Marcus was quite helpful, comforting the children and getting them ready to travel. He told stories about famous travelers in history and all the interesting places they had visited. He recited Bible verses about the Lord watching over his people as they crossed the desert to the Promised Land. Before it was time to leave, the children were almost looking forward to the journey.

At night, Josef returned to the base of the tower with Hanna, Frieder's adopted daughter. She told Miriam that the small group of survivors would depart day after tomorrow at dawn. They were trying to collect supplies for the trip, enough food for at least two weeks of travel. In order to avoid risking another encounter with crusaders, the group would not follow the river, but go directly west through the mountains. Once in Francia, they would hope to meet less hostile residents who would sell them what they needed. Then Hanna explained to Miriam about the others who would be traveling with them. These were people who had agreed to be baptized and thereby saved their own lives and the lives of their children. Hanna implored Miriam not to question them closely about their decision. Most regretted this act and would never have done it except under extreme duress. They still considered themselves to be Jews. Some had been motivated by fear for their children, that they would be killed, or equally bad, taken away and raised as Christian idolaters. Others allowed themselves to be profaned in this way so that they might bury the dead, their fellow Jews who died as heroes.

Josef asked Miriam if he could help her prepare for the trip in any way. She didn't think so. Then he told her again how sorry he was. He asked her to believe that not all Christians supported or condoned what had happened. His religion, the Christianity he loved, didn't teach such things. He himself had lain awake at night, agonizing about the events of the last three weeks. He had tried to pray but couldn't. The only place he found peace was in the Jewish cemetery. He had gone there to place stones on the graves of her parents and Ehud's father, and had been grateful that these good people, at least, had been spared the horrors that others had witnessed.

Hanna told Miriam one of the men would come for her and the children on the morning of departure. Josef bade her farewell and the two went away, leaving Miriam alone in the dark at the base of the tower.

Chapter 20

The next day Miriam and Marcus made preparations for the journey. There was little to do. The possessions they had with them were so few that packing was done in minutes. Some extra articles of clothing, Ehud's book of Psalms, and other small mementos brought from home were easily bundled into a small bag. Today they would consume most of the food Josef had brought, and if anything was left they would add it to the pack. Marcus filled the water jugs while Miriam washed the children as best she could.

Long before dawn on the following day, Miriam awoke. She was too agitated to go back to sleep. In an attempt to calm herself, she recited prayers and every Bible verse she could think of. Finally, after what seemed like hours, the gloom became a little less thick. Miriam rose and sat on the floor beside the children, watching them sleep soundly in their innocence. She gave Marcus a gentle nudge on the shoulder, and he instantly sat up. She asked him to go down and wait by the tower door for someone to come for them. Meanwhile, she woke the children. Soon Marcus came back up the walkway with a young man who introduced himself as Jonas. He and Marcus each picked up one of the younger children, still groggy with sleep. Miriam took their bag of belongings in her arms and asked Aaron and Susanna to hold hands with each other. They made their way down the spiral walkway for the last time.

The group gathered at the Andreas Gate south of the cathedral. Somehow a donkey cart had been procured, and it was already packed with food and other supplies. Blankets covered the supplies, and young children lay on top, some fast asleep. Miriam asked no questions but assumed Frieder, and perhaps Josef, had had a hand in equipping the travel party. They were about twenty people in all, including several small children. As Miriam looked for faces she recognized, she suddenly realized Josef was there, conferring with one of the men. The two were discussing the travel route and what they might meet along the way. When that conversation ended, Josef approached Miriam. He wished her a safe journey and hoped she would find a good place to live, a new home for her family. He said he'd been able to save a few items from the synagogue and school, and he had tucked them into the cart under the blankets. Before she could say more than a quick thank you, he turned and walked back into the town.

The group left soon after. As the cart rumbled out the gate, accompanied by walkers of assorted size and age, Miriam glanced over her right shoulder. She saw the outer wall of the Jewish cemetery where her parents were buried, and looming behind the cemetery, the still unfinished towers of the massive cathedral. This would be her last view of the city she had always regarded as her beloved home.

The travelers walked steadily, though not quickly, all through the first day. An elderly couple, frail in appearance, had some difficulty keeping up with the others. Their son, a strong man in middle age, carried his mother for long stretches. Miriam was proud of her children, how they walked on and on without complaining. Even little Daniel stayed on his feet most of the time, except when he joined the other small children on the donkey cart for his afternoon nap. Miriam observed the rest of the group. Hanna and her husband had three children, ranging in age from ten to two, all handsome and hearty-looking. Jonas, the young man who had come to fetch Miriam's family at the tower, and his wife Abigail had two young sons, one still a baby. The last member of the group was a man who looked to be in his forties, gruff and taciturn, with a sour expression on his face. Miriam kept her distance from him and did not even try to find out his name.

Before the sun went down, the travelers came to a soft, grassy meadow where they decided to spend the night. They ate quickly and lay themselves down in small family groups. It was warm, and all of them were weary enough that they slept soundly through the first night. Next morning they set out again at dawn. As the days passed, their progress through increasingly hilly terrain slowed noticeably. Nighttime temperatures dipped to uncomfortable levels. The families huddled together, and Miriam sent Marcus to ask the sour-faced man if he wanted a companion to sleep back-to-back. The man declined, so Marcus stayed with Miriam's family. After spotting a couple of wolves and a wild boar during daylight hours, the group decided to post a guard at night. The men took turns keeping watch, with Marcus doing his part in the rotation. At the end of each day they built a fire, which served several purposes. It provided some warmth against the night chill. It frightened away wandering predators. But best of all, it allowed the travelers to cook the occasional fish they plucked from a mountain stream. This was the most delicious food they tasted for weeks. They also caught small game to cook, and they gathered berries and mushrooms along the way. Anything was a welcome change from the food they had brought along: bread, now hard and stale, root vegetables, and moldy cheese.

In the evenings after the children had gone to sleep, the adults in the group gathered around the fire. At first they discussed only practical matters, such as their food supply and travel route. As time passed they became more open with one another about hopes and dreams for the future and about their experiences in the past. One night Jonas began to relate in detail what had happened at the bishop's palace.

"Please stop, Jonas," his wife Abigail pleaded. "I can't bear it. I don't want to think about those horrible things."

"No, my dear. It's important that we talk about them."

"But I want to leave all that behind. Can't we just try to forget?"

Jonas shook his head. "This time we've been given a nosegay of forget-me-nots. And no matter how ugly these little flowers may be, we must preserve them. For the sake of our fellow Jews, we should tell the stories. It's a way to honor the dead and forewarn the living." He turned and spoke to the group. "If anyone would rather not hear about the horrors we witnessed, I ask you to go lie with the children and begin your night's rest."

Abigail rose and left the circle of adults. The solitary man drifted farther away from the fire into the shadows, where no one could see him. Jonas began his account.

"My family and I sought refuge in the bishop's palace when Count Emmerich's mob descended on the city. We stayed in the courtyard there for about a week, along with scores of others. My friends Naomi and Abram and their son were with us." He nodded to the older couple, who were sitting to his left. "The conditions were not too bad—we had plenty of water, and sympathetic townspeople brought us bread. A banquet hall in the palace was opened for us to sleep in. Stories were circulating about how the bishop of Speyer had saved most of his Jews from the mob. We began to hope that we, too, would survive. We thought it might be just a matter of time before the rioters grew tired of waiting and moved on to another locale. But then a huge mass of them broke down the palace gates. Apparently none of the townspeople attempted to stop them. The two guards stationed at the gates by the bishop were quickly overpowered and disarmed. Our head rabbi immediately stood up and confronted the leaders of the mob. He asked what they wanted. They said baptism. Everyone must agree to be baptized. The men standing behind the leaders began shouting, 'Baptism or death!' and others took it up until it became a roaring chant. The rabbi nodded and asked for a delay. He needed a few hours, he said, to confer with his people. The postponement was grudgingly granted, with a warning they would return in two hours.

"All of us went into the banquet hall. The rabbi explained what was demanded by the crusaders. Women began wailing, and in reaction, little children cried piteously. The rabbi asked for silence. He spoke solemnly to us of Akiba, the great Torah scholar and sage who lived during the reign of Emperor Hadrian. When the emperor forbade study of Torah, Akiba continued to teach, even after they put him in prison. For his faithfulness, he was tortured to death. And now, the head rabbi said, he was willing to follow the example of Akiba and die as a martyr. Furthermore, he would slay his own son Isaak as an offering to God. Our ancestor Abraham had been willing to do the same, he said. The rabbi motioned for his son, a boy of ten, to come to his side. But Isaak did not come alone. His mother came forward as well. She fell on her knees before her husband, wrapped her arms around his legs, and pleaded that she be killed first. She could not watch her own son die by the hand of his father. The rabbi shook his head and said there could be no delay. Silently he bound his son with a piece of rope, took a knife in his hand, and raised it high over the boy's neck. He recited the prayer of benediction for slaughtering, and said that today his son would be received by the Lord and placed in the bosom of Abraham. The boy looked up to heaven and said, 'Amen.' Then the rabbi killed him. The boy's mother fell down sobbing and screaming, until she was led away by her husband.

"Upon witnessing such faith, many in the hall resolved immediately to kill themselves rather than be slaughtered by the crusaders. Others vowed to fight. They spoke of the Maccabees, who had fought for their freedom. Some of these ancient heroes were slain, but in the end they succeeded in repelling their enemies. With God's help, the Jews of Worms might also defend themselves. Miracles had happened before. Those who decided to resist the mob hurried out to the courtyard to pick up stones and sticks and anything else they might use as weapons. My wife and I stayed in the banquet hall with our little ones. What happened next was gruesome. Men in the hall took knives and killed their children, then their wives, then themselves. Others killed their parents. Elderly people without children begged to be slaughtered. Five pious men were chosen to take the lives of those who had no kinsman to do it. Our old neighbor Minna, just before she was killed, cried out, 'Heaven forbid that I should deny the Lord God! For Him and his holy Torah, take my life. Do not wait a moment longer.'

"Soon the hall became silent. Those few of us still alive sat stunned and speechless. It was too horrible to contemplate. Yet before long the bloody scene was repeated outside. At the designated hour, the crusaders returned, in larger numbers than before. First we heard shouts, then screams and groans. It must have been a furious battle. In the end, of course, the Jews were overwhelmed. No matter how hard they fought, they couldn't repel an armed force that outnumbered them ten to one. Every one of our fighters died. The crusaders then came rushing into the hall. Even they, with fresh blood on their hands, were shocked at what they saw. For a few moments they stopped and stared. Then some of them saw us. They ran to us and seized us. We and the other survivors were roughly escorted out of the hall into the bishop's chapel. We were told this was our last chance. Would we agree to be baptized? There were about ten of us who said we would. Several men in clerical dress entered the chapel from a nearby chamber. One of them identified himself as the bishop's nephew. He proceeded to baptize my family and the others. The last to come forward was a young man I had not seen before. Just as the bishop's nephew was beginning the ritual, the young man pulled a knife from his cloak and stabbed him dead. He killed two others before they could subdue him. Of course he was dragged outside and put to death. We never even learned his name."

When Jonas stopped speaking, the listeners sat quietly, most of them staring into the fire. They rose, one or two at a time, and walked away. Miriam and Marcus lay down beside the children, but neither of them was able to sleep. After a quarter of an hour had passed, Marcus whispered, "Miriam, are you still awake?"

"Yes."

"I'm afraid."

"It's okay, Marcus. We're all afraid. But at least we're getting away from the worst of it."

"Will the gentiles in Francia be any different?"

Miriam thought for a few moments before she answered. "We have to hope so. It's our only chance, really."

"Do you remember what Jonas said about not forgetting?" Marcus asked.

"Yes. He said we should tell what we saw, to warn other Jews of what might happen."

"And also to honor the dead. I want to honor my family and remember them always."

"That's a good thing, Marcus."

"But I'm already starting to forget. And if I forget, then my parents and my sisters will be lost forever."

Miriam could hear the distress in his voice. "You learned to write in school, didn't you? Why don't you write an account of what happened to them?"

Marcus spoke slowly. "I could do that . . . It would be hard."

"I'll help you get started," said Miriam. "You told me the whole story, and I think I can recall most of what you said."

"Would you?" His voice sounded almost eager. Then he seemed distressed again. "But what can I write with? We have no pens or ink or parchment."

"You leave that to me. A friend rescued some scrolls and spare parchment from the schoolhouse—he stuck them in our wagon the day we left Worms. As for pens and ink, we'll make do with what we can find. I've noticed eagle feathers by the roadside. And there must be some berry juice that would stain parchment."

Over the next few days, Miriam found feathers that would serve as quills. She experimented with different sorts of berries until she found one that stained deep red, appropriate under the circumstances, she thought. The ink Marcus used in writing a story like this might just as well resemble blood. When Jonas learned what Marcus intended to do, he asked if the boy would be willing to act as scribe for the entire group. It would be a laudable thing, he said, to compile a record of all they had witnessed. Jews in Worms would be revered for their faithfulness and courage. Perhaps they would become a model for others in the same situation. Yes, Jonas reaffirmed, this was a very good idea.

Marcus was eager to begin. Once Miriam found the best writing materials, he immediately wrote the story of his own family's fate and that of Yitzak, the young man who was dragged through the streets. Then he wrote Jonas' account of what happened at the bishop's palace. From then on, he listened for stories related by other travelers, always ready to record them if asked to do so.

Hanna told what she'd observed from the relative safety of her father's house. Looking out an upstairs window, she'd seen rioters roaming the streets, searching for defenseless Jews. One day she noticed, down at the end of their street, what appeared to be a body, lying naked and bloodied. It remained there for an entire day. Only when her father came home in the evening was the corpse removed to the cemetery. Frieder buried it himself. Hanna related another story told to her father by a wealthy citizen of Worms. Just after the massacre at the bishop's palace, this citizen and some of his friends (all Christians) discovered an elderly Jewish woman hiding in a peasant's house outside the city. They recognized the woman, who was well-known for her charitable works among the poor. She had gained the respect of Jews and gentiles alike. The citizens on sudden impulse fell to their knees and pleaded with her to "sully herself" (their own words) with baptism. They believed this was her only chance to survive. She refused. Hanna didn't know what became of the woman.

When all the stories had been told, the travelers didn't stop talking. Oftentimes, during their nightly gatherings around the fire, they spoke about sensitive topics. Marcus recorded many of the discussions. Their words, he thought, shed light on how people think and react when under threat. He was especially interested to hear the point of view of the people who had consented to be baptized. Did they regret their actions? Were they permanently stained in some way? Did they still consider themselves to be good Jews? Jonas was quite willing to speak on this topic. He had been baptized, along with his wife and children. For him, it was a completely justifiable decision.

"Yes, we are still Jews," he said. "We hold fast to the One Lord. We never believed in the Christian deity—our hearts didn't even incline in that direction. The crucified one is no more to us than dead leaves hanging on a tree."

"Would you have eaten the bread they claim to be his flesh?" asked Miriam.

"Yes, if they forced us. But it means nothing. We keep all Torah and Sabbath regulations, as before. We eat only meat that has been properly examined and slaughtered. Our beliefs have not changed in the slightest."

"What made you acquiesce when so many others chose to die rather than betray their faith?"

"Our children. Abigail and I decided weeks ago that we would do whatever we had to to save the lives of our sons. This does not mean we disapprove of martyrdom. In fact, we greatly admire those who died. But that was not the path we chose."

The son of Naomi and Abram now spoke. Miriam had seen him in the schoolhouse before and knew him to be a learned man. He was called Michael.

"The Talmud supports you in this," he said. "If the choice is given between death and transgression, a Jew is allowed to transgress. The only exceptions are adultery, murder, and idolatry, which are not permissible."

"What is worship of a man-god, if not idolatry?" came an angry-sounding voice out of the darkness. "How can you justify soiling yourself with such filth?"

Michael peered into the gloom in an attempt to see his opponent. "Come closer, sir, so that we can discuss the matter."

"What is there to discuss?" asked the gruff man as he emerged into the firelight. Miriam had hardly heard him say a word these past ten days, and she still didn't know his name.

"Well, the sages don't all agree," began Michael. "To be sure, some of them say we should never submit to idolatry of any kind, because we are commanded to love God with all our heart and soul and might. But Rabbi Ishmael dissents. He says idolatrous worship may sometimes be chosen over death. Ishmael and his supporters make a distinction between private and public worship. Idolatry in public is always condemned, they say, based on the command to sanctify God's Divine Name. However, a Jew may (and should) submit to demands for idolatrous behavior in private when the alternative is death. The recent baptisms took place under precisely those conditions."

"I don't claim to be learned like you," said the man, "but I know about the three young Jews in Babylon who walked into a burning furnace rather than bow down to a golden statue. And the righteous woman of Judea and her seven sons, who all endured torture rather than eat swine flesh. These are the heroes of our people. These are the examples we should follow." He stood frowning with arms folded.

"Well, sir, we have a difference of opinion, or perhaps of interpretation," said Michael. "My understanding is that Torah was written to preserve life, not destroy it. If this means leniency in keeping some of the commandments, then so be it."

"Bah!" said the man, and he spat into the fire.

"You have never told us, sir, how you survived the riots."

The man stared into the fire. "The less said, the better," he responded. Nevertheless, after a few nights had passed, he did tell of his experiences. He had stayed in his house when the trouble began. His sister and two of her children joined him after they entered their own home and found the rest of their family slain. The four of them hid under the floorboards of his house. The man couldn't recall the exact sequence of events. He knew they lay huddled together in this narrow, dank area, with no sunlight or fresh air. Their food grew moldy and their water stale. Rats crawled past them and over them. The children became ill, and so did their mother. Whether it was from the food or the water or the rats, he would never know. But he watched his loved ones burn up with fever. He could do nothing. If they left their hiding place, they faced death at the hands of the crusaders. At any rate, there would be no doctors to help them. All the doctors he knew in Worms were Jews, who were either dead or in hiding. He could do nothing but watch them die and hope to die himself. But he kept on living. Finally, when the stench became unbearable, he went out to face death by the sword. But that didn't happen either. The crusaders had gone. He wondered why he had survived when so many others died. As he walked the streets of the Jewish quarter and saw bodies strewn about like refuse, he knew what was required of him. He would bury the dead. Beginning with his sister and her family, he lovingly washed the bodies and dressed them in the finest clothes he could find among their possessions. He entered other houses, too, and performed similar ministrations for people he knew and people he didn't know. Soon he met up with Jonas and Michael and a few gentiles who were engaged in the same work. They had obtained a donkey cart in which to carry the bodies to the cemetery. It was hot, exhausting work and often nauseating as well. They buried hundreds of bodies.

After hearing this man's account, Miriam could better understand why he was bitter toward those who chose baptism over death. His sister's family was given no choice. Some had been killed outright and the rest died of disease. It was horrible. Yet Miriam knew that these Jews in the travel party, with their diverse backgrounds and differing philosophies, would have to stay together if they hoped to survive.

As the travelers crossed into an eastern province of Francia, they met up with another group of refugees. These Jews, fifteen in all, had escaped from Mainz, where the crusaders went after they left Worms. They had made the first part of their journey by boat. A river flowing into the Rhein near Mainz afforded them a westward channel into the mountains; though they were sailing upstream, it was still faster than walking. Miriam was glad to be traveling in a larger company, in case they should meet robbers or other hostile groups on the road. She assumed these new arrivals would have their own experiences to relate of terror and devastation, and she wasn't sure she could bear to hear any more. And yet the stories must be told. Marcus had undertaken his role as a scribe with diligence; now there would be more work for him to do.

Chapter 21

"It all started a couple of months ago," began the narrative of Rizpa, a middle-aged woman who became spokesperson for the refugees from Mainz. "We received letters from our friends and relatives in Francia, warning us of violent armies marching eastward. They advised us to fast and pray, which we did. Yet few of us took the threat seriously. We had a good relationship with the bishop of Mainz and with the citizens. Our treasuries were full, and this, we thought, would provide a measure of protection. Therefore we took no advance precautions, other than discussing the situation with the bishop and city leaders. Indeed, this approach worked for a while. Duke Godfrey and his soldiers were the first to come through. He was known to be a zealot who'd sworn to avenge the blood of his crucified god with the blood of Israel. Through a gentile spokesman, we offered the duke five hundred silver marks to buy food and supplies for his army. About the same time, an order came down from King Henry not to seek revenge against the Jews. The king's order, together with our payment, was enough to persuade Duke Godfrey to continue his march toward Jerusalem. A few in our community objected to paying what they considered a 'bribe' to an evil man, but most of us were willing to 'serve the king of Babylon and live,' as it says in Holy Scripture. Thus we hoped that negotiating and giving money to the crusaders would prevent violence in our midst. Then we heard what happened in your city."

"What did you hear?" asked Jonas.

"That the religious fervor of Count Emmerich's followers was impossible to contain . . . that they had killed hundreds of Jews in Worms and were coming next to Mainz."

Jonas nodded. "You heard correctly."

"Immediately our chief rabbi applied to Archbishop Ruthard for protection. We gave the bishop a large sum of money which he set aside, he assured us, to use in our defense. Money was also paid to certain influential citizens and noblemen. It is to this last group that we here owe our survival." The speaker nodded toward her companions sitting nearby. "All of us you see alive today were taken in by nobles who were able to hide us in their fortified houses. Others not so lucky went to the bishop's palace or the synagogue, or they lodged with gentile friends."

"What became of them?"

"It's a long, sad story. We found out the details afterwards from one of the bishop's guards and other gentiles who witnessed the events."

"Can you bear to talk about it?"

Rizpa nodded. "By the time Emmerich and his mob arrived at Mainz, most of the Jews had sought refuge in one place or another. Our gentile spokesman went out again to meet the leaders. He offered Emmerich seven pounds of gold if he would bypass the city. The offer was refused. He added a promise to provide letters to other Jewish communities along the route, encouraging them to support the crusaders on their way to Jerusalem. This also was refused. When Emmerich was reminded of King Henry's edict not to harm the Jews, he sneered and asked who was going to enforce it. He said the king had been bribed by Jews. The orders of such a king could not stand in the way of a noble cause. Whether Emmerich really believed this or whether he simply realized he couldn't control the mob milling behind him is hard to say. In any event, our efforts to negotiate failed. Nevertheless, our gentile leaders still did not welcome the crusading mob into the city. The gates were locked, and Emmerich's massive army (if you can call it that) was forced to camp outside the city wall for several days. Eventually, the main gate was opened by unknown sympathizers, but Emmerich claimed it was a miracle done by the crucified one himself.

"While all this was going on, our people were not sitting idle. Many collected weapons to defend themselves. Some renewed their commitment to fast and pray. Our chief rabbi was in frequent contact with the bishop, trying to find ways to protect Jews. You have surely heard of our rabbi, Kalonymus ben Meshullam?"

"Most certainly," answered Miriam. "One of his kinsmen was a rabbi in Worms. They shared a common ancestor in the great Talmudist and poet Kalonymus, who came to the Rheinland from Italia."

"Yes. The earlier Kalonymus also lived in Mainz. Our rabbi was a great man too, worthy of the name he inherited. As I said, he was our advocate with Archbishop Ruthard. The best plan the two men agreed upon was to send Jews away on ships sailing the Rhein. Some of our people actually boarded ships before the violence began. We assume they escaped. Other than sending people away, the bishop said, there wasn't much else he could do. He had opened his palace as a refuge for Jews, but neither he nor the secular leaders had sufficient soldiers at their disposal to defend them. Besides, he pointed out, Christian soldiers might not be willing to fight other Christians in defense of Jews.

"Once the city gates were opened, Emmerich's horde flooded into the streets of Mainz. There were thousands of them, like grasshoppers descending on a field of grain. It happened at noon on the third day of Sivan. When Bishop Ruthard saw the multitude of attackers, he told the rabbi he could not save us. He believed the Jews had been abandoned by God. Now they must convert to Christianity, he said, or suffer for the sins of their ancestors. Then the bishop left the palace and fled for his life. It was said the crusaders wished to kill him because he had spoken well of the Jews.

"Inside the bishop's palace many people were weak from days of fasting. Nevertheless, young men and old men picked up weapons and put on such armor as they had, and they prepared to fight. Led by Rabbi Kalonymus, they took their positions beside the bishop's soldiers at the gate of the courtyard. Soon the gate was breached by the mob. Almost immediately, the bishop's men ran away, leaving the Jews to face the enemy alone. When the people saw how desperate the situation was, all of them cried out, weeping and praying to the Lord. They began to encourage one another, saying, 'Let us bear the yoke of our holy religion. Blessed be God and blessed be his Name, who has given us his Torah. Happy are those who do his will. Happy is anyone who is slaughtered, who dies for the unity of his Name, for he will be ready to enter the world to come, and to live in heaven with the righteous.' Many retreated into the palace chambers to be with their wives and children. Those who remained in the courtyard fought bravely while the enemy showered them with stones and arrows. They were quickly overpowered. One of our rabbis, a righteous man, stretched out his neck, offering to be the first one sacrificed. The invaders cut off his head. Other pious men sat down in a corner of the courtyard, wrapped in their prayer shawls, filled with love for God and ready to receive his sentence. The enemy killed them all.

"When those inside the palace chambers saw what was happening, they said to each other, 'There is nothing better than to offer our lives as a sacrifice.' Women picked up knives and slew their own children, even infants they had one hour earlier suckled and played with. Men slaughtered their fiancées or their wives. Virtuous people bared their throats to each other to be killed, while they cried out, 'Hear, O Israel, the Lord our God is One. Look and see, O God, what we do to sanctify your great Name, in order not to exchange you for a false deity.' Blood touched blood as the killing went on. A man's blood mingled with his wife's and a father's with his children's; the blood of teachers mixed with their disciples' and the blood of judges with their scribes'. Are your ears tingling? Who has ever heard of such a thing? Has it happened before since the days of Adam that eleven hundred offerings were made in one day?"

Rizpa looked around at the faces of those listening. Some lowered their eyes, and others closed them as tears streamed down their cheeks. Only Marcus was looking straight into her eyes, with a serious expression. His pen was raised and he was poised to begin writing again when her narrative resumed.

"These good people had prayed for God's help. When it didn't come as they expected, many saw this as an opportunity to be martyrs for their faith. Others were not so eager. They fled into the inner courtyards and chambers of the palace. The mob pursued them. When they found people alive, they killed them. When they found people already dead by their own hand, they threw their bodies out the windows. A few who were mortally wounded but still living begged for water. The crusaders said they could have it only if they would be baptized. Feeble as they were, these dying people found the strength to say no. Some Jews, when they saw the fate of their friends, threw themselves out the tower windows into the river.

"The stories of certain individuals became well known among us. The fate of Rachel, daughter of Rabbi Isaac and wife of Rabbi Judah, will be told for many generations to inspire steadfastness among Jews under attack. It is a pitiful story. If you do not wish to hear it, please go take your night's rest and cover your ears." No one left.

"Rachel had four children. They were hiding with her in an upstairs room of the palace. She begged one of her companions to take their lives, lest any of them be snatched by Christians and brought up as idolaters. When the knife was raised to slaughter her son, Rachel beat her own chest and let out a bitter lament, saying, 'Where are thy mercies, O God?' She turned to her friend. 'Do not slay little Isaac in the presence of his brother Aaron, because Aaron will run away when he sees it.' They took the child Isaac aside. The friend slaughtered him while Rachel spread out her sleeves to catch the blood. When Aaron saw the blood, he knew what had happened. Again and again he screamed, 'Mother, don't butcher me!' The frightened boy ran and hid himself under a table. Rachel had two beautiful young daughters named Bella and Matrona. The girls sharpened the knives themselves and stretched out their necks to be sacrificed. The friend who raised the knife said, 'Perfect shall you be with the Lord your God.' After Rachel had watched her three children sacrificed to their Creator, she called loudly to her son Aaron, 'Aaron, come out. I will not spare you either.' She took hold of his foot and dragged him out from under the table. He, too, was sacrificed before God. Then Rachel laid herself down with two of her dying children on each side of her. She spread her sleeves out over them and wailed. The enemy broke into the room where she was and demanded to see the money she was hiding under her sleeves. When they saw it was only her dead children, they killed her too. At last her soul was at peace. When the father came in and saw the death of his beautiful children and his wife, he wept loudly and plunged the sword he was holding into his bowels. The enemy returned later to strip the bodies bare, in case they should find jewels. Once the crusaders had killed everyone they could find in the bishop's palace, they held a service of thanksgiving. In the name of the 'hanged one,' they gave thanks that they had accomplished their purpose.

"Soon the mob moved on to the castle of the burgrave, where another group of Jews had sought refuge. The outer doors were quickly breached. Using arrows and lances, the attackers overpowered the castle guards. As in the bishop's palace, all the Jews who had not killed themselves were slaughtered. Amongst the dead were found some scrolls of Torah. The crusaders tore them to pieces and desecrated them. Next they marched into the city, looking for houses where Jews might be hiding. A well-meaning priest had given shelter to a tax collector named David, who also distributed alms to the poor. When the mob appeared, the priest urged him to accept baptism, because he could not protect him or his family. David asked that he be allowed to speak to leaders of the group. A number of them assembled in the courtyard of the priest's house, expecting David to beg for mercy and agree to be baptized. Instead, he called them apostates and children of lust. He said the one they worshipped, the crucified one, was also born of lust. David declared his trust in the One

God who dwells in highest heaven. Immediately the mob fell on him and killed him and his whole family."

Over the next few days, as the group of refugees traveled westward, Rizpa told more stories of the desperate plight in which the Jews of Mainz had found themselves. Perhaps none was sadder than the story of Isaak, the synagogue administrator.

"On that day in Sivan, the day of the horrible massacre at the bishop's palace, Isaak accepted baptism. He hoped this action would save the life of his children and his elderly mother. Almost immediately, he regretted what he had done. He vowed to do penance and be utterly faithful to God. Perhaps, he thought, the Lord in his lovingkindness would forgive him and allow him to join his comrades in martyrdom. He went first to his mother, who was bedridden. He told her he intended to make a sin-offering to God as atonement for his deed. She suspected what he might do and begged him not to proceed. All the rest of her family had perished, and he was the only one left. But Isaak did not listen to the words of his mother. He went to his house and asked his son and daughter, 'Do you wish that I sacrifice you to our God?' They replied, 'Do what you must.' He said, 'My children, our God is the true God and there is no other.' And he took them at midnight to the synagogue and slaughtered them before the holy ark, saying, 'May this blood serve as atonement for my sins.' Then Isaak went back to his house where his mother was and lit a fire under all four corners. He returned to the synagogue and lit a fire there as well, intending to prevent its desecration by marauders. This pious man walked round and round the synagogue with his hands raised heavenwards, calling to the Lord from the midst of the fire. Some of the crusaders saw him through the windows. They shouted for him to escape and save himself. They reached in with a staff to try to pull him out, but he would not take it, preferring to be consumed by fire. Now this righteous man is surely walking with all the saintly men in paradise.

"There were other cases where crusaders tried to prevent Jews from taking their own lives. Whether they were actually trying to save them or just wanted the pleasure of killing them, we cannot know. But when they saw hundreds and hundreds of Jews perish by their own hand, they were appalled. Some of the local citizens took pity on these poor souls and on the murdered Jews whose naked bodies lay in the streets. They located the money that had been given to protect Jews and used it to bury them instead. Other townspeople were not so kind. Some joined the mob and stole whatever Jewish property they could get their hands on. Church and civic leaders warned against looting, but in vain. The horde of crusaders was so large and so unruly that any attempts to control it were futile. It is said there are at least twelve thousand men marching with Count Emmerich.

"Yet somehow Rabbi Kalonymus escaped the bishop's palace and hid himself, along with fifty-three elders, in the sacristy of the cathedral. Archbishop Ruthard, who left his palace before the killing began, was staying in the village of Rüdesheim, across the river from Mainz. He heard that Kalonymus and other Jewish leaders were still alive. Secretly, he sent three hundred soldiers to try to rescue them. In the middle of the night someone came to them and said the bishop wished to save what remnant of the Jews was left. These three hundred soldiers, he told them, had pledged to bring them safely across the river, even at the risk of their own lives. At first, Rabbi Kalonymus didn't believe the messenger, until he took an oath. Then the rabbi and the elders followed him. The soldiers put them in boats and ferried them across the Rhein to Rüdesheim. The bishop was overjoyed to see that they were indeed alive.

"But the story did not end happily. The mob found out about the escape and followed across the river. Once again, Bishop Ruthard had to admit he was powerless to save their lives unless they would consent to be baptized. Rabbi Kalonymus asked for one night to reflect upon his decision. That night some of the Jews killed themselves; others ran away or were driven out into the surrounding forest. All these were hunted down and killed."

As the Worms refugees and their new companions traveled steadily westward, they felt more secure in their surroundings. Local peasants in the fields seemed friendly enough, often greeting them with a wave. The old man Abram could speak a little French and so was able to barter some of their possessions for fresh milk and vegetables. What finally gave the refugees hope that they had eluded the worst danger was their entry into a region where Jewish communities were still intact. Abram and Naomi and their son took the first opportunity to settle in one of these communities. They were just too tired, Naomi said, to travel any farther. Others in the group made a similar decision when they came to a town that seemed hospitable. Gradually the group dwindled to a dozen or so people, then grew larger again when they were joined by exiles from other cities along the Rhein. Miriam wasn't sure how much farther she would go, but she knew they wouldn't stop until they found a community with scholars and a good school for her children. The Jews she met along the route were helpful in that regard—most of them advised settling in Troyes, home of the renowned Jeschiba (or Yeshiva, as the local people called it). Miriam knew the city by name. Troyes was the place where Rabbi Scholomo lived, the great teacher whom the Jews of Worms claimed as their own. Was he still alive? People thought so. Would he be willing to take her children, who spoke no French, into his Yeshiva? This was a harder question. Miriam used every opportunity to expose her family to the local language. She thought how proud her husband and brother would be for the children to study with Rabbi Scholomo himself, and she made that her goal.

Jews in this region of Francia were accustomed to regular visits from merchants traveling to and from the Rheinland. Therefore they knew the routes and were able to give good directions. One of the local men pointed out a fact Miriam had not thought of, namely that travel was safer now, since most of the criminals had joined the crusading mobs. It was true, they had not met a single robber on the road. At night they sat around a fire, never worrying that the light might attract undesired visitors. But this was small compensation for the horror and bereavement suffered by her people.

As they continued their journey, they heard, and Marcus dutifully recorded, more stories of death and devastation. Exiles from Köln related how an army from the low countries approached their city, intending to deliver an ultimatum to the Jews. For two days the townspeople kept them out. Meanwhile the Jews fasted and prayed, and some hid in the homes of gentile friends. Local priests and citizens tried to enforce the law and keep order, but the mob pushed relentlessly to enter the city. When Bishop Hermann realized he could not protect the Jews, he sent many of them out to nearby villages, hoping they would be safe. The ones who stayed in the city were split: some chose to resist the crusaders with force, and others vowed to kill themselves. Knowing they would surely die, these people saw martyrdom as victory. Their rabbi spoke to them at the Sabbath meal, saying their reward would be great. They would see

God in paradise, receive golden crowns, and sit on a golden throne under the Tree of Life. The people shouted "Amen!"

As for the Jews who went out to the surrounding villages, they seemed for a while to be safe. But after three weeks, the enemy discovered Jews in one village and murdered them. This gave the attackers motivation to search other villages, and soon all was finished. Miriam was especially disturbed by this last account. She thought of her brother and his family, who had left Worms to find refuge in a nearby village. Had Count Emmerich's mob been as diligent in their search as the attackers of Köln? Could anyone have escaped their march through the countryside? Miriam realized she might never know the answer, but she remained optimistic. It was better to hope than to despair. Thinking of the worst possible outcomes made her physically sick. At any rate, she had not been feeling well lately. First she thought it was the strange food upsetting her stomach. Now she began to suspect she might be pregnant. This would complicate matters for her and her family. How could she earn bread for them if she had an infant to care for? Ehud would be overjoyed if he knew, but at this moment Miriam could not rejoice. She would need to force herself to eat, as she had during previous pregnancies. It was important that she be strong and healthy for her family's sake.

Over the next couple of months other reports came to their attention, and Marcus recorded them all. They learned the unhappy fate of Jews all along the Rhein, but also in outlying places, such as Trier and Regensburg. In this latter city, the authorities knew they could not protect the Jews, so a huge crowd of townspeople came and pushed them down to the river bank. The Jews were forced into the water and baptized as a group, against their will. Thus the city and the Jews escaped destruction at the hands of the crusaders, but their honor was sacrificed. As Miriam reflected on recent events, she often repeated the words of a Psalm to herself, hoping for the fulfillment of the Psalmist's prayer.

> God is our protection and strength, a help in distresses, very readily found.
> Therefore we will not fear, even when the earth is transformed, and when mountains are moved into the heart of the seas;
> When the waters thereof roar and foam, when mountains quake before his majesty.

Nations rage, kingdoms are moved: he letteth his voice be heard,
the earth melteth away.
The Lord of hosts is with us: a defense unto us is the God of Jacob.
Come, look at the deeds of the Lord, who hath made desolations on
the earth.
He causes wars to cease unto the end of the earth; he breaketh the
bow, and cutteth the spear in pieces; he burneth chariots in the
fire.

Chapter 22

Toward the end of September, Miriam and her family arrived in Troyes. As best she could work out, they had been traveling for two and a half months, covering ten miles on a good day, but usually much less. The group had stopped for as long as a week when they came to a friendly community where they could buy supplies or do odd jobs in exchange for food. Their numbers had swollen when other bands of refugees joined them and dwindled again when families found a place to settle. By the time they reached Troyes, only eleven members of the original group from Worms remained: Miriam and her children, Marcus, Jonas and his family, and the gruff man whose name Miriam finally learned. He was called Esra. Like Miriam, Jonas and Abigail wanted the best education for their sons; due partly to her influence, they decided the best place for them to stay would be Troyes.

The first necessity when they arrived was to find shelter. Sleeping outdoors was fine in the warm summer months, but now the nights were turning chilly. It was the time of year when children catch colds, and Miriam wanted to keep hers as healthy as possible. She was now certain of her pregnancy, at present about four months along; therefore she needed to protect her own health as well. Fortunately, her stomach was more settled and she could once again eat good meals. Regarding shelter, the Jewish quarter in the center of Troyes was extremely crowded, too much so to accommodate any of the immigrants. But Jews also lived in other sections of the city. In fact, a smaller Jewish settlement was growing on the western edge of town. Here, in an open field, temporary dwellings were constructed for incoming refugees.

Miriam's family was given its own small hut. It was a primitive dwelling, one room only, with no windows. The walls were rough-hewn wooden slats with gaps showing between them. Miriam saw they would have to make improvements before the colder weather set in. She would inquire of local residents where to find clay and rags to fill the holes. Her children could do most of the work while she and Marcus looked for gainful employment. After shelter, the next most pressing matter was earning enough money to feed and clothe the family. Fortunately, none of the refugees would starve—the *tzedaka* fund of the Jewish community supplied bread, and some women of the town started a large kettle of vegetable stew simmering each day. But children need a better diet to grow and develop properly. And threadbare summer clothing would not keep them warm through the winter.

Miriam and Marcus looked for work together. In her condition, Miriam could not have hoped to find employment if she went out on her own. But Marcus was a strong, healthy-looking youth and he spoke passably good French by this time. They soon found work cleaning out stables at the house of a nobleman. It was exhausting work, and Miriam had to rest frequently. Marcus always picked up the slack and worked twice as hard when she was resting. Nevertheless, he insisted on turning over every bit of their pay to her. By the end of each day she was weary, but happy to have a few pennies to spend or save. Some of the servants in the nobleman's house took pity and donated their castoff clothes to her, another benefit of their employment. None of this would have been possible, Miriam realized, except that her responsible older daughter Susanna took charge of the younger children all day while she was away. At age eight she was almost a second mother to them. What gave Miriam the most satisfaction, however, was that a small school had been set up in the refugee camp, and Aaron was able to spend his days studying Torah under direction of students from Rabbi Scholomo's Yeshiva. She only wished her girls could study too.

Living on the outskirts of Troyes, the group of immigrants quickly learned about the commerce and customs of the region. The city was located at a crossroads of trade routes, and merchants brought exotic goods to the marketplace. Brocades, silk, pepper and other rare spices, incense, and ivory were items Miriam and her companions had rarely seen in their homeland. They also noted the variety of occupations practiced by Jews in Troyes. There were weavers, dyers, tanners, jewelers, silversmiths, doctors, porters, laborers, and merchants. Three things the newcomers found surprising: First, how very well integrated Jewish activity was into the general economy of the town. Second, that Jews owned significant amounts of land, including farms and vineyards. And finally, that women ran their own businesses. Miriam was especially happy about this last fact, since she would have to support her family independently. She heard hints that women might even find employment in the academic field, as scribes and teachers. This would be ideal for her, once she learned the local language and scholarly traditions.

The refugees living in the camp quickly became friends. Most came from cities along the Rhein and had had similar experiences fleeing the crusaders. Their families had spread in all directions, this group coming west, while many of their loved ones went to colder regions of the north and east. It was ironic that hatred and persecution should cause Jews to spread their heritage to far corners of the earth. Along with their own culture they carried language and learning they had acquired in the Rheinland. What that region lost, Miriam thought, others would gain.

Not all talk in the camp was friendly. As people conversed and their stories became known, a noticeable tension developed. Those who had agreed to be baptized were heckled and made to feel unwelcome by certain other residents. Esra of Worms headed the small group of hecklers who felt the "traitors" should be expelled from their midst. Jonas and his family were among those singled out, and Miriam felt bad for them. She stood up more than once and said she wasn't sure she wouldn't have done the same to save the lives of her children. Perhaps the question of forced baptism should be taken to the Jewish court in Troyes, she suggested. The wise men here had given rulings on many other weighty matters. They might be willing to render judgment on this one as well. Her proposal was ignored for the moment, as the refugees were fully engaged in the daily struggle of keeping their families warm and well-fed.

December was relatively warm, but a blast of cold air came in early January. Miriam bundled the children in many layers of clothing and kept a small fire burning in front of their hut. At night they carried hot stones and bricks from the fire into their dwelling. Miriam was increasingly uncomfortable in her pregnancy and knew she would have to stop working soon. How could they afford firewood and food on what Marcus earned alone? It might be necessary to send the older children to work as well, but she would put off that decision as long as possible.

Then a miracle happened. At least that's the way Miriam saw it. In mid-January, on one of the coldest days so far, a kindly old lady named Ruth appeared in the camp. She asked some of the residents where she could find a woman named Miriam who had four young children. When she found her, Ruth offered the family a place to stay in the town, in a small apartment on the third floor of her house. Miriam protested that she had no money to pay rent, but the lady waved her hand and said they would worry about that later. She insisted they pack up their few belongings and come right away. Marcus helped with the move, but once they arrived, they realized the apartment was too small for him to join them. There were three garret rooms with low, sloping ceilings, two of them barely big enough for the beds which took up the floor space, and one slightly larger room consisting of a tiny kitchen and an eating area with table. The fireplace was in this room. Miriam suggested that the table could be moved out to make space for Marcus to sleep, but he reassured her he could survive in the camp until they found a bigger place. Once the baby came (within two months), the apartment would be even more crowded, he pointed out, and Miriam had to agree. Marcus promised to check in on them every three or four days and to bring his wages. Not that they had to buy a great deal—Ruth and her husband Eliel insisted on supplying firewood, and they often contributed food as well. They even offered to babysit the younger children.

Miriam couldn't believe her good fortune. Their little home was warm and secure. She and the girls shared one bed and the boys the other. The furniture was worn, but solid and clean. Apparently an elderly couple had lived there until the wife died and the husband went to live with his daughter's family. Getting up and down the steps was difficult in her condition, but she could minimize trips by sending the children out on errands. Aaron was big enough to carry water buckets up the stairs each morning before he left for school. He was now allowed to attend classes at the boys' academy attached to the Yeshiva. Sometimes he returned home in the evening with special treats such as oranges and dried figs to share with the family. In response to his mother's questions, Aaron would only say his friends in Troyes were very generous. There was even a place for girls to study in this extraordinary town. The wife of a young rabbi conducted a class once a week for Torah study, and Susanna joined the small group of interested girls. Miriam didn't understand why all these good things were happening. First Ruth offered them lodging, now Aaron and Susanna were getting the finest education available, and everyone was showering them with generosity. Though she didn't understand it, Miriam accepted her good fortune and was grateful to God, who provides all good things.

The pressing questions concerning Jews who'd been baptized did finally come before the council of Jewish elders in the city. The leading judge on the council was, of course, Rabbi Scholomo, known locally as Rabbi Salomon, or affectionately as Rabbenu Shalmo. Miriam, intensely interested in the outcome, wanted very much to attend the assemblies. As it turned out, she was so clumsy and uncomfortable in the eighth month of her pregnancy that she couldn't do much more than sit and mend clothes or knit. Thus it was a practical way for her to pass the days, attending sessions of the council during her daily excursion out of the apartment. As a spectator sitting in the back of the room, she could keep her hands and her mind occupied without straining her body. Aaron usually attended with her, since schools were temporarily closed during the council sessions.

One of the chief witnesses was Esra from Worms. As instigator of the case, he was allowed to speak before the judges and put questions to the parties involved. He began his testimony with a general statement:

"Knowing as we do that this distinguished council of rabbis represents the Jewish community of Troyes and the surrounding regions, and that the esteemed leader of the council is the learned Rabbi Salomon ben Isaac himself, wise judge and founder of the Yeshiva that has thrived for twenty-five years in this city; and furthermore knowing that this council has rendered scholarly judgment in the past on such varied questions as dietary laws, slaves and servants, property ownership, commerce, and the conduct of worship in the synagogue, we therefore apply to you with questions of a most delicate nature."

Esra paused and cleared his throat. Miriam stared at him. She was surprised that such flowery speech came from a man she regarded as taciturn. Members of the council motioned for him to get on with his testimony. He bowed his head in deference.

"In particular, the distinguished rabbis of the council have issued regulations concerning admission of new members to this community. My understanding, gleaned from statements of long-term residents, is that your policy has been generous and that permission has been granted to nearly all applicants who wished to settle here. Only a few who refused to pay their share of taxes or who had denounced their fellow Jews to gentile persecutors were refused admission."

The rabbis nodded. One of them added that occasionally a merchant had been denied residence in one quarter of the city if his enterprise would compete directly with an established business; nevertheless, the newcomer had been allowed to settle in another part of the city. But on the whole, yes, he agreed with the speaker, that under the leadership of Rabbi Salomon, the council had been generous and accommodating.

"Now is a time to be less generous," said Esra, narrowing his eyes. "Let me explain." He proceeded to narrate all the horrors of the Worms persecution, everything he had witnessed or heard about. He told of entire families who were pulled out of their houses and butchered by gentiles, of Jews who were given "sanctuary" in the bishop's palace, only to be attacked and overrun by the mob. He recalled how Jewish husbands slaughtered their wives, and mothers their children, in order to preserve the sanctity of the Divine Name. No gruesome detail was left out. Gasps were heard from members of the audience who had no idea such horrible events had taken place. Esra continued, "The people who consented to the blasphemous ritual of baptism betrayed their fellow Jews and consorted with the devil. Now they should be left to reside with the devil. If we admit them into the community of Jews, we dishonor the memory of those courageous ones who chose to die rather than profane the name of the Lord."

A young rabbi of the council spoke up. Miriam learned later his name was Shmaya and he had been one of Rabbi Scholomo's star pupils. "In the Talmud, it says, 'An Israelite, even a sinful one, remains an Israelite.' We have operated under this premise in the past. Spanish Jews, for example, who were forcibly converted came back to the true faith once the danger was gone."

With a look of disdain, Esra replied, "As you well know, they were called by the name 'Marranos,' or swine. Do we want swine living in our midst? Or even worse, disloyal turncoats who might betray us again? Jews must keep to themselves, to protect themselves. We can't allow such vermin."

Now Rabbi Scholomo spoke. It seemed to Miriam that everyone in the hall suddenly became attentive. No sound could be heard except the rabbi's voice. "We must not overlook the fact that many Jews who were forcibly baptized later risked their lives by continuing to practice their faith. Even living among gentiles, they never ceased to keep dietary laws and observe the Sabbath, and they diligently stayed away from churches.

It seems to me some tolerance is in order. A good Jew must not be cast out if he sins under threat of immediate death, yet hastens to return when the threat has passed. After all, human nature dictates that one's life and progeny be preserved."

"Human nature is vile!" protested Esra. "We must reject human nature! It was human nature that made the gentile devils do what they did. That wicked Satan of Rome, the pope, told his legions they could go on a murderous rampage and he would pardon them all!" Now Esra was shouting. "In the name of the crucified bastard, they maimed and killed hundreds of innocent Jews! *That's* human nature!" He began sobbing uncontrollably, covering his face with his hands. The rabbis were too stunned to speak.

After what seemed a long period, Rabbi Scholomo said softly, "You have been deeply wounded, my brother. Sometimes it is harder to go on living than to die a martyr. Yet we who survive must follow the courageous example of those who died." He paused, with eyes closed. "The martyrs died steadfast in their faith, in complete innocence. Likewise, Isaiah the prophet tells of a servant who suffers, though he is innocent of any crime. We as a people have often been in this position. At times, it has looked as if we might be destroyed. Yet we survive. Each time we are able to gather strength and carry on. First, however, the dead must be mourned.

"Through the years, our poets have composed prayers and elegies to assist us in mourning. Let us end this session today with a prayer for the martyrs." The rabbi closed his eyes again and raised his hands toward heaven. "May the Merciful Father, who dwells in heaven, remember with compassion the pious and pure who sacrificed themselves for the sanctification of his Divine Name. They were swift as eagles and strong as lions in doing the will of their Creator. May the Lord remember them alongside the most righteous of history. The prophets have written that our God does not excuse the shedding of innocent blood. Therefore we know that He will judge the nations with justice and heed the cry of the afflicted. We place our hope in Him who is above all others. Amen."

The rabbis rose to leave. On his way out, Rabbi Scholomo took Esra's hand and said a few words to him, trying to comfort him.

The hearings and discussions went on for nearly three weeks. Many of the refugees were asked to testify, those who had allowed themselves to be baptized as well as the ones who escaped by other means. The former group pleaded their innocence of wrongdoing. Some told of quick decisions made as they watched friends and family members killed before their eyes. Others said they had deliberated beforehand and knew what they would do to preserve their lives. All spoke of repentance before or after the deed, and of disclaimers they had made to themselves and others regarding the Christian faith. In spite of these similarities, no two cases were alike. Some of the speakers aroused great sympathy and pity from the observers, while others seemed to them callous and self-serving.

The daily sessions took on the nature and appearance of a trial. The most obvious defendants were baptized Jews who hoped to be fully accepted and integrated into the community. Under the surface, however, another trial was taking place. Through insinuation and innuendo, certain speakers implied that those Jews untouched by violence hadn't done enough to protect victims, intervene on their behalf, or even take up arms against the crusaders. Many French Jews, for example, knew what was happening but did nothing out of the ordinary. Someone mentioned that Rabbi Salomon continued to live a quiet life, tending his vineyard and writing his obscure commentaries. What good was all this study and scholarship while people were perishing? Tension built up as members of the council perceived these accusations were directed at themselves and their leader. Rabbi Scholomo himself said nothing in his own defense. He continued to preside with complete objectivity, never changing his modest tone or charitable attitude. He was careful, even in correcting mistaken testimony, not to insult or offend. The closest the rabbi came to defending the members of the council was to say that God is just, and anyone who is guilty of transgressions will pay the consequences.

After all the testimony had been heard, the council prepared to adjourn. As with previous cases where formal "Responses" had been given to difficult legal questions, the council would take several days before rendering judgment. Much discussion would go on behind closed doors before a written statement was issued. Members of the council would read Torah and Talmud together, pray, and appeal to the Lord for wisdom.

Before they adjourned, however, young Rabbi Shmaya stood to address the assembly. The other rabbis seemed surprised at this unusual action. "Pardon me for speaking before the council has deliberated," he said. "But since our leader Rabbi Salomon will not say a word in his own defense, I feel I must speak. Some of the witnesses have implied that he and the other rabbis of Troyes were indifferent to the fate of Jews in the Rheinland. This is absolutely false! When we first heard of the massacres, we acted immediately. Rabbi Salomon led us in constant fasting and prayer for the victims. His own health was damaged by lack of proper rest and nourishment. Even so, his work load never diminished, for when he could not write he dictated to his oldest grandson or to his sons-in-law.

"Why has Rabbi Salomon not commented specifically on the horrible events? Our good rabbi has taught us that 'tracks in the sand' are not of great import, except in relation to the divine message. Historical events must be seen in their completeness, to be judged by God on the day of redemption. Everything Rabbenu has written, volumes and volumes, speaks to this question. Meanwhile, Jews are sustained during hard times by Torah and Talmud, and Rabbi Salomon's commentaries provide enlightenment on the texts. The hearts and minds of sufferers are borne up through his writings. How better could he spend his time than doing what he does best for all Jews everywhere?"

Rabbi Shmaya sat down before a silent assembly. The other rabbis looked embarrassed at his passionate outcry. After a few moments, Rabbi Scholomo signaled to them, and they filed out a side door. Miriam watched until the last one left. She was anxious to hear their ruling on the case and hoped it would be delivered before her birth pangs began.

Chapter 23

A week passed, and still the council gave no judgment. There were rumors that the members were engaged in heated discussions, perhaps even shouting at one another behind closed doors. Miriam thought this unlikely. She knew that Rabbi Scholomo, when stumped by a difficult question, often waited many days for inspiration, knowing that God might enlighten him while he slept or tended his vineyard.

Miriam's labor pains, however, would not wait. On a cold day near the end of February, a midwife was called in. Aaron was in school at the time, but Susanna stayed by her mother's side. The landlady Ruth offered to keep the two younger children downstairs with her for as long as necessary.

Upon climbing the stairs to the third floor, the midwife paused to lay out the implements and herbs she would need later. When she entered Miriam's bedroom, her eyes widened. "Madam, you are very large," she said.

Miriam grunted. "It must be a big baby. I'm so tired of carrying the extra weight."

The midwife felt Miriam's belly and nodded knowingly. "It's no wonder. You have twins." She wiped the sweat off Miriam's forehead.

Susanna clapped her hands. "Twin babies! What fun!"

Miriam thought of the extra work involved, but nevertheless couldn't help smiling. She would have six children to care for! Thus far, the Lord had provided for her family, and she would try not to worry about the future.

After four hours of labor, the first baby arrived, and it was a boy. Miriam had already decided that if she had a son, he would be called Ehud, for his father. About twenty minutes later, a second boy made his appearance, and she knew immediately what his name would be. Miriam might never see her brother again, but her new son Mosche would be a constant reminder of the blessing he had been to her when she was growing up.

Another surprise came along a few weeks after the twins. As was customary, Miriam had gone to the *miqveh* subsequent to giving birth, so that she might be immersed and purified. On one of her first trips out of the apartment following the ritual, she saw Ruth on the street conferring with a man. At first she took no notice, until he put his head down and made a move away from her. There was something familiar about his posture. She looked harder and recognized him. It was Josef! He was carrying a load of firewood. Suddenly, scores of questions raced through Miriam's head. What was he doing here? How long had he been in Troyes? Did he know where she lived? Had he seen her children? Why was he talking to Ruth? Extremely confused, she stood staring at him.

In due time, Miriam found out answers to all her questions. From the day they left Worms, Josef had been worried about the family. Frieder's daughter sent word to her father that the travelers had come safely through the mountains and into the region of Champagne. Her family had settled in a small village on the river Marne, and she thought the others intended to go a little further and stop in Troyes. This was information enough for Josef—he set out immediately for that city. Arriving there in late November, he first located his old friends Ruth and Eliel, who years before had boarded with his mother in Worms. He learned from them where the refugees were staying. One day, when Miriam was no longer going to work with Marcus, Josef followed the boy to his job and spoke with him. Marcus gave assurances that the family was in good health, though their nourishment was meager and their shelter drafty. Josef immediately inquired of Ruth whether she might help him locate better accommodations for them. By good fortune, she said, her upstairs rooms would soon be vacated. After the move, Josef delivered food and firewood to the house. A few times he ran into Aaron on his way to school, but asked him please to say nothing yet to his mother about this. Now she had seen him herself. Things suddenly came clear in Miriam's mind. She was grateful to Josef for his help, but she feared he might want to renew the relationship they'd had before she was married. That would be impossible. And she was a little annoyed with him for not revealing his presence earlier. Yet she understood his reasoning. Had she known where the help was coming from, she probably would have refused it.

Later Miriam learned more about Josef's first three months in Troyes. He had quickly found work tutoring three sons of a wealthy Christian merchant. This position afforded him room and board, plus a modest income. Clearly, he had been spending most of it on Miriam and her family. He had undertaken to visit Rabbi Scholomo but was turned away. Some of the rabbi's students were trying to shield their master from outsiders, especially gentiles. Now that the rabbi was getting older and suffering ill health, he was less able to carry on discourse with visitors. But Josef did not give up. He would try again and again, if necessary, to speak with the learned man about recent events. He needed to unburden his mind about the terrible things that had happened. The rabbi would have wise words for him, he felt sure, which couldn't make the events less horrid, but might guide him to some sort of resolution, and perhaps restitution.

A couple of days after the twins were born, Rabbi Scholomo and the council announced their decision on baptized Jews who wished to join the Jewish community in Troyes. Miriam herself could not go to the session, as she was still homebound after childbirth. Aaron attended and gave her a complete report. The council's response was divided into four parts.

The easiest judgment came in regard to those who were baptized without their knowledge or consent. This category included infants and young children, as well as adults who had been forcibly immersed in water before they knew what was occurring. No one could question the innocence of these people. For that reason, they were to be accepted immediately into the community, with full responsibilities and privileges. Eligible children were to be enrolled as students in the school if their parents wished it.

The second category encompassed those adults and youth who had considered the matter carefully beforehand, aided by Torah and Talmud. These people vowed in their hearts to be loyal to the One Lord and to continue to practicing their faith in all circumstances. In order to preserve life, they consented to a ritual which they regarded as meaningless. They always intended to return to their own religion and their own community. This group, said Rabbi Scholomo, was to be commended for their careful preparation. While only God could say if they made the right decision, at least they had used the resources he provided in the best way they knew. This was a beautiful thing, and Torah teaches that beautiful things should be protected. Therefore, these people also would be fully accepted into the community, once they had publicly renounced their baptism and professed loyalty to the One whom Jews worship.

A more difficult ruling was reached in regard to people who chose baptism at the last minute, perhaps after the slaughter had begun. They had given the question no thought and simply went along with the crusaders' demands. For a time, they abandoned their faith, participated in gentile apostasy, and did whatever was necessary to conform to the behavior expected by their captors. Only later did they understand the gravity of their transgressions and repent. For this group, a one-year waiting period would be imposed. If, during that time, they engaged in serious study, attended prayers and Sabbath services regularly, and showed themselves in all ways to be faithful Jews, then they, too, would be accepted into the community.

Finally, the council gave judgment on those applicants who, in their fear, had turned on their fellow Jews, denounced them, and even betrayed them. Under no circumstances would these people be accepted into the community.

For a few seconds after Rabbi Scholomo concluded his reading of the formal Response, the room was hushed. All of a sudden, someone cried out in a belligerent tone, "How can you justify these decisions? You are opening the doors to everyone, except out-and-out traitors, who pretends to be a Jew! Don't their actions speak against them? This community will be sullied." It was Esra's voice.

Rabbi Scholomo responded calmly. "We considered all aspects. In particular, we looked at previous rulings in similar situations. A recent case involving marriage has some bearing on these questions. Would you like to hear the details?"

Esra rolled his eyes and growled. "Go ahead," he said with evident scorn.

"A Jewish man and woman married after they, along with all the witnesses to the ceremony, had been forced by gentiles to disavow their religion. After the Jews returned to their faith, the woman claimed the marriage was invalid. However, it was decided that this woman would need a bill of divorcement before she could leave her husband and marry another man. The first marriage was deemed legal because, according to the sages, a Jew who has sinned is still a Jew. Do you see the connection?

This ruling applies to any forced converts who remain loyal in their hearts. The recent immigrants should be so characterized, because after their escape they returned immediately to Judaism."

Esra was not willing to let the matter lie. "Your rulings are pure sentimentality. Where is the strength of character that allowed our ancestors to survive when they were surrounded by Canaanites? In those days, Jews killed their enemies. Now you let them rule over you. Why do you not denounce the enemy? The idolaters who call themselves Christians should be condemned as murderers!"

"You, my friend, have suffered great losses," continued the rabbi. "But so have others in this room. All of us have lost friends and relatives at the hands of the fanatics. Some would favor our issuing a blanket condemnation of all Christians for the deplorable acts committed by the crusaders. There are two reasons why I refuse to do this. First we are called to be just to all men, Jew and non-Jew alike. Why was Moses chosen by God to be the greatest of our prophets? Because he stood against injustice wherever he saw it: When two Jews were fighting each other in Egypt, he intervened. When a gentile overlord thrashed a Jew, he killed the oppressor. And when Midianite gentiles competed to water their flocks, he stood up for the weaker side. In every case, Moses stepped in, not to extol or condemn any group, but to seek fair play for each individual. We should do likewise."

"Moses never saw thousands of his own people killed, as we have!" cried Esra.

"No, with God's help he averted that. But remember, killing Jews was not part of the plan for this crusade. The official armies led by appointed marshals did no such thing. Only mobs led by rogue priests and other rabble-rousers engaged in slaughter. Such mobs are like locusts, and locusts have no ruler. Should we censure an entire population for the guilt of the smaller part, the ones who lack humanity?"

"They're all guilty! Since any of us can remember, they've portrayed Jews as greedy, filthy blood-suckers. They've driven us out of our homes. They've stolen our property and taken away our children to teach them idolatry. What more can they do?"

"Yes, we have grievances. There are many wrongs which must be righted. In these things, we will continue to strive for justice, for ourselves and all men. However, we are commanded not to take vengeance, nor to bear a grudge."

"Bah!" said Esra under his breath as he stalked out of the room.

"Rabbi, what is the second reason you won't speak against Christians?" came a quiet voice from the front of the room.

Looking directly at the questioner seated before him, he said, "Thank you, daughter, for asking. My belief is that public complaint would not be effective just now. In fact, I'm afraid it would only increase the enmity between our peoples. Fair-minded Christians already know that a terrible injustice has been committed against Jews. Let them first have the opportunity to speak against their fellows. If their voices are not heard, there will be time enough for us to speak. We will not forget what happened, nor will we allow others to forget."

A few weeks later, Miriam was at home with her four youngest children. The twins were napping, while Eva and Daniel played quietly together. It was a rare moment of peace. As she sat watching the children play, there came a thud against the door. With curiosity she opened it and had to laugh, for all she could see was a huge pile of firewood standing before her. She peered through the cracks and thought she knew who it was, but asked anyway.

"It's me, Josef."

"Are you the new delivery boy?"

"Not exactly. Ruth and Eliel are too frail to carry loads up all these steps. They told me your supply was low."

"Yes, it is. But we can manage."

"You shouldn't strain yourself so soon after childbirth."

"Aaron is big enough to carry firewood."

Josef shifted his weight. "Well, I guess he's not here now, and this load is getting heavier by the minute. Would you tell me where to put it down, please?"

Miriam apologized and led him to the hearth. She helped him pile the wood in a neat stack. After a moment's hesitation, she asked if he'd like something to drink. He nodded.

"All we have is water and wine. I'm afraid the wine is rather diluted. It's what the children drink with their meals."

"That's fine."

She handed him a cup. "The weather will be changing soon. We won't need as much firewood from now on," she said.

Josef sighed. "Miriam, why are you so unwilling to accept my help? I'd like to be allowed to do more for you and your family."

"You've done too much already, Josef. I appreciate that you found this place for us. And Ruth tells me you've been paying the rent. I suppose you've been supplying us with firewood and much of our food as well. It's too much. We can never pay you back."

Josef shook his head. "You don't have to."

Miriam continued. "You shouldn't have followed us here in the first place. Your life is in Worms, with your own family and friends."

"I hardly have any family left. And you and Mosche are the best friends I ever had."

Miriam winced. She knew how much Josef had done for them, both here and in Worms. Yet she was afraid he would take her gratitude for encouragement she did not intend. "Look, Josef. You mustn't do any more for us. I've found work which will pay the rent, and Marcus' income is enough to feed us."

"You're working?" said Josef with evident surprise.

"Yes. Aaron brings me papers to copy from the school, mostly legal documents and financial records. I can work at night when the children are in bed. If the rabbis are pleased with my work, I'm hoping they'll give me more to do."

"As I recall, your script is neat and attractive."

"So, we'll soon earn enough to support ourselves completely. Then we can afford a bigger apartment, and Marcus can join the family."

"You don't want me to help you find a bigger place, I suppose."

"No."

"All right, Miriam. May I at least be a friend to the family? Someone you could call on when there's an urgent need?"

"We do consider you to be a friend. And thank you for what you've already done." As he finished his drink, she said, "There are a couple of questions I wanted to ask you." She hesitated. "Did anyone find . . . what happened to Ehud?"

Josef shook his head.

"And what about the people who went to the villages?"

"Like Mosche, you mean. We never heard any news. Some of them must have escaped, I'm sure. If there'd been a mass killing, we would have heard about it."

Josef rose to go. Miriam walked him to the door, then returned to her chair and thought about the loved ones she would never see again. Mosche had been her playmate, teacher, and lifelong companion. Ehud had given everything for her and the children, and she loved him dearly. Observing her mother's sadness, Eva climbed into her lap. She lay her head on Miriam's breast. There they sat, Eva embracing her mother and Miriam thinking how fortunate she was to have such good children.

In the months that followed, more decisions came down from the council concerning events relating to the crusade. All sorts of questions were raised within the community of Troyes: Did the Jews who died deserve their fate? Was this punishment for their sins? Is suicide justified, when carried out to avoid a worse death? Are those who kill themselves to be considered martyrs? The most vexing questions were those involving murder. Is it condoned in any circumstance? What about killing children? Should they be sacrificed rather than allowing them to become idolaters? More general questions came out of these discussions as well: Why have Jews suffered for so long in servitude to gentiles? Are they perpetually suffering for the sins of their fathers? Is there no end of misery?

The council could not, of course, answer every question that was raised. Some things are inexplicable, even to the wisest of men. Nevertheless, when Rabbi Scholomo attempted to address a difficult point, his conclusions were invariably clear, frank, firm, and guided by common sense; at the same time, they were governed by his understanding of Torah and Talmud. Miriam tried to attend every session when the rabbi gave an oral Response—she always learned something.

All members of the council agreed that the Jews who were killed did not deserve this kind of barbarous treatment. Nothing could justify such slaughter, especially of women and children. Nor did Rabbi Scholomo dissent from the opinion that accepting death is preferable to forced conversion. There was plenty of historical precedent for martyrdom. In the case of suicide, however, the written record was mixed. For example, ancient sages did not agree as to whether King Saul was justified in taking his own life. Some thought that a man could perhaps, by means of suicide, avoid transgression while under torture. Most of the council in Troyes felt that people who acted in this way were indeed martyrs. On the other hand, they were not able to come to any decision on the question of killing family members to protect them from apostasy. Some cited the story of Abraham and Isaac as an illustration that God might allow a parent to kill his child. Others held to the law that God forbids any murder of innocent people and requires a reckoning for lifeblood.

In the end it was decided that the names of all the known dead would be listed in "remembrance books," so that those left behind could make prayers for their souls. Certain days of the year would be designated times of mourning, especially the days between Passover and Shavuot, when much of the killing took place, and on the ninth of Ab, when the temple destruction was remembered. In answer to those who felt Jews had been abandoned by God, the council formulated a more hopeful interpretation of events. When Moses led his people through the wilderness, they were tested severely for forty years. During all this time, their clothing stayed clean and trim, never becoming frayed. How could this be? It was because, so long as the people remained true to the commandments, they were surrounded by clouds of glory that gave cleansing. The terrible afflictions of the past year should likewise be regarded not as punishment, but as testing. Thus far the people had proved themselves honorable, humble, generous, and courageous. They were heroes like the three young men who walked willingly into the burning furnace. This type of severe testing could only fall on a generation that was especially righteous. The rewards for their faithfulness and heroism would come later, as they had to Abraham and his offspring. For now, they would continue to live as a people set apart, but ruled by others. "The elder shall serve the younger" were the words the Lord spoke to Rebekka about her sons Esau and Jakob, and now it was true again in a larger sense. But the Jews would endure.

One day when Miriam came out of the assembly hall where Rabbi Scholomo was speaking, Josef was there waiting for her. He had earlier told her he had no intention of returning to Worms. Yet she rarely saw him and was surprised by his appearance. "Have you been here long?" she asked.

"An hour or so."

"Why didn't you come in and hear the rabbi's Response?"

"It's better if I don't go in the school or the synagogue," Josef responded. "Some of the people here are uncomfortable if Christians come too close."

Miriam nodded. "You were looking for me?"

"Yes. I have a favor to ask. Remember, you said you could never repay me for the help I gave you and your family? There is something you can do."

"And what is it?"

"Well, I heard that lately you've been working more closely with the Yeshiva rabbis, transcribing scholarly texts for them. I know it's a great honor for you to be considered knowledgeable enough to do this, and I wouldn't want to jeopardize your position. But . . . but, could you ask Rabbi Scholomo if he would see me?"

Miriam thought for a moment. "Yes, I think I can do that."

Chapter 24

Within a week, Miriam had arranged a meeting between Josef and the rabbi. Knowing that the Yeshiva students were still trying to protect their master from unwanted visitors, she had gone directly to Rabbi Scholomo about this matter. Carrying an armful of scrolls, she was allowed to enter his study room, presumably to ask about fine points relating to her work as a copyist. When she explained her request to him, the rabbi remembered Josef and quickly agreed to see him. On the appointed day of the visit, Josef was nervous. Miriam led him into the school, past groups of students who looked up at him as he went by. Josef could feel their eyes piercing his soul. At last they came to the rabbi's room. The learned man rose to greet them, with the hint of a smile. Miriam asked if she should leave, but Josef insisted she stay.

After exchanging polite greetings and gazing at each other for a few moments of awkward silence, Josef blurted out, "It's too horrible for words, . . . what we have done. It was like hell on earth for the Jews in Worms. I wouldn't blame you if you hated every one of us."

With quiet voice, the rabbi responded, "That would accomplish nothing."

Josef persisted. "Don't you see? We failed to protect our friends. We stood by and watched while helpless people were murdered."

"Some Jews would have me denounce you or take up arms against you. My own wife, God forgive her, thinks I should spit on any gentile who sets foot on Jewish property. She claims I am stricter with infidel Jews than with outsiders who wish to harm us. Yet our doctors have a saying, 'Never use a cure unless you can prove its effectiveness.' Would spitting, or denouncing, or fighting make things better for us?"

"How can you not be bitter?"

"If it is bitterness to ask God to avenge spilled blood, then I am bitter—I admit to that. We Jews find comfort in divine justice. Perhaps it will be postponed until a future time, or until we reach the world to come, but there will be justice. The Lord's decrees assure us of this fact."

"How long can you wait? Your communities may be wiped out before the Lord gives everyone what he deserves."

"We are a patient people. You know, after centuries of waiting, we're still expecting the Messiah. In the meanwhile, we do what is needed. Our communities will be strong if everyone works for a common purpose. Our strength is in unity."

"Do you not wish, at least, to cut off day-to-day dealings with your persecutors?"

"Where do I find them? There was no slaughter in Troyes. The people who wanted to kill Jews have left this region and gone east, on a crusade to kill Muslims. Cutting off ties with our Christian neighbors would be disastrous for us, judicially, politically, and economically. We need friends now more than ever."

"How long can Jews continue to cooperate with people who hate them?"

"Remember how many chances God gave Pharaoh before he finally hardened his heart the last time? The Lord knows whether a man is capable of repentance or not. We listen to the Lord, and so we continue to work with the people in whose midst he has placed us. One of my students asked me who were the greater sinners, Noah's contemporaries before the flood, or the generation that built the tower of Babel. He wanted to know why the people of the flood who did not actually rebel against God were killed, while the ones who challenged God's sovereignty at Babel were merely dispersed. The answer is easy. Those who lived in Noah's time robbed each other and brought chaos to society, and therefore were the greater sinners. The generation at the tower lived together in a spirit of unity and cooperation. This shows us that God hates controversy but loves peace."

Rabbi Scholomo invited Josef to attend his sermons and study sessions at the school, but Josef declined. Even if welcomed with open arms, he said, he would feel awkward and blameworthy. But he did return to speak with the rabbi a second time, and a third. He learned about the Jewish perception of suffering and its possible benefits. Suffering people tend to have more empathy with those around them, said the rabbi. And when they're not completely crushed, they emerge stronger after adversity than they were before. Most importantly, when persecuted people react righteously, they help to balance evil in the world with goodness. This is one way Jews can be a light to the nations. Josef understood from the rabbi that Jewish cohesion is based not on a common land of residence or a group of political leaders or religious authorities. Rather it springs from a body of knowledge and values long preserved and handed down from generation to generation. When Josef asked if he could do anything to make relations better between their peoples, the rabbi said he could donate to a charity fund, Jewish or Christian, that would help alleviate misery. He also said it would be a good thing if Christians knew more about Torah and Talmud, and if they learned the Hebrew language. Knowing a person's language, after all, helps one to understand his culture. Josef went away from these discussions with increased hope.

After one of these meetings, Josef recalled to Miriam how, years before when he was on his way to the abbey in Poitiers, he had stopped in Troyes and spoken with Rabbi Scholomo. At that meeting, the rabbi had counseled him to sit at the feet of a master who would guide him. Now he had done that, and the master was Rabbi Scholomo himself! Not only had he acquired insight into life and faith, but he had unburdened himself by confessing to the good rabbi his own failings and the failings of his fellow Christians. This had been more beneficial to him than any confession he had made to a priest. Though he was a Christian and would always remain so, Josef felt he had much to learn from the Jews of Troyes. God willing, he would remain here for the rest of his life.

Miriam and her family quickly adapted to the culture of the region. The land was not ruled by a faraway king, they were told, but rather by a local count named Hugues who was tolerant and protective of Jews. As full citizenship was withheld from them, Jews could not serve in the military or in certain government positions. Yet their property rights were assured and their trade protected. Furthermore, Jews were allowed to choose their own residences and to administer justice among themselves. In return for these rights, they paid taxes to the count.

The Jews of Troyes spoke French, gave their children French names, and adopted many of the customs and practices of the non-Jewish population. They seemed well-informed about local art, games, food, and festivals. The council of rabbis in the city was renowned for its wise rulings, not only on religious questions, but on practical matters as well.

From great distances, Jews and Christians sent questions about everyday affairs. Most of these questions had an ethical component, concerning qualities such as cleanliness, proper dress, or good manners. In drawing on teachings in Torah and Talmud, the rabbis found it necessary to invent many new French words to explain the Hebrew texts. Miriam again saw firsthand what an excellent teacher Rabbi Scholomo was. Aaron took part in a study group headed by the rabbi. Miriam herself attended his sermons and lectures whenever she could. In winter, sessions often lasted well into the night, revealing a deep love of learning and religion by the rabbis and their pupils. Study provided a channel for their intellectual and spiritual energy; and it was essential, they believed, for their survival.

Rabbi Scholomo used his teaching notes as a basis for his written commentaries on Scripture and Talmud. Over the years, he wrote and revised explanatory treatises for almost every book of the Bible, as well as for large bodies of rabbinic teaching. He always tried to give the clearest explanations possible, reconciling inconsistencies and anticipating questions. Sometimes he would give two different interpretations so that students of varied abilities could each learn something. Often he used legends or real-life examples to illustrate a point, and occasionally included a visual diagram. As the rabbi worked on a treatise, his students would follow his progress, taking notes through the course of his lectures. Aaron reported to his mother that when a treatise was completed, the older students brought wine and had a lively celebration.

As the years passed, Miriam and Josef remained friends. While they did not see each other often, it became a family tradition to invite "Uncle Josef" to the Passover Seder each year. With Jews everywhere, they celebrated the safe passage by Moses and the Israelites out of Egypt. But the day had special meaning for the family—as former refugees, they remembered their own escape from persecution. The memories they shared were not all unhappy ones, however. When little Mosche, the youngest son, asked the four questions of Passover, Miriam recollected how her brother Mosche had years ago asked the very same questions. The children loved to hear how their Uncle Mosche had taught Uncle Josef to read. The younger ones, especially, were eager to know about the place where their mother had grown up and their older siblings were born. Josef told about the first Jewish wedding he had seen in Worms, when he instantly fell in love with the bride sitting in her canopy. He recalled for them how he practiced Hebrew words while delivering cheeses with their uncle, and how the two of them had sneaked into church together. He told of the first time he heard Rabbi Scholomo preach, even to the details of what he talked about. And best of all, they liked to hear that their mother had been a scholar before any other women in the town took an interest.

Now and again, Josef heard reports of the crusaders' progress on their eastward march. He assumed Miriam, and more especially Marcus (who now lived with the family), would be interested in whatever news he could bring. Some of the earliest bands inspired by Peter the Hermit never reached the Holy Land. Disorganized and undisciplined, they fell into conflict with other Christians along the Danube River and were wiped out. Another group, led by Peter himself, arrived in Constantinople, where they looted and killed indiscriminately. Most were massacred by the Seljuks. A year later, an organized army from France captured the cities of Nicaea and Antioch, and two years after that, Jerusalem was finally conquered. These successful armies were not the mobs who had traveled through the Rheinland molesting Jews. They had avoided this distraction by taking a more southerly route. Nonetheless, they met and fought with other enemies they had not anticipated, including eastern Christians whose bishops they had deposed.

King Henry, who had been living in Italia when the Jews of Worms and Mainz were massacred, did at last return to the Rheinland. He once again asserted his authority, sometimes in opposition to the Church. Much to the pope's displeasure, he allowed Jews who had been forcibly baptized to return to Judaism. He chastised his local bishops and priests for not protecting Jews, or in certain cases, for actively persecuting them. As punishment, he levied fines against them, which (of course) he deposited into his own treasury. While many of his actions were in direct violation of canon law, the king nevertheless undertook to protect his Jews once again from anyone who would harm them. Most of the people who had been forced to convert did indeed return to their faith; many returned to their homes as well. Within three years, resettlement had begun in the Jewish quarter of Worms. A few years later a new synagogue was consecrated in Mainz. The communities that had not been touched by violence quickly returned to normal and assisted those areas that had.

Eventually King Henry forged a treaty with lords and landowners of his kingdom to tighten protective laws and prevent future massacres.

Josef could not understand why any Jews would return to the scene of such horror, but Miriam said she could imagine why some people might want to. Older people especially, she said, found it nearly impossible to uproot themselves, learn a new language, adjust to a new culture. Ehud's mother, for example, would certainly have wanted to return to Worms if she had escaped.

At times when Josef met with Miriam and her family, they discussed aftereffects and likely consequences of the crusade. About four years after it began, he heard that Byzantine rulers had taken back much of their territory from the western invaders. Thousands of crusaders were killed. Josef himself (along with many Jews) thought this was appropriate punishment for their misdeeds. But that was not the end of it; reinforcements were sent and the conflict continued. With increased traffic between east and west, it became easier for Jews in Francia to communicate with their brothers in the land of Israel. A few western Jews actually undertook pilgrimages to Jerusalem. Rabbi Scholomo saw this as a positive sign. He reminded his people that God had promised to give the land to the Jews. Miriam was more interested in reports that trickled in from regions to the north where Jews had recently settled. She still wondered about her brother, if he had found a good place to live, and how he supported his family. She couldn't imagine him as a farmer, but thought he might very well be a shopkeeper. In any case, she was sure he had opened a school, spreading his learning like seeds in a fertile field. Marcus kept adding to his stories every bit of news he received from survivors. His chronicles came to be known as "Deeds of the Jewish community and how they sanctified the One Divine Name." Miriam was proud of "her boys." Marcus was already a respected authority on the history of the Jews, while Aaron (and later his brothers) became promising students in the Yeshiva. They sat at the feet of one of the best teachers and scholars the world had yet known.

Nearly ten years after Miriam and her family came to Troyes, the great rabbi died. He had hoped to do revisions on his commentaries, but as his health declined, he realized it would not be feasible. In the last months, Rabbi Scholomo was at peace. He reminded visitors that the only thing necessary after six days of Creation was rest—this was God's final generous act in making the world.

Josef was able to meet with the rabbi near the end of his life. Miriam did not accompany him on this visit, nor did she get a detailed report. But she heard hints about what they discussed. Apparently they spent a long time talking about teaching and what an agreeable occupation it was. Rabbi Scholomo told his young friend he always thought Josef would make a better rabbi than priest. They talked about the meaning of fatherhood and how God himself is Father to the fatherless and protector of widows. They discussed how it is possible for a person to love God with all his heart and still find room in it for loving others. One detail of the conversation Josef willingly shared with Miriam: He had asked the rabbi why God allows evil in the world. With shining eyes, the rabbi gave a simple answer, "So that we may choose the good."

After his death, the rabbi was highly praised by his associates; everyone had something favorable to say. The other rabbis of Troyes sent out a message to Jewish communities in the region, saying, "As the owner of a fig tree knows the best time to harvest the figs, so God knew the appointed hour of our beloved Rabbenu Shalmo, when it was time to carry him away into heaven." His fellow scholars spoke of Rabbi Salomon's great learning. His knowledge of linguistic subtleties, grammar, poetic images, and historical detail was unsurpassed. He knew by memory many of the sages' explanations of Midrash and Talmud, and he incorporated their moral lessons into his commentaries. Where Talmudic texts differed, he compared versions and often included both, yet indicated which one he found most rational and convincing. By this method, the rabbi brought unity to the rabbinic tradition. Were it not for Rabbi Salomon's commentaries, some said, the Talmud would have remained a closed book.

Yet it was not only the Talmud that the rabbi opened to his people; his commentaries on the Bible became immediately popular. Already they were much quoted in schools and homes, especially where children were taught. While interpretations of Talmud were fairly common, there was hardly any precedent for this kind of biblical commentary. Rabbi Salomon wrote explanations for nearly every book of the Hebrew Bible. His most ardent admirers said his collected writings added a third foundation, along with Bible and Talmud, to Jewish learning. Furthermore, his writings appealed to both mind and heart. The style was clear and comprehensible, while the content revealed the teacher's passionate love for the Law.

In spite of his accomplishments, the rabbi himself remained modest. He did not set out to write a literary masterpiece, but merely to throw light on the accepted texts. He was satisfied to explain the ideas of other men, reconciling contradictions when possible. Of course many of his original ideas did appear in the commentaries, but they were usually disguised in his explanations. Always willing to admit his own mistakes, Rabbi Salomon appreciated when someone pointed out an error in his work. Nor was he afraid to seem ignorant, as he readily admitted when a passage puzzled him. The rabbi acknowledged receiving help in all he did, and that help came from the Lord.

And now the great man was dead. Miriam had heard stories about him since she was a little girl. In fact, she couldn't remember a time before she knew about the "rabbi of Worms." It was inaccurate to call him that now, of course, since he hadn't visited her birthplace during the last ten years of his life. Yet this was part of his identity, one which she treasured. If her brother was still living (or any other scholar from Worms) he would be teaching young Jews what he had learned there from Rabbi Scholomo. The Rheinland region of Mainz, Worms, and Speyer had been a center of Jewish scholarship for many decades, nurturing young men (and a few women!) who were thirsty for learning. Since the crusade, that center had shifted westward toward Troyes. Would it survive, now that its leader was dead? Miriam thought so. Already the rabbi's students had founded schools in nearby towns. Some of them were writing books about their teacher's life and work, and others putting together collections of his legal decisions and Responses. But what gave Miriam the most confidence was Rabbi Scholomo's own family. His three daughters all married respected scholars and had many children. Through Aaron's studies and her own work at the Yeshiva, Miriam had met some of the grandsons. They were exceptional boys, scholars all, who knew about poetry, biblical interpretation, liturgy, and Law.

Yes, Miriam was sure Rabbi Scholomo's scholarly work would endure from generation to generation. He knew how to listen to the Lord, and he wanted others to do the same. That was the aim and the outcome of his teaching.

Afterword

The year 1096 was a turning point in Jewish-Christian relations. While church and civil law had in earlier centuries restricted and regulated the livelihood of Jews in Europe, still there was a fair amount of interaction, and even cooperation, between the two religious communities. A drastic change occurred during the First Crusade. Suspicion, hatred, and violence by Christians against Jews reached new levels, spurred on by "armies" marching eastward.

Before 1096 Jews had lived together in one section of town largely by choice, but later they were forced to live in circumscribed ghettos. In many places, they were required to wear identification badges to facilitate discrimination. Time after time, Jewish communities were wiped out by pogroms. Tragically, such institutionalized violence went on for centuries.

The story told in this book is based on historical events of the eleventh century. Many of the characters, including Rabbi Scholomo, King Henry, and Bishop John of Speyer, as well as other religious and civil leaders mentioned, actually lived in Europe at that time. Other characters are invented, in order to fill in the details of daily life for medieval Jews and Christians.

Rabbi Solomon ben Isaac (Rabbi Scholomo in the story) lived from 1040–1105. As a youth he studied Torah with scholars in Mainz and Worms and later founded a yeshiva in Troyes, southeast of Paris in the region of Champagne. He is now widely known as Rashi (a contraction of his title Rabbi with his names). Rashi's work has indeed endured—his commentaries are still used today by students of the Hebrew Bible and Talmud. Several of his grandsons and great-grandsons became famous scholars, writers, and teachers. The family's legacy is immense.

This novel incorporates writings and documents contemporaneous with Rashi's lifetime. In particular, the accounts of violence committed by crusaders against European Jews are based on chronicles written by survivors or their descendants. Also woven into the plot are actual proclamations and charters issued by bishops and kings regarding rights and restrictions pertaining to Jewish residents. Some of Rashi's commentaries on Torah and Talmud and his recorded social and legal rulings are the basis for sermons and judgments given in the book. All of this lends historical authenticity to the story.

My thanks go to Rashi's biographers, especially Samuel Blumenfeld, Maurice Liber, and Chaim Pearl, and to historians such as Israel Abrahams, Salo Baron, Robert Chazan, Jacob Marcus, and James Parkes, whose writings make medieval history alive and relevant. Also I must extend my deep gratitude to the following individuals: my cousins Mieken and Wilhelm Michel for offering the hospitality of their home in Worms and introducing me to the historical figure of Rashi; my husband Sam Hammond and friend Betsy Skidmore for many hours spent helping with research, typing, and editing; my cartographer Charles Register; my early readers Beth and Gary Berman, David Brodsky, Mary Jane Morrow, Isabel Samfield, Judith Ruderman, Diane Weddington, and Betty and Charles Young, all of whom offered valuable suggestions. To my late parents, Elisabeth and Henry Katz, I owe my interest and appreciation for German and Jewish history (and much more). Last, and most importantly, I wish to thank Rabbi Solomon ben Isaac for his life and work that continue to inspire people of faith.

www.ingramcontent.com/pod-product-compliance
Lightning Source LLC
Chambersburg PA
CBHW051145030726
47504CB00004B/1051